Quiver

GIULIANA VICTORIA

Editing by Steph White (Kat's Literary Services)

Proofreading by Louise Murphy (Kat's Literary Services)

Cover art and internal images by Sonia Gx (ArtBySoniaGx on Instagram)

Typography by DisturbedValkyrieDesigns on Instagram

Contents

Content Warning

There are mentions of attempted sexual assault (attempted drink tampering and groping NOT by the MMC), family trauma, domestic violence (very brief mention), attempted homicide, gun violence (very brief mention), suicide (non-graphic), on-page seizure, and explicit language.

Chronic illness and mental health representation are a few main themes in **Quiver** and will be in each of my books in this series. This is an open-door romance with lots of consensual spice. If you aren't a fan, this book may not be for you, or you're welcome to refer to the "Table of Cocktents" on the following page so you know which chapters to avoid.

For a detailed list of events, please feel free to contact the author via Instagram DMs or email at Giuliana.Victoria.Author@gmail.com with any specific questions you may have about the contents of this book. While **Quiver** is filled with lots of light and laughter, some themes may be triggering for people. Your mental health is *always* a priority. Never be afraid to ask for specific chapters to avoid or to just avoid reading the book entirely. Please take care of your mental health <3

Table of Cocktents

For anyone who wants to jump straight to the spice, know how far ahead the "good stuff" is, or wants to skip it entirely.

Playlist

Stress Me Out – PLVTINUM
CPR – Summer Walker
La Noche De Anoche – Bad Bunny and Rosalía
Replay – Iyaz
Mona Lisa – Lil Wayne (ft. Kendrick Lamar)
Idea 686 – Jayla Darden
Come Thru – Summer Walker (ft. Usher)
Honey – Kehlani
Wine – Zae
Nervous – John Legend
in my head – thuy
Leave – CIL
Over Some Wine – RINI (ft. Maeta)
Comfortable – H.E.R.
Lost – Frank Ocean
Oops!... I Did It Again – Britney Spears
WAP – Cardi B (ft. Megan Thee Stallion)
Frozen – Sabrina Claudio
Lovin On Me – Jack Harlow
changes – XXXTENTACION
violet skies – Colette Lush
Shallow – Lady Gaga & Bradley Cooper

Lose Control – Teddy Swims
Curiosity – Bryce Savage
Beautiful Things – Benson Boone
Conversations in the Dark – John Legend

Additional songs mentioned:
Carmen Suite No. 2: Habanera. Allegretto quasi Andantino
(Act I) – Georges Bizet
Hallelujah – Pentatonix
Baby, It's Cold Outside – John Legend (ft. Kelly Clarkson)

De Laurentiis Family Tree

Gloria: Mother
Angelo: Father
Alessandro (Ale): Oldest Brother
Luca: Second Oldest
Dante: Oldest Adopted Brother
Arielle: Dante's Wife
Sammy, Benny & Lily: Dante & Arielle's Children
Gianni (Gi): Youngest Adopted Brother
Charlene (Charlie): Youngest & Only Adopted Sister
Rose: Charlie's Wife
Arlo & Sofia: Charlie & Rose's Daughters

Signature Fragrance

Katarina Narvaez:
Kayali Yum Pistachio Gelato
&
Sí Passione by Giorgio Armani
Alessandro De Laurentiis:
Gucci Guilty Pour Homme

To those who have so much love to give but weren't born into a big family or surrounded by tons of friends despite seeing these dynamics displayed on TV and in movies, always wanting what you thought you couldn't have. Create the family you want. Our friends are just family that we get to choose. So choose quality over quantity, and always remember, the love you choose to give is precious. Don't squander it. Reserve some of that love for yourself, and be gentle and kind to yourself too. For the gentle souls with a wild side, this one's for you.

&

For anyone who's ever felt like they need to tone down their personality for people to like you. The right people will know your worth, and you'll never have to dull your shine for them. <3

Chapter One

Katarina

Friday, November 3, 2023

It feels like there must be one of those "Nor'easters" coming our way that I always heard my parents talk about as a kid if the windchill threatening to freeze my body like a popsicle is any indication. I had checked the weather before deciding on what outfit to wear, but it seems the fleece-lined leggings and chunky knit sweater aren't enough to keep me warm on a day like this.

It's thirty-four degrees in Philly, and I'm quickly realizing that I need to buy some more substantial winter apparel if I want to make it through my first winter back.

The plane ride from San Diego was what you'd expect from a six-hour flight purchased off of a website called "CheapoFlight-sRUs." The experience was complete with the quintessential screaming children sitting behind me, kicking my seat and blowing out my eardrums. Honestly, I didn't mind that nearly as much as others seemed to. They're just kids, and I imagine I was no delight on my first flight either. Plus, the pressure differential popping their little ears would be annoying for anyone, especially when you don't know what's happening.

The worst part was definitely the annoyed passengers who kept judging the parents and making unnecessary comments under their breath, and of course, the flight was delayed by about four hours. I'd still consider that a win when the delay could have been so much worse, and again, the tickets were extremely inexpensive.

Thankfully, I thought ahead for once, so my brother, Kas, dropped by my new apartment and picked up the keys from management so he could mail them to me ahead of time. At least now I can take all of my luggage back and get a good night's rest before I have to settle into my apartment and start my new job on Monday.

As I approach the thirty-eight-story high-rise that I'll be calling home for the foreseeable future, it becomes glaringly obvious that I wouldn't have been able to afford the rent on this place on my own. When I first started discussing the move to be closer to Kas, he vetoed every one of the hundreds of listings I sent him in the area. Granted, many of them *were* pretty sketchy.

I appreciate that he wants me to be safe, comfortable, and close to him, but buying one of the two penthouses in this massive building and charging me the average cost of rent in Philly for a studio apartment was excessive, even for him.

He swears that it's just a drop in the bucket for him now that he's playing for the Philly Scarlets, and that when I decide to move someday, he'll make a killing off of the sale of the apartment, so he's calling it an investment property. I think what he's really doing is investing in his twin sister.

Kas lives about two blocks away in a similarly designed building but said they didn't have any availability that was "to his liking."

Which probably means they were reasonably sized apartments and actually affordable for me, so he wouldn't be able to spoil me how he wants to. He chose this building on the recommendation of a couple of his teammates.

I'm sure I'll be able to quickly decipher which of the hundreds of people living in my building are hockey players as they all seem to be six foot four and three hundred pounds of solid muscle and are usually missing half their teeth. Essentially, they're built like brick shithouses, and it's hard to miss someone who looks like that.

As I look up at the sprawling building in front of me, my stomach fills with butterflies from the anticipation of being back here. I have so many memories of growing up here, both good and some very, very bad. Still, I'd always intended to come back for Kas, even as it simultaneously broke my heart to leave him and thrilled me that I'd be moving toward a major step in my career.

The building is covered in panels of mirrored glass, which, I'll admit, does add a nice opulence and some much-needed privacy. I love the look of floor-to-ceiling windows, but it's always made me a little uncomfortable that people could see directly into my apartment. For someone with so much anxiety, I listen to a lot of true crime podcasts that do nothing but fuel my reeling mind.

I walk toward the sliding doors under the covered red awning, literally taking my first steps toward my new life, and notice that the building has a concierge as well as building security, which is a far cry from the dingy studio apartment Aiyana and I shared. If I'm being honest, it was less an apartment and more an attic above an older woman's garage, but it was cheap and safe, which were our two highest priorities when we chose the place.

After taking in the brightly lit lobby with its upscale decor, I turn my attention back to the concierge; he's an older gentleman, probably in his mid-sixties, with white hair and kind brown eyes. I find myself mindlessly toying with the gold pendant of my necklace, a nervous habit I've used as a coping mechanism for my anxiety for as long as I can remember.

He smiles at my arrival, and he must be good at his job as it's obvious that he knows who I am when he says, "Good evening, Miss Narvaez. I'm glad to see that you've arrived safely, though a bit late in the evening, it seems." He gives me a slight frown as he looks down at the watch on his weathered wrist, brow crinkling as he realizes the time. "Unfortunately, the manager is out for the evening, but if you have any troubles, please don't hesitate to call the office." He gives me a small smile, and his brow smooths.

I smile at the man, whose name tag reads "Ralph," and thank him before I start heading toward the huge glass elevator doors placed in the center of the sprawling lobby with high ceilings resembling those of the promenade deck on a cruise ship. Unfortunately for me, there's an "out of order" sign on the one that reads, "penthouse."

I groan internally. I'm definitely not asking Ralph, or anyone else for that matter, if there's an alternative, so I head to the door to the right labeled "stairs" and begin my ascent to the thirty-eighth floor with my rolling suitcase in tow. At least I'm a pretty light packer, and I work out, so it isn't until around the twentieth floor that I start to really slow down from exhaustion.

By the time I get to the thirty-eighth floor, I'm panting, keeled over with my hands on my knees, and my suitcase tossed to the side. It's clear that I need to start using the stair climber at the gym to build my stamina, or I might just die up here if there's a fire. Here's to hoping this fancy schmancy building has some super high-tech safety measures and I'll never have to worry about that. Now that the thought's in my head though, it feels like something I'll be thinking about in the middle of the night when I can't sleep. Hell, I'll probably end up researching a collapsible window ladder to buy with all the money I *don't* have because spending money at strange hours of the night gives me a solid dopamine rush and sets my mind at ease, just long enough for me to fall asleep.

Once I catch my breath, I walk over to the door on the right that has a giant cardboard cutout of my face taped to it. Clearly, Kas wanted to ensure I wouldn't have trouble deciphering which door was mine.

Or he wanted to embarrass me and make sure that whoever lives across the hall has zero desire to seek me out, based on the horrific photo he chose. It's a picture of me on our twenty-sixth birthday wearing a huge grin with a giant corncob in my mouth and cotija cheese and mayo covering my cheeks.

He can be such a clown sometimes, but hopefully, whoever lives across the hall hasn't seen it yet.

I pull out the key Kas sent me, which, of course, he sent on a keychain that says, "If sisters were boogers, I'd pick you first."

I slide it into the keyhole, and it doesn't seem to fit right. Turning it over and trying again, that's *definitely* not right. I give it one last go, and the key finally slides in, but I can't get it to turn. Resting my forehead against the door, I allow the annoyance I'm feeling to seep in after the long day of travel I've had.

Blowing out a breath and straightening my spine, I inspect the door, trying to distinguish if there's anything I could possibly be doing wrong. The door also has a keypad on it, but management said I would have to wait until I checked in with them to select a secure door code, so the key was all Kas could get at the time. And it appears that isn't working.

Deciding to try out some random combinations of door codes just in case I can somehow pick one that'll let me into my not-so-humble abode, I start with the classic, "one-two-three-four." That doesn't work, not that I had really thought it would, so I move on to the building number, my date of birth, and the door number. When none of those options work either, I Google the name of this apartment complex and try to find out the year that it opened. While I thought that was a genius idea, it *still* doesn't work.

Anxiety and frustration are seeping in, but I try to ground myself. I'm doing my best to remember that this is just a small blip in my plans; I'm alive, safe, and healthy, and so many worse things could be happening to me right now.[1]

Releasing another long breath, I consider my options, hands on my hips in determination and the tip of my tongue poking out of the corner of my mouth. This is my "deep concentration" stance—I *swear* it helps. I can trek back down the stairs and not be able to get myself back up here; I can try to find the number for the concierge and hope they can do something for me even though I know the manager isn't here. Another option would be to try to make it to my brother's apartment and hope he isn't asleep on the plane coming back from his game in Memphis so he can tell me what his door code is.

None of those options sound all that great, so I weigh the pros and cons one by one. Going downstairs doesn't necessarily mean I'll get any answers, so that's out of the question. It doesn't hurt to call the concierge and see if there's another option I hadn't thought of, so I'll probably do that regardless. And there's no guarantee Kas will answer me about his apartment, plus I'd have to get myself there. Settling to call Ralph, I find the number, and to my surprise, he answers on the first ring.

"Hello, Miss Narvaez, this is Ralph. How can I be of service to you?" His voice is chipper and smooth, and I imagine he's a level-headed person most of the time.

"Um, hi, Ralph. I can't get into my apartment. The key won't work, and I haven't had a chance to set up the door code yet. Is there someone who could let me in?" I try to keep the exhaustion out of my voice. It isn't his fault that this trip has been long and with so many obstacles along the way.

"I'm very sorry to hear that you're having difficulty, Miss Narvaez." I hear him typing and assume he's checking to see what can be done. After a brief pause, he sighs, "Unfortunately, for security reasons, our manager is the only one who is able to handle these kinds of issues, and as I mentioned earlier, he is out of the office. He will return at 6:00 a.m., and we can get you all sorted then. Do you have anywhere to go in the meantime?" He sounds regretful, and I can't say I don't return the sentiment.

Without a second thought, I reply, "Uh, yeah, I do," not wanting to worry or inconvenience him. "Thanks so much. Have a nice night, Ralph, and please call me Kat."

"Good evening, Katarina," he says before ending the call.

---

1. **Stress Me Out - PLVTINUM**

Chapter Two

Katarina

I slump against the door to my new apartment, and contrary to what I just told Ralph, I don't have anywhere to go. Not until Kas gets home from his game, anyway.

It's just past 11:00 p.m., and their games usually end around 9:00 p.m. Then, they have to take turns on the bikes, shower, get changed into their suits, and board the plane. I figure he should be back around 3:00 a.m., and then I'll call him to come by and grab me.

He may need to bring an AED to resuscitate me after I make it down those stairs into the lobby though.[1]

Until then, I'll make myself comfortable up here. Staring down at the pastel-pink suitcase, I mentally prepare myself for the task and can't help but think over and over about what'll happen if whoever lives across the hall sees me out like this. Trying to brush away the thoughts, I start by opening my suitcase and taking out all of my coats to lay down as padding in front of my door, doing my best to stack them in a way that'll cover enough of the floor for my whole body to lay on while also providing enough cushioning.

When I'm satisfied, I work on unfolding my shirts, laying them down flat on top of one another before rolling them into a shape that *should* be comfortable to use as a pillow.

Here's to hoping my hallway mate doesn't come out and see me like this. Talk about a bad first impression.

Settling onto the stack of clothing, I clench my eyes shut and try to picture my next steps. Sometimes, my brain works too quickly toward a goal that doesn't really get me to the end result I want, and just the idea of that alone then makes me anxious. It's a vicious cycle that I've learned to control somewhat, but medication helps, and with how my day was going, it only made sense that I'd forgotten to take my pills this morning. It's such a dumb mistake for something I do every day, but I live by routines, and moving across the country wasn't exactly a part of my carefully curated routine.

I settle into the nest I've made myself and make a little checklist in my mind. First, I'll write this checklist. Yeah, okay, that's helpful; I roll my eyes at my own thought. Okay, starting again, first I'll pick a book to read, then I'll set an alarm for 2:55 a.m. so I'll remember to text Kas. I'll set it to vibrate mode though because I wouldn't want to increase my chances of having a run-in with my hallway mate. Then I'll just read until Kas lands, and the time should fly by.

I've had an ever-growing TBR on Goodreads since I moved to San Diego for physician assistant school, and then spent another two years doing a neurology fellowship. I have plenty of books to catch up on now that I have some time to read for fun. I probably could've fit some fun reading into my schedule, but having ADHD makes it really difficult to juggle multiple aspects of personal and work life, so I was afraid I'd accidentally fall into a hyperfixation and end up reading smut every night when I should've been studying. It was just better to avoid the temptation.

Opening my Goodreads app, I scroll through the covers, settling on a sports romance by a Latinx author I adore. The mention of a strong female lead, who also plays soccer and falls in love with her interim coach, is one of my favorite tropes, so she has my attention already.

***

I awake with a startle to the sound of the heavy stairwell door slamming shut, my body practically levitating off the floor as my eyes snap open, heart pounding in my chest. When I look up, I'm greeted by the face of a man who makes Jimmy Garoppolo look like the discount version of *himself*! The guy is easily six foot five or maybe even taller; it's hard to tell from my precarious position on the ground. His wide eyes meet mine, and a small smirk curves the corner of his full lips. His dark curls hang slightly over his forehead, grazing his thick brows, one of which is arched slightly with amusement, dancing above his striking light-green eyes.

I'm forced to stop my perusal, okay, outright ogling him, when his deep, silky smooth voice wraps around me in my dazed stupor. "Is everything all right?" he asks me with that same smirk, and his eyes shine brightly under the cool hall lights.

I work to pick my jaw up off the floor, fighting the urge to check whether or not I've got drool hanging out of my mouth. My brain short circuits for a moment before I finally answer. "Yeah, I actually live here, I promise. I'm not just loitering in the halls. If that's your apartment, I'm your new neighbor," I say as I point to my giant head taped to the door. Who would've guessed I'd be actively drawing attention to that ugly picture? "See? It's me. I'm your new hallmate, I guess? Is 'hallmate' even a term that people use?" God, now I'm rambling. He's either going to think I'm intoxicated or suffering from a traumatic brain injury at this point. Why else would I be lying in the hallway?

As I wait for his answer, my fingers make their way back to the pendant, toying with the cool metal as I work to calm my shaky breathing.

"That unsightly picture of you has been hanging on the door for the last three days, but I'm glad to see that you're much more beautiful than that picture of you deep-throating a corncob would suggest." His voice has a lilt to it, and the lopsided grin he gives me nearly makes me forget the reality of what he just said.

I choke on my own saliva and probably add to the "unsightly" scene before him.

Did he just say that I was *deep-throating* a corncob?! I need my brother to come drag my ass down those stairs and rescue me so I can crawl into his apartment and hide in a closet like the troll that I've evidently become. That way, I can search for a new place for myself because there is no chance I can live across the hall from this guy! Not after repeatedly embarrassing myself, and in such a short time frame too.

Oh shit, I've just been staring at him with panic in my eyes for a solid thirty seconds. Speak, Kat, speak!

My eyes are quite literally bugging out of my head, my chest heaving with the effort necessary to stand up as I sink deeper and deeper into my panicked thoughts.

I decide it's best to ignore his comments altogether and instead say, "My brother sent the key to me a few days ago, and it's not working. The manager isn't back until the morning, so I'm just waiting until he gets in, and I promise I'll be out of our mutual hallway. Can we pretend this never happened?"

He takes a moment, studying me and digesting my words before replying, "Listen, it sounds like you've had a rough introduction to Philadelphia, and judging by your apartment door, your brother is giving a new meaning to 'the city of brotherly love.' So I'll give you a break, and we can pretend I didn't find you lying in a heap of laundry in our hallway." He gives me a small but genuine smile that makes it look like he may be holding in a laugh.

Continuing, he adds, "Would you like to stay at my place until the manager gets back? You can stay in my guest room; it's got an en suite and a lock, so you don't have to worry about your safety." That's... oddly considerate.

I'm hesitant to accept his offer, but frankly, I'll take my chances that this guy is an axe murderer if it means I can avoid going down those stairs tonight or spending another minute on this hallway floor. I'm already starting to feel pain lancing its way up my spine, punishing me for the time spent on this hard floor after a day spent on an airplane.

So going against my better judgment, I say, "Do you promise you're not going to murder me in my sleep?"

His brows shoot upward before lowering, and that same cocky grin spreads across those gorgeous lips. He brings his right hand up, palm facing me, and tucks his pinky under his thumb, the three middle fingers pointing upward, and says, "Scout's honor," with a deep chuckle.

"Well, all right, if you were backed by the good ole Boy Scouts of America, what, two decades ago, you must be a pretty trustworthy person," I tell him with a wink. "Offer accepted."

---

1. **CPR - Summer Walker**

CHAPTER THREE

Katarina

SATURDAY, NOVEMBER 4, 2023

A fter he helped me toss all of my clothes back into my suitcase, we made our way inside his apartment.

I'll admit, I'm not expecting it to be as nicely decorated as it is. All of my previous experiences with ex-boyfriends had led me to believe that most men live in untidy apartments and rarely understand that countertops should be wiped daily. Frankly, if I hadn't been treating my ADHD, my apartments would probably have not looked as clean and tidy as they did either, especially not with the long hours I was working and studying.

This guy, though? His floor-to-ceiling wall of windows is spotless, not a speck of dust anywhere, and yet it's also super cozy with throw blankets tossed over the plush charcoal-gray sectional and even a few decorative pillows. The living room is an open concept with a massive kitchen and an island connecting the two rooms, and the kitchen is spotless with marble countertops, white cabinets, and gold finishings. There are three additional doors that I'm guessing are the bedrooms and maybe a laundry room.

He probably hired an interior designer and has a cleaning service or something. At least, that's what I tell myself to lessen the jealousy creeping its way into my exhausted brain.

I imagine my apartment will be pretty similar to this one, but I honestly haven't seen more than a few photos, opting to trust my brother's opinion because I'm just glad to be near him and finally back in Philly. It didn't seem I had much of a say in the decision anyway.

I'm hoping my best friend, Aiyana, will be moving back here too, and we can share the overly extravagant penthouse.

"Hey, so before I stay the night here, I just realized I never introduced myself. I'm Katarina, but you can call me Kat." I smile brightly at him, extending my hand.

He quirks his brow at me, but his expression shifts into a panty-melting smile that shows off the dimple in his right cheek. He takes my hand in his own extremely large one, giving it a firm shake. "It's nice to meet you, Kat. I'm Alessandro, but you can call me Ale." He says it with a smirk that tells me he clearly recognizes that I'm affected by his charm, and my nervousness is apparent. I can feel my cheeks heating under his teasing gaze.

He leads me over to the left of the living room and opens the door to a guest room with white walls, a gold metal bed frame, a queen-sized bed covered in the softest-looking white duvet, a matching quilt folded over the end of the bed, and a soft, faux fur throw blanket tossed over the corner of the mattress. There's a gold dresser across from the bed with a TV mounted to the wall above it and a tan velvet chair in the corner of the room. It's simplistic but luxe at the same time, and if he actually decorated this room himself, I'll be extremely impressed. Heck, I'll have to ask him to decorate my place too.

"This is the guest room; the en suite is the door to the left of the dresser, and the closet is to the right of the bed. Feel free to toss your luggage in there if you'd like. Make yourself comfortable and knock on my door if you need anything."

He turns on his heel, heading out of the room, and I'm finally starting to recover from my shock at the strange turn of events for the evening when I realize I've been super rude. "Ale," —he turns around to face me— "thank you so much for this. I really appreciate it. I could've spent the night in the hallway, but I'm really thankful not to have to," I tell him with an expression that I hope conveys how grateful I am.

"Don't mention it, Kat. Have a good night." He gives me a grin that crinkles the edges of his eyes, those sage-green orbs twisting my stomach. He leaves and heads to his room after turning off the lights in the living room and kitchen. When I hear his door shut, I close my own and lock it, just in case he does turn out to be a serial killer.

God, I really hope he's not an axe murderer. I just finished a whole lot of school only to be offed by my trusting stupidity.

I make my way to the bathroom and clean up before crawling under the plush duvet and quilt. Something starts vibrating, and I'm reminded of the alarm I set to text Kas. Swiping the notification away, I put the phone on the nightstand, turn on my side, and doze off quickly. I wake up with nightmares often, usually replaying the same horrifying stream of events, but tonight? Tonight, I dream about a mysterious stranger with beautiful eyes and an incredible ass.

Chapter Four

Katarina

I wake up to the sun streaking through the blinds, the smell of food wafting under the door, and I swear I hear a Bad Bunny song playing from the kitchen.[1]

It doesn't take long to realize I'm not in my old apartment in San Diego, and the events of last night come flooding back to me.

"Gosh, how long did I sleep?" I groan to myself, still groggy.

I reach for my phone on the nightstand and frown, realizing I forgot to charge it last night, so I'm not sure what time it is. But based on the sun glaring into the room through the soft, white curtains, I'd say it's definitely after six, so I should be able to set up the door code to my apartment and get out of Alessandro's hair.

After using the restroom and brushing my teeth, I take my meds with some water from the faucet and make the bed, feeling a little awkward because I'm not sure if I should strip the bed before I go.

I shake my head at the intrusive thought; I'm always overanalyzing my every move, thinking people are judging me for totally normal things that don't really require the extra thought.

I head out to the kitchen, and I'm greeted by the sight of Ale's tall, tan form, his trim waist, massive shoulders, and bulging back muscles on full display as he cooks. From the smell of it, he's making eggs and veggies of some sort.

I clear my throat and try to suck back some of the drool pooling in my mouth, and not just from the smell of food. "Good morning, Ale." I give an awkward little wave before he's even turned around and abruptly snap my hand back down to my side, realizing how dumb the gesture looks.

He turns around, and if I thought he was gorgeous from the back, the front of him is even more impressive. His abdominal muscles are the definition of "washboard," and it's clear his body has been honed by years of physical labor and hard work. His muscles look like they serve a purpose, not just meant to look pretty like that of a bodybuilder. He's got a tattoo of a Medusa head with three legs in the shape of a triangle on his right outer arm, but there are some details that I can't quite make out though. Again, he smirks when I stare at him a bit too long and says, "Morning? I'm not sure when you last checked the time, but it's two in the afternoon, *gattina*."

Gattina? I make a mental note to look that up later. It must be Italian or something. Now that I think about it, he does have sort of an Italian American accent, like a lot of northerners do around here. It's really faint though, almost undetectable.

How is it possibly two o'clock in the afternoon? I look at him sheepishly, embarrassed that I've overstayed my welcome. "Gosh, I didn't realize it was that late. I hadn't charged my cell last night, so it's dead. Do you mind if I use your phone to call downstairs so I can get my apartment situation worked out, and I'll be out of your hair?"

He looks over his shoulder at me from his place at the stove. "No rush, my cell is on the counter. Call them and then take a seat at the island. Breakfast is almost ready. You don't have any allergies, do you?"

"I really appreciate it, but that's not necessary; you've already helped me out so much."

"Kat, it's okay to accept kindness without feeling like a burden. Besides, I've already made enough for us both," he chuckles. "I'm Italian, and my mom has always taught me never to let someone leave my home hungry." So I was right; he *is* Italian. "Besides, she'd probably castrate me if she found out I let you leave before feeding you," he chuckles, turning back to the food on the stove.

"That'd be a damn shame," I mutter under my breath; my cheeks heat when I realize he's heard me. His shoulders shake almost imperceptibly, attempting to contain the laughter from my comment.

I stand by what I said though—he's too gorgeous to lose the ability to procreate.

I'm clearly not getting out of here without eating, and the frittata he's making looks incredible, so I walk over to his phone sitting on the counter. "The password is one-two-two-five," he calls out to me without looking, obviously knowing where I'm headed.

That catches me off guard; his password is... Christmas? And he's actually giving me his password? I wonder if he'll change it after I leave. I've had some pretty long-term boyfriends who wouldn't even give me the password to their phones. Granted, they were either cheating or doing some other shady crap.

As I unlock his phone, I see him lean over and lower the volume on the Reggaeton music he's got playing over a Bluetooth speaker. I do an internet search for the manager's number and give them a call. A gruff-sounding man answers the phone, and after some explanation, he agrees to head up shortly to set up my apartment with the new door code. I tell him what I'd like it set to, stepping out of earshot so I don't have to give myself a panic attack worrying about Alessandro sneaking in and killing me someday. The manager says I don't have to be present, so I guess I'm free to eat before I head over. When I'm done with the call, I lock his phone and place it back on the counter before sitting down at the island.

Ale leans down and places a plate of food in front of me, and the smell is incredible. I haven't eaten anything since before my flight yesterday, and I'm ravenous; the way my stomach gurgles at the sight of food only confirms that. The frittata is plated with a little parsley for garnish, which makes me grin thinking about the extra care he put into it. "What can I get you to drink? I've got orange juice and coffee," he tells me, standing only a foot from me, his clean, masculine scent filling my lungs and short-circuiting my brain for a moment.

"Oh, uh, orange juice would be great. I actually don't drink coffee." I smile at him but internally cringe at the extra information he didn't need. If word vomit were a sport, I'd be a damn Olympian.

Ignoring my awkwardness, he gives me a reassuring smile and turns to pour me a glass of orange juice. "So why don't you drink coffee? Just don't like the taste?" Turning, he sets the clear glass of orange juice in front of me and takes a seat to my right.

"It's less the taste and more the caffeine. It makes me jittery and more anxious than I already am at a baseline, so I drink tea." Divulging more information about myself than anyone ever wanted to know is also a sport I'm great at.

He nods his head. "What kind of tea?" I hadn't really anticipated him wanting to know more; most people would've brushed off my awkwardness without a second thought.

Eyes never leaving mine, he uses his fork to cut off a piece of frittata and brings it to his mouth, chewing while I answer. "I like Earl Grey. It has some caffeine but not much." That's a decent answer. Just enough information without going into the logistics of how I froth my oat milk or the specific lavender syrup I use to make it a London Fog. I give myself a small smile, proud of the accomplishment, and turn my gaze away from his to dig into the food.

My taste buds are hit with the savory flavors of spinach, onion, zucchini, and goat cheese. I can't help the moan of pleasure that escapes me, and his head snaps to attention. I can feel my cheeks heating as he eyes me quizzically.

"This is so good, Ale; how'd you learn to cook like this?" I'm genuinely curious but also deflecting a little, trying to steer his thoughts away from the inappropriate sounds I just let slip past my lips.

Now I think *his* cheeks are starting to turn pink, but he seems so confident and self-assured that it must be my eyes playing tricks on me.

He ducks his chin before replying and says, "My mom taught my younger brother and me how to cook when we were little. She was diagnosed with multiple sclerosis when I was twelve, and it progressed pretty quickly." I remain quiet, urging him to continue, hoping my silence will suggest that he does.

Relief floods me when he continues speaking. "She and my dad didn't think they'd be able to have any more children biologically but wanted a large family, so they adopted my three younger siblings. My dad is the worst cook on the planet, so when it became difficult for Mom to keep up with cooking for all of us, I took over the role, and it seems to have paid off."

He gives me a grin, and the way his face lights up when he talks about his family just adds to his disarming personality. So far, he seems very different from how I perceived him based on his looks alone. I guess you truly can't judge a book by its cover, even when the cover is so handsome.

I also realize that most people would've probably considered what he just said to be oversharing, so it takes everything in me to contain the grin I feel coming on, thinking he might also be a little nervous around me.

"I'm sorry to hear about your mom's diagnosis, but it sounds like she's done an amazing job raising you and creating the family she wanted." I pause, giving him a reassuring smile. "How is she doing now?" I ask, my tone curious.

Without hesitation, he smiles and says, "My mom is the best." My chest floods with a sense of longing for that kind of parental relationship. He continues, "She's doing pretty well now. She has limited mobility but is completely intact cognitively, and she established with a really fantastic neurologist in the area who got her on a medication regimen that seems to be working pretty well." He hops off the barstool and starts clearing the island to wash our dishes, clearly done with the personal moment we just shared.

I can't let him cook for me and do the cleaning after letting me crash here, so I get down from the stool, following him over to the sink.

"I'll get those; it's the least I can do." I make my way around the island and accidentally brush up against him while reaching for the dishes. I take a step away to give us some distance, but he bumps my hip with his while grinning and says, "I'll wash, you dry."

The way he says it makes me feel like there was some kind of innuendo there, but I don't care to dissect it. I'm probably just imagining things.

However, I can't help the thought that blooms in the forefront of my mind. *Would it be so bad to have sex with an attractive guy who lives so conveniently close to me*? Then again, if things go badly, that could be an issue. Better not to cross that line.

---

1. **La Noche De Anoche - Bad Bunny and Rosalía**

CHAPTER FIVE

Alessandro

A s Kat leaves my apartment, I let my head fall to the door-frame and clench my eyes shut in frustration, hands fisted above my head. I am so *utterly* screwed. I was really hoping that my new "hallmate," as Kat calls us, would have resembled the woman on the door with the freaking corncob in her mouth, covered in food. But truthfully, even in that picture, she was gorgeous.

The real-life woman though? Simply stunning.

She's average height, probably around five-six if I had to guess. I still tower over her at six-six though, and frankly, her height is the only thing about her that *is* average.

When she looks at me, her bright honey-colored eyes gleam with interest, and that white streak of hair running through her eyebrow quirks each time she appraises me. Those soft, pouty lips turn up into a heart-stopping smile, and while it's not the only reason I can't stop staring at her, it certainly doesn't help.[1]

When she walked out of my guest room this morning in those tiny silk night shorts and black tank top, my jaw nearly hit the damn ground. Inappropriate images of her toned thighs pressing against my cheeks while I make her come with my tongue flood my mind, and I'm instantly hit with a wave of guilt. This is Kas's sister. Don't be dumb, I try to remind myself.

She's my teammate's twin sister, and while he hasn't mentioned anything about her to me, I know that's a line I shouldn't cross. It's kind of an unspoken rule to avoid sleeping with any of your teammates' siblings or any family members, for that matter.

Kas and I have been playing for the Philly Scarlets together for about four years now, and we're a part of the team's starting line. I play center, and he plays defense. With so many people on the ice, the speed of the game itself, and the dangers associated with the sport, it's important that we all remain in sync with one another if we want to win and keep everyone safe.

Which means I can't be fooling around with his sister and creating an unpleasant situation for either of us if things were to go poorly.

Besides, I don't do casual, which is why I'm so damn horny at just the sight of a beautiful woman in my apartment. Granted, Kat isn't just any woman, she's fucking stunning, but if I wanted a casual lay, I could have my pick, but I want more than that. I've seen what my parents have together. They're madly in love with each other, and if I'm not actively seeking that out in every relationship I have, it's just not worth my time.

Still, images of this gorgeous woman in my apartment, nervously chewing the side of her lip and toying with that gold necklace draped around her elegant neck, won't seem to leave me, so I head to my room to shower and *hopefully* relieve some of the tension that's been building since I first saw her last night. Fingers crossed, I'll gain some much-needed "post-nut clarity," as my teammate, JJ, calls it when you have calm, clear thoughts about a situation you were initially conflicted about after you've had an orgasm.

Since when do I follow any of JJ's suggestions? He's an incredible asset to our team, but he's also very young and sometimes says shit that boggles my damn mind. *Fuck.* I roll my eyes at my lapse in thought.

Bringing my thoughts back to what matters, I go over what needs to happen today. I have to head over to my parents' house to prep for Sunday dinner tomorrow and make sure Mom is doing okay. I also have to call and schedule an appointment with my *own* neurologist for this week because my headaches have been getting worse, and I haven't been able to shake the fatigue I've been feeling the last week. Both of these negatively impact how I train and play, so they need to get sorted out quickly.

Hopefully, Dr. Shah can see me this week before our next home game.

---

1. **Replay - Iyaz**

Chapter Six

Katarina

M uch to my delight, my apartment is the mirror image of Alessandro's.

I have a lot of plans for how I'm going to decorate this place, but they'll have to wait until I've had a few paychecks come in. Student loans are a beast, and I've managed to live off of the absolute bare minimum the last two years so that the measly pay I made from my fellowship covered my expenses. Most of my loans have been paid off, but I'm still not out of the hole just yet. I won't feel truly secure until I've got a sizable savings account.

You never know what could happen, and I want to be prepared, just in case. Having that security net will definitely help curb my anxiety a bit; plus, I'd like to buy a house someday.

I enter my bedroom expecting to have to sleep on the floor for a while or purchase an air mattress, but I really should have known better. My brother had a bed sent over. Because, *of course,* he did.

Kas really is the best, but sometimes he's just so over the top with his gift-giving. He spoils me, and I think it's his way of making up for what happened to our mom, even though it wasn't his fault. He's been dealing with that guilt for a long time and doesn't seem to have fully let it go. Pushing the thought from my mind, I redirect my attention back to the excitement I was feeling moments before.

I take in the rest of the room and see that the bed he purchased is a massive king, but the owner's suite in this penthouse is big enough that it looks like a twin. The gorgeous yet minimalistic pecan wood platform bed frame with tiny brass feet matches the two bed stands on either side, and each one has a unique lamp that he probably had to thrift to find.

Ever since we were little, I've loved intricate lamps. It seems like a strange thing to appreciate, let alone collect, but our Lola had us on the weekends because she lived across the street from us. Things weren't so great with my parents for most of our childhood, so it was a nice reprieve. She used to take us to garage sales and estate sales on Saturday mornings and then thrift shops on Sunday mornings because she said, "All the old farts are at church on Sunday morning; that way, we don't have to fight someone else's grandma for a good deal!"

Obviously, I never needed tons of lamps as a kid, but it was something we were both drawn to. She and I would admire the different shapes, textures, colors, and fabrics. Some would be blown glass with a mercury finish or with strange velvet shades; others looked homemade or filled with items like shells.

Occasionally, there was a lamp so unique that we just had to buy it and add it to her ever-growing collection. She always let me decide where I wanted the lamp placed, and thus, my love of lamps was born. It speaks volumes about my relationship with Kas that he'd take so much time out of his busy schedule to search for these lamps, knowing that they'd make me feel more at home and closer to our grandmother. I seriously have no idea where he found the time to hunt these down.

The lamp on the left side of the bed looks like a giant glass mushroom, probably about eighteen inches tall, with shades of greens and muted pinks throughout the clear glass and the occasional swirl of white. The lampshade is the top of the mushroom, and when I turn it on, the entire lamp illuminates. It's gorgeous and matches the room so well.

The lamp on the right side of the bed more closely resembles one that my Lola had on her office desk when we were kids. It's a brass banker's lamp with a matching pull string and an oblong green glass shade. There's a pile of satin, sage-green linens, a matching duvet cover, a huge duck-down duvet that I'll need to wrestle the cover onto soon, and a plush cream throw blanket, as well as a mountain of down feather pillows.

I also smell fresh paint, which must mean Kas is responsible for the muted sage-green walls that match the bedding.

Our father wasn't very handy, but Mr. Kaan, Aiyana's dad, was a carpenter before he got sick, and he taught Kas a lot about woodworking, painting, and other skills that I'm glad to see he didn't forget after becoming a professional hockey player.

There's also a note taped to the inside of the door that reads:

Hey, Kitty-Kat, I didn't have time to finish making the bed before I left for my game, but I washed the bedding after it was delivered, so it's safe to sleep on. I also ordered you a couch, which should arrive Monday evening after you get back from your first day of work. Don't worry, the couch isn't ugly. It's the dark,

> *olive-green monstrosity of a sectional you sent me a link to last*
> *year, saying how much you loved it and that you'd buy it for your*
> *new home someday. Consider it a housewarming gift.*
>   *Eternally proud of you, Kas.*

A groan slips past my lips. I don't want to sound ungrateful, but this feels like way too much. On one hand, it's amazing that I don't have to worry about this stuff, and I really do love that couch... on the other hand, I feel overwhelmed with a need to repay him for his kindness and feel like I can't be upset with him because he's just showing his love. Gift-giving has always been one of his love languages, but that doesn't stop the wave of guilt I feel.

Taking a deep breath and closing my eyes, I try to harness some positive energy, reminding myself that Kas never judges me for anything and definitely isn't expecting anything in return. Maybe I'll take him out to that new sushi spot he's been mentioning for weeks when I get my first paycheck.

I start setting up my bedroom, hanging up the clothes I brought with me, and placing my toiletries in the bathroom, which has a massive window that I imagine is one way so I don't give anyone in the buildings across from me a peep show. There's a shower stall with pebbled floors and glass doors and a soaking clawfoot bathtub with a white ceramic base and brass feet. I don't think I'll ever want to leave this place.

Once I've got the apartment set up with the little I brought with me, I buy some stuff online that'll be delivered in the next day or two. I need to figure out the public transportation situation around here, but based on what I've seen online, my job is less than a ten-minute walk from here, and there's an even closer grocery store. It's got everything I need nearby, and for anything else, I can take the train or bus, so there is no need to buy a car just yet.

Now that all of my necessities are put away, I figure it's time to set up potentially the most important thing of all—my vibrator.

Yes, I went through TSA with my favorite vibe in my backpack because I was afraid something would happen to it if I put it in my checked bag. That sounds ridiculous, but masturbation is normal and healthy and quite possibly the best anxiety relief I have at my disposal. Besides, my favorite vibe is not some huge schlong, not that I'd be judging myself if it were. It's four inches long, made of waterproof black silicone, USB rechargeable, and has ten different settings.

I was also paranoid that it would accidentally get turned on while in-flight, so I made sure it was dead before packing it.

I plug it into the USB port on my nightstand and get to work making my grocery list and figuring out what I need to get done before my first day of work in two days.

It's Saturday afternoon, and Kas had a game last night, which means he doesn't have one this weekend. And since they won, I imagine they'll be celebrating tonight. I'm not in the mood to go to a rowdy bar though, so I send him a quick text and place an order for grocery delivery. Kas quickly texts back with:

Kas

> Sure thing! Takeout at your place at 6?

I let him know that sounds like a plan and get changed to check out the gym here before my groceries get delivered. I want to get in a better sleep schedule, and working out helps me get out some of the excess energy.

Chapter Seven

Katarina

As expected, the gym is the size of the ones I've seen on cruise ships, and similarly, the entire place has floor-to-ceiling windows. The floors are covered in black foam padding, and everything looks well-kept. I haven't had a chance to work out in a few days, and the nervous energy has been building, especially since my encounter with Alessandro this morning.

I scan the room again, making sure no one else is in here and trying to make a mental map of where everything is. It's just one floor below me, which makes it even more convenient, plus it has everything I could hope for—a spacious room with wooden floors for stretching and yoga, weight racks, benches, free weights, stair climbers, all the usual cardio equipment, and, of course, my favorite piece of equipment, the squat rack.

No one is in here, which isn't super surprising on a Saturday at four in the afternoon, so I put my earbuds in and set up my favorite playlist for lifting. It's mostly a lot of rap, R&B, and some rage metal.[1]

Relaxing into the space, I bend forward, letting my hands dangle to the floor as I stare down at my white Converse sneakers. They're my favorite for lifting but not as great for cardio.

After a few moments, I right myself, allowing my arms to ark over my head, elongating my spine before bringing my hands back down to rest on my hips as I lean forward. I do a few hamstring stretches, then several squats without any weight to ease into the movement and let some of the tension from yesterday's flight leave my body.

Setting up my weights, I decide to start light with a forty on either end of the bar and do two sets to warm up. The strain on my muscles feels good, but I'm definitely ready to add more weight.

I don't have a spotter, so I can't go super heavy today, but I'm confident that I know where my limit is, so I add another forty to either side. I figure I can go up to two forties on each side of the bar before it's no longer safe to keep squatting on my own.

I get into position, keeping a wide stance as my hands wrap firmly around the hard metal bar, holding it securely to the top of my shoulders as I maintain my position, squatting low and ensuring my knees don't go over my toes. I have little difficulty with the weight, but I know I shouldn't push myself too far today, so I place the weight back on the rack, feeling both the literal and figurative weight on my shoulders ease immediately.

Turning to grab my water, a large, firm hand grips my shoulder, and I can't help but let out a high-pitched wail as my lungs seize inside my chest, fear and panic filling me, grinding my thoughts to a screeching halt. I twirl around and see a very miffed Alessandro towering over me.

My pounding heart starts to ease, but only the tiniest bit, as the fear wears off and morphs into something different entirely. Annoyance, confusion, and a little anger.

I take my earbuds out with a huff, pressing pause on my music as I do my best to contain my emotions and ask, "Hey, Ale, what's got your panties in a twist this afternoon?" Irritation still manages to lace my words as I grit my teeth.

His eyes widen slightly, and his hands are on his hips as he stares me down. I can't seem to keep my eyes from roaming over his body. He's got the sleeves of his burgundy athletic shirt pushed up to his elbows, and his tanned, corded forearms flex when he catches me staring.

A shiver of desire travels through me, but my earlier annoyance fights its way back to the forefront as I run my gaze back up his large body, meeting those piercing green eyes, now filled with the tiniest bit of amusement.

---

1. **Mona Lisa - Lil Wayne (ft. Kendrick Lamar)**

Chapter Eight

Alessandro

W e won our game last night but got in so late that we all just went home, so tonight, we're meeting at a local bar in Center City that doesn't usually have too many puck bunnies hanging around.

The majority of the guys on my team are married or in committed relationships, so we don't have a lot of the typical problems I hear about from other teams. We also have fewer scandals posted on the internet since we don't tend to be messy in our professional lives or our personal ones. It's a nice change of pace from the team I was on in my first year in the league when I played in Chicago.

The players were all pretty young and very interested in the attention they got from both men and women. A lot of them slept around and took a new date home every night. There was a lot of media coverage about it, and I couldn't stand it because it took away from how talented those guys were.

Luckily, a recruiter for the Philly Scarlets appreciated that while I was young and new, I kept my nose clean. He had heard that I was hoping to play for them and stay close to my family. When I received the offer that next year, I was thrilled, and I haven't looked back since.

I figure I should get a workout in before we head out. I don't drink often, but I'll probably grab a beer or two, and while I don't think that will negatively impact me in any real way, I still like to be cautious with how I treat my body. It's my temple and all that, plus I genuinely enjoy training, especially since during the three years I've lived in the penthouse, there's never anyone in here after noon or before seven in the evening. So that's when I usually head down to work out if I'm not training with the team.

When I walk into the gym, my feet grind to a halt as I'm greeted by the sight of a newly familiar-looking backside, and I struggle to take in everything in front of me. Kat is at the squat rack, and from the looks of it, she's got two hundred and five pounds of weight on her back with *no spotter*. As usual, there isn't anyone else in the gym except her, and it's becoming clear that I might not be able to avoid her as I had initially intended to.

Worry and irritation take hold of me despite both being emotions that I really have no business feeling for this woman. But why the hell is she squatting alone? It's clear that she can handle the weight; frankly, she could probably handle more, but she's squatting this with no one around to ensure she's safe. For some reason, that lights more than just a protective spark in me.

With my hands balled into fists at my side, I stalk over to the rack, but her back is to me, and she has earbuds in, so she hasn't heard my approach. As much as it annoys me to wait until she's done, I don't want her getting hurt because I startled her. Instead, I take in her incredible round ass as she engages her glutes, her golden-brown legs bent at a ninety-degree angle. Another inappropriate thought makes its way into my mind. I can just imagine the sound it'd make when I smack it and how firm it would be under my grip. Shaking the thought away, I do my best to look anywhere but at her and wait until she's done and has placed the bar back on the rack. Once she has, I put my hand on her shoulder gently, trying to alert her to my presence, but evidently, that doesn't go as planned.

She makes a loud sound that's almost like a kitten after its tail's been stepped on. The irony of the analogy brings a smirk to my face, but her pissed-off expression reminds me of why I was annoyed in the first place.

Kat glares at me and deadpans, "Hey, Ale, what's got your panties in a twist this afternoon?" I see she's not as socially awkward as she seemed when we first met. Or maybe her irritation is just outweighing her social anxiety.

Based on her tone, she's frustrated at the situation. But as soon as the words leave her mouth, her eyes trail down my chest, landing on my forearms, and my dick twitches as I watch her full bottom lip jut out the tiniest bit, parting those delicious lips before she snaps her mouth shut and brings her attention back to my face.

She makes it really fucking difficult to remain annoyed with her recklessness when she's practically eye fucking me.

I let out a huff, keeping my hands on my hips. "You shouldn't be squatting alone. Do you know how dangerous that is? Absolutely no one is up here, and there aren't any staff. There aren't even people on this floor." I realize I'm practically reaming her out like I'm speaking to a disobedient child, but the words keep pouring out of me, unable to stop as the fear that something bad could've happened to her makes my following words come out more somber. "You could have gotten seriously injured, and absolutely no one would have heard you screaming for help. Hell, you could have paralyzed yourself or worse." I make an effort to smooth out my expression, dragging in a deep breath.

She eyes me speculatively, her fingers toying with the gold pendant of her necklace, an anxious habit I've picked up on pretty quickly. She's probably deciding how she's going to respond, and frankly, whatever she chooses will be better than I deserve. I feel like an asshole for chastising her like that, but the image in my head of her laying there injured as she cries for help is one that makes me damn near sick. My stomach churns as I await her response, and the moment the words leave her lips, I'm relieved she doesn't give in to me. I don't want her to. I *need* her to tell me I'm being an asshole and to leave her the hell alone. Maybe if she does that, it'll be easier to do the right thing and actually stay away from her. It's only been a day though, I do my best to remind myself.

You've got this; be strong.

"Ale, I am a grown woman. I can do as I please." I'm about to interrupt her, but she continues. "While I truly do appreciate your concern, I'm not doing anything that I'm uncomfortable with or not confident in," she tells me with an exasperated huff. "I can easily squat twice my body weight, and I knew I didn't have a spotter, which is why I decided to go light today." She rolls her eyes at me and takes a deep breath, steadying herself before saying, "And think twice about speaking to me like I'm a child in need of reprimanding."

My mind is reeling with so many thoughts but gets snagged on one word in particular. "*Gattina*, if I were reprimanding you, you'd know it. I'd have you bare-assed, lying over my lap as I spank the defiance out of you."

Jesus Christ, did I just say that?

Her expression is the only answer I require. Her jaw drops in shock, but she recovers quickly, nervously biting her lip. I continue, trying to avoid any awkwardness that'll follow that statement, "So clearly, I wasn't 'reprimanding' you; I was merely voicing my concern, though I'll admit, I could've been less of a brute about it." I soften my words, giving her a small smile that I hope comes across as apologetic. "I'm sorry."

She finally releases her hold on that damn necklace, clasping her fingers tightly together in front of her stomach as she formulates a response. She blinks up at me several times before letting her hands drift to her sides, her posture relaxing and a smirk playing across her lips. "Do it again, and *you'll* be the one bent over *my* lap for a spanking." Her smirk grows into a full-blown smile as my expression morphs from shock to sheer fucking joy at her words.

I can't help but keel over with laughter, the absurdity of what she just said hitting me like a Mack truck, and I do my best to drag in some deep breaths. She's chuckling lightly beside me, and it's the sweetest sound I've ever heard. God, I need to get a fucking grip. Standing and straightening my posture, I chuff out one last laugh, and her eyes remain fixed on mine, those honey orbs alight with laughter.

Shaking her head, her cheeks turn pink under my gaze as she keeps that mega-watt smile plastered across her face.

Redirecting my attention to the reason we're having this conversation in the first place, I tell her in a rush, "Text me next time. I'll work out with you and be your spotter." So much for getting a grip. I resist the urge to shake my head at myself, and I await her answer.

"I'm sure you have better things to do than act as my spotter," she says while rolling her eyes, placing her hands above her hips, and popping a hip out as if I'm ridiculous. And I can't say she's wrong. I don't even know the woman aside from the fact that she rambles when she's nervous, latches onto that necklace like it's a literal lifeline, and her cheeks turn pink for just about every reason.

"I work out a lot and like to do it around this time before everyone gets out of work and heads here after seven," I explain.

"Ah, I see. So a big strong man like you can lift without a spotter, but a weak woman like myself can't; is that right?" Her brow quirks in challenge.

I think she's teasing me based on her smirk and the lilt in her voice, but just in case, I say, "You know what, you're right. I *absolutely* need a spotter. Thanks for offering!" My cheery smile grows at the shock evident on her face. "Hand me your cell, and I'll give you my number so you can text me next time."

The shock on her face matches my own thoughts because it appears I have no filter with this woman. And I'm certainly not going to tell her that I reserve my weight training for my mandated training days with the team. I just do cardio here, so I've never actually needed a spotter.

There's that eye roll again. "Fine, here's my cell, but I'm not promising I'll ever text you."

That makes *me* want to roll my eyes at *her*, but instead, I grab her phone and enter my number, setting my contact as "Hottie Hallmate". I save it and hand it back to her after sending myself a text from her phone so that I have her number too. I don't trust that she'll text me the next time she wants to lift, and I want the option of texting her myself.[1]

I mean, what if I need a cup of sugar or something? Always good to have your neighbor's contact info.

By the grace of god, we fall into a comfortable silence free of my internal monologue making its way out against my will.

---

1. **Idea 686 - Jayla Darden**

Chapter Nine

Katarina

After returning from the gym, I hop in the shower and quickly change. Kas should be here soon, and my groceries just got delivered outside my door.

I wrench the door open, leaning over to grab the ten-pound bag of rice I ordered and using it to hold the door open. I fill my arms with bags of groceries, bringing them into the kitchen and dumping them on the kitchen island. I've got more of the groceries in when I see Kas head out of the elevator, turning toward my door. A huge smile spreads across his face, and he quickens his pace when he sees me.

I grab the rest of the bags and move the rice out of the way to close the door when Kas gets inside. He carries several bags of takeout, and it smells like Thai, one of our favorites.

Once both of our arms are free, he rushes over to me, giving me a suffocating bear hug. "Hey Kitty-Kat, how do you like the place?" he asks with a huge smile.

I beam up at him. "I'm loving it so far. It feels really good to be back in Philly, and this apartment is insane!" I gush, hoping he hears my excitement. "I just finished at the gym, and it was incredible down there."

I leave out any interaction I've had with my new hallmate, avoiding a potentially awkward conversation. He chuckles. "I knew you'd like it, plus with Aiyana moving in with you soon, you needed the extra space," he says as he starts helping me put away the groceries, already knowing exactly where I like to keep things.

The thought of Aiyana being here with me soon sends my heart soaring; it's only been a day, and I already miss her. "I just hope she gets the job offer. If not, she won't be moving in until she's secured employment," I tell him as I pop open the top of the Styrofoam containers and lay them out on the kitchen island.

I don't have any chairs yet, so we're standing and eating.

He quirks a brow at me. "When have you *ever* known her not to get exactly what she wanted out of life?"

That makes me chuckle because he's absolutely right. "I know, I know, but there's a lot of nepotism and sexism in STEM, so anything could happen."

Pulling a pair of chopsticks out of their paper wrapping, I lean against the counter and start inhaling the food. I hadn't realized how freaking hungry I was until the food was actually set out in front of me.

"So when exactly *does* she get here?" he asks, continuing the conversation.

"Oh, she gets here on the tenth," I say, the flavors of panang curry and drunken noodles dancing on my tongue.

Kas has one forearm planted on the counter as he eats with the other, his dark brows drawn together. "This Friday?" he asks. "We've got a game on Friday. You wanna bring her with? I'll drop off jerseys for you both." He smiles playfully—as if Aiyana would miss the opportunity to be at one of his games. Truthfully, Aiyana would watch them or record them to watch later, but if I was around, I was usually studying and not really paying much attention.

Rolling my eyes at him, I say, "Of course we'll go! Her flight should land way before your game, so it shouldn't be a problem."

"Great," he says with a smirk, "I'll make sure those 'Narvaez' jerseys are at your door well in advance."

"Why thank you," I joke. "So I saw you guys won last night; how'd Memphis's team play?" I start, trying to catch up with him. There isn't a ton of newness despite living across the country from one another for the last five years since we talk on the phone several times a week.

His lips quirk up in a wide smile. "The other team was pretty good, but our center, Alice, was better, thankfully. He played a really smooth game last night and scored two of our three goals. He had to switch off more than usual though; I think he might be coming down with something, but he made his time on the ice well worth it." He talks about this "Alice" guy pretty frequently, but unfortunately, I've never met any of his teammates. I'm excited to change that now that I'm living nearby and have the time to attend his home games and watch the away ones on TV.

"I know it's only the beginning of the season, but it seems like you're off to a good start! No losses yet."

He smacks his palm against his forehead, lightly shaking his head at me before letting out a sigh. "Kat," he groans, "you just jinxed us."

My eyes widen. "Isn't it just the goalies who get superstitious? You've never believed in that stuff before." I roll my eyes at him, but the smallest drop of anxiety manages to slip in, worrying me that maybe I really *did* just jinx them.

"The goalies are weird, but they're important, so it's allowed. I, on the other hand, need to keep that shit to myself, but it doesn't keep me from thinking about Lola's superstitions." He pins me with a joking glare, unable to keep a straight face. His referencing our grandma makes me smile though, and we move on from the hockey talk.

"Are you excited to start your new job on Monday?" he asks me, eyes bright with curiosity. He's been one of my biggest supporters throughout all of my education, even when I told him for the hundredth time that I wanted to quit as I was being hazed during clinicals while I *literally* paid to be there. He'd give me whatever I needed at the moment, whether that be a pep talk or something more akin to, "Get your head out of your ass and do the damn thing, Kat." I'm just glad he never saw my old studio apartment. He'd have lost his mind and paid for something a whole lot nicer.

"I'm excited to finally get to work somewhere with a normal paying salary that I worked my ass off for, but I'm a little anxious." I'm not new to the throws of anxiety, having dealt with it most of my life, but it only got worse once the nightmares started after our father's death, and new situations always make me nervous.

His smile drops momentarily before picking back up. "Okay, let's work through it. What is it about the new job that's making you anxious?"

I nod, deciding it couldn't hurt to get his perspective. "Well, I'm worried about the staff not liking me or being super awkward and making a fool out of myself. You know I'm not great with first impressions." My cheeks heat slightly thinking about last night's encounter with Alessandro. "Mostly though, I'm worried about being late because I'm not familiar with the public transportation around here anymore."

He takes a moment, digesting what I've said before giving me his insight. Years of therapy have taught him how to handle not only complex emotions but also when to take the time to process someone's words and avoid a knee-jerk reaction. "Okay," he says finally, "well, the public transportation piece can be dealt with pretty easily. I can help you come up with the best route, and you can try using it tomorrow so you're somewhat familiar before your first day, though I think it's pretty walkable." I'm glad he doesn't offer to drive me. He continues. "And you know you can't do anything about how other people feel about you. You're a very likable person, just like your incredibly charming twin,"—he grins, winking at me—"and not everyone is going to like you anyway; that's life. Besides, your awkward first impressions are part of your charm."

I push my food away, finished with the drunken noodles and curry, walking around the counter as he opens his arms for me. I wrap my arms around his waist and lean my head against his shoulder. His arms wind around me, and I'm hit with an onslaught of emotions. I've missed Kas so damn much, and talking on the phone just wasn't the same.

"I've missed you, sis," he tells me, squeezing me tightly before letting me go.

I peer up at his hazel eyes, smiling. "I've missed you too. Thanks for talking me down from my impending panic attack." I nudge him with my elbow.

"Anytime," he says with a grin, "but I should head out. The guys are meeting at Rocco's at seven."

I nod, cleaning up the food and placing the leftovers in the fridge before walking him out. He stops in the doorway, eyeing me with a tender expression. "You sure you don't want to come out tonight? You could meet all the guys. Their wives usually come out too."

I shake my head gently. "I'm honestly pretty tired, and I'm hoping to fix my crappy sleep schedule before going back to work on Monday."

"Next time, then." He smiles, pulling me into another crushing hug before heading over to the elevator.

I lock the deadbolt on the door and turn out the lights in the kitchen and living room, leaving the light under the microwave on as a nightlight. I know it's super early, but tomorrow, I'm going to be completing some online modules to familiarize myself with the electronic medical records system we use at my new job. I want to be well prepared and, hopefully, impress my boss a little bit.

I get ready for bed and crawl under the covers, leaving one of the lamps on so I can keep reading the book I started last night. I figure I won't have too much time for "fun reading" for the first few weeks as I acclimate to this new job, so I want to enjoy it while I can.

***

The sexual tension in the book has reached a peak. While I tend to read books by authors with a slow burn but still lots of spice, I happen to know that this author doesn't give us what we want until almost the end of the book.

My mind starts to wander to the attractive giant living across the hall from me. His shirtless form was already impressive when I saw him this morning in his kitchen, but at the gym, covered in sweat? I can't lie; I was openly ogling him when he *finally* took his shirt off.

I swear, he didn't even notice. I hope.

He's got this truly spectacular body that I barely know how to describe. He's cut and muscular, and watching sweat dribble down his chest is almost mesmerizing. The thought of trailing my tongue down his firm pecs and licking it off flickers in my mind before I push it away.

I toss my e-reader to the side and grab my vibrator off of the charger, bolting out of bed and heading to the bathroom to clean it off in the sink before sliding back into my lush bed. I close my eyes and slip my hands under the covers, lifting the waistband of my silky night shorts and nudging my panties to the side. Setting the vibe to a medium buzz with pulsations, I drag the tip down my abdomen, sending a trail of goosebumps in its path. Placing the smooth silicone tip to my clit, a jolt that feels like an electrical current races through me. I'm already wet, either from the book or thoughts of Ale. *Maybe both.*

My core quickly starts to tighten, and my inner muscles clench around nothing as I hasten my pace.

I picture Ale lying in bed with me, his muscular arms wrapped around my thighs, fingers digging into my flesh, and his face buried between my legs. I can practically feel his stubble scraping the inside of my thighs as I ride his face.

The thought of him lapping me up, his tongue sliding along my wet center and groaning from his own pleasure and what's next to come makes my toes curl.

I imagine him lifting his gaze to me as I'm hanging just off the edge of my orgasm, approval lighting his eyes, and it does me in. I come careening off the edge, my muscles spasming and a long moan of pleasure slipping past my lips. I ride the wave until I'm lying in a heap of satisfaction before finally turning my still-buzzing vibrator off and sliding out of bed to clean up.

I'm exhausted and maybe a little embarrassed that I just came in under three minutes to the thought of my neighbor, who I just met, eating me out like I was his last meal.[1]

But that's a problem for later when I'm awake enough to really dwell on it.

When I'm done, I climb back into bed, roll over to turn off my lamp, and quickly drift asleep.

***

My chest is heaving, eyes screwed shut as I shriek, "Stop! *Please* stop!" The words rush out of my mouth, my throat raw as the strangling sensation I'm feeling starts to subside, and I realize, much as I do most nights, that it is just another nightmare.

I usually don't have nightmares when I'm really exhausted like I had been when I stayed over at Alessandro's, thankfully. It would've been so embarrassing to wake him up with my screaming.

Running my hands through my hair, I work to calm my breathing, practicing my grounding techniques. I finally open my eyes and look around the room.

1. I see my new bedroom.

2. I see the city skyline through my windows.

3. I see the old banker's lamp...

I continue on like that for a couple of minutes, following the five-four-three-two-one routine, listing what I see, feel, hear, smell, and taste. It works well, and usually, I don't have to go all the way through the motions because I'm much calmer by the time I'm at the "hear" portion.

Grabbing my phone off the nightstand, I check the time, and when I see that it's only 4:00 a.m., I shake my head, rolling back over to try again.

---

1. **Come Thru - Summer Walker (ft. Usher)**

CHAPTER TEN

Alessandro

SUNDAY, NOVEMBER 5, 2023

I groan, my arms stretching over my head, a wave of pleasure from the stretch rolling through me. Waking up before the sun has risen isn't my idea of a good time, but I have no choice. I have to get ready to meet the guys for team training before hauling ass back home to get ready for Sunday dinner with my family.

Rolling out of bed, I use the bathroom and head toward my dresser, tugging on a pair of sweats and a long-sleeved athletic shirt.

After grabbing my water jug and making a protein shake, I get my sneakers on, grab my coat, and make my way toward my SUV parked in the garage below the building. As I pass Kat's door, I can't help but think about the woman on the other side—when I'll get to see her next, under what circumstances, and what mood she'll be in.

Being a professional hockey player, it gets old having the people around you act so excited to see you, even if they don't really follow the sport. Kat's transparency is refreshing, and it makes me want to spend more time in her presence, even knowing it's a horrendous idea for us both.

When I pull up to the huge black-and-red arena, I park and head inside, the heavy door slamming shut behind me. My footsteps boom across the floor as I amble over to the locker room, dropping my bag in front of my locker and greeting the guys.

"Morning, Alice," they all hoot at me, making me smile with a repressed laugh, refusing to encourage them.

"Is it a good morning? Can we call it that when the sun still isn't up?" I ask with a groan, and they all chuckle. Matt Bowman, our team captain, passes by me, clapping a hand on my shoulder in greeting as he makes his way over to the training room.

"Morning, Cap'," I say, nodding my head in greeting. He smiles over his shoulder at me and saunters off to wait for us.

"My sister staying out of your hair?" Kas asks beside me as we enter the facility together, and I give him a tight smile. I'm trying to keep the groan from slipping past my lips as I think about his sister's tight ass and gorgeous smile.

"She seems to be settling in well," I say in lieu of a real reply. I can't exactly tell him that she's fucking trouble or that I've fisted my cock twice to the thought of her pretty face as she slides her pink pussy down my shaft despite having just met her. I can't imagine how obsessed I'd become if I actually had the memories to back those thoughts up.

He smirks, a glimmer of something in his eyes making my brow quirk, but I brush it off, not wanting to dissect whatever fucked-up thoughts just crossed his mind. Because it's always something that'll leave you in a tailspin for days when it comes to Kas. The guy is *not* fucking normal. He should've been a goalie.

We start our lifts, everything feeling so damn heavy as the fatigue continues to drag me down. My body aches, and it's hard to lift the extra weight we've added this week as my muscles quiver, begging me to stop.

JJ's acting as my spotter, waiting for me to need him, but as that becomes a real, distinct possibility, his dark eyes snap to mine. "You good?" he asks, his voice low and quiet, worry lacing his words.

I grunt a response, finishing one last rep before I let the weight fall to the ground with a loud thud. My lungs are heaving with the exertion, and I'm suddenly desperate to see Dr. Shah this week. These meds just aren't working, and I don't know how much longer this can go on before people start asking questions or, worse, demanding answers.

***

I pull up to the modest three-story brownstone home I grew up in, parking and heading up the short driveway. Unfortunately, it's no longer practical for my mom.

I had a contractor come and install a wheelchair lift for the stairs, and Mom's occupational therapist came over a couple of years ago to recommend some adjustments to make life easier for her. I've been working with a buddy of mine who builds homes. I know Mom won't let me spend the money on her now, but eventually, I'll wear her down and have the most accessible home built exactly as she deserves, maintaining her artistic flair and old rustic Italian style.

There are four main types of MS, and they're definitely not all created equally. Mom has secondary progressive MS, which basically means that after a period of having another more common type called "relapsing-remitting," where she would have periods without symptoms and then acute exacerbations of them, she is now in a chronic state of progressively worsening symptoms with no more periods of remission.

Still, some days are better than others, and since she had my brother and me in her early twenties, she's young and still all there cognitively, but she's wheelchair-bound and can't participate in a lot of the activities she loves. She doesn't let it get her down though, and we're hopeful that science will progress before things get really bad and she starts struggling with her thoughts and words.

I let myself in, and I'm greeted by the smell of garlic wafting through the air. I can hear my parents chatting with my siblings in the kitchen while my nieces and nephews play in the living room.

I head straight back through the long corridor bathed in warm overhead lights from the ancient chandeliers that Mom had installed to add to the old-timey feel of the home, and I enter the kitchen to say hello and see if anyone needs me before I check in on the kiddos.

The kitchen still has the original wallpaper trim near the ceiling with painted red and green grapes on vines and bottles of wine in between. The dark wood of the cabinets makes the entire space feel warm and inviting, if not a little run down from years of wear and tear.

"My sweet boy is home! Come give your momma a hug, *rattino!*" my mom nearly shouts when she sees me, her arms immediately coming out to her sides for me.

Maybe someday she'll stop calling me her "little rat," but I have my doubts about that. Her reasoning for the nickname is much sweeter than the actual name would make you think.

I give her a big hug, and pulling away, she grabs my cheeks and says, "Let me get a good look at you. I haven't seen you in two weeks." Her hands are starting to wrinkle, age spots mottling the tan skin. I place mine on top of hers, pulling them off my face and holding them in my own, giving them a gentle squeeze.

"Ma, I had a game last weekend and couldn't make it here, but it hasn't been two weeks, drama queen," I say, rolling my eyes at her but allowing her to fawn over her eldest child.

"*I'm* the drama queen? Hah!" she laughs loudly but shifts gears quickly, much like she always does. "You look tired. Are you tired? Have you been sleeping? A good meal with your family will make you feel better," she tells me, her voice boisterous as she looks me over, her hand firmly patting my upper arm.

My sister Charlie, short for Charlene, comes around the kitchen island and gives me a hug, saying, "Leave him be; he looks no different than he did last time you saw him."

"I don't know, I agree with Mom; you're lookin' a little rough there," my brother Luca says as Charlie smacks him on the shoulder with annoyance. I know he's just joking as his eyes light with mischief, and he lets out a laugh.

"Okay, everyone, settle down. This house is entirely too small for you all to be roughhousing in my kitchen." Dad clears his throat and says, "I mean your mother's kitchen. Now, Dante and Alessandro, go get the kids ready for dinner while the rest of you set the table and get the food set up."

We all chuckle at his slip-up, and I spot Rose wrapping her arms around Charlie from behind, planting a kiss on her shoulder. Rose is hard to miss in a crowd, her bubblegum-pink hair always standing out.

Before I can make my way out of the kitchen to follow Dante, my eyes snag on Luca. His usual smirk is not present; instead, it's replaced by a look of worry, his dark brows pulled together in an expression that I rarely see on him but often see on myself. Luca's heterochromatic eyes finally catch my green ones, and he smooths his expression, working to put that easy smirk back on his face, but something feels off. I've never known him to worry much about anything, but his look of concern is churning the bile in my stomach.

I give him a tight-lipped smile and follow after Dante to help him with the kids.

We work together, dragging the three older kids up the narrow stairway. "Straight line kids," Dante tells them in a stern but caring fatherly voice.

"By alphabet or age this time, Dad?" Sammy asks Dante, knowing the routine.

Dante thinks for a moment as he taps his index finger jokingly to his chin. "Age this time; we did alphabetical order last week. Youngest first."

Arlo gets in line first, followed by Benny and then Sammy. I unfold the step stool, place it in front of the sink, and help lift my niece onto it, her straight chestnut hair in tangles from all the roughhousing these kids do. She looks up at me as I chuckle, turning the faucet on for her and grabbing the soap to pump into her tiny hands. Those glittering gray eyes peer into mine, and a small smile grazes her lips. "Whatcha laughing at, Uncle Ale?"

She sticks her hands out in front of me so I can pump the soap into them, then turns her attention to the sink as she washes them, doing her best not to get the suds everywhere. I pick up a strand of her knotted hair and ask, "You get into a fight with a grizzly bear or something?"

That makes her giggle, a sound that none of us heard for a long time when Charlie and Rose first adopted her. "Of course not, Uncle Ale!" she squeals, laughter filling the small room. "I've just gotta show Sammy who's boss sometimes!"

Dante lets out a low chuckle, Benny represses a laugh, and Sammy rolls his eyes, but I can't help the pride that spreads through my chest. This tiny little creature would have *never* spoken that many words in one day, let alone in one sentence. And for it to be filled with so much sass? It's honestly incredible how much she's come out of her shell.

When she's finished drying her hands, I pull off the hair tie I keep on my wrist. "Turn around, I'll put it up for you so your nano doesn't complain about your hair getting in your food." She turns her back toward me, remaining on the small stool. I do my best to gently gather her long hair, raking my fingers through the tangles to loosen them before pulling her hair into a high ponytail.

"All done," I tell her, holding her hand as she steps down from the stool and then zooms out of the room, her feet thumping down the stairs.

Benny waddles in next, hands gripping the sink as he steps up onto the stool. He's always been a clumsy kid, having been born with a very mild form of spina bifida. His balance is a little off, but thankfully, he's healthy and happy with very few residual health complications.

He reaches over the sink, turns the faucet on, and faces me with outstretched hands, his chubby cheeks permanently dimpled from the smile that never seems to leave his face. I give him the pump of soap. "Thanks, Uncle Ale!" he says as he proceeds to make a massive mess, just like he always does.

He blushes, reaching for the hand cloth and sopping up the mess. "It's okay, Benny, you're doing great, buddy," I try to reassure him, knowing he's self-conscious about things like this. His brother is a lot more meticulous in his actions, and it affects Benny to watch things requiring hand-eye coordination come more easily to Sammy.

That smile brightens at my words, and he jumps down, running past Dante, who ruffles his dark curls on his way down the stairs.

"I don't need the step stool anymore," Sammy whines, always wanting to prove he's grown up. Some days, I really believe he is. He's the embodiment of a wise, old-souled grandfather with a grumpy spirit.

"All right, little man, if you say so." I fold the stool back up, place it beside the sink, and leave the soap on the counter for him to dispense himself.

He washes his hands methodically, his nimble fingers moving in the same way they always do. He starts with his fingernails, then moves between his fingers, his palms, and then onto the tops of his hands before rinsing and drying, not a single drop of water or soap leaving the basin. He turns without saying a word and heads downstairs.

Dante shakes his head, joining me in the bathroom. "You know, as a child psychologist, it's really fucking soul-crushing not to know how to help your own kid," he tells me in a hushed tone, his voice cracking.

I grab his cheeks in my hands, bringing his dark eyes up to meet mine. "You are a *fantastic* father, Dante, the best as far as I'm concerned, but you know as well as I do that you can't push him to open up." I release my hands from his face, and the instant I do, his head hangs low as he shakes it back and forth, exhaustion setting in.

"I know, A, but he just won't talk to anyone. He's always angry about something, and he tears Benny down any time he does something he deems incorrect, and he's got all these fucking rituals. It takes us forever to leave the damn house because he's busy rechecking shit in his room. I really think he's got OCD, but when I've taken him to childhood psychiatrists and therapists, he won't speak. He just sits there and stares at them until they finally let him leave."

My heart aches for him and Arielle. I know it wears on him, and they don't want it impacting Benny or Lily when she's older either. I lean back against the sink, my hands gripping the edge. "I don't know, Dante. I've never had kids, though when you three were first dropped here, it wasn't all butterflies and roses either."

When Mom was diagnosed with MS, there was a lot of uncertainty surrounding whether or not it was safe for her to continue having children. We now know that it's really a case-by-case situation, but either way, they had wanted to adopt.

So a few years after Luca was born, they were finally contacted by one of the adoption agencies they had applied to, and it turned out that there were three children from the same family who couldn't be separated and needed a home urgently.

Dante was the oldest of them and only a year younger than me, the same age as Luca, who was four years old at the time. Gianni was two, and Charlie was the baby of the bunch. She was only nine months old when the adoption took place, and they all came to live with us on Christmas Day.

It was a while before we had passed all of the home checks and the adoption papers were finalized, but we got to spend that first Christmas together, navigating the newness of it all. It was a really big change for us all. I was only five, so I had a general grasp on what was going on but didn't comprehend much aside from the fact that I now had three strangers around my age living with us.

Dante, Gianni, and Charlie were put up for adoption when their parents had been driving home from a holiday party and a drunk driver came swerving into their lane. We've been told that they died on impact after being thrown off the road into a densely wooded area.

The way we became a family definitely doesn't give you the warm fuzzies, but I honestly feel like they were sent to us by their parents. It even turned out that they're half Italian, hence their names fitting in so well with ours.

Unfortunately, they didn't have any close relatives who could afford to take in three young kids, and they all felt it was important not to separate them. They keep in contact with the family they have in the area, and we celebrate Christmukkah together every year. Several of their aunts and uncles are Jewish, so we combine Christmas and Hanukkah and celebrate them at the same time, so we've become one large, blended family.

Dante groans, "That's for fucking sure. Charlie wouldn't stop crying, Gi was a depressed wreck, and frankly, I don't think much has changed there, and I was just pissed off at the world. I don't want that for my son. I've done everything I can to help him, but there has to be *something*. I must be missing some key thing here." He runs a hand through his black hair, tugging on the roots and letting out a huff of frustration.

We hear a knock at the door. "Come on, you two. Mom says her blood sugar's getting low and to get your asses downstairs before she passes out," Charlie calls out.

"Coming," I holler through the door and wait until I hear her descend the stairs. Gripping Dante's shoulder, I give it a reassuring squeeze. "We'll talk about this later," I tell him, and he nods, straightening his spine and exiting the bathroom.

We head down to the kitchen, seeing that everyone is already seated at the table. Because there are so many of us, we have a long, dark wooden table in the center of the dining room that seats twelve, and then a kiddie table set up right beside us. Mom sits at the head of the table with Dad seated to her left. I'm on her right with Dante and his wife next to me, Charlie and her wife next to him, Luca and his new girlfriend, Tiffany, seated by Dad, and Gianni and his best friend across from Charlie and Rose.

No one sits at the end of the table directly across from Mom so that we can see clearly over to the kids' table. We say grace, and everyone starts piling food on their plates.

Sunday dinner is standard for us, and it usually includes something similar to what we're having today: lemon and caper butter branzino, fresh pasta with homemade red sauce, fried calamari with lemon wedges, banana pepper slices, and a garlic aioli dipping sauce, as well as huge bowls of spinach salad with sliced mushrooms, warm goat cheese, dried cranberries, and chopped beets.

We talk about our weeks, with Charlie gushing about how proud she is of Rose for her accomplishments at work, where she helps formulate vaccines.

Luca and Tiffany banter with everyone, but it's clear that Tiffany doesn't have much to add to the conversation, and honestly, she probably won't be back next week anyway. Luca is a serial monogamist, but only for a couple of weeks before he moves on.

Gianni and Alex fill us all in on their game schedule for next year, what they know of it anyway. Soccer usually runs through several of the months that hockey doesn't, which makes it convenient for me to attend their games and vice versa.

Dante and Arielle are pretty quiet this week, but they take everyone in, listening attentively and smiling when appropriate, but the gesture doesn't reach their eyes. They look at each other the same way my parents do, and sometimes, I think they can read each other's minds.

I'm incredibly lucky to be surrounded by couples who clearly love each other deeply. It's set a foundation for what I see for myself one day.

Just as Arielle's shoulders start to relax, I hear Lily's cries from the room upstairs. Before she has time to react, I stand abruptly, the wooden feet of my chair scraping along the floors. "I'll get her; just eat and relax," I tell them, and Dante and Arielle give me a grateful smile.

Heading up the stairs, I check my phone and see that Kat has texted me.

Gattina

> Delivery person left a package at my door, but it was for you, so I put it in front of your door.

Gattina

> I guess that didn't really require a text. Obviously, you would've seen it when you got home.

Gattina

> Sorry to bother you! Have a good rest of your day.

Her embarrassed texts make me smile, but I don't have time to respond just yet, so I put my phone back in my pocket and open the door; a teary-eyed Lily stares at me from her pack n' play, red cheeks matching her hair.

"Baby Lily, what's wrong," I coo, leaning down to pick her up, cradling her against my chest. I rub her back gently, little hiccups leaving her throat as she recovers from her wailing screams. "Everything's okay; Uncle Ale's got you." I continue bouncing on the balls of my feet, rubbing her back until the hiccups stop, and she falls back asleep. I'm too afraid to put her back down, so I settle into the rocking chair in the corner of the room, bringing out my cell and turning down the brightness before replying to Kat.

> You're a gem, Kat! Thanks for not stealing my package. ☒

> And no need to apologize. I'm glad you decided to use my number.

Gattina

Ugh! You're a brat. ⊠

Correct. ⊠

How's your Sunday going?

Gattina

Good! Just settling in before I start my new
job tomorrow. You?

That's sounds exciting, you nervous?

And just Sunday dinner with my family.

I open up my camera app, ensuring the flash is off, and take a
picture of Lily on my chest, sending it to Kat. She seems like a kid
person, and who wouldn't love this little bean?

Gattina

Alessandro...

Gattina

If you're trying to get in my pants, you're off
to an excellent start. ⊠

Not so anxious behind a screen now, are we?
Katarina... are you a keyboard warrior?

Gattina

If by "keyboard warrior" you mean that I troll people on the internet, then no. But if you mean that I can actually speak my mind when I don't have to see your reaction, absolutely, yes.

What if my reaction to you is always good?

Gattina

We'll see...

I shake my head gently, holding in a chuckle at that. She's always so skeptical of my intentions.

Lily's little snores start up, telling me it's safe to lay her back down and rejoin my family downstairs, but I'm unnecessarily hesitant to do so, wanting to continue talking to Kat but thinking better of it.

We definitely will...

I've gotta get back downstairs. Enjoy your night, Kat.

Gattina

You too, Alessandro.

Gently placing Lily back down, I close the door, being as quiet as possible. I head down the hall to peek in at Sofia. She's sleeping silently, and it makes my heart hammer in my chest with anxiety. I creep into the room, squinting my eyes in the dark and crouching down beside her to watch her chest rise and fall. The movement sends a sigh of relief out of my lungs, and I head back out, closing the door behind me.

I hate it when they're so small and you can't tell if they're breathing or not.

Entering the kitchen, I see that the table's been cleaned up already, and desserts are laid out for everyone. I pick up a cannoli, and Dante squeezes my shoulder, leaning in to whisper in my ear, "Thank you, A."

I nod at him, brushing him off. He doesn't need to thank me for taking care of *my* nieces and nephews.

When everyone's finished eating and chatting, we clean up, and Gianni, Alex, and I head outside to play soccer with the older kids. Arlo has gotten really good at soccer, while much to my disappointment, the boys are starting to love football, which is a damn shame.

We kick the black-and-white ball around the small fenced-in backyard using a large tin trash can as our goal.

These days, it seems that Gianni has really made quite the impression on Arlo because she doesn't wear her Philly Scarlets jerseys or shirts anymore unless attending one of my games. Instead, I catch her wearing Messi jerseys and all sorts of other soccer apparel.

What happened to the little girl who couldn't stand to be without her favorite uncle Ale for even a second? While I'm selfishly disappointed that she took to soccer more than hockey, I really think we could come to some solid middle ground with field hockey.

I watch as Arlo laughs with the boys, scoring a goal and getting tackled by Benny in an affectionate hug. Their moms, Arielle and Rose, have been best friends since before either of them met Dante or Charlie. They were both happy to enter the same family, now becoming real sisters after feeling like they already had been for years. They were also ecstatic when they found out they were pregnant at the same time, and both with little girls.

Sammy, Benny, and Lily are Dante and Arielle's, while Arlo and Sofia are Charlie and Rose's. Arlo was adopted when she was three, and Charlie and Rose decided to use a sperm donor because Rose had always wanted to experience pregnancy, and they wanted to grow their little family. I'm glad it worked out for them all because I'm filled with joy every time I think about these kids.

Parenthood must be truly amazing, but being an uncle? Unbeatable, though hopefully, time will tell.

I watch as Gianni smiles at the kids, he and Alex playing with them as I say my goodbyes, letting them know I've got to head back home. I'm hit with a sudden wave of exhaustion, and being out in the cold isn't helping. I just want to go home and crawl into bed.

I give everyone hugs once all the kids have settled onto the couch; they usually sleep over at my parents' house after Sunday dinner, with one of us also staying to keep my parents sane. As I lock up the house and head to my car, I find myself thinking about what, or who, I might find in my hallway when I get home.

Chapter Eleven

Katarina

Monday, November 6, 2023

I woke up at six so I could shower, eat, make sure my meds had time to kick in, and ease my way into my first day at my new office. I haven't gotten to meet any of the staff because my interviews were conducted via video call, so I'm excited and nervous for the day ahead.

I toss on my black scrubs and grab my white coat, which honestly, I find a little pretentious to wear, especially with the number of people who suffer from "white coat syndrome," but my boss asked that I wear it, so I will. Hopefully, that's something I can discontinue with time.

I grab my Earl Grey tea and lock up before heading out. Thankfully, the elevator was repaired before Kas came over the other day, so I don't have to toss my body down those thirty-eight flights of stairs to get to work. Is it thirty-eight? Don't some places pretend there isn't a thirteenth floor? I take a look at the number panel as the elevator descends, and sure enough, there's a thirteenth floor.

I'm maybe a little disappointed that they don't have some strange superstitions here, though it honestly might add fuel to my anxiety, giving me something to ponder at night when I'm unable to sleep.

Once off the elevator, I wave to Ralph and head in the direction of my new job. I'm practically vibrating with nerves and excitement before I get to the building. This area of Philadelphia is sprawling with tall buildings of all kinds. There are old and new buildings, religiously affiliated ones, tons of medical buildings, along with news stations, banks, and anything else you can think of.

I'm originally from the area, but five years away results in a lot of change and unfamiliarity.

I'm also glad that, thanks to Kas's suggestions and my paranoia surrounding being late, I researched everything about the area, including the best routes to take to get here. Yesterday, I even took the walk here and back to avoid getting lost on my first day.

The sidewalks are cluttered with people making their way to work while clutching their jackets to themselves for warmth. It reminds me of one of those holiday movies centered in New York City with the bustling streets and the skyline in the background, people everywhere, car horns honking, impatience skyrocketing, and wind whipping through the scarves and hair of everyone around.

I walk through the automatic glass doors and head over to check in and take a picture for my hospital-issued ID. Thankfully, it turns out a lot better than my driver's license photo had, which honestly rivals the corncob photo for the worst picture of me.

Afterward, I scan my new badge and make my way through the turnstile before pressing the button and waiting for the first available elevator. I make my way up to the ninth floor, making stops along the way to let people come and go before stepping out onto the floor of my new job.

***

Dr. Howell gets me set up in an exam room, telling me it will be my designated room for my scheduled appointments, though I'll be seeing patients in other areas of the hospital when needed as well.

The exam room is spacious, with a table that has a tan padded top and white metal base. The walls are a light-beige color, and I've got white cabinets along one side. The wall to the left of the bed is the entrance, and it consists of a solid, light wooden door, but the walls are made of thick, clear glass. There are privacy curtains in colors similar to those seen on the elevator carpet.

Dr. Howell seems like a really nice guy, and I look forward to working with him. I was a bit apprehensive because there are a lot of big personalities in healthcare, but he seems great so far. He goes over rules and expectations before telling me how the job became available in the first place.

"We're happy to have you here, Kat. Your resume is impressive, and I can tell you've got a good head on your shoulders. I understand the value that PAs provide, so it's not much of a hardship that you're replacing Dr. Shah. You'll do great, Kat. Let me know if there's anything you need."

"Will do, thanks." I smile at him, feeling dumb because his back is already to me as he exits the room.

He heads out, and I start to see patients throughout the day, occasionally responding to a stroke code, where I meet several of the RNs I'll be working with.

The day goes by smoothly, as do the days that follow.

I decided to text Alessandro a few times this week and ask to work out together; he was available twice out of the three times I texted him, and we fell into a nice, quiet rhythm of shy smiles and sneaking glances at each other when we weren't actively spotting one another.

Ale asked me to send him my playlist so we could listen to it together while we work out. I'm also not convinced that I could help him in any way if he suddenly couldn't handle the weight he was lifting. I'm strong, and I know it, but I'm definitely not lift-three-hundred-fifty-pounds-off-a-guy strong.

At least I could call for help though. Other than my encounters with him at the gym and briefly in the hallways when we're coming and going, I don't see him much, but I sure do see my vibrator a whole lot more since meeting him.

Chapter Twelve

Alessandro

Wednesday, November 8, 2023

I'm sitting at the kitchen counter in sweatpants, finally able to relax and read. We had back-to-back games Monday and Tuesday, and I was so beat afterward that the moment I got home, I was knocked out for the night.

But today I've got some time, so I'm enjoying a decaf coffee, not willing to disturb my sleep schedule for my caffeine addiction, and reading when my phone pings with a message.

Setting my book down, I take my glasses off, place them on top of my book as a placeholder, and reach for my cell on the opposite end of the counter. A wide grin settles on my lips when I see who it's from.

Gattina

Gym in ten? Full transparency, I'm just doing some Pilates today.

Did you know that I'm actually a certified yoga instructor?

Gattina

How exactly would I have known that???

Fair point.

Yes to yoga, no to Pilates.

Gattina

If you're offering me a free private lesson, my answer is yes.

I'll give you any lesson you want, gattina. ⬛

Gattina

Don't make me blush! See you in a few.

This is such a bad idea, but I just can't seem to stop myself. I've enjoyed every interaction I've had with Kat, and I'm just so damn drawn to her. Standing, I push in my chair and move around the counter, dumping out my coffee and rinsing the mug before placing it in the dishwasher.

I make my way to my bedroom, grabbing a short-sleeved dark-green shirt and pulling it over my head before slipping my sneakers on and heading out the door to wait for Kat. Her door snicks open as soon as I'm outside, and she pops out, smiling at me as she exits.

"You have a good day at work?" I ask her, and she nods.

"Good but stressful, so the yoga is much needed." She gives me a small smile as her cheeks pinken. "How was work for you?" she asks me as we take the stairs down to the gym below us.

"I actually had the day off, so I was able to catch up on some reading and clean up the apartment."

"That sounds like a perfect day; I love to read." Her voice takes on a longing quality.

"You don't get to read much?"

"I'm hoping I will now that I'm not studying all day, but the last few years in school were just a lot, so I didn't really have much free time." I nod in understanding.

Holding the heavy metal door open for her, she steps out into the hall before pulling on the glass doors to the gym.

Her sneakers squeak a little when we get inside the quiet room with wooden floors. She heads to the corner of the room where all the equipment is set up and takes two black yoga mats off the rack, handing one to me. She also grabs a bottle of disinfectant while I pull out several paper towels from the dispenser. She tosses her mat to the ground, spraying it liberally before motioning for me to drop mine for her. I do, and she sprays it down while I wipe hers off, ensuring it's completely dry before moving on to mine.

When we're ready, we both take a seat, facing one another with our mats only three feet apart. She had initially moved hers a few feet over, but I couldn't help myself and moved mine closer.

We're seated in a crisscross-applesauce position. "Do you have a playlist you'd like to put on?" I ask her before we get started. After lots of begging on my part, she finally sent me her lifting playlist, which was definitely not what I had expected from her.

"Uh, I'm not sure you'd really like the music I listen to when I want to relax," she says hesitantly.

"I'm not sure there's anything about you that I wouldn't like," I tell her truthfully, even knowing I shouldn't say the words, but every time she blushes, I get such a rush that I keep chasing it like an addiction.

Deflecting, she rolls her eyes and pulls out her phone, taking a moment to find a playlist. She peers up at me through thick lashes before pressing play.

The first lines of the chorus play softly through the speaker, the lyrics describing how the singer likes their women sweet like honey—just like Kat and those honey eyes of hers, so sweet.[1]

She's biting on her bottom lip, and I want to pluck it out from her teeth with my thumb so I can do the honors myself. The next line filters through about being a beautiful disaster, a vibrant mess. Again, this line sounds just like Kat. She's always so nervous, her personality colorful and bright, but her sense of humor always catches me off guard.

Once again, the words coming through her speaker perfectly describe my current predicament. Out of all the pretty girls in the world, I find myself with Kat. The flame between us is always stoked, burning brightly as if by fate. The song ends with a mention of the heartache that would take place if that fire were set free.

And that's exactly what I'm afraid of. If we were to date, and something went badly, we'd both suffer and so would her brother. I'd do well to remind myself of that.

My smile starts to slip, and she notices, pressing pause abruptly on the music, the room filling with an unsettling silence. "Sorry, I said you wouldn't like it." She toys with her necklace, and I can't help it. I reach out, grasping her hand and gently pulling it away from the pendant, letting her hand fall to her lap.

"No, I really like it, I do," I reassure her. "My mind just drifted off for a moment there." I smile at her and lean over, pressing play on her screen. "What's the significance of that necklace you're always toying with?" I ask, the words falling out of my mouth.

She looks down to where the pendant has fallen between her breasts before gazing back up at me. "It was my mom's; the pendant has a sea turtle engraved into it. It's a Filipino symbol for adaptability, something I'd really like to master, but it honestly just makes me feel closer to her." She gives me a small smile, which I return before moving on, not wanting to pry further or make her uncomfortable, but she surprises me, nodding her head to my bicep.

"What's the meaning of your tattoo?" she asks, her tone thoughtful.

I lift my sleeve up, extending my arm out so she can see it in its entirety. Seemingly without a thought, her fingers jut out, tracing the lines of the Medusa head and leaving a trail of goosebumps in their wake. "It's a Sicilian symbol called the 'Trinacria;' the three legs form a triangle because of the shape of the island of Sicily. They represent the three capes of the island, and the stalks of wheat are because the island was a major producer of grain during the Roman Empire, so they're considered a symbol of fertility and prosperity. And the Medusa head in the center was thought to keep evil spirits away, so the people of Sicily would etch this symbol above their doors. I had it placed at the bottom of a larger Medusa head because some days, I feel like I need my own protector." I answer her honestly, if not in a little too much detail, but judging by her enthralled expression, she's not the least bit bored.

Her brows pull together as she studies the symbol, still raking her lithe fingers over the fine lines before seemingly coming out of her thoughts. Her cheeks pinken with realization, and she pulls her hand back abruptly. I have to rein in the frown that threatens to morph my expression, not enjoying the loss of her touch.

Clearing my throat, I nod. "You ready to start?"

"Yep," she says, her voice feigning confidence.

"Okay, we can just do an easy flow today from the floor," I tell her, hoping she's okay with that because my muscles ache, and I hadn't planned to do anything but lay in bed all day, which I had all but accomplished until she had texted.

"Sounds perfect," she tells me.

I spend the next thirty minutes walking her through several positions, ensuring she faces me the entire time because I can't trust myself not to lose my damn mind if her ass somehow winds up in my face. It doesn't help that the playlist she chose sounds like the theme track to a night of incredible sex, and my dick has definitely gotten the message. It's probably best that we finish up and relax into the last pose so I have time for my semi to relax too.

"This last pose is called 'Savasana,' but it's also known as 'corpse pose'. Lay down on your back." I wait as she does, and I follow suit. "Loosen your limbs, let them lay beside you limply," I coax. "Release the tension in your neck and shoulders and unclench your jaw, letting your tongue release from the roof of your mouth."

A new song filters through her phone speaker, talking about the singer taking her partner on a trip to her body and mind, finding more pleasure than what can be seen with the naked eye.[2]

So much for calming my hard-on.

I keep my eyes screwed shut, trying to calm my mind but failing miserably. I'm flooded with images of Kat riding my cock, her perky little tits bouncing, head tossed back as she screams my name.

My dick is at full attention now, so I peel my eyelids back, peering over at her before adjusting myself, tucking myself into the waistband of my sweats and hoping that'll do the trick.

I close my eyes again, loosening my jaw and doing as I had instructed Kat to, but just as I'm settling in, she shifts slightly beside me, her pinky grazing the side of my hand. A rush of heat sears me at the small touch, but she doesn't move her hand away. I work to calm my breathing, but when her pinky twitches beside me again, I can't help my body's response. I curl my own pinky around hers, locking it with mine and not letting go until the next song has ended.

We blink our eyes open, the small tether I had to her now broken as she gently pulls out of my grasp.

She gives me a nervous smile. "Thanks, that was really nice," she tells me shakily, turning her music off and moving to clean off her yoga mat.

"Anytime, Kat," I reply, unable to formulate a wittier response with my cock still tucked into my waistband.

When we finish getting the room cleaned up and putting the mats away, I walk her back to her apartment, and she hurries in, calling over her shoulder to me, "Night, Ale."

"Goodnight, *gattina*."

***

I'm lying in bed, restless, thoughts of Kat constantly leaking in through the cracks in my resolve. What is my obsession with this woman?

I think it's obvious that this pull I feel toward her goes far beyond a physical attraction alone, but my heart aches with the thought that this isn't right. Over and over, I've tried to remind myself that, just in the last few days alone, but something about her keeps drawing me in.

Having spent the last hour tossing and turning, I give up on the idea of sleep, for now, anyway. Grabbing my cell off the nightstand, I unplug it and open my messages, seeing Kat's name at the very top.

I groan internally as my thumbs take on a mind of their own, opening the message thread as I scroll through our brief interactions so far.

My thumb hits the text box, and I find myself typing out a message to her.

> You awake?

Gattina

> It's only eleven, Ale. I'm not ninety years old...

> Hey there, some people need their beauty sleep.

> Some people being me, definitely not you.

Gattina

> Are you saying I'm ugly beyond repair?

> Hell no.

> I'm saying you're fucking stunning. Magnificent. A goddamn vision, and if you become any more beautiful, I'd be simply blinded by you.

> So please avoid that at all costs...

What the hell is wrong with me?

Nothing I just said is a lie, but why can't I seem to stop flirting with her?

Nerves take over as I watch the three dots move across the screen, indicating she's typing. They stop, then restart, and my anxiety grows, nervous energy flowing freely through me now.

I let out a long sigh of relief when her message finally comes through.

Gattina

> While I appreciate the compliment, that sounds like a line you stole from a book... and it's untrue, but that's beside the point.

Gattina

> No worries from me though because I'm not all that great at sleeping.

Gattina

> Or... are you fishing for a compliment, Alessandro?

> What do you mean by that? Do you have trouble falling asleep, or is it staying asleep?

> And yes. I'm always fishing for compliments from you...

Gattina

> I just have trouble falling asleep sometimes, and I wake up a few times each night. Nothing huge.

Gattina

> You know, I never took you as someone with such low self-esteem...

Gattina

> But since you apparently need the boost, here goes nothing...

The fact that she struggles with sleep bothers me for some reason. Her brother says she has a stressful job, and the idea of her struggling to get through the day because of exhaustion nags at something in my chest.

> If you ever want to talk about the sleep situation, I'd be happy to let you bounce ideas off of me. Sleep's important.

> I'm waiting with bated breath, gattina...

Gattina

> You look like one of the heroes from my romance novels (this is the highest compliment you could ever receive, btw). Your eyes are my favorite color, and you've got an ass I could bounce a quarter off of.

Laughter bubbles out of me, and I shake my head, a huge smile plastered across my face as I consider this. *I'm glad I'm not the only one staring at the other's ass.*

> I think I'd like to hear more about these men you fantasize about in those books of yours...

Gattina

Not a chance.

Sensing that she's ready to withdraw from me, her moment of freedom from that anxiety I see creeping into her every interaction is waning, so I change direction.

Tell me something about yourself that no one knows.

Gattina

Um… like what?

Anything.

Gattina

Okay…

Gattina

I collect lamps, or at least I used to.

What made you stop?

Gattina

When I moved, I had no room for them, so I had to leave them with my best friend's parents, and I haven't had the time to ask about them yet.

> How'd you start collecting them in the first place?

Gattina

My Lola (grandma) and I would go to estate sales on weekends, and I just loved how many varieties they came in.

> And no one else knows this about you?

Gattina

Almost no one. Kas and Aiyana do, and now you.

> Well, I'm honored to be included in the list.

Gattina

Your turn.

> Okay. Let me think.

My mind wanders back to our *lesson* earlier today, and a thought strikes me.

Gattina

Take your time.

> Okay, I've got it.

> The reason I became a yoga instructor was to help my mom with her physical therapy.

> She was having a lot of trouble with mobility when I was in my early twenties, and a friend had suggested yoga.

> I took her to some classes, and she really liked them, but she felt anxious, thinking people were judging her.

Gattina

So you got certified and took the classes to her?

> In a nutshell, yes.

Gattina

That's really sweet, Alessandro.

Gattina

How'd she feel about having you as an instructor?

> She loved it and had the whole family join in, but eventually, she became entirely wheelchair-bound and couldn't keep up well.

My heart tears a little at the memory—the day she started using the wheelchair and was never able to regain the strength she needed to keep herself upright, even with a walker.

Gattina

> I'm so sorry, Ale, truly. That must be incredibly difficult for your whole family, but I'm glad she has your support.

> Sorry, I didn't mean to bring the mood down.

I feel awkward, having brought us down this particular path to memory lane.

Gattina

> You know how you told me to stop being afraid to accept kindness from others?

Gattina

> Well, stop being afraid to show your emotions. Especially with me. I've had enough heartbreak and loss in my life to recognize when someone needs a safe space to talk things out. I just want you to know that I'm happy to be that for you.

Gattina

> You know, as a friend.

Her admission hits me like a fist straight to the gut, and her reminder that we can only be friends fills me with sorrow that I can't even begin to uncover the reasoning for.

> Thanks, Kat. Really, I appreciate it.

> I should probably try to get some sleep. Early day tomorrow.

Gattina

Goodnight, Alessandro.

Goodnight, gattina.

---

1. **Honey - Kehlani**

2. **Wine - Zae**

Chapter Thirteen

Katarina

Friday, November 10, 2023

It's Friday morning, which means it's a purple scrub day. I *always* wear purple scrubs on Fridays; it's kind of like a good luck charm. Plus, Aiyana should be arriving in a few hours, which means it's going to be an incredible end to my first week back in Philly. The week passed by so quickly that I hadn't even realized the weekend had almost rolled around already, or I wouldn't have if it weren't for Aiyana's incoming stream of memes this morning reminding me of her arrival. I smile at the thought.

I have work till five plus however long it takes for me to finish charting for the day, so I gave her the code to the penthouse, and she'll let herself in. She and I will be sharing my bed while she's here since she's in town for some job interviews, and her bed hasn't been delivered yet.

She's brilliant, so I'm sure she'll get snatched up soon and be here with me full-time. I can't wait; my heart swells with pride for her. It's only been a week since I left San Diego, and the apartment feels so lonely without her in it. It's been years since I've stayed anywhere that she wasn't. Aiyana's been my best friend, neighbor, and later, my roommate for as long as I can remember.

Tonight, Kas has a home game that starts at six, but the rink is only a few minutes away from work by car. Aiyana got a rental since her interviews are all over the city, and it wasn't worth trying to figure out the public transportation system for each one. Which means she'll be able to pick me up from work and head to the game with me.

It's been years since I've gotten to see Kas play in person because my schedule never allowed for that much time off, and he didn't have any games close enough to me in San Diego.

Last night, Kas dropped off jerseys for Aiyana and me to wear tonight, so I packed mine, as well as some black leggings and a pair of black-and-white Converse to change into before I head out after work.

***

As I'm working on my notes from this morning, my cell vibrates in my pocket. I pull it out, inspecting the screen, and see "Aiyana" flash across it several times with a series of matching vibrations buzzing in my hand. Shaking my head at her, I unlock my phone and start reading her messages, each one sounding more and more like the ramblings of a lunatic. She starts by gushing about the penthouse, but that's quickly followed up by messages about Alessandro. I'd wondered how long it would take before they met. She texts with:

My Pain In The Ass

> HOTTIE ALERT ON FLOOR 38!

My Pain In The Ass

> Are you fucking kidding me, Kat???

My Pain In The Ass

> Wtf is wrong with you???

My Pain In The Ass

> Why was I not informed that we're sharing a floor with a literal fucking GOD!?????

My Pain In The Ass

> You must not have seen him yet, right? Because if you had, CERTAINLY you would have told your BEST FRIEND about him, RIGHT?????

My Pain In The Ass

> Also, when are you fucking him? Wait, am I fucking him?! OMG, is he my housewarming gift?

For some reason, that last text sends a jolt of jealousy through me that I know I have no business feeling, but it's there all the same. I see my attending heading toward me, so I shoot her a quick text and plan to tell her all about him later.

My Pain In The Ass

OH

My Pain In The Ass

MY

My Pain In The Ass

GOD

My Pain In The Ass

He introduced himself and said YOU AL-
READY HAVE HIS NUMBER?!?!?!

My Pain In The Ass

This feels like adultery, Kat! You fucking
cheated on me! :'(

SORRY! Please forgive me, for I have sinned!
I'll tell you all about him tonight. Tata, love
you. BYE!

And another text to be safe.

AND NO TOUCHY TOUCHY!

I receive a quick text back with, "TTLYB!!!!!" just as Dr. Howell appears in front of me.

He's a nice guy, mid-fifties, and happily married. He's got salt-and-pepper hair, kind gray eyes, nice straight teeth, and dimples in both cheeks.

"Hey Kat, do you mind if we have a word privately?"

My hands start to get clammy, and I can't help but wipe them on my scrub bottoms as nerves settle in. I haven't even finished my first week here, and I'm already being pulled away for a private chat.

"Uh, yeah, of course, Dr. Howell; what can I help you with?" My voice is shaky, anxiety leeching in, my hand making its way to my necklace.

He lets out a huff while shaking his head and says, "Kat, we've talked about this before; you can call me Jeff. We're co-workers, you're not really my subordinate; you see patients on your own just like I do."

I smile at him shyly, still a little nervous, but I figure if he wants me to call him Jeff, that must mean he's not planning on getting rid of me. "Sorry, Jeff, what is it?"

"There's a patient I added to the schedule for today that's pretty last minute. He used to see Dr. Shah, and I haven't had a chance to go through his chart entirely, but it's pretty heavy. He called a few minutes ago and begged to be seen urgently. I don't have any room on my schedule for today, but you had a cancellation for three. Would you mind seeing him?"

Without a second thought, I respond. "Of course I don't mind. Do you have any idea what he's coming in for? Also, next time, lead with that; I thought I was getting fired!" I tell him, a little louder than I meant to, and a nurse walking by eyes me warily.

He lets out a rumbling laugh. "Fire you? Kat, you're the first person here to learn how to use our EMR in less than three months, and your patients love you. The staff does too, which is incredibly rare. Some days, I'm not even sure if they like *me.*" He lets out a quick huff that sounds like a mix between exasperation and a laugh.

"I'll let you get back to it, and I'll let the front desk know you'll see him. I believe they said his name is Alex. He's coming in for symptoms related to a recent exacerbation of his multiple sclerosis. I think just fatigue and maybe some generalized pain."

I nod. "Okay, that should be easy enough to manage."

I head back to my desk to finish my notes from my earlier patients, and it doesn't take long until my medical assistant, Cindy, lets me know my add-on is here.

"I just roomed your next patient. He was previously seeing Dr. Shah, but I forgot to tell him he isn't here anymore." She looks down at her feet, her cheeks flaming from a blush of embarrassment. "Should I go let him know before you come in?"

"Oh no, Cindy, it's totally okay. Did you get his vitals or any more information on what's bringing him in today?"

"Yeah, vital signs are normal; the guy has muscles for days, so his BMI was almost thirty-three." Her comment makes me chuckle as she continues. "The EMR automatically marked him as obese, but you can tell he's in excellent shape. Other than that, everything appears normal. He said he's been feeling fatigued the last two weeks and can't seem to shake it, and he's experiencing some muscle pains." Her earlier embarrassment has worn off, and a huge grin has taken residence on her youthful face. She's nearly shaking with excitement; she must be happy about the upcoming weekend.

"Thank you, Cindy. You ready to head in?"

CHAPTER FOURTEEN

Alessandro

I'm sitting in an exam room waiting for Dr. Shah to come in when I hear two semi-familiar voices chatting outside the room. I can't make out what they're saying behind the thick wooden door. I can't tell who the second voice belongs to; everything's muffled, but I believe the first voice is Cindy, Dr. Shah's medical assistant. The voices quiet, and I hear a knock on the door.

"Come on in," I call to him. "I haven't given you a peep show yet, Dr. Shah," I add, chuckling. These appointments don't usually require me to undress into a gown or anything.

Who I see walk through the door with Cindy in tow is definitely *not* Dr. Shah. My chest squeezes as soon as she enters the room. "Kat? What are you doing here? And where is Dr. Shah?" My brows climb up my forehead, confusion jumbling my mind.

"I, um, are you here for an appointment about your MS symptoms?" Kat's face is becoming increasingly more red, and she's obviously flustered. How does she know what I'm here for?

Dr. Shah signed an NDA; he literally can't tell other staff members what I'm here for. Even Cindy isn't allowed in the room with me after she takes my vitals. I can't have information about my condition leaked to the press because of someone's big mouth; they'll have a field day with it. My career will be over when my team finds out I have a degenerative illness that could result in a fucking loss of motor function.

The only person even affiliated with the team who knows is my athletic trainer, and she definitely won't say anything. She'd rather know and keep quiet than not be aware of my medication regimen and further increase my risk of injury.

"Where is Dr. Shah?" I say it a lot more harshly than I should, especially based on how frightened Kat looks right now.

Cindy pipes up, "I'm so sorry, Mr. De Laurentiis, this is all my fault! I completely forgot to tell you that Dr. Shah won't be your provider anymore because he's left the practice."

Shaking my head vehemently. "I can't see you. I need to see Dr. Shah; he's been my provider for years." I'm gritting my teeth and getting more frustrated by the second. How is it possible that he just left the practice, and no one bothered to tell me? Didn't they think that was important? Granted, I haven't been seen in a few months, but there should be a protocol for these types of situations.

I'm beyond flustered. I knew Kat worked in healthcare since her brother never shuts up about her, but I hadn't known she worked in god damn *neurology*.

Straightening her spine, Kat pins me with a look that tells me I'm on thin ice. "I'm sorry that this comes as a shock to you. I saw your name on the chart, but you and I had never exchanged last names before, so I hadn't realized you were the patient I'd be seeing."

She's speaking through gritted teeth, and I'm getting the feeling that she has no idea why I wouldn't want to see her. Maybe she thinks it's because she's a PA or a woman? Either way, neither of those is true. She continues, "Unfortunately, there is no way for you to see Dr. Shah as he's no longer a member of this practice."

I huff out a frustrated sigh, trying to calm myself before I continue speaking. "Fine, I'll see you, but Cindy needs to leave. She was never in the room when Dr. Shah saw me." Not that it matters anymore; she already knows what my diagnosis is now.

Kat speaks up immediately. It's clear that she won't be letting anyone make her staff feel belittled in her presence, and I feel the warmth of pride for that seeping into my chest despite my annoyance at the situation.

"That's because Dr. Shah was a man; our office policy states that there needs to be a chaperone in the room when dealing with patients of the opposite sex. Though, I suppose if you'll allow us to draw back the curtain and leave the windows viewable, Cindy can sit in the hall and chaperone from there, since you don't need to remove your clothing for this exam. Is that all right, Alessandro?" Kat's tone is stern; she has a no-bullshit air about her that I've never seen, and under any other circumstances, I'd find it sexy as hell.

However, against my better judgment, I keep talking, sounding more and more like a complete jackass. "Just to clarify, you both are fully aware that you cannot under any circumstances mention my presence in this office today nor the reasoning for my appointment, correct? I just want to make sure my rights in accordance with HIPAA are well known and followed."

"Yes, Alessandro, we are both very well acquainted with HIPAA." She looks like she wants to roll her eyes but holds it back while she remains as professional as possible despite my shitty attitude. "Right, Cindy?"

Cindy nods and leaves the room while Kat opens the curtains and closes the door. Kat takes a seat and places her tablet to the side before facing me.

"All right, so what brings you in today?"

"Kat, you know what brings me in today. I'm fatigued, and I've had some muscle aches," I tell her, exhausted already.

Her tone softens as she speaks her next words. "All right, tell me a bit about that, like when it happens, how it feels, and if anything makes it better or worse."

We go on like this for the next ten minutes or so until she's satisfied. She prescribes me a new medication and goes over a plan with me in the event that it doesn't work. She said that she's not a huge fan of my current regimen, but if it seems to be working for me, she's okay with maintaining it and working on something new in the future. She's incredibly professional, making me feel understood and ensuring I'm aware that this is a conversation about my medical management, not her just telling me what and how we're going to go about my treatment, but actually including me in it. Honestly, I already like her a whole lot better than Dr. Shah, even on his best days. Guilt settles in, and I know I need to apologize because none of this was her fault. I was being a total douche; I was just so overwhelmed by the situation and, honestly, pretty embarrassed that she had to see me ask for help, which left me feeling weak and frustrated.

As she gets up to leave, I grab her hand quickly before saying, "Kat, wait. Can we talk real quick?"

She looks down at her tiny hand in mine and gently pulls it out of my grasp. It feels like a huge loss when she breaks the contact, but I'm relieved when she takes a seat again. Clearly, Cindy isn't paying attention anymore, or she probably would have busted down the door seeing me grab for Kat like that.

As she settles into her chair, I lean forward, resting my forearms on my thighs, gazing up into those honey eyes as I prepare myself for the potential that she won't accept my apology. And she'd be completely valid in doing so. "I shouldn't have spoken to you like that," I start, her posture relaxing further. "Outside of my family, almost no one knows about my diagnosis, and I want to keep it that way. When I saw you come in with Cindy, I was shocked and confused, but I shouldn't have behaved like that."

She visibly softens, that soft blush brightening the tan apples of her cheekbones as she looks at her feet, her long lashes fanning out on her cheeks before she peers back up at me with wide amber eyes. "I actually really enjoyed this office visit. Your bedside manner is a lot better than Dr. Shah's, and you're definitely easier on the eye than he was." I chuckle a little when her eyes widen, her blush deepening and spreading to her ears. I was trying to lighten the mood, but it seems that may not have been the most sensitive thing to say. I'm fucking this up left and right.

"I'm glad I exceeded your incredibly low expectations, Alessandro." She says it with a hint of anger in her tone, but when my cheeks start to heat, she smirks before giving me a somber look. "Why didn't you tell me that you had MS? You said your mom has it but never mentioned yourself, not that it was my business in either regard." She's letting her guard down a bit for me, so I decide to do the same.

"I know that it's more rare for men to be diagnosed with MS, and even less common that it's inherited, but my mom and I both have it, though I don't exactly love talking about it. She has secondary progressive while I'm told I made out easier so far."

She's nodding, digesting my words. "You're right; both of those occurrences are rare." Her eyes are wide, and I can read the surprise and empathy all over her face. "I'm right across the hall if you need anything, okay? I mean that—HIPAA applies no matter where we're at."

"Thanks, Kat. I'll get out of your hair so you can see your next patient."

Chapter Fifteen

Katarina

What the hell just happened? I feel dazed and confused, like one of the characters from the romance books I read where the main character finds out something crazy about her main love interest. Though that isn't real life, and Alessandro isn't my love interest. At least, he definitely can't be *now*.

"Oh my god, Kat! You know Alessandro De Laurentiis?" Cindy gushes when he's left the office.

"Uh, yeah, Cindy, we've met briefly. So briefly, in fact, I didn't even know his last name." I leave out the fact that he lives across the hall from me. Those are details she definitely doesn't need to know. And I'm not sure why she's acting like some crazed fan.

He's just a hot patient. We get those periodically, and we even have a pretty attractive male RN working in the psych unit who comes down from time to time for consults.

We get back to work, and luckily, I only have one more patient to see, which ends up being a quick appointment for a refill of migraine medication that has been working great for them.

I'm always happy to hear when something's working and that there's no need to make any changes. Not just because it makes things easier for me but because changes can be frustrating for the patients, and I obviously want their symptoms to be well managed.

I finish writing up my notes and head to the locker room to get changed. I toss my giant black winter coat over my Philly Scarlets outfit and head downstairs for Aiyana to pick me up.

***

"I'm so happy you're here!" Now that we're seated only three rows up from the glass on the home team's side, I can't help but throw my arms around her and squeeze her tight. It's only been a week since we last saw each other, but having lived with her for the last several years makes any time apart seem so much longer than it is.

"Me too! I've missed you so much! But this conversation will have to wait until after we get back to the penthouse with the dreamy giant across the hall because hockey is on." Aiyana loves hockey; it's one of the things we first bonded over, and when she found out my brother was a hockey player, the two of them became inseparable until she and I moved.

She watches all of my brother's games from home, either recorded or live, so it's nice to finally see him play in person with her. And I think she's had a crush on my brother since we first met in middle school, but she's never admitted it, so I haven't brought it up in case I'm misreading the situation. I wouldn't want to make things awkward between them.

"I don't know if you've noticed or not, but hockey isn't 'on' because it's not TV. This is an in-person game." I say it playfully so she knows I'm joking, but she side-eyes me and sticks out her tongue before regaining her focus on the game before her.

I'm just glad that Kas chose a sport that isn't slow-paced because there's absolutely no way I'd be able to keep my attention trained on something like golf or tennis.

***

"I'm gonna go grab a beer before the third period starts; want anything?" The game is tied one-one, and fans all around are getting restless and weary as we approach the final period.

"Yeah, could you grab me a water and popcorn, please?" I bat my lashes at her, making a big show of it. She laughs and heads over to the concession stands.

While she's gone, I decide to text Ale and see if he wants to work out tomorrow. Truthfully, I just want to see him again, especially after how awkward today ended. After giving it some thought, I can understand why he'd be so upset. I took a deeper look at his chart after he left and realized he'd been seeing Dr. Shah for several years. People form an attachment to their providers, but more than that, having to open up to someone new about a chronic illness with no cure as of yet? That'd be extremely difficult for anyone, but especially when your new provider is someone you already kind of know.

Looking down at my cell, I try to figure out what to type, settling on the simplest text possible as the best way to avoid any further anxiety for either of us.

> Workout tomorrow?

Aiyana gets back with our snacks and drinks and settles in beside me. I check my texts again, but he still hasn't responded. "Whatcha lookin' at?" she asks, reading over my shoulder like a nosey child.

"Oh, I just texted Alessandro while you were at concessions to see if he wanted to work out tomorrow since I know you hate any kind of physical activity that isn't sex. And unfortunately, I'm still not interested in your offer of the former, so the gym will have to do."

"Mhmm, well, you'll have to tell me *all* about these 'workouts' you're doing." She makes air quotes around the word "workout."

I shove her shoulder, chuckling at her. "He usually replies back within a couple of minutes, so maybe he doesn't want to or he's busy." I shrug, trying to act as nonchalant as possible, but I feel anxiety welling up inside me. Maybe today was just too much for him, and he doesn't want to be friends anymore?

Cutting off my anxious train of thought, she replies, "Hmm, 'hottie hallmate,' huh? I thought you said you didn't really know the guy well?" She's peering over my shoulder again. "Also,"—she takes a swig of her beer— "based on your previous conversations," she says, dragging her finger up my screen to quickly scroll through them, "it doesn't seem like he's ever *not wanted to.*"

I can't exactly tell her why things have changed, but they have, so I deflect.

"That's what he saved his contact as in my phone. It makes me laugh when I see it, and it's not like he's wrong, so I haven't bothered to change it."

Her thin brow quirks, a knowing smirk spreading across her ruby-red lips. "You know, he looks sort of familiar, but I can't seem to place him."

My brows pull together, considering this. "Maybe he went to school with us? I think he's a few years older, so it'd make sense that we wouldn't know him."

"*Maybe,* but I think I'd have noticed him." She chuckles but redirects her attention to the ice, and the game starts up again.

***

Buzzers go off; everyone is either screaming out of anger or cheering with joy because someone scored a goal on our side. Shit, I can't believe I missed it! I was too busy checking my phone for a text from Ale.

I hear the announcer come over the intercom, "And another goal for the home team! Courtesy of number twenty-six, Alessandro De Laurentiis!" More cheers from our side and angry screams from the other team's. And all I can do is stand here with my mouth hanging open, jaw practically scraping the ground.

"Babe, you okay? What'd you say our hallmate's name was? Wasn't it Alessandro?" I guess she takes my look of utter disbelief and silence as a "YES, IT'S HIM!"

"Oh my god! *That's* where I know him from!" She's got a shit-eating grin on her face as she starts jumping up and down with excitement. She grabs my shoulders, shaking me out of my shock, and continues vibrating with laughter. She's absolutely delighted by this change of events. "Kas never mentioned him! Never once did my brother say anything about an Alessandro, and wouldn't *you* have recognized his name as someone who never misses a game?"

She chuckles. "Babe, I never see these guys without helmets on, so I couldn't place the name to the face, especially not after our brief hallway encounter. Like I said, *he looked familiar.* Besides, I'm usually more focused on the player I *actually* know in real life!" She says it almost defensively, but her smile remains intact.

I manage to pick my jaw up off the ground and take a seat, barely paying attention as the last few minutes of the game go by, and the Philly Scarlets win two to one—Ale's goal securing the lead.

Aiyana and I head down to meet my brother after he's showered and changed. It usually takes a while since they all have to take turns riding the stationary bikes to help release the built-up lactic acid from playing for so long. It's not totally necessary, but my brother has always erred on the side of caution when it comes to his physical fitness, so he does it every time.

A while later, he emerges from the locker rooms with a few other players, including Alessandro.

Aiyana runs over to my brother, jumping up and giving him a huge hug. He shakes with laughter, wrapping his arms tightly around her in one of his signature bear hugs.

Aiyana's pin-straight, raven-black hair falls just above her butt, the ends tangling in Kas's grip. I've never met anyone with such long hair, though her father used to give her a run for her money. Aiyana's family is Cherokee and incredibly proud of it. She's explained to me that her hair represents a strong cultural identity for her.

While my brother and I are Filipino on our mother's side and Puerto Rican on our father's, our features don't lean too heavily to either side. We haven't remained super connected to our heritage, especially not after the incident. Not how Aiyana is anyway, though Qaletaqa, her dad, spent a lot of our childhood teaching Kas and me how to carve wood and weave baskets.

Once Kas has released her from his clutches, I walk over for my hug. He steps back after and smiles at me as he waves his arm behind him theatrically toward the group of giants huddled there. "Guys, meet my sister, Kat, and her best friend, Aiyana. Kat and Aiyana, meet the guys."

Everyone chuckles and starts passing by us with a smile, a wink here or there, and the occasional smirk of interest.

Everyone except Alessandro.

I walk over to him, still a little dazed, and on a whim, decide to throw my arms around his neck and give him a hug. I can't say for sure why I do it other than I want to know what his hugs are like, among other things. That and I'm desperate to erase the awkward haze that's descended upon us.

He's easily a foot taller than I am, so I have to stand on my toes to reach him. That should have been the first warning sign that he was a hockey player.

I knew there were some of Kas's teammates in my building, but for some reason, Ale being one of them hadn't crossed my mind. I just found it doubtful that my brother would be okay with me living across the hall from one of them, and he had mentioned that the majority of them are happily married or in relationships. I definitely haven't seen any women coming or going from his apartment.

Plus, there's the fact that he seemingly has all of his own teeth. That in itself threw me off.

He seems a bit startled at first, so when I hug him, his arms don't immediately go around me.

I guess he shakes out of his surprise because his massive, warm arms come around my back, and he clutches me close to his chest. He tucks my head under his chin, and I can't help but sigh into him, leaning my body weight against him and nuzzling my nose into the base of his neck in a gesture that's more intimate than appropriate.

I take a deep breath in, and the smell of him is intoxicating. He smells faintly of soap from his shower, a little salty because I'm sure he's still a bit sweaty, and something so uniquely him. It's warm, a little spicy, and masculine but clean, and I'd buy it if it were a cologne so I could spray everything I own with it.

It reminds me of perfumes I've purchased with Fougere pink pepper in them, and I love it on him more than I ever did on me.

I hear a throat clear from behind me, and we break apart from our little moment. Kas stares at me with confusion, and Aiyana has a smirk on her face that very clearly broadcasts, "We'll be talking about this tonight, little lady."

"Sooo, I guess you've met Alice, huh?" My eyes go wide with recognition. *Alice*! He's been telling me all about this great guy he plays with who's very family-oriented, sets the standard for all men, and plays better than anyone he's ever known for the last *three* years. Kas has been playing on the same team for four years now, and never once has he called him by his real name.

I hear a groan from beside me. "Can you please stop with that god-awful fucking nickname? It was *one* time!"

"Wait, what was one time? How'd he get the nickname?" Aiyana voices exactly what's going through my head right now. She's almost bouncing with the anticipation of hearing a potentially embarrassing story.

I guess Ale decides to save himself from whatever messed up version of events my brother is about to give when he says, "I told you I have a big family, and I have a lot of nieces and nephews." His eyes are focused on me. "My niece, Arlo, was adopted by my sister and her wife when she was three. She was the first of my nieces; up till that point, we had only had the boys, Sammy and Benny. So when she arrived, she was a timid little thing, afraid of her own shadow and didn't like anyone. Including her moms."

His face brightens, a cheerful grin widening his lips, and that damned dimple pokes out, as if he could get any hotter. Or any more *off-limits*. "But when she met me, she latched herself to me and refused to let go. To the point that I had to take her to practice with me pretty much Kas's entire first year on the team. My sister and her wife even lived with me until Arlo finally trusted them enough to let me get back to life as usual. Her therapist says it's likely I remind her of someone she knew before being adopted who made her feel safe," he explains.

"So one of the last times she had to come to practice with me was on her fourth birthday. She had just watched the animated version of Alice in Wonderland, and I'm sure she had no idea what was going on outside of there being a tea party, a guy in a crazy hat, and a white bunny with a blonde girl. So for her birthday, she demanded that we have a tea party, but instead of her being Alice..."

Aiyana interrupts him abruptly, snickering, "Let me guess; she wanted *you* to be Alice?"

His cheeks turn pink, and he continues, "Yep. I was Alice, my sister Charlie was the Mad Hatter, her wife Rose was the Cheshire Cat, and Arlo was the White Rabbit. We lost track of time, and I didn't have a chance to change before leaving, so I took Arlo to practice with me looking like that, and we almost had to cancel practice because everyone was laughing so profusely that Coach got pissed and made them all run drills. Luckily, Coach Allister loves kids and took a liking to Arlo. She reminded him of his granddaughter, so I didn't get in any trouble for showing up like that, and he let me and Arlo sit in the stands while we watched the guys run a bunch of bullshit drills that were too exhausting for them to laugh at us."

"That is probably the cutest thing I've ever heard! Kassian, you are an asshole for making fun of this poor man!" Aiyana gushes. She loves men with a soft side, so she's probably already thinking of trading my brother in for a new model in Alessandro's honor.

Shaking my head with a small smile, I add, "That is pretty cute." I peek up at Ale, and he grins down at me before looking away quickly and excusing himself to go meet up with his family.

"So you and Alice have gotten pretty friendly then, huh?" Kas asks me, his elbow nudging me as I fight the blush threatening its way up my neck.

I roll my eyes at him with a look of annoyance. "We've spoken a few times. Now let's go eat; I'm starving."

I'm also gaining a lot of clarity as to why Alessandro was so adamant about HIPAA compliance earlier. Anxiety is starting to bubble inside me because Ale said his episodes of relapse have become more and more frequent.

He also admitted to previously experiencing muscle weakness and some numbness in his extremities, though he said this time it's mostly just fatigue and some pain. It isn't easy to combat the two when your body requires a lot more rest than the average person, but your job literally entails fatiguing your muscles daily.

I'm concerned that an episode of weakness or numbness could result in an unsafe environment for the whole team. And one very important person on that team is my brother, who I can't say anything to. I'm hit with a sudden wave of nausea, and my appetite is officially gone, but I put on a smile and head out for dinner.

Chapter Sixteen

Katarina

Saturday, November 11, 2023

I wake up with a sheen of sweat coating my skin—breath ragged as I come out of the familiar nightmare that leaves me unsettled, and my stomach is in knots. The nightmares haven't been as intense in recent years, but high-stress situations tend to increase my chances of having them.

Thankfully, Aiyana's already in the bathroom getting ready for the day, so I didn't wake her.

After yesterday's strange stream of encounters, my head was still spinning, so when we got home from the game, Aiyana and I just went right to bed. But we have plans to go to this cute Mediterranean café a few blocks away for brunch, so I should get up anyway.

***

As we head toward the café, wearing a light sweater and jeans and enjoying the sunny weather, I wring my hands with nerves, not knowing how I'll explain everything I need to without telling her too much. I know she's doing her best to contain the many questions she has running through her head right now, which I truly appreciate because I think it's physically hurting her.

We stop outside, the hostess leading us to our seats, where we find a round two-person table with mismatched Spanish tiles and fake grapes hanging over our heads. I order a tapas tray with vegetable crudités. Aiyana orders the Turkish eggs and a lemon ricotta-filled Dutch baby to curb her sweet tooth.

As soon as the waiter finishes taking our order and heads out, the dam officially breaks. "Okay, I've been so good waiting for you to finally tell me all about this guy, but *I can't take it anymore!* Spill the beans, lady!" Her tone is high-pitched with poorly contained excitement.

"All right, all right," I start and proceed to recap every detail since my arrival in Philly a week ago, leaving out anything pertaining to his healthcare information. I don't care that Aiyana is my best friend; I'm not breaking the law or the trust of my patients for anyone—not her and not Kas.

When I'm done speaking, she sits back, lets out a sigh, and slumps against the chair. She makes a face that tells me she's mulling everything over, digesting it, and choosing her next words very carefully. Or not so carefully based on what she says next: "And you haven't jumped his bones?"

"Was that what you had expected me to tell you? That we had sex?"

"Well, not entirely, but with the chemistry you two were giving off last night, I had at least hoped." She says it like I should have already known that.

"I'm sorry to disappoint you, but nope, we have not. I barely know the guy—it's been a freaking week, he's my brother's teammate, and he lives across the hall from me." I put my hand up in a "stop" motion before continuing because I know she's about to interject. "I know what you're about to say, and I don't care that it's convenient for him to live so close. If we did date and things ended poorly, he's *right across the hall*. It's as convenient as it is potentially disastrous."

I wish I could tell her that he's my patient. *That* might actually make her stop for a moment and agree that it's a bad idea, but again, I won't.

"Okay, I hear you, but I didn't say shit about dating the guy. I said, 'jumping his bones.' Very different things." She seems very proud of herself for making that distinction, giving me a full smile that shows both rows of her teeth. That has always been her trademark "I'm up to absolutely no good" smile, and it makes me nervous every time.

"Aiya, I can't deal with you getting involved right now, okay? I'm serious; I don't want any added temptation." I *already* want to tear his clothes off and have my way with him, but as previously determined, that would be a *bad* idea. Or would it? Okay, okay, yes, it would definitely be a bad idea, and the sooner we both come to terms with that, the better.

"Temptation, schmemtation, fine." She rolls her eyes. "If you want to live a sad, boring life and never clear those cobwebs out of your coochie, be my guest, but I swear to all that is holy, if I hear you scream his name while using your vibrator, I'm tossing it in the garbage disposal."

I let out a fake gasp of outrage. "You're a cruel lady, you know that?"

"You're the cruel one, letting your lady parts shrivel up like that." She rolls her eyes again, and I guess that's the end of that conversation. For now, anyway, until she decides to torment me some more.

Chapter Seventeen

Alessandro

I recognize that Kat can't tell her brother about my situation, but they're twins, and I'm just having a hard time trusting that she won't say anything to Kas.[1]

Especially considering how dense my file is and the numerous times I've gone to physical therapy for numbness and weakness in my extremities.

I'm fully aware that if things get bad, I'll be putting my teammates, including her brother, in danger, and my career will be over.

That said, I'm also prepared to do the right thing when the time comes. I feel very confident that I'll be able to tell when and if I need to hang up my skates, but that doesn't mean that the concern isn't still there, looming over me.

I'm constantly overwhelmed with this weight that seems to hang over me, but I've never had to put my trust in someone outside of my family who has as much skin in the game as I do. Now that Kat knows, it's really up to her discretion as to whether her professionalism will win out over her desire to keep her brother safe. I can't say I'd judge her too harshly if she did decide to tell him, and I'm not sure he'd say anything to anyone besides me, even if she did.

I think of Bryan Bickell, who played for the Blackhawks for nearly a decade before he was traded to the Hurricanes and was diagnosed with MS that same year. Granted, I never really knew the guy, so I'm not sure of the exact circumstances surrounding his retirement, but I can't help but fear the same for myself. In a few interviews I've seen of him, he's stated that he decided to retire in order to focus on his health, and he's started a foundation to help others navigate their diagnosis and the new world they're learning to live in. Maybe when I retire, I'll be able to do something similar.

I think the best thing to do is hope that the medication Kat added to my current regimen keeps working and do my best to show her that there is nothing to worry about.

Maybe if I actively show her that I'm fine, she'll start to believe it and forget about it entirely? Yeah, probably not, but it's worth a shot.

On that note, I remember that Kat texted me last night during the game, presumably before she realized who I was.

I forgot to respond after our encounter and dinner with my family after the game. I'd like to see her, partially because everything that happened yesterday must've been a lot for her, but also because I enjoy her company.

I head to my room and grab my cell off the charger, sending her a text. When a couple of minutes go by, I realize it's easier to just knock on her door, so I get changed and do that. She doesn't answer, so I knock again. After the third time, I realize she's not home, so I send her a series of semi-embarrassing texts and head to the gym by myself to do some light stretching and cardio.

1. **Nervous - John Legend**

Chapter Eighteen

Katarina

After brunch, we head back to the apartment so Aiyana can get her talking points ready for a dinner interview she has set up this evening.

When we arrive, I see that I've got a few new texts, all of them from Alessandro.

Hottie Hallmate

> Hey Kat, forgot to respond last night. Gym in ten?

Hottie Hallmate

> Decided to knock, no answer. Sorry if I bothered you.

Hottie Hallmate

> Ignore that last text. Obviously, I didn't bother you if you weren't home.

Hottie Hallmate

> Ignore that other last message too *insert facepalm emoji* Can you tell that I'm clearly *very* smooth? Anyway, if you want to hang out tonight, text me.

I read his texts, and each one causes a new emotion to form in my chest. The fact that he was concerned about how I'd perceive him makes my heart clench and butterflies take flight in my stomach. His nervous energy puts a huge smile on my face because he makes me feel just as nervous.

It's super endearing, but that's the problem. Nothing can happen between us, but I'm not going to ignore him and make him feel more self-conscious either, so I opt for cordial friendliness. Or at least as cordial as I can be with him.

> Hey Ale! Sorry, went to brunch with Aiyana and left my cell at the apartment. She's heading out for an interview tonight. Wanna go on a run with me around 6?

Running is safe, right? You can't talk while running if you go fast enough.

A minute later, I get a response.

Hottie Hallmate

> I'll be at your door at 5:59 :)

I head to my room to read for a while and take a nap before getting ready for our run.

Chapter Nineteen

Katarina

Friday, November 17, 2023

K as will be here any minute, so I busy myself in the kitchen making a London Fog.

He has an away game tomorrow and won't be back until Sunday. I have quite a few PTO days to use before the end of the year despite my late start at the hospital, so I took today off to go on a hike with him.

He had invited Aiyana, but not only does she not believe in exercise in any capacity, she just started at BioMedics and didn't want to make a bad impression by taking the day off. Even though I've only been at my job for two weeks, Dr. Howell assured me it was fine with him.

We decided to make the drive upstate for a hike at The Pinnacle. It's the highest point in Pennsylvania on the Appalachian Trail. It's been on our bucket list for years, but obviously, with my absence, we had held off, so I'm excited that we get to do it now.

A knock raps at the door, so I pop the cap on my to-go mug and grab my backpack, which I have filled with granola bars, fruit cups, soft pretzels, and a variety of other snacks. I might have gone a bit overboard, but the last thing I want is to be hungry. *Ever.*

I answer the door, and to my surprised delight, Alessandro is standing behind Kas with a big grin spread across his handsome face.

"Good morning, Kitty-Kat, I hope it's okay that I brought a friend. Alice here hasn't stopped talking about you all week, so I figured we could put him out of his misery." Kas knows exactly the effect his words will have on us both. My lips spread into an embarrassed smirk, and my heart stutters, realizing how pleased I am to hear that he's been talking about me.

Ale's cheeks heat, but he doesn't deny it.

God, he's gorgeous. It's cold out, and the elevation will only add to that, so Ale's sporting a pair of khaki utility pants, well-worn hiking boots, a button-down Henley, and a fleece Columbia over the top. Despite how early it is, his green eyes glimmer when they meet mine, and his face is bright, not showing any signs of the exhaustion I'm already feeling.

"It's not a problem at all," I tell them both, "let's get a move on. I don't want to be hiking in the dark."

After locking up, we make our way out to Kas's truck and begin the hour-long drive.

***

We all get situated, ensuring we have everything we need before starting the ascent to the top of the trail.

"So Ale, do you hike a lot?" I figure it's an easy question to break the awkward silence that's descended upon us.

He smirks at me, clearly having regained his confidence, and says, "Almost never, but I couldn't resist the opportunity to see you."

Now my cheeks are red, and Kas is looking at us quizzically, but he's got a look on his face that tells me he wouldn't be upset if things went further between Ale and I. Honestly, it seems like he's trying to play matchmaker.

I grin at him sheepishly, trying to remember all the reasons we can't be together before I answer. "We live across the hall from one another, Ale; you see me every day," I finally tell him, shaking my head slightly as I direct my attention elsewhere to hide my grin.

We continue to walk, talking about our plans for the week and the team they're playing this weekend. I won't be going since it's a Canadian team, and I don't have the time or energy to make a trip like that right now.

The trail is relatively flat, and the view is beautiful, overlooking a seemingly endless expanse of trees with their leaves in varying shades of red, orange, and yellow. I love this time of year—it's *usually* not too cold out, and it triggers a literal season of change.

"Hey," Kas shouts at us, having trailed a few yards ahead, "look over there!" He points to a clearing on our right that boasts a beautiful waterfall we hadn't been expecting. I don't think I ever heard of one mentioned by previous hikers before.

Ale and I head toward the edge of the trail to get a better look, but my focus is no longer on the path beneath my feet. My foot catches on a root, and my ankle twists as I fall with a yelp, but before I can hit the ground, Ale's strong arms are under mine, supporting my weight.

"You all right, *gattina*?" he asks me, his face scrunched up with worry, hands still clutching me.

"Yeah," I tell him breathlessly. "I tripped," as if he doesn't already know that.

His lips spread into a beautiful smile, the dimple in his right cheek appearing. "I saw,"—he's fighting a laugh—"but is your ankle okay?"

Before I can answer him, Kas finally sees us, not having heard my screech of pain. "You guys good over there?"

"Yeah!" I shout back at him, "I just tripped!"

He's pretty far up ahead, but I can still see how he shakes his head at me, knowing I've always been clumsy. He's clearly not surprised.

Kas starts walking back toward us, Ale's attention snapping to my face. "Can you walk, or do you need me to carry you back to the truck?"

My eyes widen slightly. "I can walk. I swear, it barely hurts at all now." It really doesn't, but when he releases my arms and takes a step back from me, assessing my face for anything that could indicate that I'm in pain, the loss of his warm hands on me is exponentially more bothersome than the discomfort in my ankle.

That soft look of concern is still etched into his brow, and I want to kiss him there. I want to kiss him everywhere, but before I can do something I'll regret, Kas is at my side.

"You good to keep going? We're almost at the top, but it'll be a few hours till we get back to the bottom."

"I think I'm good," I tell him because I really think I am. Besides, we've been looking forward to this trip for so long, and we're almost at the top anyway.

"I can give you a piggyback or carry you up the rest of the way," Ale tells me, his straight lips indicating he's serious.

"Uh, thank you, but seriously, I'm good." My face is bright-red, I'm sure. I'd love nothing more than for Ale to carry me around bridal style, but we can't go there, especially not with my brother around.

"All right, let's get going then so we don't have to make the trip back in the dark." Kas starts leading us back up, and Ale takes the opportunity to grab my hand before quickly releasing it, his lips pulled taut as he levels his eyes on me.

He looks like he's battling something, his expression a mix of longing and annoyance. He bends his head toward me, Kas too far away to hear regardless. "Just tell me if you need me, or just want me for that matter." His expression turns sheepish as he lowers his eyes to his feet.

***

About an hour later, we make it up the sixteen hundred feet of elevation and are standing at the top—*The Pinnacle.*

Overlooking the vast valley beneath us, the wind sways the trees, causing leaves to flutter all around us.

My ankle is starting to throb a bit. I know it isn't broken, and it's probably not sprained either, but after I twisted it, I kept walking, which wasn't one of my better ideas. I let inflammation set in, and it'll probably take a few days of icing it and rest before it feels normal again.

I'm a little nervous about the hike back to the bottom, but I'm trying not to think about it. I don't want to ruin this moment. The view was worth every step.

"Damn, look at that, Kat; it's fucking gorgeous up here. Absolutely worth the wait," Kas tells me, reverent with a look of awe on his face.

I completely agree. "I wish Aiyana could be here. I know she hates hiking, but this view is worth it."

"You guys stand right there, and I'll get a picture. Maybe you can convince Aiyana to go sometime once she sees this view." Ale ushers us to stand with our backs facing the valley below; smiling at him, he takes several photos with Kas's arm draped over my shoulder. "There, perfect!" he tells us before handing Kas the phone to inspect the pictures.

Kas's smile turns wide, his eyes bright with mischief as he looks at me. "Dude, these are just close-ups of Kat's face." Kas is chuckling as he hands me the phone.

I swipe through the photos, finding roughly twenty of them. I have to scroll through fifteen or so of my face before I finally make it to a few of Kas and me together.

"I said I'd take a picture of the incredible view, and I did," Ale says with a soft smile, eyes twinkling at me. Kas laughs, shaking his head and patting Ale on the shoulder as he passes by him to start the descent back to the truck.

This guy is so damn sweet, and I never would have guessed that Kas would be okay with one of his teammates hitting on me so blatantly, but I think even he's been won over by his charm.

We follow after Kas, and Ale slips his arm around me, placing his warm palm against my lower back and sending tingles down my spine. He leans into me, his lips so close to mine that I could turn my head an inch to the left and they'd meet his.

"I see you limping, and I *am* going to carry you. I'll give you the choice—bridal carry or a piggyback ride?" His eyes glint and his teeth dig into that supple bottom lip. "I know which one I hope you'll choose," he tells me, sending a surge of electricity through me and straight to my core.

"I'm really fine," I tell him as I hobble my way down the side of the mountain, Kas not letting up his grueling pace. I'm starting to think he's doing it on purpose.

"You're not," he says with mild annoyance, and his face lacks all amusement. "Stop being so stubborn, Kat; I can carry you. I don't mind even a little bit, and if you're hurt, you won't be able to work next week. It's no skin off my nose if I get to carry you down this mountain."

He's not wrong. My ankle is bothering me, and frankly, I wouldn't mind being held, but I'm worried about putting the extra strain on his body. He says he's felt great since we swapped out his meds, though I know if I wasn't trying so hard to fight this attraction between us, I would have zero qualms about having him trudge down this mountain with me on his back.

"Fine, turn around," I grumble at him, hoping my displeased tone will deter him, but I know he won't change his mind. It's so damn hard to keep doing this when he's so sweet and shows no desire to give up any time soon.

A grin lights his face, the sun catching in his eyes, making them look even more green against the fall foliage. He turns around, humming contentedly, pulling his backpack off and wearing it around his front instead. Chuckling lightly, he says, "Piggyback it is."

I wrap my arms around his thick neck, resting my forearms along his built traps, and as I'm about to hoist myself up, his long arms come around the backs of my thighs and pull me up his body. My legs wrap around his trim waist, and his hands stay securely around my thighs as he starts walking us toward the truck. I have doubts that he'll be able to maintain this for long. I'm muscular and pretty heavy as a result, and this trail is about two hours from the top back to our vehicle.

Kas smiles at us with a cocky, knowing smirk as he looks over his shoulder, seeing me on Ale's back. He seems extremely pleased by this and finally slows down long enough that we can walk beside him.

***

I finally see Kas's truck ahead of us, and much to my surprise, Ale managed to trudge along the entire time, actually cutting down our time to just over an hour. I know going down the mountain is faster and easier than going up, but I hadn't anticipated cutting that much time off. He did have to change positions, swapping from a piggyback ride to me on his shoulders for the last ten minutes or so. I tried to convince him I could walk, and I'm nearly certain he didn't actually *need* me to swap positions, but I didn't push.

"I'll run over to the truck and get it warmed up." Kas doesn't wait for our reply as he sprints toward the car, holding my backpack against his chest. He had offered to take it a while back so Ale wouldn't have to carry the extra weight.

I think the exhaustion must be setting in because now that Kas is out of sight, my resolve is too. I've been dying to run my fingers through Ale's dark, silky waves, and I finally do. He releases a deep belly laugh that shakes me, rubbing my core against the back of his neck. Every time the terrain started to get a little bumpy, I'd be pressed up against him in a way that sent sparks of pleasure to my clit, and it's been driving me wild.

"I'm just directing you to the car," I laugh, hoping he'll get the reference.

"I was already heading there, Remy, but feel free to tug on my hair some more." His teasing tone lights me up all over, and I can't help the way my thighs try to squeeze together to dull the ache. But instead of the desired effect, I just end up squeezing Ale's head, and it's pretty apparent that he knows why. He turns his head to the side, his stubble scraping along my inner thigh through my leggings, before he plants a soft kiss on the inside of my knee.

We're almost at the truck, so before this can become any more inappropriate, I say, "Okay, time to get down; thanks for the ride." My cheeks flame. "I mean, thanks for returning me safely."

He helps me down, and before he can respond, I'm practically catapulting myself into the back of the truck, against my better judgment and my angry ankle's best interests.

Chapter Twenty

Katarina

Monday, November 20, 2023

I fell asleep early last night, so I'm up uncharacteristically early today. I've got about thirty minutes before I need to head out for work, thirty-five if I decide to take an Uber, which really might be the safer option. My ankle feels significantly better, but I don't want to push it.

I take the Earl Grey and vanilla tea bag out of my mug, tossing it in the trash before adding honey, a pump of lavender syrup, and cream. The mug warms my hands as I take it to the couch to sit and read for a while before heading out.

Twenty minutes later, I hear a knock at the door. Aiyana already left for work, and she obviously has the code to the door, so it couldn't be her.

I set my mug on the side table and head to the door. Looking through the peephole, I see Alessandro's wet, dark hair lying across his forehead in a messy pile of waves, like he just got out of the shower.

I open the door. "Morning Ale, I'm about to head to work, but do you need something?"

His lips spread into a wide smile. "I just came to take you to work. I'm heading that way anyhow since I'm gonna go drop by my parents' place."

I'm not sure where his parents live, aside from knowing that they're close, but it'd be rude to decline his offer, and I was going to order a ride share anyway.

"That'd be really nice, thanks," I say, smiling. "Come on in. I just have to grab my coat and rinse out my mug, and we can head out."

He follows me in, but before I can make it to the side table, he sidesteps me, grabbing the mug. "This smells good; what is it?"

"It's a London Fog. It's Earl Grey tea with lavender, vanilla, honey, and some cream." He gives it another sniff before pressing his lips to the mug and taking a big gulp. When he pulls back, my eyes are so wide I'm afraid my lids will get stuck.

He lets out a low moan. "No wonder you don't drink coffee; this is so much better." He looks pleased with my reaction.

"What if I had herpes or a cold or something, and you just infected yourself with my germs?" I'm seriously shocked. I'm also intrigued because that's the closest we've been to kissing. My ChapStick is lining the mug, now coating his glistening lips.

"Well, do you have any of the aforementioned contractable illnesses?" His brow quirks, but the smirk remains on his lips.

"No, but my point still stands. Don't be a smart ass." I roll my eyes at him—his smirk turning to a full-blown, shit-eating grin as he pours the rest of the tea into the sink, rinsing it and placing it in the dishwasher. I grab my coat, pull it on, and we head out to his car.

***

The drive to my office is short. Too short.

He asked me if I had anything interesting going on today, and I barely had time to tell him I wouldn't know until it happens.

He pulls up outside of the building, and I'm about to hop out, but he leans across me, holding the door shut with one hand. His warm, minty breath dances across my cheek, and it takes everything in me not to tremble with the need that ricochets through me.

I think he might kiss me, but instead, he just says, "Have a good day at work, Kat," before he runs out of the car and around to my side, opening the door for me.

I get out on shaky legs, thanking him before I nearly sprint inside to get some much-needed air. Less than five minutes in Ale's car, breathing the same air as him; it's too much. I want to cuddle him and sink down on his hard length almost with equal measure, but the building I'm standing in reminds me of all the reasons that can't happen.[1]

---

1. **in my head - thuy**

Chapter Twenty-One

Alessandro

Sunday, November 26, 2023

I've been seeing Kat quite a bit, but it's never enough. Every moment spent with her feels right, and no amount of time seems to curb my craving for more.

There isn't anything about her I don't like.

Well, except maybe her ability to hold strong, avoiding anything more with me despite the way she looks at me with happiness, desire, and admiration in her eyes.

I wish she'd just give us a shot. I haven't felt this way about anyone before, and now that I do, she has it in her head that we can't be together.

Truthfully, I had thought the same at first, but it became clear pretty fucking quickly that Kas is trying to set us up. Now that that isn't standing in our way, I'm not sure what's really holding her back. It can't be *that* big a deal that she handles some aspects of my healthcare, can it?

I've spoken to my mom about her. She says to just give her time, and she'll eventually come to terms with her feelings for me and finally admit that they exist in the first place. I'll wait as long as it takes. I can be patient. At least, for Kat, I can. I'll wait as long as she needs.

I can't get her out of my head. Her soft voice, boisterous laughter, and smart mouth drive me wild with need. Of course, I'm attracted to her, but it's so much more than that.

***

I can't help but keep checking in on her. She says she'll text me if she needs me, but I have my doubts. I think she actively goes out of her way not to need me.

Her ankle seems to have made a full recovery, but until Kat tells me she's going to start walking to work again, I've made up an excuse for why I was headed in that direction every day this week and taken her myself.

Those extra five minutes with her each day fuel me. They give me just enough to push me forward until the next time I get to see her.

Chapter Twenty-Two

Katarina

Thursday, December 7, 2023

T he last few weeks flew by in a compilation of work, hockey games, and personal time with my vibrator.

Ale and I have been seeing each other a lot, but mostly just when other people are around, like my brother. I've been avoiding seeing him alone because the more I've gotten to know him, the more I genuinely like everything about him.

It's not just his good looks but his fierce love for his family, his incredible sense of humor, and, most of all, his insanely humble personality. He's kind to every fan who greets him in public, speaks highly of his teammates, and would quite literally give the shirt off his back to anyone in need. He's going to make a special person really lucky someday, but unfortunately, it can't be me.

And a lot has changed in the five short weeks since I arrived in Philly. Aiyana landed that job at BioMedics from her dinner interview, and it turns out, Ale's sister-in-law, Rose, is the lead biomedical engineer for the vaccines Aiyana is helping manufacture.

She also finished moving in, so her room is officially set up, and our penthouse has gotten a major makeover. Not only have we been hanging paintings, pictures, metal art, and just generally filling up the space, but Ale was so tired of hearing me threaten to sneak into his apartment and steal all of his gold fixtures from his kitchen that he came over while Aiyana was home and installed new brass ones for me.

I had had a really tough day at work and was exhausted when I got home that day; when Aiya pointed it out to me, I broke down in instant tears. His kindness broke down all my walls that day. It probably wasn't the response he would have wanted, but it's what he got.

***

I make it into work with just enough time to run to the café downstairs and grab myself a tea. I place the order and wait in line for pickup when I see a familiar face approaching.

"Hey Kat, how's it going?" Ante is an RN who works on the psychiatry floor in my building. We cross paths every now and then, and he's always been friendly. I've overheard some of the nurses on my floor mention that he has a bit of a reputation, but if I looked like him, I probably would too. He's built and just over six feet tall with dirty-blond hair, bright-blue eyes, and a clean-shaven face. He's nice to look at and certainly the kind of guy I'd normally go for if I were interested in a one-night stand.

"Hey, Ante, everything's going well. I'm settling in, and all of the staff have been really great so far. How've you been?" I say to him, my expression neutral as I wait for my name to be called so I can hurry back to my floor.

He gives me a smile that seems genuine, though maybe he doesn't really care about how things are going at work. He was probably just being polite. "I've been good, but I've missed seeing you. I haven't had a reason to go to your floor, and it's definitely put a damper on my week." He says it with a smirk, and his eyes are slightly hooded as if he's trying to tell me with his face alone that he wants to fuck me. Trust me, dude, we can all tell from more than just your facial expressions.

"Aw, that's sweet," I say, trying my best to sound interested in this conversation but doing pretty poorly. I don't really have much to add other than that, and the awkward conversation makes me feel like I'll break out in hives at a moment's notice. My hand makes its way to my necklace, fingers toying with the smooth metal. I haven't missed seeing him, so I'm not going to lie and say I did. I honestly haven't thought about him at all.

He chuckles, his gaze raking over my body in a way that makes me feel exposed. "Would you like to go out with me Friday night?"

My brows shoot to the ceiling, not expecting how forward he's being. "Like on a date?"

"Up to you. We can go as just friends, or I could be persuaded into a date." He gives me another one of those smirks before continuing, "It'd be fun to just grab a drink, right?"

"I guess one drink wouldn't hurt. Where should we meet?" We are technically coworkers, and maybe there's something more beneath his leering smile. "I can't go until after the hockey game though; it's a home game, and my brother plays." I also don't really want to go out with him at all, but I figure maybe saying he'd have to wait until several hours after work might deter him.

It seems I'm incorrect. "That works for me. I was planning on going with a few buddies anyway. We can meet at that bar across from the rink when the game is over. Sound good?" he asks, his hip resting against the counter, looking completely relaxed.

"Yep, sounds great." Thankfully, my name was just called, so I grab my drink and haul ass out of there. That was super awkward. He had always seemed nice enough, but he was really laying it on thick despite my lack of responsiveness. I thought we were mere seconds away from him calling me "baby girl" and luring me to his sex dungeon.

***

"Hey, babe! How was work?" Aiyana calls from the couch when I get in. I really do love that couch. Kas was right—totally worth every penny he spent.

Placing my bag on the hook by the door, I remove my coat, hanging it in the coat closet. "It was okay, long but good. I got asked out on a date." I decide to drop that bomb right away so we can get it over with.

Her head pops up over the back of the couch, excitement gleaming in her eyes. "Oh my god! Best news ever! Are you going? Please tell me you're going! Is he hot? Do you have pics?"

Shaking my head at her, a small smile tugs at my lips as I toe off my sneakers. "Calm down, lady, I'm going. It's with a guy at work from the psych unit. He's an RN named Ante, and he asked me to grab a drink with him at Rocco's after the game tomorrow."

"Mmm, okay. Did you forget that you don't drink?" She rolls her eyes and gives me an incredulous look as if I had really forgotten.

"No, asshole." I roll my eyes back at her, exasperated already. "I'll be getting a drink... of water."

"As long as he doesn't try to pressure you into drinking or make it into a big deal, then I hope you have a fabulous time!" she tells me cheerily. "Make sure your location tracker is on, and text me when you get there. Give me updates throughout, and let me know when I should come pick you up." She pauses, drawing out her next words. "Or, you know, not pick you up." She gives me a dramatic wink, hopping off the couch and doing a little dance, shaking her hips and thrusting animatedly.

I can't help but laugh at her theatrics. "I won't be going home with him; it's just a drink with a coworker."

Her smile drops almost imperceivably. "Yeah, okay, but would it be so bad if you had someone clear out those cobwebs for you? It's not like he works on your floor; is he attractive?"

"By society's standards, sure. He's not unattractive, but I care more about personality than anything else. Though I guess you're right. We don't technically work together, so it wouldn't be so bad if the mood was right and we both consented." That's a thought. Maybe one night of fun in the sheets is all I need to get Alessandro out of my head.

Unlikely.

Chapter Twenty-Three

Katarina

Friday, December 8, 2023

I nstead of waiting for Kas, I head straight out of the ice rink and walk over to Rocco's to meet with Ante. It's not too packed yet because the hockey team hasn't gotten here since they're all showering and changing. The team usually heads over after home games to celebrate their wins, and once they've arrived, the bars are packed with fans hoping to get a glimpse of the players off of the ice.

I send Aiyana a text letting her know I got here safely, and just as I hit "send," I see Ante walking through the doors, prowling toward me. He's wearing a bright-red button-down paired with fitted black jeans. I assume that means he doesn't own any Philly Scarlets attire but made the effort to dress in the team's colors.

As soon as his eyes meet mine, his mask slips into place, sending unease jolting through me. My stomach drops as his hand wraps around my waist, and he leans in for a hug. I take a seat at the bar, and Ante orders a beer before telling the bartender, "She'll have a Mai Tai," ordering a drink I won't be ingesting.

My gaze flicks to the bartender, and I give him a closed-mouth smile. "I'll actually just have a club soda with lime, please." He grunts, nods his head, and bends, grabbing two glasses from beneath the bar.

Although Ante doesn't make any comments about me not drinking, his smirk says he has questions.

The bartender is a tall, rugged-looking guy wearing jeans and a plaid flannel over a white V-neck. He's got a full beard and light-brown hair pulled back into a low bun. He wears a serious expression, and when he brings our drinks back to us, he eyes us speculatively, paying close attention to Ante before sliding our drinks forward on white cocktail napkins. His eyes flicker between us, lips pursed, and Ante shifts uncomfortably under the man's scrutinizing gaze.

When he turns his attention back to the other bar patrons, Ante's shoulders relax, and he leans himself up against the bar top. That same calculated smirk returns. "So Kat, what was it like growing up with a hockey legend?"

I'm taken aback at first, mostly because I can't believe how dumb that sounded, but also because I'm shocked and a little disappointed that he doesn't have anything else to start with. I work to smooth my wrinkled brow. "Kas and I are actually twins, so I didn't grow up with a hockey legend. He's always just been Kas to me." I do my best to not sound snarky, but when his lips pull taut, I know he took it exactly how I had initially meant it.

In an effort to clear the awkward air that's surrounding us, I continue. "He wasn't well-known in hockey until he joined the

Philly Scarlets four years ago, and by then, we were twenty-four. It's been really cool seeing him on TV and being around when he gets recognized in public." I smile at him, a genuine one this time, brought on by fond memories of how my brother has managed to ease into the limelight.

He lowers his gaze to my lips, staring as he raises his glass, taking a big gulp of the frothy golden liquid. Some remains on his lip when he places the glass back on the counter. His tongue darts out, swiping across his lip in a move that makes me so uncomfortable that my gaze shifts to my shoes, staring at a scuff on the white rubber of my sneakers.

He still hasn't answered me or made any effort to converse further, and I'm considering hiding in the bathroom until he leaves or flinging myself out the window.

Tension leeches into my shoulders, spine ramrod straight, and I fight the need to release a sigh of relief when he finally breaks the silence. "Hmm," he says, humming as he takes in my appearance, making a show of his perusal. "Is your brother all that brings you to the area?" he asks, but his words are laced with a hidden meaning. His eyes dart over my shoulder, looking at something behind me.

I clear my throat, not wanting to dive too deeply into my reasoning for ever having left in the first place, so I give him the most simplistic answer I can think of that isn't a lie, just skirting around the whole truth. "Yeah, to be closer to Kas, and then I was also really excited to be offered a job working with Dr. Howell."

He nods, feigning interest. "Dr. Howell must really love working with you; getting to see that pretty face of yours every day must be a real treat."

My cheeks flame with outrage, brows skyrocketing up my forehead. "Dr. Howell is *married,* and I don't appreciate you insinuating that he has any kind of intentions toward me aside from the professional kind." My voice hitches with anger.

He puts his hands up, palms facing me. "Hey there, killer, I was just complimenting you." He takes another sip of his beer, rolling his eyes at me as if *I'm* the one who just said something outrageously insulting.

I take a deep breath, calming the wave of anger that's threatening to take hold of me and drag us both along with it. "Okay, topic change," I huff out. "Are you from the area?"

His eyes light up at the opportunity to talk about himself. He drones on and on about growing up with wealthy parents, how they were never home, and it was his neighbor, who was a retired RN, who took care of him and inspired him to become a nurse. I don't ask questions—like how the hell a retired RN could afford to live next door to a supposedly extremely wealthy family in the suburbs of Princeton, New Jersey.

He doesn't give me the opportunity to speak either; instead, he continues to talk and sip on his beer, acting like a male peacock preening his feathers.

When he stops talking long enough to finish his beer, I hurry to excuse myself to use the restroom. I text Aiya telling her that I'll be going home pretty soon, clarifying that I'll be by myself since I know that's the next question she'll ask. She's always got sex on the brain, but she texts me back quickly, asking if I'm okay taking a cab home. She's sleeping over at some guy's house and won't be back until the morning, so I let her know I'm happy to grab a cab, and I put my cell back in my pocket.

I see the hockey team seated at the bar and scattered between several tables, but I don't see Kas anywhere. He must have decided to stay home tonight, or maybe he figured it would be awkward to be here with me on a "date."

Alessandro's sitting with a couple of his teammates, who I've gotten to know over the last few weeks. He's seated facing the bar, his gaze locked on me while Kyle and JJ are on either side of him.

They're chatting away, but Ale doesn't seem to be listening at all. He's got his eyes firmly planted on me, and he doesn't seem happy, judging by the hard scowl on his face and the sharp line between his crinkled brow.

He has no reason to be jealous. We aren't dating, and I have no interest in Ante either.

Ignoring him, I head back to my seat, where Ante waits with a fresh club soda for me. "Hey, I got you a refill, extra lime." Bile claws up my throat, and the fizzy water looks entirely too carbonated.

Avoiding conflict, I opt for an easy smile. "Oh, thanks." I grip the glass, having absolutely no intention of drinking it. I'd really like to believe he wouldn't drug me, especially since I work in the same building as him, but his leering gaze and overall sleazy personality don't fill me with much confidence.

I take my seat next to him, thinking of excuses to leave soon, as he starts talking again. He tells me how much he hates his floor, can't stand any of his coworkers, and his patients are "the absolute worst."

At this point, I'm crawling out of my skin, the red flags glaring so heavily over him, and I can't take it anymore. I have zero desire to placate him, so the next words just pop out of my mouth with little thought to the potential consequences: "If you hate people so much, why don't you find a new career? Healthcare is about helping people, which means engaging with them and caring about them." I pause for a breath and continue before he can cut me off. "The nurses I know love their patients and work their asses off to ensure their well-being, even when management is still paying them in pizza parties." I roll my eyes exaggeratedly and let out a big sigh of annoyance.

In case he didn't get it already, I think his opinions are horrendous piles of trash and add to the problems being experienced in the US healthcare system. It's one thing to vent about your day because, frankly, it gets exhausting bottling it all up, but to outwardly make statements about hating your patients? Absolutely not something I'll tolerate.

His face is turning red, and if smoke could literally whistle out of his ears, it would be. "Yeah, that's an opinion for sure." He rolls his eyes more aggressively than even I had managed and continues staring down at my hand wrapped around the glass of water, untouched, and finally says, "Aren't you thirsty?"

If the alarm bells hadn't already been going off in my head, this was like a foghorn straight to the ear followed by a mariachi band coming out waving giant red flags in the air singing "La Cucaracha." Which is pretty fitting, considering this guy is definitely the human equivalent of a roach.

"Oh, I guess not. I was just so enthralled by your storytelling"— I was not—"that I must have forgotten I even had it in my hand. But you know, I should be heading out. It's getting late, and I'm starting to feel a headache coming on." My voice goes up an octave as I finish.

His brows scrunch together, anger etched into his expression. "Oh, well, maybe you're just dehydrated," he tells me, not at all concerned about whether I'm aware of his efforts to drug me. He's more focused on pressuring me into drinking the clearly tampered-with liquid.

My temper is rising, and he seems to be getting more and more agitated as the seconds tick by.

I nearly throw myself out of my seat, feeling Alessandro's gaze practically burning a hole into the back of my skull.

Dodging his poorly veiled suggestion, I say, "I think I'm gonna head out." I work on pulling my coat on, trying to remain casual and appear unbothered, but Ante grips my forearm tightly, so tightly that my arm is on fire, and I can feel his nails cutting through my flesh.

I let out a yelp of pain, and he yanks me toward him, lowering his mouth to my ear, snarling as he says, "It would be rude of you to go without a goodnight kiss, wouldn't it, Kat?"

I rear back, eyes wide with shock. I can't believe he still thinks he has a shot at getting anything out of me tonight.[1]

Not without a fight, anyway. Gritting my teeth, I tell him, "Get your hands off of me; you're hurting me." I look at him with tear-filled eyes, silently pleading for him to just let me go. I'm pissed off and overwhelmed, adrenaline coursing through me as I prepare my body for a fight. I refuse to let this guy see me cry.

He loosens his grip on me slightly, his eyes pretending to soften, going through the motions of his usual manipulation tactics. "I'm sorry, Kat. I would never hurt you. I just think we had a lot of fun tonight, and we should continue it at my place." My eyebrows shoot up my forehead in shock; I know he can't be this delusional.

"Ante, I am not going home with you," I emphasize, ensuring he hears me loud and clear. "I'm not interested. Get your hands off of me, and let me leave."

Instead of backing off like I desperately hope he will, he moves the hand that was wrapped around my arm to my lower back, tugging me aggressively to him, and uses the other hand to grope the front of my crotch through my jeans. I let out a screech, and several of the bar patrons turn toward us to see what's going on. I busy my free hand, pushing him off of me, bending forward and biting down as hard as I'm able to on his shoulder.

I fall back against the counter at the abrupt loss of contact with his body, catching myself before I can hit my head.

I frantically look to my side, and there he is, red-faced and nearly frothing at the mouth, whimpering for Alessandro to release his grip on his throat. I'm staring with my mouth hanging open as Ale leans forward and whispers something in Ante's ear that makes his eyes go wide with shock.

He shoves him backward. Ante loses his balance and falls to the ground, ass first, before flipping over onto his hands and knees. He frantically rights himself, running out of the bar looking like Taz from Looney Toons.

Ale comes charging over to me, eyes ablaze, and as soon as he's close enough, I catapult into his arms, feeling myself melt into the safety of his embrace. He automatically cages me in, smoothing my hair with his palm.

All of the emotions I'd been bottling up, trying to keep from making a scene and potentially putting myself in even more danger, start to rush out like a broken dam. I'm suddenly clutching the front of Ale's shirt, crying and getting snot all over him while he holds my shaking body, whispering over and over again, "It's okay, you're okay, I've got you. I promise. You're okay now."

---

1. **Leave - CIL**

CHAPTER TWENTY-FOUR

Katarina

After several minutes of emotional relief, Ale pulls back to look at my face, concern etched all over his own. "Are you hurt?" His eyes are blazing with repressed anger.

I shake my head; though he did hurt me, it isn't worth mentioning right now. I just want to go home, cleanse my skin of his, and crawl into bed.

He looks slightly relieved, but I can tell he isn't really buying it. He gives me one more once-over before letting out a huff, as if he had been holding that breath in for hours, not seconds. "I'm gonna text your brother to let him know I'm taking you home, okay? He said he was having someone sleep over tonight, so I don't want to worry him. I'm gonna bring you home, sweetheart, all right?"

I nod my head and turn to grab my scarf and purse from the back of my chair. Ale grabs a twenty out of his wallet and tosses it on the bar to pay for Ante's beer. I look at him skeptically before he says, "It's not the bartender's fault that guy was a fucking prick, and someone has to pay for those beers." God, he's so thoughtful all the time. I never would have thought about that in my current state of mind, but when I did later, I'd have felt guilty for it.

We head out into the cold air, and of course, it's drizzling and windy—potentially the most uncomfortable combination known to man. Huddling on the sidewalk, Ale pulls the hood of my coat up over my head as we wait for a cab.

Arriving in front of our building, Ale opens the door for me and follows me into the brightly lit lobby, heading up to our floor.

We exit the elevator, and Ale stops, pulling me to him again gently. Not at all like how Ante handled me at the bar. "I want to take care of you tonight. Can I do that?" I lift my head abruptly, eyes widening because I have no idea what that means.

"You already did, Ale. Thank you for that, by the way. I just realized I hadn't told you that."

"No, Kat, baby, can I take care of you tonight? I don't mean pulling some sorry excuse for a human being off of you at a bar or taking you home. I mean, can I grab a pair of sweats from my place real quick and then take you to your room, run you a bubble bath to soak in while I make something for you to eat, and cuddle you on the couch until you fall asleep?" He's looking at me with that same crease between his brows, agony lacing his words as if the thought of leaving me to stay in my apartment alone tonight would be physically painful for him. And truthfully, I'm done fighting it. This thing we have, this connection that's been simmering since I arrived over a month ago, is exhausting to try and ignore.

I don't have the energy to say all of that, so I just nod and give him the best smile I can manage. If it were anyone else, I might not have even bothered.

He holds out his hand for me to take and opens his door. We step in, and he walks me to his room before letting go of my hand. I'm too tired to stand, so I walk to his bed and take a seat on the edge while he grabs a duffle bag from his closet and makes his way around the room, tossing clothes and toiletries in the bag. As he does that, I take in his room, and frankly, it's everything I expect now that I know him a bit better than when I was first here.

While his guest room is all whites and creams, his bedroom is in complete contrast—there is nothing but variations of steely-grays and blacks. He has a huge four-poster bed in the center of the room, which looks like it must be a super dark wood with black stain judging by the grain and the intricately etched designs scrawling throughout. Touches of gold foil are layered tastefully throughout the design, which adds a subtle embellishment that suits the room.

There's a long dresser with matching nightstands on either side of the bed. His lamps are golden mercury glass with black velvet shades that complement the aesthetic of the room without taking away from the uniqueness of the furniture. He also has some framed paintings hung up, but I can't tell what they are from where I'm sitting, and I don't want to outwardly snoop.

His bed has a black duvet with black satin linens, and the floor is a dark-gray vinyl wood plank. The walls are painted a slightly lighter gray to match, and the ceiling is painted black with what looks like tiny holes for lights throughout. Are those constellations, maybe? I can't really tell.

When Ale finishes whatever he's been doing in the kitchen, he comes back to his room to retrieve me. Jutting out his hand for me, I take it, and he leads me across the hall to my place.

I let us in and head to my room, where he follows behind, then lifts me up and sets me down on my bed. He tosses a blanket over my legs and strokes my cheek with the back of his knuckles before leaving a quick peck on my temple and strolling over to my bathroom.

I hear the sounds of running water and realize he's running the bath. He comes back a few minutes later, leaving a robe draped along the bed, which is definitely not mine, and judging by the monstrous proportions of it, it must be his robe. He brought me his robe?

He leaves the room with his duffle bag in tow and gently closes the door. I don't get up until I hear him rummaging around in the kitchen. Walking into the bathroom, I see that he's lit some lavender candles, which again, are not mine, and the tub is nearly overflowing with steam and bubbles that I'm almost certain are not from anything in my bathroom either. He must have brought all this stuff over from his own bathroom.

I didn't take him as a bubble bath and candles kind of guy, but we have the same bathroom, and it would really be a shame to let that tub go to waste. I'm glad he gets some use out of it because, unfortunately, this is my first time in mine.

I undress, assessing myself in the mirror. My eyes are bloodshot, and my hair is a mess, with the elastic barely containing my waves. My cheeks are swollen, and the arm I was grabbed by has a giant purple bruise blossoming, along with five distinct nail marks, though thankfully, none of them broke the skin.

I head back to my room, pull out my phone from my purse, and take pictures of the bruises to file with the police report I plan to make tomorrow.

I climb into the tub and sink down into the steaming water until I'm fully submerged, letting the tension soak away as I lay here. The floral-scented bubbles surround me, calming my racing mind.

My eyes flutter open, and I realize I must have drifted off because I hear a gentle knock on the door, and the water surrounding me is now lukewarm.

"Sorry, I'll be out in just a minute," I call to Ale before climbing out of the tub, draining it, and toweling off.

Once I'm dressed, I drag myself into the living room, where I find Ale sprawled out on the couch with a tray of food, a pile of blankets he must have grabbed from the linen closet, and a rom-com on the TV, waiting for me to sit down and watch.

Without a word, he takes one look at me and opens his arms in invitation. I walk over to the couch, which he has set up like a giant bed with the ottoman tucked in the middle where legs would normally dangle. I crawl over the cushions to him and slump into his chest when his arms wrap around me. He holds me for the next several minutes until I finally get myself to move out of his tight grasp.

"We don't have to talk about it right now, but we will talk about it, Kat. That guy needs to be reported." His voice is rough and strained with tension.

"I know, Ale. I promise I'll report him to the police and to my hospital. If not for me, then for everyone before me who he's ever tried that shit with or been successful with in his attempts." That seems to subdue him, and we slip into a comfortable silence. He turns the TV on, which I now realize is playing *How to Lose a Guy in Ten Days*, and he grabs a few blankets from beside him, tucking them around me before handing me a mug of hot chocolate absolutely brimming with whipped cream and scooching the tray of food closer to me. His choice of movie would ordinarily make me laugh, considering I've been trying to lose this one for *five weeks*, and somehow, we've both seemingly become more attached to one another, just like in the movie he's chosen.

I can now tell that he's made a charcuterie board with all sorts of cheeses, some grapes, blackberries, truffle honey, crackers, and dark chocolates. At least half of these items came from my own kitchen, but the rest must have been from his. How he knows I'm obsessed with charcuterie, I'm not sure, but I guess it makes sense, being that most people love cheese, right?

I'm not one to shy away from eating when I'm hungry, and since lunch was my last meal, I am absolutely famished. I eat my weight in cheeses and berries before lying back in the corner of the huge velvet couch and hunkering down.

I'm perfectly content to stay here with Ale, just like this, all night.

***

I start to drift asleep and am startled awake by screams, which I quickly realize are my own, as Ale frantically fights to soothe me for the second time tonight. "It's all right, *gattina*, you're safe. It was just a dream."

I pry my eyes open, chest heaving as I get my bearings. He continues trying to soothe me, and a knot forms in my stomach when I realize how much he's been affected by this entire night.

I give him a gentle smile, doing my best to reassure him. "I'm sorry." I peer up at him. "I sometimes have nightmares. It used to happen a lot more often, and I'd wake up but be pushed straight into a panic attack. I'd wake up screaming, which is one of the reasons Aiyana demanded to move to San Diego with me when I got accepted into PA school. She knew she'd get in anywhere she applied—her grades were that good, and she had a mountain of extracurriculars."

"Do you know what started the nightmares?" Without realizing it, he just asked me a very loaded question.

I think my silence speaks volumes, indicating that fact because his face starts to scrunch up again, so I rush to answer him. "Uh, yeah, I do. It's not so bad anymore, like I said."

He looks at me skeptically, seemingly deciding whether to push the subject or not, but I guess he can't help himself when he says, "You know about my mom and my diagnosis. You've never judged me for that, and I won't judge you for this." Second guessing his boldness, he says, "But you don't have to tell me anything if you don't want to; I'm here to listen if it'll help though."

I let out a long breath before tossing my legs over his and scooching closer to him. This isn't something I talk about with almost anyone, but something compels me to open up to Ale in more than one way.

"Kas and I grew up near here; did you know that?" He says nothing but nods.

"Well, we lived with our parents, and some days were good, and others weren't so good. We lived across the street from our grandma, who we'd spend every weekend with, and it was easily the best part of our entire week." I pause, looking at him for assurance that I should go on.

He's listening intently, so I do. "Our father was an addict, mostly just alcohol. Like many others who struggle with addiction, as I'm sure you've heard or maybe witnessed yourself, he was the sweetest guy when he was sober, but when he wasn't, he had a mean streak. He never hit any of us, but he and our mom would get into screaming matches that ended in Mom taking us over to our Lola's house, and we'd have a sleepover while Dad cooled off. He eventually went to rehab and was clean from the time we were seven until we were fifteen. He stayed sober for so long that we didn't think anything would change that, and things were mostly really good."

I pause for a moment, getting a hold of my emotions before continuing. "When Kas started showing real potential to play hockey professionally, he was getting scouted by colleges all over the Northeast, and with that came more stress and more money necessary to make his dreams a reality. Dad started drinking again, and he lost his job shortly after relapsing, and seemingly out of nowhere, things went very bad, very quickly." I struggle to continue for a moment as my eyes rim with unshed tears, but I take a steeling breath and trudge on. Alessandro rests his hand on my thigh for reassurance, and I'm sure he's regretting his decision to ask about this now.

"Kas woke up because he heard our parents screaming at each other, which wasn't uncommon." My gaze flickers downward at my hands, and I start to play with the pendant on my necklace. Ale notices but doesn't say anything.

"I had woken up too, but I stayed in my room and hid in the closet with my phone, waiting to call the police if things started getting really loud. Kas didn't hide though." Images of that night flood my mind, making me wince.

"He left his room to see what was going on and found our father with a gun in his hand, aimed at our mom's head. When he heard Kas come around the corner, he took his shot before turning the gun on himself and dying by suicide." A shudder wracks me, and Ale squeezes my thigh again, leaving his warm palm stroking comforting circles. "Kas saw the whole thing and immediately ran to our mom, who, to everyone's immense shock, was not dead. As soon as I heard the gunshots, I called the police and then Lola, but I never left my room. Not until our father was taken away in a body bag and our mom was airlifted to the nearest emergency room."

A tear slips free, trailing down my cheek, and Ale wipes it away with the pad of his thumb. "Kas came to find me after they were gone so I could talk to the police but wouldn't let them get me until our parents were gone. He was covered in blood because he was applying pressure to the entrance hole and trying to prevent her from dying of blood loss, but before the paramedics arrived and took over, he lost her pulse and started chest compressions, saving her life." I can't help the sob that climbs up my throat, more tears slipping free, my throat raw.

"He and I had been taking CPR and basic first aid classes since we were twelve, and he was actually able to remember it in the moment." The tears pour freely now, unable to stop them, but I'm not even crying for myself. I'm crying for Kas and the hatred for himself he held onto for so long because he thought it was his fault. "He thought that if he hadn't wanted to go pro so badly, our father would never have started drinking again, and the truth is that if it wasn't money, it would have been something else. He was sick in more ways than one, and I think after years of therapy, Kas finally understood that. It's why he finally accepted the offer from the Philly Scarlets to play with them when we were twenty-four. They had been scouting him for years prior."

Ale looks at me with an inscrutable expression, not of pity or even sympathy but something else. Pride? He looks proud. Of what or who, I'm not sure. But I am damn proud of Kas and everything he's overcome to get to where he is.

"What happened to her?" he asks, his voice thick.

"She lived. She's still alive, living in a twenty-four-hour nursing facility, oddly enough, being paid for by our father's life insurance policy payout." I shake my head, still in disbelief all these years later. "The bullet got lodged in her brain, and it was too risky to remove. She had lost a lot of blood, and there was definitely a chance she'd die whether they took it out or not, so they left it in. She can still speak, but her sentences are broken, and she requires a lot of speech therapy. She isn't ambulatory, so she can't walk or bathe herself, and she suffers from major depressive disorder, but she has a boyfriend in the facility, and she seems to get along well with the staff."

I cast my gaze away, still fussing with my necklace, shame coating my next words. "We used to visit her, but we stopped entirely when one of the staff members sat us down and explained that she only gets worked up and angry when we visit; she's pretty okay otherwise. And her being content is all we can ask for, so we stopped going."

"That's beyond miraculous that she lived," he says with clear shock written all over his face, but it morphs into something softer, his hands gripping mine. "I'm so sorry you and Kas had to navigate that; it sounds like an overwhelming amount of trauma for anyone, but especially a couple of teenagers."

"It was, but we had our grandma to help us along the way, for a while anyway. She passed a couple of years ago. Truthfully, I think she was only able to live as long as she had so she could take care of us. She was the absolute best." I give him a small smile, my mind flooding with all of the incredible memories we shared with her before she passed. Even through all of the bad, she was still a light to this world.

"Is that why you decided to work in neurology?"

"Yeah, it wasn't because I thought by doing so, I'd somehow be able to fix my mom or save her from what had already been done though. It was more that I found her ability to live at all with a bullet lodged in her brain absolutely fascinating. The brain holds so many intricacies that I wanted to explore and help others by doing so."

He shifts beside me, resting his arms around me and gently tugging me closer to him before planting a kiss on the top of my head. We sit there in silence for a while until I think we're both starting to feel a bit better. It's been a really long night, but talking about everything was incredibly cathartic, and it's a good reminder for me to establish with a new therapist here. It definitely helps to let some of that go.[1]

"Hey,"—I look up at him, grinning with mischief—"what would you say to watching the new season of that trash TV show where twenty strangers talk to each other behind a wall for weeks, getting to know each other and proposing at the end of the two weeks before they're allowed to actually see each other?"

He lets out a bark of laughter before grabbing the remote and looking for the show. He finds it so quickly that I think he must know the show better than I had expected. "My sister and her wife love this show, and honestly, I kind of do too. We watch it after Sunday dinners, usually when a new season gets released. One year, I started watching at home without them because I couldn't wait anymore, and you should have heard the threats Charlie was spitting at me that Sunday." He chuckles with the memory, and I join in. I've never known a man who enjoys reality TV as much as I do, and definitely not one who will actually admit it.

---

1. **Over Some Wine - RINI (ft. Maeta)**

Chapter Twenty-Five

Katarina

Saturday, December 9, 2023

We've managed to watch six episodes of this show, laughing and pausing to complain about the cast when they do or say something particularly cringey or annoying. One minute, I'm bawling my eyes out in front of him while he comforts me, and the next, I'm laughing until I cry and he's red in the face. I've dated a few guys, but no one has ever made me feel the way Ale does already.

It's this moment I decide to say *fuck it*. If a bunch of random strangers on TV can manage to give their relationships a shot, we can too.

Tomorrow, I'm going to the police station to report Ante, and on Monday, I'm going to HR to report him too. When I'm done,

I'm going to speak with Dr. Howell about transferring Alessandro into his care.

I'm breathless from laughter as I scoot closer to Ale, the outside of our thighs touching now as we lay horizontally on the couch. I look up at his face to find that he's gazing down at me; his eyes look heavy with lust, which makes me lick my lips in an automatic response. I roll onto my side and place my hands on his chest, scooching up his body to angle my face over his before saying, "I'm transferring your care to Dr. Howell."

He looks startled, seemingly because that is definitely not what he thought I was going to say. "Why would you do that?" His brow is furrowing again.

"Because I have no intention of getting involved with my patient, which means..."

He finishes the sentence for me. "I can't be your patient." He looks me over, assessing and mulling over what I just said. "Is that why you've been actively avoiding being alone with me?" He cocks a brow at me, and my cheeks burn with embarrassment. Obviously, I hadn't been as sneaky about that as I had hoped. This man makes me feel like a giddy teenager, and I seem to have had a lot of inappropriate reactions to situations involving him since we met.[1]

"Yep," is all I manage to say.

He continues appraising me, and when he realizes what I've just implied, his eyes flare with heat, and there's that heavy-lidded look again. Groaning, he wraps one hand around my waist, and the other cups the back of my head. "Thank fuck," is all I hear him grind out before his lips are on mine.

His fingers twine through my hair, the tension on my roots creating a dull ache that makes me dizzy with anticipation. I slide my hands up and around his neck, holding on. His lips are soft and supple, though they're demanding as he kisses me feverishly—first with a closed mouth and then using his tongue; he slides it along the seam of my lips, coaxing them open. My mouth opens voluntarily, seemingly of its own accord, and his tongue dives in, tangling with mine. He tastes like truffle honey and chocolate, and I can't help the needy moan that escapes me. It spurs him on, his hand angling my head for better access before he loses his patience, and he flips me on my back, reversing our positions.

"Is this okay?" he asks so breathlessly, it's almost a whisper.

"Mhmm," is all I can say. I just need his mouth back on me.

He chuckles as I try to pull his mouth back to mine, but he stops me, saying, "Use your words, baby, or I'm not touching you."

I let out a frustrated sound that's a cross between a groan and a whimper. "Yes, it's perfect. Now keep kissing me." God, I sound needy, but I don't care because *I am* needy.

That's all the answer he needs. He grips the front of my neck, my hands automatically going behind him to scrape my nails over his back. I want more contact, but I'm trying not to rush this.

His fingers dig into my throat, the weight of them just enough for my breathing to become shallow and to make my inner muscles clench. I can feel myself becoming wetter by the second. He moves his mouth from mine, pressing searing kisses down my jaw, my neck, on the soft skin behind my ear, and finally, nipping at the sensitive skin of my chest and the base of my throat. I can feel his cock hardening along my thigh, and I have to fight the urge to grip him in my hands. Instead, I find myself angling my center toward his, rocking my hips, seeking the pressure I desperately need from him.

He lets out a series of curses under his breath, looking at me intently with need in his eyes. "You tell me to stop any time you want, okay, Kat?"

"Okay, but *don't* stop," I rush to say so he won't quit; my plea-sure is building, and my clit is aching with the need for release. That elicits another low chuckle from him.

"How far do you want this to go, *gattina*?" He's sliding the tip of his nose up the bridge of mine; the hand that was on my throat is now drifting toward my hard nipples. His other hand acts to support him so he doesn't lower the weight of his whole body, crushing me.

I take a moment to think, which is difficult given the current situation, before saying, "As far as you want. I want all of you." I know he needs me to be sure, and I am, so I pour as much confidence into my words as I can.

He lets out a grunt and slides his hand under my shirt, squeezing my breast before pinching my nipple and flicking his thumb across it. He leans back completely, and the loss of his body heat would make me grow cold immediately if it weren't for the need running through me, overheating my skin.

"Take off your shirt," he demands, and who am I to argue with this guy? I sit up and take my shirt off, tossing it behind me. He looks at me hungrily. "Lay back and lift your ass up." Again, I do as I'm told, and he slides my night shorts and panties off before leaning forward to kiss me in another hurried tangling of tongues and lips. His lips travel down my body, leaving molten hot kisses in their wake that scorch my skin.

He stops to pinch my nipples, sucking on them and biting down hard enough to elicit a cry, equal parts pain and pleasure, but he immediately runs his tongue over the sore bud, licking the sting away while heat floods my core.

How does this man read my body so well? I've never been with someone who knew exactly how to please me. They were always too afraid to hurt me, not realizing that that was exactly what was missing.

He continues trailing kisses down my abdomen until he gets to my core. His hands are on my thighs, pulling them apart; he settles in between them, his broad shoulders causing me to stretch my legs out so far to the side that I feel like I'll split in half. He realizes this and scoots down a bit so his mouth is angled right where I need it. Gazing up at me beneath hooded lids, he says, "Look at you, Kat, you're already soaked for me." He's right—I'm already dripping onto the couch.

"Do you want me to eat this pretty pussy of yours, *gattina*?" I'm practically purring already; if that isn't answer enough, I don't know what is. My patience is running thin, so I tug on his hair and direct his mouth to my needy clit.

Another chuckle, and he dives right in, his tongue running up and down the seam of my folds before stopping to suck my clit between his lips. I cry out, my back arching off the couch and my eyes rolling to the back of my head.

"Oh god, yes. *More.*" He lets out a low rumble of approval before slipping a finger inside me, curling it to hit my G-spot as he continues sucking on my clit. He alternates movements, slipping another finger in that fills me with a fullness so satisfying that it has me nearing the edge. Then, he laps me up, hums against my folds, and says, "You taste so good, Kat, exactly how I knew you would, just like honey. Be a good girl and come for me."

If that weren't enough to coax me, the onslaught of his tongue swirling and slipping between my folds and his fingers pumping faster inside me sends me toppling over the edge of a cliff with no parachute. I'm moaning and pressing his face into my core, literally riding him as I start to come down from the most intense orgasm of my life. If that's what he can do with his mouth, I can't wait to see what he can do with his dick.

Once I've regained control of my body, I release his head. He climbs back up, bringing his mouth close to my ear, nipping the lobe, and says, "Such a good girl." I let out a long groan. Fucking hell. Is *praise kink* written across my forehead in neon lights?

"That was incredible," I say, still a little lightheaded but eager to return the favor.

He lets out a low chuckle, shaking his head, his mussed hair lightly sticking to his forehead that's slick with sweat. "The pleasure was all mine," he tells me, and somehow, I know he means it.

My cheeks flame, and I playfully smack his shoulder. Dragging my hands down his abdomen, I try to gain control and flip him onto his back, but he won't budge. He's too damn big for me to toss around, so I settle for gripping his length through his gray sweats, which sends a quiver through him that I feel immediately. He shakes his head at me. "Not tonight, Kat. I just want to hold you."

He makes it very apparent that going down on me was for both our pleasure and not just mine. I'd argue with him, but I'm exhausted and just want to head to bed.

"Take me to bed?" He scoots off the couch, extending his hand toward me, the black-and-red Medusa tattoo peeking out from under the sleeve of his white T-shirt, but I can make out the heads of the snakes crawling down to the crook of his elbow.

I latch onto his hand; he hoists me up into a bridal carry that has me giggling as he walks me into my room. Ale tucks me under the covers and turns out all the lights but leaves the lamp on the opposite side of the bed illuminated before moving to exit the room.

"Stay with me?"

His eyes widen at first, but then he tells me, "I'm just cleaning up in the living room. I'll be back in a few minutes. Don't worry, I'm not going anywhere." He says it with complete sincerity.

1. **Comfortable - H.E.R.**

CHAPTER TWENTY-SIX

Alessandro

I wake up Saturday morning in Kat's bed with the sun filtering in, highlighting her gorgeous high cheekbones. She's tucked her body in snugly next to mine, and her ass is pressed firmly against my cock, which is currently sporting morning wood that's trying to tunnel its way between her cheeks. I've got my arm slung across her waist, and I'm making a real effort not to move so she won't wake.

Last night was... a lot. I was jealous as hell when I saw her at the bar with that guy, but the rage that I felt when I came out of the bathroom to find her pinned to the bar by him had smoke nearly billowing out of my ears. Kat allowing me to take care of her afterward sent my heart soaring. Getting to know her better while also digging up some pretty heavy memories for her wasn't where I had thought the night would go, but I'm glad she felt comfortable enough to be vulnerable with me.

Then I found out that she's obsessed with the same reality TV shows as me and my sister. Most people hate those shows, and most *men* are afraid to admit they actually like them. It was refreshing to find someone who matches my love of those shows, and her sense of humor? God, she's hilarious, and she's got this laugh that tells you exactly how she's feeling. When she thinks something is cute-funny, she lets out an airy giggle like a Disney princess would, but when she thinks something is truly hilarious, she outright cackles, which sends her into a fit of snorts. I find it unbelievably endearing.[1]

But the way she moans and responds to my words and not just my touch? It leaves me unhinged. I want to devour her every sound.

We left things off in a good place last night, but we still need to discuss expectations. She said she was going to transfer my care to Dr. Howell, which I don't mind. She speaks highly of him, and I know she wouldn't transfer me to someone she didn't trust implicitly. That said, I wouldn't let things go any further last night until we established that this is more than just fooling around for convenience or because of nothing more than an intense physical attraction.

I want to take her out on dates, tell her brother about us, bring her to Sunday dinners with my family, and, more than anything, get to know everything about her. Every detail. Every small, seemingly insignificant piece of her. Last night was just a taste of that, and it left me wanting so much more.

She's one of those people who wears her heart on her sleeve; you can read all of her emotions clear as day as if they're literally written on her face, but I want her to *want* to tell me what she's thinking.

When she wakes up, we can talk about it and then grab some breakfast. Maybe she'll agree to invite Kas and Aiyana so we can tell them about us too, assuming she agrees to there being an *us* at all.

God, I hope she does.

---

1. **Lost - Frank Ocean**

Chapter Twenty-Seven

Katarina

After having the most restful sleep I've had in what feels like forever, I wake to a heavy arm slung over my waist, holding me firmly to his thick shaft, which is practically pressed between my cheeks. The memories of last night's events come flooding back to me in a wave of emotions.

Looking over my shoulder, I see Alessandro gazing down at me with a content smirk on his face. "Good morning, gorgeous. How'd you sleep?"

"Amazingly, better than I have in forever. You?"

"With you by my side, safe and sound. I slept like the dead. It was incredible." He presses a kiss to my temple before saying, "Now that you're awake, we have some things we need to talk about."

Well, doesn't that sound friggin' ominous? "Look, we already went over this. I'm going to report him today. That hasn't changed, so we don't need to keep reliving it," I rush to tell him, trying to avoid yet another recounting of last night's horrible encounter with Ante.

"What? No, *gattina*." I lift his arm and shuffle myself so I'm sitting up and looking at him. This feels like something we need to talk about face to face, not cuddled up in bed. "I'm talking about *us*. We need to talk about *us*."

"Us?" I ask, not understanding what he's referring to. He moves to sit up and face me as well, taking both of my hands in his much larger ones as he continues.

"Yes, Kat. I want to take you out on dates, show you off, cuddle you every night, get to know you, bring you home for the holidays, and have you meet my family." The lightbulb finally goes on in my head. *Us*. He wants to discuss a future together.

"Good god, Alessandro!" I let out a relieved chuckle, smacking his chest. "You didn't have to preface this conversation with 'we need to talk.' You gave me a freaking heart attack! Of course I want to date you; I don't really do casual. That's why I said I'll be transferring your care to Dr. Howell. I want all of those things you just mentioned... and more."

I realize now that I'm still naked from last night; heat is starting to simmer in my belly as he seems to realize the same thing.

Ale wraps his arms around me, pulling me back down with him, his hand skimming over my hip and trailing down my outer thigh. He brings his lips to the base of my neck, placing a kiss there before sliding his tongue all the way up to my ear, eliciting a shiver from me. But instead of continuing, he leans over me, wrenching my nightstand drawer open. My eyes widen in shock, my mouth popping open.

"What are you doing?" I nearly shriek as he starts digging through the drawer. "Don't you know nightstands have people's most personal belongings in them?"

He chuckles, his body still angled over mine as he continues digging. My panic attack meds are in there, along with smutty books, my e-reader filled with much of the same, and, of course, my fucking vibrator!

"I *do* know that, *gattina*; that's why I'm going through it. I want to know the inner workings of that beautiful brain of yours." He smirks down at me. "Don't worry, you can go through mine too."

"I'm holding you to that," I grumble.

"I'm looking forward to it," he says as he finally lays back against the pillows, his hands filled with books, and sitting on top of the stack is my vibrator.

He looks positively radiant as he lays out all of his findings, making my cheeks grow pinker by the second. "Let's see what my girl's been reading, shall we?" *My girl.*

"Which one of these is your favorite?" he asks me, and I don't know which book would be least embarrassing for him to read. Not because they're all pretty spicy; that isn't really the embarrassing part at all. Frankly, I think we should all just let people read whatever the hell they want as long as it isn't hurting anyone else. That said, every single one of these books is about getting fucked by a *hockey player* or three.

"That one." I point to a book with shattered ice and a hockey puck soaring through it, and he smirks as he picks it up.

"How appropriate," he says, voice laced with amusement. "Pick a number"—he flips to the last page in the book—"through three hundred fifty-six."

"Twenty-six," I tell him immediately, picking his jersey number but also knowing there's no sex in the first several chapters.

He tsks at me, "That's too low of a number. How will I know how you want me to fuck you if you've got me stuck reading the intro?"

I flop back on the bed, eyes clenching closed as I throw my arm over my face, heat searing through me at his words. "Two seventy-seven," I grumble, uncovering my face.

He smiles, reaching over to his bag on the side of the bed and pulling out a pair of reading glasses. He places them on his face, and if I were wearing panties, they'd be melting right off my body. Good god, he looks hot. I resist the urge to fan myself as he picks up the book, sifting through the pages until he finds the one he wants. He clears his throat theatrically before beginning to read.

"I shouldn't be pursuing her, and I know it. She's completely off-limits, and somehow, it makes me want her more." He peers over at me, a brow quirked with interest.

"Coach will fucking slaughter me if he finds out I'm seeing his daughter, but I'm past the point of caring, especially when her body is pressed against mine. She's looking up at me with those hooded baby blues, and I lose it, all control snapping when she bites her bottom lip. I lose all thought, pressing the pad of my thumb to her lip, pulling it free before taking her mouth with mine."

His voice is so smooth and sensual. "You should be a book narrator; people would pay good money for that," I tell him, heat pooling at my core.

"I'll narrate for you any day, *gattina*," he tells me before continuing. *"She moans into my mouth, my hand trailing down to her breasts, pinching her nipples as she releases a cry of pleasure, my mouth capturing the sound. My hand snakes down her body, finally finding that sweet pussy of hers."* I'm starting to squirm, unable to control myself.

He catches the movement but does nothing to ease the pressure building between my thighs. *"My fingers slip beneath her panties, sliding through her slick folds."* He snaps the book shut, tossing it onto the nightstand beside him and gathering the rest of my books, hastily shoving them to the side too. Ale grabs the vibrator that's been sitting in his lap and turns on his side to face me, gripping the covers draped across me and tossing them toward the foot of the bed.

He sucks in a breath as he takes me in, his eyes landing on the bruises littering my arm, and his expression turns to rage. Gently grabbing my hand to pull my arm to his mouth, he presses kisses along the bruise. "No one will *ever* touch you like this again, Kat." His words are a promise, and I have no doubt he'll keep it.

Not liking where this has headed, I drag his attention back up to my eyes, wanting his hands on me desperately. "I need your hands on me," I tell him, his eyes looking down and snagging on my pert nipples. He dips his head, dragging one into his mouth and tugging hard. "Ale." A surprised moan leaves my lips.

Swirling his tongue along the sensitive bud, my back arches off the bed. I hear the familiar buzz of my vibrator as he drags it down my sensitive skin, leaving a trail of goosebumps in his wake. He drags the tip of the toy to the apex of my thighs, pressing gently on the skin just an inch above where I actually want it, but I can tell he's fully aware of that.

His nose drags along my jaw, stopping at my ear. "Take it and show me how you like to fuck yourself when you're thinking of me." He presses the toy into my hand, so I wrap my fingers around it, changing the setting to a high, steady buzz.

Ale's calloused hands run up the inside of my thigh, parting my legs and making me feel even more bare than I had before. I fight the urge to pull the covers over myself, seeing how turned on he is. Before I do as he told me to, I turn my face to his, bringing our faces mere millimeters from one another as I say, "Only if I get to watch you too."

He releases a long groan but does as I asked, pushing his briefs down his tan, muscular thighs, and his cock springs free. Gripping it at the base, he begins pumping his fist up and down the hard length, and my mouth waters with the need to choke on it.

"Be a good girl and fuck yourself, *gattina*." He jerks his chin to my unmoving hand. I trail the black silicone tip downward, sliding it between my swollen pussy lips, gasping as my core tightens and clenches as it buzzes over my clit, the motion making my body sing. "Fuck, you're perfect," he grunts.

"If I'm so perfect, then put that pretty cock of yours in me and let me come around it," I whine, the ache in my core begging for more.

His strokes become rougher as he grips himself more tightly, squeezing precum out of the swollen tip. "We're supposed to ease into this," he moans.

I quicken my pace, losing myself in the feeling. "Exactly," I pant, "ease into me." My eyes burst open as I feel the heavy weight of him hover over me. He grabs the vibrator out of my hand, slipping it through my folds and applying pressure exactly how I want it.

"Keep talking like that, and you won't be doing anything with ease for at least the next week," he grits out, the implication making me shudder.

He continues working me, my muscles tightening as pleasure sears through me, and I come hard and fast under him. I haven't finished riding the wave of my release when I feel his hot come spurt across my stomach, my eyes widening with shock as I look down. He wasn't even touching himself, one hand holding himself up and the other still *in* me.

"Did you just come without even touching yourself?"

"It wasn't difficult with you under me making those little sounds," he tells me, removing his hand from my center and caging me in. Leaning his forehead against mine, he closes his eyes, just enjoying our proximity, until he finally releases a sigh and rolls over to get up from the bed.

I watch as he pulls his briefs back up his thighs, heading to the bathroom. I hear the faucet running in the bathroom, and a moment later, he returns with two washcloths, one wet and one dry. "Spread your thighs, baby," he coaxes me, then wipes me clean and pats me dry, the gesture both erotic and so tender.

When he's finished, my stomach rumbles loudly, and we both laugh. "Okay, get up and get dressed. I'm taking you to breakfast, and then we can head to the police station to file that report together. Sound like a plan?" He presses a chaste kiss on my cheek.

"Yep!" I hop out of bed with Ale following closely behind; he swats my ass, making me jump, but the surprise is trailed by a jolt of pleasure.

"Mind if I invite your brother and Aiyana to breakfast too, so we can tell them the good news? I'll need to get Aiyana's number from you, but I figure if we tell Kas first, there'll be hell to pay." Judging by the playfulness of his tone and the chuckle he lets out after he says it, I know he doesn't mind my best friend's quirks.

I give him my cell to text them and head to the bathroom to freshen up and get changed before heading to the living room. To my surprise, it's absolutely spotless. The couch looks and smells like it was wiped down with a wet cloth or something, the dishes are put away, and all surfaces appear to have been wiped as well. I look up at him quizzically. "What? I figured it was best if Aiyana didn't come home to find a puddle of your come on the couch, with a pile of clothes on the floor and dishes everywhere."

There he goes, making me blush again.

Strangely, neither Kas nor Aiyana answer our texts about breakfast, and my stomach can't wait for them to finally reply. So we head to a café nearby that has amazing chocolate croissants and eat before heading to the police station to file the report.

Chapter Twenty-Eight

Katarina

"Okay, so tell me all of the juicy details about last night! I want to hear every last detail." Aiyana is lounging in the corner of the couch in a pair of red sweatpants from high school and a white tank top, with her long, dark hair hanging in two loose braids. She just got in from her late night out with her mystery date, and she's ready to delve into what should have been a relaxing Friday night for me.

I shift uncomfortably in my seat and grab the blanket off the side of the couch to drape over my legs, stalling and also using it as a literal and figurative security blanket. I finally meet her eyes, and she must read the situation on my face because she scowls and looks visibly upset. "So that RN I met up with ended up getting handsy"—stopping her before she can dive into the role of the protective best friend—"and I really don't want to talk about it right now, not in detail at least. I promise I'm okay though, and Ale and I went down to the police station this morning to file a report."

Her eyes go wide with disbelief, either at the fact that I had such a horrible experience or at my mention of Alessandro and me together. "I don't even know where to start with that, so go on..."

I let out a huff because I know the first part of this conversation will be pretty uncomfortable, but the second half, she'll be all over with excitement. Which is good because I honestly just want some girl talk without any of the sad parts. "I think he drugged my drink while I was in the restroom, so I didn't drink it because I already had a bad feeling. The guys all went to Rocco's after the game to celebrate, so Alessandro was there with them, and when he noticed what was happening, he came over and scared the guy off." I pause, taking in a deep breath before continuing. "If I weren't so skeezed out, I'd probably have been turned on by the way he took charge of the situation."

"And that's when you texted that you were going home?" Her brow quirks at me in question.

I shake my head. "No, I texted you from the bathroom. I was already planning to leave before that, but when I got back, things got so much worse."

She nods slowly, lips pinched together. "You know you could have told me, right? I'd have dropped everything to come get you, babe. I don't like that you took a freaking cab home after that!" Her voice hitches up a notch at the last few words, her frustration growing.

"I know you would've, but you didn't need to. Alessandro took me home." My eyes lift to hers, and I don't miss the switch in her moods, her eyes turning wild and her lips curling up in a cheeky grin.

"Mm, and things just got interesting." She shifts her position on the couch, shuffling closer to me and crossing her legs, looking expectant.

I laugh at her, shaking my head before recounting all of the good parts of last night. "He took me home, ran me a freaking bubble bath, and made me a cheese tray." I pause again, then add, "I told him about my mom." I breathe, emotion tearing at my chest.

She wraps her arms around my shoulders and squeezes me tightly, releasing me quickly. A blush takes over my cheeks when I think about what came next, and her eyes start to go wide with recognition. "Oh my god, Kat, there's more, isn't there? Tell me, tell me!" she chants at me.

"He ate me out like I was the last meal on Earth and the world was in flames, so all in all, I'd say it was a pretty fabulous night if you can get past all the shit that was... not."

"Babe, we're really gonna have to work on your delivery there. I just went on a rollercoaster of emotions with you in the span of two minutes. It was like watching a lecture on double speed while trying to track every detail needed to pass an exam." Shaking her head at me, she scoots over again and tosses her legs across my lap. "For your sake, I'm going to ignore the first parts of that because it sounds like you don't really want to talk about them, and I trust that you *and Alessandro,*" she says, drawing out the "o" for dramatic effect, "sorted it all out and that you'll talk to me about it all when it isn't so fresh. Now, what about that last meal?"

She always has a way of reading the situation and diffusing it before it gets too heavy; it's one of the many things I adore about her. Letting out a chuckle, I relay some of the highlights of Ale's incredible mouth on me. "And then this morning, he wanted to talk about being exclusive and actually dating one another, which is why he didn't take things any further last night."

"I'm on the edge of my damn seat here, Kat; what did you say?!
Are you guys dating?"

"Yep." I grin, knowing that simple answer won't fly with her but
doing it anyway to see how far I can push her patience. "That's all
the detail you get until you tell me about the new mystery man or
woman from last night," I say playfully, wagging my eyebrows at
her, "and there *is* more to tell, so you'd better get talking."

Something I've never seen before happens. Her cheeks flame instantly, and for the first time ever, I believe I'm actually witnessing
her feel... *embarrassed*? "It was nothing, really. I'll tell you about
him if anything comes of it, but it's not worth talking about right
now. Besides, we have a date to plan!"

"I'm glad that neither of us believes a man should be the one in
charge of planning the first date, or every date for that matter. I'd
rather plan a date I know I'll actually enjoy, and if we're going to
be equals in a relationship, I should be spoiling him too."

"Absolutely agreed, so where should we start?"

We begin by calling my brother to let him know about us dating
and ask him to send over their training and game schedule so I can
pick activities that work on his next available day.

***

After some extensive planning, we land on a date that makes my
stomach twist in knots. "And you are absolutely certain that you
don't want to do anything for your birthday? We could at least stay
home and watch movies, order takeout, that sort of thing?"

"Babe, I do have plans that night"—she rolls her eyes at
me—"plans to lay in bed, listen to some audio erotica, try out
the new vibrator I gifted myself, and wait to hear about my
best friend's incredible first date with the hottie across the hall."

She waggles her brows at me suggestively, and I grin, my cheeks pinkening.

It doesn't take long before we have all the details worked out, so I text Ale and let him know when to be ready for our first date before heading over to the shelter to volunteer for the night.

Chapter Twenty-Nine

Alessandro

Tuesday, December 12, 2023

As I pack a bag with street clothes and finish getting my tie on straight for my date with Kat tonight, I think back to all of the dates I've been on and can honestly say that I've always been the one to plan them. I've also never been on a date that required an outfit change in the middle, so that's definitely new.

I called my mom earlier and gave her the good news about Kat and me making things official, to which her only reply was, "Thank god, *rattino*. I'm not getting any younger over here, and I need a grandbaby or seven out of you! Those gorgeous green eyes on a little curly-haired thing? Oh, can you imagine?" I didn't bother explaining that this is our *first* date because she already knows that. It would be futile because she doesn't care how long I've known her; she just wants more grandkids.

I'm slow to finish getting ready due to some pain and numbness I've been having recently, but I'm eager to see Kat, which keeps me going.

I check myself in the mirror, ensuring my clothing isn't wrinkled. Kat said to "dress nicely" and bring "street clothes" to change into, which was oddly vague.

So I went with navy dress slacks, a white button-down, a matching navy sports coat, and brown leather Oxfords. I grab my coat before heading out but realize that maybe I should tidy up a bit more.

I have a few minutes before I'm supposed to meet Kat anyway, and maybe she'll want to come back here tonight? Not that I'm expecting it or anything, but you never know if she wants to cuddle and watch TV here or maybe sleep over without any funny business. Obviously, because I am the perfect gentleman. Clearly.

I roll my eyes at my internal monologue and wipe down the kitchen counters before placing the sneakers I had slipped off by the door in the hall closet.

All right, the penthouse is presentable, and it's officially 5:59 p.m.

I head to the hallway, and just as I step into it, Kat is leaving her apartment dressed in a satin emerald-green dress that cinches at her waist and hits her at about mid-calf. Her hair is in some sort of updo with loose tendrils curling around her gorgeous face, framing it beautifully.

She's wearing strappy beige heels, and a matching winter coat is hanging over her forearm. Meanwhile, I'm officially sporting a semi, and I think I've got drool coming out of the corner of my mouth. I manage to scrape my jaw up off the floor and compliment her instead of just staring at her like a buffoon.

"You look gorgeous, *gattina*"—I wrap a hand around her hip and cup her cheek with my free hand—"simply stunning." My heart is pounding out of my chest. She looks fucking *delicious,* and I'd be more than happy to skip dinner and have her instead.

"Tell me about it, stud." That gets a chuckle out of me immediately.

"Did you just quote *Grease* after I complimented you?" As I've come to expect, her cheeks heat, and she directs her gaze toward our feet.

"Yeah, not one of my finer moments. I'm honestly a little nervous." I'm not sure why, but I am too. My hands are starting to get a little clammy, and I can't wait to get outside for the cool breeze to calm my heated skin.

"Hmm, you don't say? I couldn't tell." She knows I'm joking and reaches up to lightly smack me on the shoulder. This form of playful banter is becoming a regular part of our encounters, and I love every second of it.

"You look really handsome, Alessandro, but did you bring a change of clothes?"

Lifting the arm holding my duffle bag to show her evidence of my compliance, I reply, "Yep, 'street clothes,' just like I was told. I'm pretty good at following directions when they're coming from that sweet mouth of yours." I wink at her, eliciting another flare of pink across her cheeks before pulling her into me and taking her mouth with mine.

She lets out a startled gasp before melting into me and raking her hands across my chest, deepening the kiss of her own volition. We break apart, leaning in with our foreheads pressed against one another, breathless. Somehow, she manages to make me forget my own name every time we're together.

"Off we go, my lady," I say while dramatically extending my arm for her to take. When she does, we head to the elevator, and from there, she takes the wheel on the rest of the night's events.

***

As we step outside onto the sidewalk, we're greeted by a short, stout man in a black tuxedo waiting in front of a sleek, black Rolls-Royce with gold rims. Kat grabs my hand and tugs me toward him, and after introducing us, she climbs in first. I bring my lips to the shell of her ear and watch as she instantly reacts, squeezing her thighs together. Seeing how she responds to me is undeniably satisfying. I whisper in her ear, "A Rolls? I thought I was the one who should be spoiling you?"

She places her hand on my thigh and squeezes, looking up at me but keeping her face forward. "I know a guy." She winks and continues, "I wouldn't get too excited yet. The fancy part isn't even the best." She gives me a knowing smirk that insinuates I have no idea what I've gotten myself into, and somehow, I think that's potentially what I like most about her. Her emotions are so impossibly easy to read, but the inner workings of her brain, how she operates, and why she makes the decisions she does all remain a complete mystery. It's addicting getting to peel those layers back.

We're driving through Center City—it's December so it's cold out but not snowing yet. The streets are glowing with bright holiday lights hanging from buildings of all sizes, strung around the leafless trees, and people are lining the sidewalks dressed in thick winter coats. It's a Tuesday evening, which isn't exactly the most common date night, so everyone is heading home from work, but I have a game tomorrow night as well as Friday night's away game. So today was the only day this week that worked well for both Kat and me.

I still have no clue what she's got planned, but seeing the city lights has Kat's eyes glowing with anticipation, her leg bouncing and full of excitement. "Care to tell me what we're doing tonight?"

"Nope." Popping the "p" and looking back out the window, that's all the answer I get. I see the corner of a sly grin spreading across her lips as she keeps her gaze trained out the window.

A few minutes later, we pull up to a very unassuming-looking building with several small shops attached. The driver opens our door, letting me out first. Standing, I reach for Kat's hand, helping her out of the backseat. The driver closes the door and heads around to his side, getting in and taking off immediately.

Kat pulls me toward a small shop that looks vacant, with a check-in counter that is entirely void of everything. There isn't even a computer or a pencil. Eyeing her from the side, I wonder if this is where she intended to take us or if it's the result of a Google review that hasn't been updated recently. She approaches the door. A large man who looks like he's straight out of a mafia crime movie is seated at a small round table with a single flameless candle in the middle. He appraises us before bowing his head and holding the door open for us.

Whispering to Kat again, I say, "I don't know if I should be saying 'thank you' or begging for forgiveness before being slowly tortured by your mob boss father..." She lets out a high-pitched squeak, trying to contain her laughter, and walks me behind the desk. Except, it isn't a desk, and this definitely isn't an office space...

"You know, I *was* joking about the whole mob boss thing, but now I'm not so sure. Why are we heading into this guy's underground dungeon?" We descend the steps that were hidden behind the "desk." Each step becomes more and more narrow, the stairs in a spiral formation though they're concrete, and we can't see where we're headed. The lower we go, the more I realize I'm hearing music and not some ancestral buzzing in my ear to "get out." We make it roughly thirty steps before being faced with a wall of smoke and, finally, flat ground.

We're standing inside an upscale, underground hookah lounge with a large wooden bar up against the back wall. The bartender is a woman with brown hair, probably in her thirties. The walls are covered in Moroccan-style tapestries, and they hang from the ceilings too. There are booths tucked away in corners with sheer curtains separating them from the rest of the room. The air is smokey but doesn't smell bad—it's actually kind of a sweet smell, and the air isn't thick with it, thankfully.

Kat nods over at the bartender with a small smile. When she gets a broad smile in return, her hand squeezes mine, and she tugs me toward a booth tucked in the innermost corner of the place. There's a square table in the center covered in a mosaic top with whimsical patterns along it. The wooden booth is shaped like a square, missing one wall where the entrance is. It's built into the walls, and there are brightly covered cushions tossed atop the benches. She slides in first, and I take a seat after her and pull her to me, not able to wait another minute without my hands on her.

The bartender arrives, greeting Kat warmly before handing us menus, and when we're ready, she takes our orders. Kat takes the lead, ordering us a grilled salmon dish and a seafood and saffron rice pilaf dish. She also orders a lavender mocktail for herself, and following suit, I get a Moscow mule mocktail.

When the drinks arrive, I'm incredibly impressed. Not only are they delicious, but they're each served on a different plate or small tiled tray with a mug or glass that matches the drink, as well as a dried lavender garnish for her drink and a curled piece of ginger for mine. On the trays, we each have two cookies that complement the drink. It's such a small touch that really adds to the experience. I can definitely understand why she was shaking with excitement about coming to this place.

Our food arrives shortly after, and it's even more delicious than the drinks. "How'd you find this place?" I ask her, then take another bite of the rice pilaf that's rocking my fucking world right now.

She stops stuffing her face. Another thing I really like about Kat is that she can eat and has no shame about it either. "It's kind of a long story, actually."

"I've got time," I tell her; hanging onto every word she says will hopefully make her realize that. I've always got time for Kat.

"Okay, well, when Aiyana and I were eighteen, we had decided to go out for my birthday in October to celebrate, but all of the clubs around here were really strict about age restrictions, and she wasn't turning eighteen until December, so we couldn't get in." Her eyes cast downward with guilt. "Today is actually her birthday, but she insisted we go on our date." She smiles at me gingerly before continuing. My eyes widen with shock, piecing together something Kas mentioned about a date he has tonight. I remind myself that it's none of my business and continue listening to Kat's story. "We were walking around, probably looking impossibly sad, when the guy from outside saw us.

"He actually went to school with us, if you can believe it. He recognized us and told us to come check out his cousin's new bar. His cousin is the bartender, by the way; she opened this place when she was only twenty-two. We thought we were about to have a Hannibal 'It puts the lotion on its skin' moment when we first saw the set of stairs but then we made it down to this place, and you can imagine how much trouble two young women could get into down here." She gives me a sheepish grin. "We never did though. Clarice, the owner, always made sure to keep us safe, called us a cab when she'd see us heading out, and we made this our going-out spot. I haven't been back since I moved to Cali almost five years ago, but I'm glad to see it's still as incredible now as it was to me then."

"So this place didn't have an age restriction policy?"

She laughs at that. "Of course they did, but Jared wanted to get in our pants, so he didn't even bother checking." I scowl, immediately thinking about that guy, or anyone else for that matter, getting to touch her the way that I now get to. "I didn't say he was successful," she clarifies, chuckling. Clearly, my disdain was written all over my face.

***

We finish eating, all the while talking about her grandmother, her job, our likes and dislikes, and I tell her all about my family and what it was like when Dante, Gianni, and Charlie were adopted.

Her eyes gleam with affection when she speaks about her Lola, Kas, or Aiyana.

She listens intently when I speak, and the more we converse, the clearer it becomes that we want so many of the same things out of life.

We both love dogs and want to rescue as many as we can. We'd love an old Mediterranean-style home with limestone walls, two-story high ceilings with wooden beams, and a fenced-in yard. My thoughts on the home are a bit more specific than hers, but she's brimming with excitement with every added detail of my fantasy.

She wants at least three children, and I'd be happy with anything more than two. We'd both love to adopt but wouldn't be upset if we also have a biological child... or four.

She's also got dreams of opening a free clinic in Philly with a greenhouse attached, where she can have volunteers host classes to teach those experiencing homelessness and those living in low-income households how to grow their own food.

She's absolutely radiant when she speaks about this project—her passion for giving people the tools they need to help prevent and modify their risks of illnesses at their roots, with high-quality, homegrown produce, is something I'm already proud of her for.

It's definitely a plan I'd love to help grow and fund someday. Talking with Kat is like speaking to an old friend whose voice you haven't heard in ages. It's nostalgic and fills me with a sense of longing. It just feels right being with her.

CHAPTER THIRTY

Katarina

After the check arrived, I fought with Alessandro over who was going to pay for so long that I eventually gave in, but then I remembered I had the upper hand here. I went to the bathroom and gave Clarice my card to pay with instead. Ultimately, I won but told him he could repay the favor later.

I take his hand and lead him outside, making a right onto the sidewalk along Main Street, and I pull us to a stop. "One sec, I just need to check in on Aiyana real quick."

"Take all the time you need," he tells me, smiling and pulling my knuckles to his mouth, pressing a kiss there that sends a shiver through me.

When he releases my hand, I unzip my purse, digging through it until I find my cell.

> Hey! We're here. Let your uncle know we're ready, please!

My Pain In The Ass

> You got it! You crazy kids have fun!!!

A minute later, a horse-drawn carriage pulls up in front of us. The horse is a pure-white Lippizan, and he's got red jingle bells tied to his harness. The carriage is the perfect size for two—it's open along the side where there'd normally be windows but has a white covered top with twinkly lights hanging along the sides.

"Your literal chariot awaits," I tell him with a flourish and flutter my lashes at him. The wave of emotions striking across his face is giving me whiplash. He looks shocked at first, then touched at the gesture before he settles on unadulterated delight.

He suddenly wraps his hands around my waist, lifting me up, my feet dangling as he spins me in circles with my body pressed to his chest.

Onlookers are smirking as they see us—some of them seem to recognize Alessandro and pull out their phones to snap a few pictures, but neither of us could care less. We're giggling together, and when he places me back on my feet, he moves his hands to my cheeks, tilting my head back and pressing his lips to mine for a maddening kiss.

A soft moan escapes me, and I'm suddenly hyper-aware that we're in public, being watched, maybe even recorded, and yet I'm absolutely soaked.

Alessandro lets out a deep groan before pulling away and taking my hand. "Let's go, trouble," he grunts out and helps me into the carriage.

I can't help the smile that has been a permanent fixture on my face since having met him. He's like a cinnamon roll—hot on the outside but oh so soft and gooey in the center.

The inside of the carriage is pretty simple, but the seat is covered with a cream-colored faux fur blanket, and I'm perfectly comfortable pressed up against him.

He snuggles up next to me, wrapping his arm around my shoulders and checking to ensure the coachman, aka Aiyana's Uncle Terry, is looking straight ahead and not at us before turning into me so his back is to the road. He places his other hand on my thigh, edging my dress up, and suddenly, I'm cursing myself for wearing a tea-length dress instead of something skimpier.

That doesn't seem to deter him though, and he manages to bunch the material up high around my thighs before leaning in to whisper in my ear, "This is the perfect way to end a perfect night, even if there is a thousand-pound animal carting us around while he steps in his own shit." He chuckles deeply.

I can't contain the cackle that erupts out of me. Terry turns to eye us warily, seemingly unaware of our precarious positioning, before focusing his eyes back on the road.

"You can't say things like that unless you want to risk me laughing so loud I blow your eardrums out!" I snort, still shaking with laughter.

He smiles at me, a broad one that shows off the dimple in his right cheek. "I'll risk a blown eardrum any day if it means getting to hear that laugh."

His voice is suddenly husky as his hand lands back on my thigh; he's about three inches from my dripping heat. Sliding his hand to my inner thigh and hiking it up, his pinky grazes me, and his eyes turn molten. "And just when I thought you were a good girl..." He trails off, tsking at me, "No panties."

I take a look at my surroundings and realize we're less than five minutes from our next destination. I know I should tell him to stop as I feel him slide his middle finger through my slick folds, but the words get stuck in my throat as a moan climbs through me.

My bottom lip juts out, and I'm letting out little gasps, frantically grasping his forearm because I need something to hang onto. My nails dig into him, my mouth going to his shoulder to muffle my moans.

He's letting out soft grunts of approval, and when he inserts his middle and index fingers inside me, I think I'll shatter. He's pumping them in me, dragging his thumb through my wetness and teasing my aching clit.

We're seconds from our destination when he finally gives me the pressure I desperately need, pressing down on my clit, and as soon as the carriage stops and I'm about to go off like a bomb, he withdraws his hand, sucking his fingers into his mouth.

My mouth drops open in shock, lust, disappointment, and even a little anger until he leans into me and says, "You taste so good, *gattina*, but I'm not risking another man getting to hear those sweet sounds of yours. I'll finish you later."

I flush and nearly catapult myself out of that carriage, dragging him behind me. We walk up to Pawsitively Purrfect, the shelter Kas and I grew up volunteering at. It's late, but Louri gave me the code to let us in as long as we promise to lock up.

"Katarina Narvaez, did you bring me to cuddle puppies?!" His face is lit up like a damn Christmas tree, and it's more beautiful than anything I've ever seen. That dimple in his right cheek is on full display, making my heart thump against my chest.

"Yes, but not just puppies. Old dogs too, and cats and kittens if you aren't allergic."

"Not to be dramatic, but I'd literally *die* if I were allergic to dogs or cats because that would ruin my damn life."

Shaking my head at him and grinning like a fool, I unlock the door and let us in, the smell of antiseptic hitting me like a wall.

We head past the run-down front desk, and I lead him to the bathroom to get changed. Once he's done, I change real quick, eager to play with the dogs, and we head down the corridor toward the adoptable pet section. We start in the elderly dog section, which consists of about twenty runs, each housing just one dog with a small patio that allows them to sun themselves when staff are here.

Alessandro walks down the rows, petting each dog and speaking sweetly to each one along the way until he approaches a timid old pitbull affectionately named Tank.

"What's this big guy's story?"

"We aren't sure where he came from, but the vet estimated he's around thirteen years old. He's got no teeth as they were all riddled with issues due to the periodontal disease he had developed, which is common in older dogs, especially those without routine dental care. He walks with a limp, and his tan fur is patchy from dermatitis," I inform him, but his eyes are glittering, and a smile is tugging at his lips.

"He's not the prettiest, but he's so sweet when given the time to cuddle up to you. He doesn't get particularly excited about meeting new people and usually shies away from men, but if you're lucky enough to earn his trust, that big gummy smile of his will brighten your whole day. I just hope someone adopts him soon." Shaking my head and letting out a tired sigh, I add, "Louri runs this place as a no-kill shelter, but he shouldn't have to live here like this."

Ale crouches down in front of Tank's run, extending his fingers slowly toward the bars. Tank sniffs the air, peering over at Alessandro, and starts to scooch himself very, very slowly over to him, as if by making small movements, he won't be seen at all. When he gets up to the bars, Ale slips his hand inside entirely, leaving his palm up, and Tank drops his head right in his hand, allowing Ale to hold the weight of it.

"Can we take him out to get to know us a bit?" Ale turns his attention to me, still supporting Tank's head as he looks at me with hopeful eyes.

"Of course," I tell him excitedly and grab a leash from the back and open his run—leashing him and walking him to one of the adoption rooms where potential owners can meet and play with the animals to ensure they're a good fit for one another.

Ale plops down on the ground immediately, forgoing the couch in the corner and opting to be at eye level with Tank instead. I unleash Tank, who sniffs the room, eyeing Alessandro as he does. When he finishes his perusal of the room, he comes to me for head scratches before moseying over to Ale, who's sitting in a relaxed position, keeping his hands to himself and allowing Tank to seek him out first.

And then, something rather miraculous happens, as if his trusting Ale while in the safety of his run wasn't already a huge surprise—Tank wags his tail; it's not fast, but it's there. Almost like a flicker. Just when I think my entire night has already been made, Tank stands between Ale's legs, looks him dead in the eye, and slumps to the ground, laying his entire body against this giant of a man.

My mouth pops open in surprise. "Oh my gosh, that is the cutest ever!" I'm giddy with excitement just watching the two of them interact.

Ale's rubbing Tank's belly, giving him head scratches, and planting tiny little kisses all over his face as he lounges there in his lap. "I'd say he likes me," he says with a smirk. "Come over here and give my new buddy some tummy rubs."

I sit on the floor in front of them and leisurely stroke Tank's back. He relaxes into my hand, his eyes drift shut, and soon, he's lying in a puddle, snoring away.

"I know we had big plans of cuddling every animal in here, but I don't think I can leave him. Do you think he'd like to live in a penthouse?"

My eyes are wide with shock. "Really? You want to adopt him? What about your hockey schedule?" I hadn't necessarily brought Ale here thinking he'd adopt a pet. I was really just trying to show him one of the happier pieces of my childhood.

"I don't say this to brag, but I make enough money to afford to have someone take him for walks, and he's an older guy. He's probably got a lot of health issues, and I imagine the cost to care for him will be more than a lot of people can afford in the current economy. I could get him on a high-quality raw food diet, pay for his supplements, and get him cold laser therapy to help with his limp. Besides, my family loves dogs, so I know he could stay with any one of my siblings or my parents during away games, assuming you don't want a cuddle bug staying with you on those nights." He looks up at me excitedly; it's clear he's thought this through already, but he continues, "That said, I value your opinion, Kat. So if you don't think I'd be a good fit for him, I'd at least like to sponsor his adoption and all that comes with that for someone who'd give him a good home."

My eyes prick with tears that I can't help but let overflow. "I think you'd be a perfect fit for him," I say through choked sobs, my voice cracking.

"Kat, baby, this is a good thing, right? Please don't cry. You're killing me here, sweetheart." His brows pinch with concern, but he looks down at his lap as if wanting to reach out for me but not wanting to disturb the sleeping pile of goo lying there.

"These are happy tears," I choke out, laughing at how ridiculous I probably look right now. He joins in the laughter, Tank shifting in his lap.

After we spend about an hour with Tank, we put him back in his run for the night, and I send Louri a text with the good news. She's elated to hear this and tells me that I should bring the whole hockey team over to clear this place out. I might just do that.

We walk through the other rooms, petting puppies, kittens, and cats of all ages and sizes along the way before heading outside to lock up and wait for our Uber.

On the ride back to our apartment, Ale is looking out the window at the holiday lights whizzing by, and he holds my hand the entire ride as we sit in comfortable silence. Usually, silence makes me nervous. This is why I tend to fill those potential silences with rampant thoughts and end up sounding like a blabbering mess, but it's always been easy with him. Even since we first met. I just hope this doesn't end up blowing up in my face.

Chapter Thirty-One

Katarina

We exit the elevator hand in hand. Ale places his hands on my hips after we approach my door, spinning me to face him. He's looking at my lips with hooded eyes, and my body buzzes with electricity. He cups my cheek with his warm hand, my eyes dipping to his parted lips. Somehow, his breath still smells minty despite having eaten hours ago.

He tilts my head back, pressing kisses along my jaw, then the corner of my lips, breathing me in, and I'm weightless. A useless blob of a person with jelly bones and zero balance. Thankfully, he's holding me up against my door because I think I'd melt to the ground if he let me go. He absolutely undoes me, and I love it.

Finally, his lips are on mine, soft and gentle, unlike the other kisses we've shared. Those were charged with need and felt desperate, almost punishing, but not now. Now, we take our time, pressing closed-mouth kisses to one another until he swipes his tongue along my bottom lip, nipping at it and urging me to open. I oblige, his tongue sweeping into my mouth, that cool mint flavor of his heightening my senses and sending me spiraling.

Our tongues dance together, a moan escaping from me and a deep rumble following from Ale. My arms wrap around his neck, my hand tangling in his hair, frantically pressing him closer to me. I need more of him. My body is on fire, heat radiating throughout my aching core.

Our kiss is no longer leisurely—we're desperate and wanton. The dam has officially burst, and I'm drowning in desire. He pulls away from me, trailing kisses to my ear, his length pressing against my leg, branding me. His voice is low and husky. "My place or yours?"

"Yours; Aiyana's home," I say breathlessly, eager to continue this.

And right on cue, the door to my apartment swings open, the loss of support dragging me down, but Ale catches me before I can smack my ass on the ground. "I thought I heard... Oh, oops." She's wide-eyed and surprised, her expression quickly shifting to amusement. "Carry on, don't have to drop—sorry, sorry, I mean stop, don't have to *stop* on my account."

She closes the door, but the mood is gone. Effectively doused like a bucket of ice water thrown over us.

Adjusting himself, he says, "Well, I guess that was bound to happen at some point. Wanna watch some TV, and I'll make us hot cocoa?"

I chuckle. "Yeah, I'll be right back. I need to change, and I'll be over in a few."

Before I duck back into my place, he says, "Let yourself in when you're ready. You know the code." I do?

I rush back into the apartment, and luckily, Aiyana is nowhere to be found. She must have gone to hide in her room in case we decided to take our little party in here. That's uncharacteristically thoughtful of her.

Quickly changing into a pair of black joggers and a white tank, I toss a change of clothes and some toiletries in my bag. I know I'm right across the hall, but I'd rather have the option to change there than not have it. As I head to leave, stopping in front of Aiyana's door, I hear muffled voices on the other side. She must be watching TV or something. Knocking, I say, "Just stopped in to change. I'll see you in the morning!"

Silence, and then an overexcited, "Tata, love you, bye!" Wow, she must be really excited that I'm finally "clearing out my cobwebs."

"Tata, love you, bye!" I shout back at her before heading to Alessandro's. Standing in front of his door, I'm nearly scratching my head, trying to figure out what he meant.

I know his door code? Had he given it to me before? I could just knock and ask, but I like problem-solving, and this feels like a fun puzzle.

Then, a lightbulb clicks on in a real *aha* moment. He gave me his phone code once; maybe it's the same? If so, we're really going to need to have a talk about cybersecurity.

Punching in the code one-two-two-five, it flashes green and un-latches. Yep, we definitely need to have that chat.

Walking into his penthouse feels surreal—like we're really an official couple now, and I can come and go as I please. It's both thrilling and nerve-wracking. I head into the apartment, walking straight over to the couch, when I see Alessandro sitting with two mugs of hot chocolate and our favorite show loaded up on the screen. I head over to him, placing a kiss on the crown of his head and giving him a small smile before hesitating. I'm not sure whether I should assume I'm sleeping in the room with him tonight or not. Then I decide to just go for it and head to his room, dropping my bag by the nightstand on the side that I normally sleep on in my room.

I make my way back to him, plopping down next to him and grabbing the throw blanket off the back of the couch, laying it over my legs. He wraps his arm around me, pulling my back to his chest and placing a kiss on my temple before handing me a mug.

"Mmm," I nearly moan. Sex is great, but chocolate might be better. However, my opinion might change where Alessandro is concerned.

"I'm glad you like it, but you might want to start saving those breathy moans for me." He winks at me, grabbing the remote and starting the show.

"So your door code *and* your phone password are both one-two-two-five? I get that it has a deeper meaning for *you*, but to most people, that's a pretty popular holiday in the Western world. And it sounds like a surefire way to get broken into," I chastise him jokingly.

He turns a wide smile on me, those pearly-white teeth gleaming under the low lighting of the living room. "You're probably right," he says with a chuckle. "I'll speak with management tomorrow and have it changed if that'll make you feel better. How's your birthday sound?"

Grabbing the nearest pillow, I chuck it at his head, giggling as he tosses it back and reaches over to grab me, hauling me into his lap. I curl my arms around his waist, resting my cheek on his pec, and turn my attention back to the TV, watching the drama unfold between the couples who are just on the show for clout.

After a while, he pauses the show, turning his gaze to me eagerly. "I know I'll need to get Tank a kennel because I want to make sure he's comfortable in a crate, just in case he ever needs to stay in one, so I'm thinking I'll get a nice big one for that corner over there," he says, pointing to the corner of the right side of the room. "And I'll have to interview some dog walkers to let him out during the day while we're gone. What do you think he needs? I'm definitely going to order a snuffle mat, some puzzle feeders, maybe some soccer cones to do some rally training with him—gotta keep his mind sharp." His excitement makes me giddy, and I love that he's now the one going off on tangents, not just me. "Oh, and he'll need lots of blankets, and I'll need to get some fragrance and dye-free laundry detergent since he's got dermatitis. I don't want to make him extra itchy. One of my nieces has eczema, so I know a bit about the dry, itchy skin situation."

"And you thought about all of that in the last thirty minutes? You weren't even paying attention as poor Sarah got her heart ripped out by Eric!" I joke, and he presses a kiss to my temple.

"Sorry, I've just really wanted to adopt a dog for a long time but was waiting for the right opportunity, and now that it's really happening, I can't stop thinking about it. I also feel guilty as hell for leaving him there tonight." He looks down at our intertwined hands. "He probably thinks I'm not coming back for him."

His voice sounds strained, and it pulls at my heart, making me feel sick for him.

I can feel my eyes getting glossy; his thoughtfulness never ceases to amaze me. So many people adopt an animal without putting any real thought into it, especially around the holidays. They adopt a dog as a gift and then forget that they're a real, living being and not just a cute, fuzzy toy. They come with responsibilities, but the love they give is so worth it.

I'm so glad he isn't one of those people. "Dogs are intuitive, and he didn't seem too upset when we left. I think he knows you'll be back for him." I squeeze him tightly, and he presses another kiss to the top of my head.

"Truthfully, I've been planning to adopt for several months now that I've gotten comfortable with my team and good at managing my time. I just hadn't started looking yet, and Tank both literally and figuratively fell into my lap. He's such a good boy, and he just needs some extra TLC." His eyes soften as he speaks about him—love at first sight is an understatement.

"I'm really glad you found each other," I say, looking up at him.

"And I'm really glad we found each other." He's now speaking about us. He runs his thumb across my lower lip, stroking it gently. His eyes are heating with desire, and suddenly, that damp heat is rushing back to my core.

He holds me tightly against him as he swings his legs over the side of the couch, standing and swinging me over his shoulder as if I'm weightless. I'm giggling and half-heartedly squealing, "Ale! Put me down!" I can feel his shoulders shaking with laughter.

He carries me to his room, nudging the door open with his foot, then kicks it closed. "Alexa, lamps on." Suddenly, the room is flooded with warm lights, and those little bulbs I thought I saw on the ceiling? They really are constellations. It's beautiful.

He swats me on the ass, pulling me out of my dreamy state before tossing me in the center of the bed and crawling up to me. His body is pressed against me, his forearms on either side of my head, holding his weight so he doesn't crush me. I'm lost for words. He's so gorgeous, especially in this lighting. The lamps cast shadows across his chiseled face, his green eyes flaring with heated desire.

He's gazing down at me, slowly making his way down my face, my neck, my chest, and finally to my breasts. Goosebumps erupt under his gaze. Letting out a hum of appreciation, he devours me in a kiss that makes my head spin. His tongue flicks against mine, swiping through my mouth, punishing me.

I wrap my arms around his neck, then my legs around his waist, pressing my heat into his growing length. Breaking the kiss, he whispers in my ear, "So eager," as he presses wet kisses to my blazing skin, breathing me in, and I feel his dick twitch against me. "All you have to do is ask, Kat."

I can't speak. My tongue is suddenly thick in my mouth, and I'm so aroused that I can't form a coherent thought. Finally, I'm able to squeak out a quiet, "Please, Ale."

Immediately, his control snaps. He reaches between us, causing me to loosen my legs on him before he grips his length, letting out a strangled grunt before releasing himself and cupping me right where I want him.

He trails his hand up to the waist of my sweats, dipping his hand in, and luckily, I opted to not wear panties... again. He moves the hand that isn't currently occupied over to my breast, pinching and teasing the hard pearl through my thin top. Pressing his forehead to mine, he takes a deep, steadying breath, trying to regain control. I'm wound so tight, my muscles are clenched and practically screaming for release. Finally, he sweeps his fingers through my slick entrance, and my head bows back.

"Tell me what you want, Kat," he says, sliding a finger inside me. I let out a gasp of pleasure, involuntarily moving my hips, milking his fingers. "God," he grunts, "you're so fucking tight. I can't wait to find out how this sweet pussy feels strangling my cock." I'd probably die of embarrassment if any of my previous boyfriends had said something like that to me, but Ale carries himself with so much confidence that it sounds natural, sending shivers down my spine.

Finding my confidence, I say, "Then let's find out."

"Sweetheart, if we go there right now, I'm so fucking hard I'll blow in two seconds." He slips a second finger inside me, curling his fingers as I arch off the bed, eyes practically rolling to the back of my head.

Before he can take this any further, I tease him, "Hmm, I didn't take you as a two-pump chump."

His eyes flare, the corner of his mouth lifting in a lopsided smirk. He shifts the hand that's inside me, pressing his thumb to my needy clit, giving me every bit of the pressure I'm craving. "Normally, I'm not, but I've wanted this since the day I laid eyes on you, and I'll be damned if the first time I'm inside you doesn't rock your fucking world." His words wash over me, further heating my skin, setting me ablaze.

He increases his pace, leaning forward to angle himself differently and pull my tank down before enveloping my pebbled nipple in his warm, wet mouth. Flicking his tongue, he's nipping and sucking my entire breast into his mouth before releasing me. The hand between my thighs picks up an almost crazed pace as Alessandro is nearly shaking the bed, relentlessly filling me with his fingers.

Just as I'm arching off the bed, damn near levitating from pleasure, vision becoming fuzzy, he removes the fingers that were inside me, swiping them up my folds, and finally, pinches my clit. I'm skyrocketing into space, nails digging into his biceps. I'm coming down from the high just as he slips his fingers back in me, pressing a kiss to my lips, and says, "Such a good girl."

He removes his hand from me and places his fingers to my lips. My eyes are wide with surprise. Before I know it, he's plunging his fingers in my mouth. "Taste yourself, *gattina*, so you know why I'm so obsessed with your sweet cunt."

I taste the salty-sweet flavor of my arousal before he pulls them out and sucks them clean himself. Head tilting back, eyes closing, he promises, "I'll never get enough of you."

After a few minutes, my heart rate has returned to almost normal, and my only concern is him. He's lying beside me, his thumb drawing lazy circles on my stomach. Swinging my legs over and straddling him, he shifts and grips my hips.

"Just can't help yourself, can you?" He winks at me. Shifting down his body, I begin to rock my hips along his shaft. He's still hard, but not rock solid like he had been. Definitely time I rectified that issue.

I'm grinding myself onto him, all humor erased from his face as he stiffens, gripping my hips to try and slow me down. The strong ridges of his abdomen are taught like a bowstring.

"Remember what I said about blowing in two seconds?" My eyebrows shoot up my forehead; I know he didn't mean to suggest it, but now all I can think about is sucking him off.

I lean forward, kissing him enthusiastically, tasting myself on his lips, and that cool mint flavor of his mixes with the hot chocolate we just had. Releasing his mouth, I shift down him, gripping the waistband of his pants and sliding them down.

His throbbing cock bounces out, slapping against the skin of his hard abdomen. I smirk up at him. "No panties?" He lets out a hoot of laughter. I use the distraction to surprise him, gripping him in my hand and directing the head of his cock to my mouth. All laughter abandoned, his hand travels to my head, fingers twining through my roots to steady me.

I suck him eagerly while pumping him with one hand as I balance my weight on the other. I can't take all of him, even deep-throating, so I continue using my hand to help me tend to every inch of him.

He's now propped up on his forearms, one hand still in my hair, letting out grunts and moans of appreciation. I swirl my tongue along the tip, then lick from the hilt up, my mouth wetting him all over, and I watch as his eyes become more hooded.

I cup his balls, eliciting a groan from him as I tuck my thumb into the palm of my free hand, laying the fingers over it and effectively tamping down my gag reflex. Moving the hand that's cupping his balls so I can steady his shaft, I look him in the eyes as I take him as far as he'll go, hollowing my cheeks out around him. He's gripping my hair, trying to pull me back. "Fuck, I'm gonna come..." He tries to pull me back again, but I want to taste him.

Releasing my thumb from my hand, I start gagging and fighting the urge to come up for air. That does him in. Salty warmth slides down my throat as he grunts and quivers beneath me. He releases my hair, and I let him out of my mouth with a pop, effectively sucking him clean. He's still managed to retain most of his erection, but he suddenly looks exhausted.

"God, baby, that was incredible." He's lying back against the pillows, his arms out to his side forming a T. I climb off the bed and head to the bathroom to clean up, and when I get back, he's sitting on the edge, bracing himself with his hands, head down and looking pained.

My stomach sinks as I run over to him. "What's wrong? Are you okay? Do you have pain anywhere?" The questions rush out, his back stiffening.

"Kat, I'm not your patient anymore." He says it through pursed lips. I think I'm experiencing whiplash from the shift in his mood. My eyes are wide with anxiety.

"I know that, but I can help. I'm here to help." His eyes soften, and he scooches further onto the bed, supporting himself better. He takes my hands in his and pulls me to him so I'm standing between his legs.

"I'm sorry, *gattina*, I'm just frustrated. I should have told you sooner, but I didn't want to ruin our night." I'm suddenly plagued with fear of what he's about to tell me.

"I've been in some pain recently," he says, looking up at me, gauging my expression before continuing. "The paresthesia and weakness are back with a vengeance. It's getting harder and harder to play without getting thrown into the boards. I just need to make it a few more months," he tells me, that same pained expression gutting me.

"I know we can win the Stanley Cup. Our stats are incredible; the team works like a well-oiled machine, and we haven't lost a single game since the season started October tenth." He's pleading with me to understand, but I'm nearly shaking with anxiety.

I'm overwhelmed and caught in the middle of two people who are so important to me, but even if I chose to tell Kas, I'd be breaking the law.

"If you're going to keep playing"—I let out a huff of disapproval; he doesn't need to quit playing—he just needs to get help so we can avoid things like this—"then you're going to need to see Dr. Howell tomorrow morning before you fly out on Friday because I'm not going to just stand by as you deteriorate and continue putting your entire team, including my *brother*"—I emphasize with annoyance—"at risk for your own selfish reasons, Alessandro."

"It's not selfish, Kat. Do you really think I'd still be playing right now, risking the game and the safety of my teammates, who also happen to be my closest friends, if it weren't important? My parents were barely making it before I went pro, and it was a while before I was making enough money to help them out. I've been saving, and yes, I live in a nice penthouse, but this place is definitely not anywhere near as extravagant as the places some of my teammates live," he tells me, his tone reverent.

"I'm paying my parents' mortgage, saving to build them a house that will actually be accessible for my mom as her condition continues to worsen, setting money aside for her impending medical expenses, and saving for my own future because I can only assume that a day will come where I'm not able to work anymore either. When that day comes, I want to be prepared. I want to have enough money for our children to play sports and get involved in whatever hobbies they want, no matter how expensive. I want you to not have to struggle to afford those things while working in such a mentally and physically exhaustive field." My eyes are pricking with tears at the reality of the situation. He said, "our children" and not, "my children."

He grabs my cheeks. "Kat, baby, don't cry, please. I promise you, I'll pull out of the game if it starts to become dangerous for me or the guys. Just let me make it one more season; let me help them win that Cup, and I'll tell them and let my coaches decide if I can keep playing. I already have an appointment with Dr. Howell on Thursday morning, but I'll even let you pull some strings and get me in tomorrow if it makes you feel better." He gives me a small smile, trying to lighten the mood. I will *absolutely* be having Dr. Howell see him tomorrow. He's not waiting.

I genuinely trust that he wouldn't knowingly put anyone at risk, which is why I nod my head, melting into his lap. It's the thought of him unknowingly hurting someone that makes my heart sink to my toes.

CHAPTER THIRTY-TWO

Katarina

FRIDAY, DECEMBER 15, 2023

W ork was exhausting. I ran three stroke codes and lost a patient who had been hanging on in the ICU, hoping her family would make it to see her in time. Unfortunately, they didn't.

The emotional and physical stress of the day is crushing me, and all I want is to curl up on the couch with Alessandro, but he's in New York for an away game. Aiya texted me earlier to see if I wanted to check out a new sports bar that opened up nearby and watch the guys' game. I told her I'd have to get back to her because I wasn't sure how I'd feel. I gave her the gist of how my day was going, and she replied with a GIF she made of her in a Care Bear costume hugging me.

I'll admit, her GIFs are my favorite, and it did cheer me up a bit, but the day was long, and I'm beyond exhausted.

As I enter the apartment, I dump my bag on the entryway table and slip out of my coat. Heading to the kitchen, I grab a snack before I shower and crawl into bed. Mood decided, no sports bar for me.

Aiyana sees me in the kitchen and heads over, enveloping me in a crushing hug. She's strong for someone so small. Pulling back with me still in her arms, she says, "Sooo," drawing out the "o," indicating she's about to be in trouble. That same grin shows both rows of her teeth, and I'm filled with dread.

"Don't be mad at me, but"—she begins rushing through her next words at such warped speed, that I barely make them out—"I figured you'd be sad and wouldn't want to go to a rowdy bar tonight, so I reached out to Kas and got him to send me tickets for their game tonight. And I may or may not have exploited my friend Sean's massive crush on me to get him to let us use one of his planes. He owns a charter company and said they'd be able to get us there before the game starts at six, which means you need to change and hurry the fuck up because we've gotta leave in"—she checks the time on the stove—"seven minutes."

I don't know how I'm supposed to react to that, so the emotion that's most potent rears its head. Excitement.

I turn on my heel and sprint to my room, a sudden surge of energy leading me to strip down and grab my usual Philly Scarlets attire. I change with lightning speed, leaving my purple scrubs in a heap on the floor before running to the bathroom to brush my teeth. When I'm finished, I yell to Aiyana, who has suddenly appeared to lean against my doorframe, "Do I need to pack anything? How and when are we getting home?"

"He's just dropping us off. I got us a room in the same hotel as the guys, and Kas spoke with Coach. He's letting us fly back with them tomorrow morning after the press conference. Speaking of which, after last week's game where the press made it known that you and Alessandro are official, I suggest preparing your poker face because once they catch a glimpse of you tonight, they'll be unbearable."

"You're right, but I can handle it. Kas loves Alessandro, and he was happy when we told him." There shouldn't be too much drama for the media to post about since there isn't any in real life. How much can they truly fabricate?

"Oh, I know. But the media doesn't. Just be prepared." She heads to the kitchen to grab her things as I toss some clothes in my duffle and head out behind her.

***

Forty minutes later, we're on a private jet with tan leather seats and shiny round wooden tables anchored between them, preparing for landing in just a few short minutes.

"Your negotiation tactics must be better than I thought because this is incredible." I gape at her, still in awe.

Winking at me, she says, "Don't ask questions you don't want the answer to, babe." Smiling, I shake my head at the implication, knowing fully well she didn't give out any sexual favors for this.

"Flight attendants, prepare for landing," the pilot says over the intercom. The two women take their seats after ensuring we're buckled in ourselves. A couple of minutes later, we're on the ground, parked a few minutes from the arena.

My pulse is beating more rapidly, Aiyana's earlier words about the press digging into our relationship snagging in my thoughts, nerves clawing at me.

We hurry off and shuffle into a car that Aiyana also apparently had set up for us. My hands are clammy as we wait, Aiyana chatting with the driver, and my thoughts spiraling. When we pull up to the arena, I slip out of the back seat of the car and am rushed by curious reporters, wondering who we are. It only takes a second before several of them are shouting, "That's the sister! It's De Laurentiis's girlfriend!"

Acrid bile climbs my throat, my fingers rubbing vigorously on the pendant around my neck as I keep my head down, allowing Aiyana to drag us through the crowd of people, her arm firmly around my waist.

"Miss Narvaez!" they shout, trying to get my attention as if I could possibly ignore their presence. "Miss Narvaez! Do you have a statement about your relationship with your brother's teammate?" and "Did he approve of the relationship?"

Aiyana gives them all a glare, and if looks could kill, they'd all be six feet under. She continues tugging me through the throng of reporters, meeting a man at the door, who I recognize as Kas's agent, ushering us in and toward our seats.

"This way, ladies," he instructs as he holds the door open for us.

Aiyana stops, looking around to take in the scene and spotting our seats. "We're over there, babe." She points somewhere in front of us, and I follow behind her.

We take our seats, the cold metal seeping in through my leggings, chilling to my core. My anxious thoughts start to calm as we see the guys get out onto the ice.

The calm only lasts momentarily though. I feel several pairs of eyes set on us, or more specifically, me. "That's her, his new girlfriend," I hear someone whisper behind me.

"What do you mean by *new*? By all accounts, it seems she's his *first* girlfriend. And what a shame, at thirty-two years old and looking like *that*," the snarky woman sitting next to the first says. At this point, they're not even bothering to whisper, and I'm tempted to turn around and give them a piece of my mind, but the anxiety I'm feeling would never allow such blatant confrontation.

I've never had to deal with something like this before. Most people don't care that I'm Kas's sister because the novelty seems to have worn off, and honestly, I'm not sure most of his fans even realize I exist.

I've never been more thankful that the Scarlets aren't constantly in the tabloids for something dumb. Even my two minutes in the spotlight have been overwhelming, and I feel like there's a two-ton elephant sitting on my chest, and my hands are beginning to shake. I'm taking deep breaths in and out, trying to practice some grounding techniques, taking account of my surroundings, what I can see, touch, smell, and, unfortunately, hear.

Aiyana shifts her glare on them, knowing I can't and won't say anything, and she says, "You know, we can hear you, you fucking idiots." Turning back around, she rolls her eyes before she looks at me and says, "Ignore them; they don't know him or you for that matter. Their opinions don't matter. Besides, they're not really saying anything bad. I think they're all just curious since he's never brought a woman into the limelight before."

I nod, her reassurance helping soothe the anxiety bubbling in my stomach.

After pictures and videos from our date on Tuesday night went viral, the internet has seemingly blown up with people trying to uncover all of my dirty secrets, which means Kas's too. I have nothing to hide, really, but I like to keep my private life private, and I don't love the idea of the press finding out about what happened to our mother. Kas has gone through too many years of therapy to have his progress ruined by a media scandal bringing it all to the surface. Besides, reality always gets twisted in favor of a more interesting take on a story.

***

We're four minutes into the third period, and fortunately for us, the home team advantage hasn't seemed to matter because the Scarlets are up two to one. It's not a landslide, and it could definitely change, but we're feeling good.

At least I was, until I saw Ale slip, catching himself before he could go down. It happened so fast, I doubt anyone realized it, but I haven't taken my eyes off him all night. I'm hoping it was due to a divot in the ice and not his legs.

He saw Dr. Howell Wednesday morning after I spoke with him about having him seen sooner. Dr. Howell was happy to get him in, and luckily, he had a cancellation, so he didn't even have to shuffle his schedule around.

They completely reworked his medication regimen, just like I had wanted to after our first office visit. But I'm always tentative about changing too many things at once, opting for a slower approach to see what makes a difference, either positive or negative.

Ale called me this morning while I was on my way to work and said he felt eighty percent better already, so hopefully, the ice was just uneven. He's been skating well all night, so I shouldn't really be too concerned.

Precisely ten seconds after the thought passes through me, there's a guy on the home team's side banging against the boards with his buddies, yelling at Kas, trying to rile him up. I hear them yelling something about me, and my ears perk up, trying to make out what he's saying. That familiar prick of anxiety takes place in my chest, not that it ever fully left.

He's screaming at the top of his lungs, but it's pretty packed in here, and he's about thirty feet away from us. I make out the words, "your sister, De Laurentiis, fucking," and "dirty girl."

My eyebrows shoot up my forehead. I realize he's just trying to get him off his game, not realizing Kas was practically starring in his own version of *Millionaire Matchmaker*, trying to set Alessandro and me up together from the very beginning. Kas also hasn't addressed his feelings about us to the media, so as far as they know, he can't stand that we're together.

Then, for a second, I almost believe it myself. Kas whirls around, skating toward Alessandro, and pushes him into the boards. My heart drops to my toes watching as Ale almost loses his balance but manages to grab Kas's jersey and steady himself. They back away from each other slightly, raising their fists, and the entire arena quiets down into an eerie silence before erupting in a roar of chants. "Fight! Fight! Fight!"

One of the reasons people love hockey so much is the fights. Players get riled up; it's a physical sport that causes a lot of emotions, and the refs don't break up the fights immediately. It's a common occurrence in the game, but what isn't common is for fights to break out among teammates.

The refs are rushing to break it up, but then I see a massive grin split across their faces, only for a second before it vanishes.

It looks like they're about to pummel each other, their gloves, sticks, and helmets tossed to the side as they begin grappling. But then Kas wraps an arm around Ale's waist, Ale propping his hand on Kas's shoulder, and they take each other's free hand before beginning to dance around the rink, performing their own version of a waltz.

Laughter fills the arena, everyone on the ice stopping to watch their little charade as they twirl each other around, Ale lifting Kas off of the ice, spinning him like he would in a pairs ice skating routine, though with the weight of Kas's gear, he only gets him a few inches off the ice.

The speakers suddenly flood with music, a slow melody trickling in, adding to their antics.[1]

And finally, the refs catch up to them, breaking them apart and sending them to the sin bin for "holding." They take their punishment with big, goofy grins plastered on their faces, clearly proud of themselves.

A smile spreads across my face, and Aiya presses into my side as she whispers, "That was fucking adorable."

I nod my agreement and turn my attention back to the game.

Luckily, the team still won despite the loss of Kas and Ale for their two-minute penalty.

---

1. **Carmen Suite No. 2: Habanera. Allegretto quasi Andantino (Act I) - Georges Bizet**

Chapter Thirty-Three

Alessandro

It's become glaringly clear to Kas and me that people *want* him to hate me being with Kat. I understand that the media are out for the most drama possible in order to sell their story, but it's shitty that him hating me is more exciting than him being happy for us.

I know hockey players don't have the best reputations when it comes to relationships, as much of the media coverage is on our personal lives and who's sleeping with whom. However, that has never been how our team works—we're low drama, so drama has to be created purposefully. The same can't be said about my brother Luca.

He's been playing for a team in New York since he finally got the offer for an NHL team five years ago. New York has two NHL teams—one of them is good, and the other, not so good. Unfortunately, Luca plays for the not-so-good team, which is putting it lightly. Total transparency? They're utter trash.

He wanted to play for the Scarlets with me so he could limit travel and time away from our family, but our team manager decided against it due to his reputation as a hot-headed womanizer. He's actually a really sweet guy, and he's very up-front with his dates about his intentions, but the media paints a story how they want, and he isn't doing himself any favors by playing into it.

Speaking of Luca, I hadn't anticipated Kat's arrival at our game tonight, so she doesn't know about my dinner plans with him and Kas. I'd love her to meet him, but if she's uncomfortable with that, I can understand that too. She's probably feeling extremely overwhelmed by the reporters swarming her and by our little charade on the ice. I wouldn't be surprised if she thought Kas was about to deck me, because truthfully, I did too for a second there.

I finish changing after my shower and head out to meet up with everyone. I see Kat smiling brightly, chatting with Kas and Aiyana. When she sees me approach, she rushes toward me, throwing her arms around my neck. My heart clenches in my chest; seeing my girl so happy to see me is a whole new level of joy I never knew existed.

My body reacts to her instantly, squeezing her tightly to me. I whisper, my lips grazing the shell of her ear, "I've missed my girl."

She pulls back from me gently, shifting her hands to my chest. "Good game, De Laurentiis, but maybe you should take up ballroom instead?" Her eyes are glittering with mischief, challenging me.

I take her hand and usher us toward Kas and Aiyana, who are waiting for us at the exit. "You should know better, Kat—I've already got years of ballroom classes under my belt." I swat her butt playfully, which seems to surprise her.

"*Really?*" She's smiling so hard that her cheeks must hurt.

"Yes," I tell her, rolling my eyes. "My mom made all of us take them because the lady that moved in at the end of our street when I was in middle school was a dance teacher. Suzanna was elderly and lonely, so she offered to teach us for free. It gave my parents some alone time and helped us bond. Not that Gianni or Luca saw it that way at first, but they grew to love it too."

Her eyes grow, glittering with excitement. "How long did you take classes?"

"We were at Suzanna's house every Sunday until she passed away during my senior year of high school." The memory causes conflicting feelings to flood me. I loved the classes, but my heart aches. I miss Suzanna every time I think about dancing, which is one reason I don't do it often. That and I haven't had time or a partner.

Doing my best to shake the sorrowful thoughts away, I lean forward, placing a kiss on Kat's forehead. "So I didn't know you'd be here today." I give her a small smile.

Her face immediately looks stricken, so I rush to explain. "Meaning your brother didn't tell me until we were getting on the ice. I'm happy you're here," I say, looking her in the eyes to ensure she understands. I never want miscommunication between us.

Her expression shifts quickly, a gentle smile curving her lush lips. "I'm glad I'm here too," she says, leaning back into me and tucking her head under my chin.

"That said, Luca plays for the other NHL team in New York, so while we're here, I made plans to get dinner with him and Kas. There's already a lot of media coverage on us right now, so I understand if you don't want to go, but I'd love for you to meet him. If you want to, that is." Suddenly, I'm unsure of myself. I don't remember the last time I introduced a woman to my family, but I know I want Kat to meet them all eventually. I just don't know where she's at with our relationship, and I don't want to risk running her off.

That smile stays etched into her tan skin as she looks up at me through those black-and-white lashes. "I'd love to meet Luca! Plus, I'm starving! I didn't get to eat after work before being tossed on a plane."

Her excitement fucking *thrills* me.

"Well, then, allow me to rectify that issue." I'm guiding her through the crowd when we're swarmed by reporters from all directions vying for our attention. She's clinging to me, and her visible anxiety ignites a fierce protectiveness in me.

I pull the hood of her jacket up and over her head, keeping her as concealed as possible as she tucks herself under my arm, trying to make herself appear small. I think she's shaking, and I just hope it's from the cold and not stress. "Baby, it's okay. Ignore them; we'll be old news soon, I promise," I say as I press a chaste kiss to the top of her head, guiding her to the bus. Non-players aren't usually allowed on it, but Coach had told Kas it was fine this one time only.

We get on the bus, and she moves to sit next to me before I grab her hips and sit her in my lap. I can't imagine how anxious she's feeling right now. Her life is relatively quiet, and this is all new to her. I want to wrap her up in my arms and hope she doesn't run.

"Kat, baby, are you okay?" I ask her softly, my lips hovering just above the sensitive skin of her neck. She shivers beneath me, so I hug her tighter.

She hasn't responded yet, so I'm getting worried just as she looks up at me. "Yeah, I'm okay. Just overwhelmed is all. It's a big adjustment for me, and I like to keep my private life private." That's got my back ramrod straight, my muscles coiling with tension.

My voice cracks as I whisper to her, "I can't give you a quiet, private life, *gattina*."

Her teeth sink into her bottom lip, those small, cold hands of hers reaching up to hold my face. "I didn't mean it like that. I just meant that this is new to me."

My pulse slows at her words, and she leans in, still holding my face as she presses a firm kiss to my lips.

***

We ride the bus the rest of the way to the hotel with Kat in my lap. She's started to feel better, her demeanor changing, becoming more relaxed. By the time we get to the hotel, she's made friends with all the guys on the bus, making them laugh at her and Aiyana's antics. They have a playful banter that would be borderline malicious if you couldn't hear the laughter from both of them as they tease one another while telling stories about the last five years that they've been living in San Diego.

We all get off the bus, and I see my brother's black Yukon pull up; thankfully, no one's in the passenger seat from what I can tell. The fewer new people to introduce Kat to tonight, the better, and the last thing we need is her being pictured with a puck bunny my brother picked up on his way here.

With my arm slung across her shoulders, I point over to Luca. "My brother's right over there. Do you want to head straight to dinner, or do you need to freshen up before we go?"

"Where are we going for dinner? I'm dressed pretty casually in comparison to you and Kas." She peers down at her outfit, scrutinizing her appearance.

"Well, it's super late, so it's less dinner and more just bar food." I add, "You look perfect," in case there was really any doubt.

"Just what every girl wants to hear—she looks perfect for cheap bar food," Aiyana butts in teasingly.

"Well, you know, I aim to please." I chuckle and lead the four of us over to Luca's car. We all pile in, with me taking the seat at the front, reluctantly separating from Kat.

We give each other a side hug before I introduce everyone. "Luca, you know Kas already." Kas reaches over, grabbing Luca's shoulder for a quick squeeze of acknowledgment.

"That ugly mug back there? Of course I know him." Luca tosses a wink at Kas. They've known each other since before I joined the Philly Scarlets with Kas.

"That's Aiyana." I gesture toward her, seated in the middle. She gives him a wave that seems oddly shy, given her usual outgoing personality.

"And the gorgeous woman hiding behind your seat is Kat; she's the one I'm trying to take home for Christmakkuh." He gives me a knowing smirk, and Kat grabs the back of his seat, leaning around to introduce herself.

"Hi, Luca, it's so nice to meet you," she says with a genuine smile lighting her face before she looks over at me. "Christmakkuh?"

"Oh god, man, you haven't even asked her if she wants to come or not, and you're already laying it on this thick?" Luca huffs, rolling his eyes at me. "Kat, it's really great to meet you, but if you want someone fun who won't make you go to huge holiday celebrations with our family, I'm really the one you want." He's really doling out the winks today, and usually, this type of crap wouldn't bother me, but it does where Kat's concerned.

Before I can even respond to him, Kat says, "Sorry, Luca, but I'm not really looking to downgrade." She lets out an airy chuckle as she says it, but I can tell she also means it. She doesn't like his implication any more than I do, even if we both know he's joking.

Her remark is immediately met by Kas and Aiyana's resounding "Ooooh" and "Burnnn," as if we're a bunch of teenagers. Their carefree nature lightens the mood even further, and we all laugh at Luca's expense.

Luca grips his chest over his heart. "Kat, how you wound me!"

"I've got a feeling you have no shortage of people willing to apply some ice to that burn. I, for one, am all on board." I'm turned around a bit in my seat, and while Aiyana looks playful and seems to be genuinely interested, I don't miss the disbelief that flashes across Kas's face. They've never really suggested they're together, but there have been more than a few occasions where I've gotten the idea that they are, secretly, anyway.

A few minutes later, we pull up to a brightly lit karaoke lounge, with next to no parking available. "I thought you said we were getting bar food?" Kat asks.

"Someone recommended this place to me recently, so I figured we could give it a try if everyone's cool with that. It's a Korean karaoke lounge where you pay by the hour for private rooms with your own setup, so no one outside of this car has to listen to Ale serenading you. The guy sounds like a screaming walrus when he sings, and it's horrendous." Unfortunately, he's not wrong.

"Ah, and there it is," she says, smiling broadly as she shakes her head in mocking disbelief.

"And there *what* is?" I ask her, my voice hesitant.

"Your flaw." She says it as if she's just stating facts. "I've been waiting for some major personality flaw to make me feel like you're a real person and not a figment of my imagination, but I'll take 'screaming walrus' too." She smiles at me smugly, arms crossed over her chest, and a repressed laugh shakes her shoulders.

"I could say the same about you, but instead of finding flaws, I'm finding more and more reasons to fall madly in love with you."

Her cheeks pinken, her eyes locking on mine as her jaw goes slack with surprise.

Before we can add to the embarrassing display of affection, Kas says, "While I'm really, truly enjoying this proclamation of your undying affection for one another, can we please get out and go eat? I'm fucking starving." He sounds grumpy as hell, probably because he's hangry, but I'd bet it's primarily due to Aiyana's comment about my brother, even if he won't admit it.

"Come on, grumpy face, let's get your hangry ass some food." Aiyana pushes him to open the door and let her out.

I jump out of the SUV, running over to Kat's side and opening the door for her. She looks up at me with a goofy grin on her face, and I take the opportunity to reach over her lap and unbuckle her seatbelt, wrapping my arms around her and pulling her out of the seat to carry her across the parking lot.

Luca whistles at us, smiling as we pass by him. Aiyana and Kas are smiling as they roll their eyes at us. Kat keeps her fingers clasped behind my neck, holding onto me like a koala bear. She kisses my cheek softly as I set her back on her feet outside the door of the karaoke lounge.

We head inside and are greeted by the hostess, who takes us to a private room with six seats, a long rectangular table, a small stage, and a projector screen behind it with a tablet on the table for music selection. The walls are covered in colorful paintings that look like the artist threw balloons filled with paint at them.

"Oh my gosh, this place has spicy rice cakes!" Kat and Aiyana go to work selecting everything they want off the menu, and I pick a song to sing with Luca and Kas. We land on "Oops!... I Did It Again" and hop on the stage to give the performance of our lives.[1]

Once up on the stage, I look over to see Kat and Aiyana leaning against each other, laughing and smiling conspiratorially. I quirk a brow at Kat, and she turns her gaze away, whispering something to Aiyana.

"All right, dude, get your head in the game." Luca swats my chest to get my attention.

I nod at him, and the music starts playing. Kas takes the lead, belting out the lyrics with Luca and me leaning into him, vying for the microphone. Does anyone really sound good singing this song?

As my gaze catches back on Kat, she and Aiyana are recording the whole thing, laughing hysterically at our expense. Luca sees where my eyes are set. Grinning, he grabs the microphone from Kas, leaving him with a pout as he stomps after Luca, who runs over to the girls seated at the table, dropping to one knee and sliding across the floor to them, his arm outstretched to Aiyana as if serenading them.

Their laughter grows, and Aiyana grabs her cell phone off the table and turns the flashlight on, swaying it over her head until the song comes to an end.

Kas and I head back to the table just as the waitress comes over with a tray of drinks.

Taking a long swig of his water, Luca takes Kat's hand when he's finished, places the glass back on the table, and says, "All right, Kat, pick a song so I can have my do-over. I require redemption!"

She turns her gaze on me, laughing but looking to ensure I'm okay with it. I nod at her, giving her a broad smile as she follows after him to pick a song.

I can't say I'm surprised when, moments later, they're up on the stage singing "WAP," and Aiyana runs to the stage, yelling at them for leaving her out.[2]

She hops up on the platform with them and starts belting out the lyrics. If I didn't know any better, I'd think they *were* drunk.

Kat's treating my brother like she's known him forever, and it further solidifies what I already know. The rest of my family will *adore* her.

I'm grateful for her kindness because Luca can be annoying as hell, but he deserves to be surrounded by people who'll show him that he's more than fun for a night and good for a few laughs.

A few songs later, the waitress comes out with plates full of spicy rice cakes, fish cakes, japchae, kimchi, Honey Butter Chips, and Kat's favorite, corn cheese. I don't know that I could call this random hodgepodge a meal, but when Kat sits in my lap instead of in her chair, I think I know what I'll be eating tonight.

She piles food on a plate and hands it to me, then makes her own. My heart dips a little because the only person who's ever made a plate for me is my mom. It's a sweet gesture that's dueling with the very unsweet thoughts I'm having about her right now. I wrap my arms around her waist, give her a quick squeeze, and place a kiss on her shoulder.

I'm sure she can feel me getting hard as she rocks her hips, leaning forward to add more corn cheese to her plate. This woman is a conundrum. She's sweet, sometimes timid, caring to a fault, sensitive, and unbelievably understanding, all while being boisterous, stubborn, a real shit-talker, and a sassy pain in my ass.

Every one of those qualities has me falling, *hard*.

***

"They seem to be closing up, so we should head out."

"Yeah, I'll drop you guys off at your hotel," Luca agrees, then turns to Kat. "I expect to see you at our house for Christmas. If you don't come, you'll ruin Christmakkuh for everyone because *rattino* over here"—pointing at me, he finishes— "will mope the whole time like a big baby." I can't even deny it—it's true.

"*Rattino*? Did you just call him a little rat?" Kat asks, Luca smirking as my cheeks start to turn pink. That's a nickname I'll seemingly never rid myself of. And if she's figured that out, I think she probably knows exactly why I call her *gattina*—my little *kitten*.

Dodging her question, I ask, "Are you planning to come for the holiday?"

"That'd be really nice, but we usually spend it with Aiyana's family," she tells me, turning to Aiyana for confirmation.

"Actually, I've been meaning to talk to you guys about that. My parents decided that they want to take a cruise to Alaska for the holidays, so we're on our own this year," Aiyana informs Kat and Kas.

"Perfect, then it's settled. You three will join us for the holiday. You're all welcome to stay the night, I'm sure. Festivities go well into the night, and Ale can't leave the kids. They latch onto him and make him their personal bed, so he's forced to sleep over." Luca effectively convinces them to agree to come, all while setting an adorable look of admiration on Kat's face that I know is from her picturing me with a bunch of babies and young children. I'll have to thank him for that later.

He drops us all off at the hotel, leaving Aiyana with his number and effectively pissing Kas off. I'm not going to be asking him about that because I mind my own business, but there is definitely something going on there.

We all head into the hotel. It's a nice building with red brick and twinkling lights hung up for the holidays, probably about twenty stories high, and there's a small courtyard in the back with a firepit. Hopefully, it's still lit, so I can sneak off with Kat later since I'm rooming with Kas tonight.

1. **Oops!...I Did It Again - Britney Spears**

2. **WAP - Cardi B (ft. Megan Thee Stallion)**

Chapter Thirty-Four

Katarina

"Damn, this room is nice!" Aiyana says as we enter the hotel room, which is really a massive suite with two queen-sized beds, each covered in fluffy white linens, a charcoal-gray couch in the corner, a desk, and a nice-sized window on the far wall, surrounded by brick. The room even has an electric fireplace under the mounted TV.

Laughing in agreement, I walk over to the bed closest to the door and flop down on my back. "I'm exhausted."

"Don't get too comfortable there, girlfriend—Ale looked like he wanted to lick you from head to toe the entire night. I'd give it ten minutes tops before he's texting you to meet him or just showing up at our door."

Shrugging my shoulders, I say, "I'd argue, but you're probably right. I'm gonna hop in the shower real quick and change."

***

Once I've dried off, I brush my hair and braid it into one Dutch braid down my back. I pull on my favorite black sweater-knit joggers and an oversized gray hoodie. I've just gotten my socks on when I hear a knock on the door. Rolling my eyes, I straighten and head out of the bathroom to answer it.

Aiyana is already at the door, letting Alessandro in. He must have showered again because he's now wearing a pair of gray sweats that aren't leaving anything to the imagination. He's also wearing a cable knit light-blue sweater that makes his green eyes look even more sage. His hair is damp and messy, and that damn dimple is out for the world to see, effectively making me weak in the knees.

I catch Aiyana staring at the outline of his dick; she's never been one for subtlety, but before I can tease her, Ale says, "My eyes are up here, Aiyana." He's pointing to his eyes, smirking at her.

She lets out an embarrassed breath but recovers quickly, saying, "Well, maybe have some decency and wear clothing that actually covers that third leg of yours!" She's got her hands on her hips, exaggerating just how ridiculous this entire conversation is, her lips pursed and her chin jutted out, looking smug.

Ale keels over, hands on his knees, laughing so hard his face is turning red. It just makes it even funnier. Aiyana deflates, and we look at each other and burst out laughing with him.

He finally recovers, regaining control of his breathing and straightening. "Jesus, woman, third leg? I'll have to take that as a compliment, I guess."

"Oh, it's most definitely a compliment," I say, still giggling.

"Well, you guys go have a grand old time with that third leg of his, and don't be afraid to stay out late." Aiyana gives us an exaggerated wink before shooing us out the door.

Ale extends his hand for me to take; it's large and warm in mine, leading me to the elevator. As soon as the doors shut around us, Ale presses the emergency stop button and pushes me up against the wall with my butt on the handrail. He grasps my face, bringing his lips to mine. My arms wind around his neck, fingers curling in his hair as our lips dance together. His tongue swirls in my mouth, lapping at me, teasing and tasting.

I can feel my nipples pebbling, and I'm getting wet and impatient. I release a whimper as Ale snakes his hand into my waistband, cupping me. He pulls back, his lips to my ear now. "I've been waiting for this all night."

Just as I think he'll take things further, he removes his hand entirely, fixes his shirt, and presses the button for the elevator to continue our descent.

"What was that for?" I ask him, my voice full of frustration at him for stopping, eyes wide with annoyance.

He chuckles lightly, ignoring my temper tantrum. "I saw the hotel has a nice little courtyard with a firepit. I spoke with the front desk and asked if we could have it lit for us despite the time." It's nearly three in the morning.

"That sounds nice, but it still isn't an explanation for why you're such a tease." I'm rolling my eyes at him, which is a childish thing to do, but I've read a lot of books with steamy elevator sex scenes, and I'm completely up for seeing if that fantasy is really that good.

He chuckles, wrapping his arms around me, and presses a chaste kiss to the top of my head. The elevator opens, and he leads us through a set of sliding doors in the back of the hotel. We make a left past the pool and head down a sidewalk that ends in front of a gas-lit firepit, where there's a metal bench under a covered awning and three chairs with a couple of blankets stacked on them.

"Did you have them set this up too?" I ask him, curious as to how much planning went into this.

"No, *gattina*, I came down here before I got you and brought the blankets out so I could tease you in that elevator instead of carrying down an arm full of blankets." My heart does a little flip.

"Go ahead and take a seat; I'll adjust the height of the fire," he tells me as he turns to the firepit, messing with the knob on the side before bringing his gaze back to mine. "I haven't seen you in a couple of days"—he pauses, looking down at his feet before continuing—"and I missed you."

There goes my heart again. Maybe these aren't warm and fuzzy butterflies in my chest. *Maybe* I'm having heart palpitations and should get an ECG or something.

I know I'm being ridiculous, but I've truly never been with anyone who's made me feel like this before.

I grab a blanket, draping it over the bench to give us some cushioning before taking a seat, sitting crisscross, and laying a blanket over my lap. It's around twenty degrees outside, but it hasn't snowed yet this year.

He takes a seat next to me, angling himself to look at me.

He gently grabs my chin, tilts it toward him, and places a soft kiss on my lips. "How was work?"

"Work was meh. I love what I do, but it's emotionally exhausting sometimes, and today, there were just so many losses." I clench my eyes shut, shaking my head gently at the depressing thoughts pushing their way to the forefront of my mind. "I don't know how I'm even still awake right now." I rest my head on his shoulder as he wraps an arm around me, pulling me into his side.

"I'm sorry you had such a draining day, but I'm glad you could be there for those people. I know firsthand what an amazing provider you are to your patients. They're lucky to have you."

"Thank you." I peek up at him. "I just wish I could do more. I'm glad I got to come to your game tonight, and I loved meeting Luca. I didn't realize he played for one of the New York teams," I say, hoping he will fill in some of the blanks I've got rattling around in my head.

"He's a good guy, Kat. He doesn't seem to think so, and neither does the media, but the bad-boy act is just that. An act. He's great with our nieces and nephews. Once he cares about someone or something, he gives everything he's got," he tells me, voice reverent.

"The press just doesn't find that interesting enough, and he enjoys sex entirely too much to hold out for a meaningful, long-term relationship. Frankly, I don't blame him. It's not my thing, but he always makes sure his partners know that while he'll remain monogamous with them over the course of their *very* short relationship, it won't be a long-lasting one. And they agree to it." He shrugs.

"You know, he wanted to join the Scarlets, but our manager turned him down because we don't deal with the drama. He's an incredible goalie though, and not as weird as some of them are." He lets out an exasperated huff. Clearly, there's a lot going on in his head.

"It sounds like he's being judged harshly for things that have nothing to do with who he is as a person and have no impact on how he performs on the ice. That must be really frustrating for all of you, not being able to have him around as much." My tone is soft. I understand some of what Luca is going through. I never would have left Kas if I didn't have to, but PA school is highly competitive, so I had to go wherever I was accepted, and ensuring the schools I applied to met my moral standards meant my choices were even further limited. Though, I didn't have the added pressure of millions of people watching my every move.

"It's really difficult because my mom isn't doing any better, and thankfully, Luca doesn't have MS, but he does feel a lot of guilt surrounding that fact. He's mentioned that it should have been him instead because I'm the 'better brother' and I'll make a better parent, husband, whatever. I think it's like survivor's guilt because none of that stuff is even remotely true." His face is scrunched up, anguish crossing his handsome features.

"Do you think he self-sabotages because he feels unworthy?" Now we're getting into some pretty heavy stuff that isn't really my business, but I care, and if he's uncomfortable, he can always say so.

"Oh, he definitely does. I just hope that someday he'll realize that it's not like I'm dying. Sure, things are slowing down for me, and maybe I won't get as many years out of hockey as I want, but honestly? I really want kids, Kat. I want to start a family. I'm thirty-two; the average age at retirement for a hockey player is thirty-six, so it's not like I'd have too much time left anyway." He seems content with that, knowing where he wants his future to go, all while dealing with these overwhelming feelings for his brother. "I just want to win that cup, and then I'll probably retire and maybe take up coaching instead." His head is hanging low as he peers up at me and says something that stops my heart for a beat.

"I'm just so damn worried that the new meds won't keep working, that I'll be wheelchair-bound like my mom." He chokes out something like a cut-off sob, but no tears flow. He's squeezing his eyes shut. I push his arm off of me and toss my arms around him.

I'm whispering to him, "It'll be okay; there's so much that can be done to help you. If these meds don't work, we'll try something new. There is always *something*, Alessandro, and I won't stop until we find it." I'm pleading with him to understand my words, to trust me.

He's shaking his head. "I know, it's just really difficult to stay hopeful when your body randomly decides to fail you." He looks up at me, eyes crinkled at the sides. "I slipped today. I noticed when I skated back over to the same spot that there was a divot in the ice, and I can't even begin to tell you how elated I was to know it wasn't my legs giving out. I know I said I was sure I'd know when it was time to give it up, but what if I don't? What if someone gets hurt first?"

"You need to try to trust yourself—you know your body better than anyone. If it had been your legs, you would've known for certain." He nods, not saying anything else as we sit there for a while longer, and I rub his back, comforting him. Eventually, his shoulders relax, and he sits up straighter.

"Dance with me?" He stands up suddenly, pulling me to my feet with him. There are warm café lights hanging all around us, and the only sounds are the few cars passing on the road.

"But there's no music," I tell him, a little thrown off-kilter from the change in topics.

He pulls out his phone, swiping through his apps until he finds a song and presses play. Setting the phone on the bench, he takes me in his arms, and we begin to sway. "Conversations in the Dark" by John Legend is trickling through the phone. Ale is spinning me around, and as he pulls me close to his chest, it starts to snow.[1]

He's got his hand on the back of my head, pressing my face to his chest. I'm breathing in his warm, masculine scent as we sway to the music, the snow falling gently around us, his body heat keeping me warm. It's like a literal fairytale come to life, and it couldn't be more perfect.

The song abruptly switches to a club track, and I can't help but flip around, grinding my ass into him. We're laughing until he grips my hips from behind, and I feel his quickly hardening length against me.

My breathing becomes more rapid—my earlier arousal coming back in full force. I drop my head back behind me onto his shoulder. He's placing kisses along my neck, and I feel the slide of his tongue as it swipes over the line of my ear and nips at my lobe.

He spins me around to face him, still gripping my hips as he backs us up until his legs hit the bench, and he takes a seat, placing me on his lap.

His hand is in my hair, the other arm holding me tightly against his body as I grip his sweater in my hands. I move to straddle him, forgetting entirely that it's snowing and we're outside where we could be caught at any moment.

"Take those pants off and get back on top of me just like you are now." My eyes widen with shock, but I'm so turned on that I do exactly as he says, tucking my thumbs into the waistband of my joggers and sliding them down my thighs until they pool at my feet. I pull them off, along with my shoes, and climb back onto his lap. My legs have to stretch beyond the point of comfort because his thighs are so massive, but he grips my hips, helping to hold me up.

He nuzzles my ear, and in that deep, husky voice that undoes me, he says, "Good girl. Now touch yourself for me."

"You want me to touch myself?" I'm in disbelief because I'm oddly excited about the potential of getting caught, and I'm unsure as to why he isn't doing it himself.

He chuckles at me softly. "I want to watch you touch yourself, Kat. Give me a show before I take over."

My whole body heats at the thought of him taking control.

Reflexively, my hand goes to my center. I drag my middle finger through my folds and start rubbing small circles on my aching clit, my other hand resting on his shoulder, providing me with much-needed leverage. The pressure in my belly is growing, and I feel Ale getting harder beneath me as I'm rocking my hips against him.

My nipples are so hard and sensitive that when Ale bends forward, sucking one into his mouth through my top, I buck under him. He's gripping my ass to him, watching hungrily as my finger continues working me to the edge. His eyes flare. "Insert two fingers," he demands.

Again, I do exactly as he says, my head falling back as my muscles coil tighter and tighter. I'm pumping my fingers, the movements becoming more erratic the closer I get to release.

I'm just at the edge when he pulls my hand away, grabs my waist, and hauls me over his shoulder. My bare ass is out for anyone walking by to see, and that same frustration from earlier hits me like a brick wall. He grabs for the blankets on the bench, tossing them on the ground haphazardly with me still in his arms, and lays me down on top of them, careful to ensure we're under the awning.

He lowers himself over me. "Spread your legs, baby."

When I do, he supports his weight on his forearm as he makes his way down my body. Dipping his head over my center, he drags the flat of his tongue along me. My hands shoot out to grip the blankets around me, my knees bending up on instinct. A chill zips down my spine, but Ale's mouth warms me, heat pooling between my thighs.

I'm practically panting as he twirls his tongue, moving between my clit and my core. And again, he pulls away, traveling up my body to kiss me, but this time I'm so pissed that I bite down on his lip hard.

He pulls back sharply, wiping the small amount of blood from his lip, looking down at it in disbelief. "Did you just *bite* me?" He says it with a low chuckle, his expression a mixture of disbelief and excitement.

"You're edging me, you asshole. I could have had *three* orgasms already tonight." I can't help myself, so I smack him across the head without any real force, which makes him let out another laugh.

"This isn't funny. I need to come." The words escape me in a desperate, frustrated plea.

His eyes turn hard, and he bends forward, nipping at my throat as he pulls his hard length out of his sweats. "Do you want me to fuck you, *gattina*? Here? Outside, where someone could see us?" With anyone else, I'd say they're crazy, but with Ale? Absolutely. That's exactly what I want.

A breathy "Yes" is all I manage.

"Good," he rasps, lining the swollen head of his cock up against me; he's dripping in precum. His head snaps to me, eyes wide with worry. "I don't have a condom."

"I'm on the pill, and I got tested after my last relationship," I tell him without hesitation.

"I do too, and I've always tested negative. We get mandatory testing every few months, and I haven't been with anyone in over a year." There go those butterflies again. I knew he'd said he doesn't do casual sex, but hearing that it's been over a year fills me with joy.

"I trust you," I say, meeting his gaze as he realigns himself, entering me. It's been a while for me too, and he's stretching me, filling me with aching pleasure. I wrap my legs around his waist to give him more room as he settles into me. He's going slow, allowing me to adjust to his size before his hips *finally* start rocking.

"Just like that," I pant as he increases his pace, reaching down between us to apply pressure with the pad of his thumb, my clit swollen with need.

The veins in his neck are straining against his skin as if he's holding back, concentrating on not being consumed by his own pleasure too early. His hips are thrusting relentlessly now, and I'm circling my own, deepening his movements. He abruptly pulls out of me, grabs my waist, and flips me over onto my stomach before pulling my ass toward him so I'm leaning back against him, balancing on my forearms with my legs bent. The motion knocks the air out of my lungs, and my limbs scrape across the ground with the force of his movements.

Suddenly, his cock is plunging back inside me, even deeper than it was before, but the stretch feels incredible. "God, yes!" I nearly scream the words.

He grips the ends of my hair, wrapping my braid around his fist and pulling tightly. He's thrusting into me, bent over me, and says, "If you want to come, you've gotta be a good girl. Rub your clit, and don't stop until you're coming around my cock."

I do as he says, my cheek resting on the navy-blue blanket beneath me, supporting the weight that my arm isn't able to.

"Keep fucking me, just like that," I moan before begging him again, "*please.*"

"Don't worry, baby, I won't stop," he grunts as he continues thrusting into me. My core is clenching around him, my scalp on fire from how rough he's being, and I nearly collapse when he smacks my ass. Grunting again, he releases my hair, hands going to my hips to steady me.

"Such a good girl, *gattina*; you feel so good, this tight pussy clamping around me as I fuck you like the dirty little slut you are with me." His words should anger me, but they don't, and his next words absolutely undo me. Whispering directly into my ear, he continues, "Only me, baby; this pussy is all mine."

"I'm about to come," I moan as he adjusts his position to hit my G-spot. Pulling my hair even more tightly than before, he wraps an arm around my waist, dragging my body up so I'm kneeling on my shins. His cock is buried so deeply into me, I'm trembling before him, working to sink myself up and down his shaft as I shatter around his hard length, milking his release with my own.

"Fuck," he groans, increasing his pace as he pumps into me harder. I'm riding the wave of euphoria, moans escaping my lips as he stills.

I feel him about to pull out. "Come inside me," I rush out.

"God, you're fucking hot." He draws a shaky breath as he fills me.

***

"We'd better get back to the room. We've been out here awhile, and the bus leaves at eight," he tells me as he stands, stretching to his full height. We've been cuddled up by this fire for hours, and I couldn't be more content despite the lack of sleep.

I stand to follow him, but he collects me into his arms, his warmth seeping into my bones. I could stay here, just like this, forever.

"Come on, *gattina*, let's get you to bed. Aiyana probably thinks I kidnapped you." He chuckles, taking my hand and escorting me back to my room.

Once we're standing in front of my room, he presses a kiss to my forehead and says goodnight.

1. **Frozen - Sabrina Claudio**

Chapter Thirty-Five
Alessandro
Saturday, December 23, 2023

It's been over a week, and I haven't had my cock buried in Kat's tight cunt again.

Between having several games before the holiday break and Kat's work schedule, we've been so exhausted, opting for cuddles and sleep each night. Just sleep.

I adore those sweet moments with her, waking up to her body pressed against mine, but that doesn't mean it doesn't leave me wanting more of her.

When I picked Kat up for this party, I was practically drooling when I saw her golden skin and those hip-hugging jeans.

My birthday was a couple of weeks ago, but I hadn't wanted to make a big deal about it, so when Matt, our team captain, asked if it was okay to throw me a party once we were on break for the holidays, I felt bad saying no. Ever since I joined the team, Matt has done something for me, and I appreciate it, but this year, I really just hadn't thought about it. I'm more excited for this year's party than I have been in previous years though because Kat agreed to go with me as long as she was allowed to take Aiyana.

Aiyana was just settling into the penthouse when her birthday rolled around, so she plans to use tonight as a make-up day, and I have no issue with sharing the spotlight with her.

The four of us—Kas, Kat, Aiyana, and I—head into the two-story home that Matt and his wife, Jessie, own. They've got two daughters, who are four and six. Matt said the kids are with their grandparents tonight, so we don't have to keep the noise down.

Their home is really nice. It's tastefully decorated, Jessie's doing, I'm sure. It feels a little out of place, considering there aren't a lot of farmhouse-style homes in Pennsylvania, but they have a lot of land and a literal white picket fence. The house has a modern feel with light-gray walls, and everything seems to be in various shades of gray and white.

I introduce Kat and Aiyana to Jessie before heading further into the house to see the rest of our teammates.

"Do you guys want anything to drink? We can go look for water or soda." I direct the last part at Kat, knowing she doesn't drink alcohol.

She smiles at me knowingly. "Yeah, I'd love a Coke." She turns to Aiyana, asking her what she'd like, and we return to her and Kas a few minutes later with three beers and Kat's soda.

We played a few rounds of beer pong with the team, no one saying anything about Kat's Coke, and I learned that Kat has incredible precision with a ping pong ball.

"All right, Kat, you've gotta go find another game to play because you keep whipping our asses, and I need to beat *someone* tonight, or it'll hurt my pride," JJ tells her from the other side of the table, accepting his third loss of the night.

Her cheeks are flushed from the warmth of the house, so many bodies crowded around, heating up the place. She smiles at him. "I need to use the restroom anyway, so I *guess* I'll put you out of your misery," she tells him with a sly grin.

I wrap an arm around her waist, incredibly aware of her bare skin touching my own. She's wearing light-wash denim jeans that fit her like a glove, which she paired with a slinky crop top that is being held on by two barely-there straps.

I kiss the top of her head. "I'll show you where the bathroom is."

Leading her up the steps, I show her to the bathroom at the end of the hall to the right. I wait outside the door for her, and when she steps into the hall, I'm overcome with the need to take her up against the door and fuck her right here.

Chapter Thirty-Six

Katarina

Alessandro's waiting outside the door to the bathroom when I emerge, and his eyes are sweeping over me, devouring me from a few feet away.

I feel a sudden rush of dampness flood my core from his perusal. I can't say I didn't wear this outfit for his benefit. I look good, and I know it, but I also knew he'd love it.

I saunter over to him, my eyes hooded as I place my hands on his chest, his growing erection giving me a newfound confidence. He grips both of my hands in his, pulling one up to his mouth to place an open-mouth kiss on the inside of my wrist.

Both of our heads snap behind us as we hear voices and the creak of the steps. Ale sweeps me into his arms, dragging me into the nearest room and turning the lights on for us to see. We realize he just pulled us into a hallway closet, and we're surrounded by jackets, and Matt's hockey gear is tossed in the corner.

Ale chuckles, stopping abruptly when the voices grow nearer. His hand snaps back, turning off the lights, and his finger comes over my lips as he dramatically whispers, "Shh."'

He pulls his hand away, stepping closer to me, and begins working at the buttons of my jeans before pulling the zipper down and sliding them down my legs along with my panties.

I step out of them, popping my shoes off and tossing them to the side. He doesn't even kiss me—just falls to his knees and hoists me up against the wall, my legs wrapping around his neck.

God, his strength is so damn attractive. He throws me around like I weigh nothing.

He doesn't pause to ask permission like he has before, knowing I'm fully on board any time he wants me. He runs two fingers through my slick folds, pressing kisses to the inside of my thighs. My fingers thread into his hair when he licks a path from mid-thigh up.

Groaning, he takes a deep inhale. His hand moves to grip my ass cheek, spreading me and pressing the tip of his pointer finger to a spot I've never been touched. Surprise and laughter fill me.

His forehead is pressed against my thigh, and enough light from the hallway trickles under the door for me to make out the beaming smile he's wearing, lips spread wide as he laughs as quietly as possible.

"Is this your way of saying you wanna put your dick in my ass?" I've never done that before, and I have no desire to now...

He lets out another laugh, this one louder, and his head falls back, eyes squeezed tightly shut, his body shaking, and I start slipping off his shoulders with the movement. His eyes snap open, hands gripping me tightly and catching me before I fall on my ass into Matt's pile of hockey gear.

I right myself as he stands, eyes suddenly flaring with heat again. The muscles of his jaw work back and forth as he fights to regain control, but I see the thick ridge of his erection twitch in his pants.

I reach forward to grip him, but he digs his fingers into my triceps, turning my whole body and pushing me against the wall. My hands splay out in front of me, and my cheek presses to the wall. His hands slide up my arms, one hand wrapping around my wrists, pinning them to the wall above my head. His other hand trails down the side of my breast to my ribs and then travels lower.

I feel the loss of contact only briefly before I hear the pop of his button, the lowering of his zipper, and then I feel it.

The thick head of his erection angled up against my center. He runs his nose along the side of my neck, nipping at the sensitive skin behind my ear.

"Do you want me to fill that sweet pussy of yours, *gattina*," he asks me in a low whisper.

A moan slips past my lips as my hips jut backward to meet him, urging the head of him inside me. He presses into me agonizingly slowly.

My head falls back against his chest, and my legs feel weak like jelly as the full length of him continues to fill me, my hands still pinned above me.

He suddenly pulls all the way out, the loss an emptiness that jolts me before he plunges back into the hilt. My abs clench, and my clit aches to be touched.

I'm panting as he fucks me relentlessly; he's releasing deep groans of approval. His free hand snakes around my front to lazily draw circles on my clit. I buck up against him, my hips seeking the extra friction I need.

"Mmm, so eager," he whispers, his hips driving deeper into me.

His movements halt when we hear voices approaching the door, but he continues his onslaught as they grow quieter.

The slapping of our skin together and a chorus of wet sounds surrounding us and mixing with our moans spurs me further toward my release.

"God, you're so damn wet. Your needy cunt is milking my cock so well." He suddenly pulls out, and before I can protest, he spins me around, releasing my wrists. My arms fall to his chest, tingling with the blood flow that was restricted for so long.

He pushes me to my knees and abruptly lifts my shirt, exposing my lace-covered breasts as he continues to pump himself in his fist. He groans loudly as hot come spurts out of the tip of his engorged length, landing on my chest and dripping down the swells of my breasts.

Ale's eyes are squeezed shut, the muscles of his thighs straining to keep him upright as he finishes pumping the last bit of come from his swollen tip.

His eyes open, looking down at me with hooded lids. A smirk pulls at his lips as he leans forward, gripping my chin between his thumb and forefinger, tilting my head back and opening me to him. His tongue slips in, lapping at me, and my hunger grows.

I'm growing feral with need for this man as he devours my mouth in his. Ale sinks to his knees in front of me, lips never leaving mine.

Two fingers slide through the sticky mess he's left on my chest, his opposite hand planted above my head as he steadies himself. Those come covered fingers swipe between my wet folds, and his mouth leaves mine with a guttural groan rumbling through his chest.

"I'm fucking obsessed with you and this gorgeous needy pussy," he tells me as his fingers dive deeply into me, spreading himself throughout my cunt, taking everything he has to offer. I'm panting; his desire to absolutely own me leaves me writhing against him.

He angles his thumb to rub against my clit, drawing me closer to the edge of release.

"Oh god, just like that," I urge him on, and he releases another groan, tilting his head to suck my nipple into his mouth, sucking his own arousal off of my heated skin.

I'm climbing higher, my knees jutting to the side, opening myself to him further. My abs tighten, and my legs are shaking as I reach euphoria. Ale nips at my neck as I thread my fingers in his hair, tugging at the roots.

"My good girl loves it when I fill her hot aching cunt with my come." He pulls back, and, looking down at me, he groans, "*Fuck,* Kat, you're a goddamn wet dream."

Chapter Thirty-Seven

Katarina

Sunday, December 24, 2023

The last few weeks have been a whirlwind of date nights with Alessandro, his birthday party, the occasional brunch with Aiyana, dinners with Kas, lots of work, gift shopping for the holidays, and following up with HR about Ante.

Thankfully, after conducting an investigation while he was put on a leave of absence, it was discovered that he had done similar things to some of the nurses here as well, who were too afraid to say anything. I'm not glad it happened to me, but I'm happy something was done to stop him. He was fired, and all of the reports were sent to the police department in order to back up the story I gave them, along with the photos I took of my bruises.

Alessandro had also gone back to Rocco's at some point and spoken with the bartender, who gladly agreed to make a statement about what he'd seen that night, further solidifying the validity of my report.

The relief I felt when I had that meeting with HR, the police chief being present to assure me he wouldn't just be losing his job, was unlike anything else I've ever felt. A two-ton boulder lifted from my chest.

I'm so ready for the next few days. Dr. Howell doesn't celebrate any specific holidays, so he told me I could take Christmas Eve through to the twenty-sixth off to spend the holidays with Alessandro's family.

I just finished packing, and I'm shaking with anxiety. On one hand, I'm super excited to meet the rest of his family, but on the other, I'm afraid they won't like me. Kas and I grew up very differently from Alessandro, so I wouldn't hold it against them if they thought I was too awkward or didn't fit in well with the family. I did pick out gifts for everyone with Alessandro's help and doubled down on the presents for the kids. I'm excited to meet the people who made him who he is.

I hear a knock at the door, and before I get out there to answer it, I see Aiyana running to it, shouting, "I've got it!" at me. She opens the door wearing a pair of black thermal tights and a burgundy sweater dress that hits her just below the knee. Kas is standing at the door with Alessandro, both of them carrying black duffle bags. Tank is sitting at Ale's feet, wearing a holiday sweater that reads, "Feliz Navidog," and his tail is thudding against the floor with excitement.

I meet them at the door a moment later, leaning down to squeeze Tank's cheeks and pressing a kiss to the top of his head.

Kas heads in with Ale trailing behind. "You ladies almost ready to go?" he asks us.

"I'm ready, just need to put my shoes on. Your sister, on the other hand? She's still not packed, and when I checked on her last, it looked like she had taken up residence at Santa's workshop. Her room is filled with presents, and I bet your ass not a single one of them is for us." She says it cheerfully but playfully rolls her eyes at my nervousness.

"I'm just trying to make a good impression!" I explain, adding, "And I'll have you know that I just finished packing." I stick out my tongue at her as Alessandro approaches me for a hug, wrapping me in his arms from behind.

"All right, children, let's go," he says, laughing. He lowers his voice. "You know you didn't have to buy so many gifts, Kat; my family is going to love you," he tells me seriously.

"You say that, but I bet gifts will increase my chances of being in their good graces, and I love giving gifts! It's even more fun than actually receiving them myself."

He releases me from his hold, shaking his head. "Of course you'd say that." He smirks at me as he heads to my room to grab my bag. "Good god, woman, we're gonna need to take ten trips to get all this shit downstairs!" he calls over his shoulder at me when he sees the massive pile of gifts, each neatly wrapped and sitting in baskets and laundry baskets on my bed.

I follow after him, stomping childishly. "Nope. I called Ralph. He's bringing up a bellhop cart for me."

A minute later, we hear a knock, and Kas opens the door. True to his word, the bellhop cart is waiting at the door with no Ralph in sight. That man really is like a ghost. A really sweet, wonderfully on-time ghost.

We all work on loading up the cart, and when we finish, Ale grabs my duffle, and Kas grabs Aiyana's bags. Yes, I said bags, with an "s."

"Did you need to bring two suitcases and a duffle bag? What the hell do you have in there anyway?" I ask.

"You'll find out soon enough. Besides, you can't judge me, Miss 'I bought out the entire mall.'"

We all head downstairs once our apartments are locked up, and we pile into Kas's SUV. Thankfully, he has enough room for all of our stuff, plus the gifts I brought.

We start heading toward one of the Philly suburbs, and a little over twenty minutes later, we arrive in front of a gorgeous three-story brownstone. I'm vibrating with nervous energy, but I'm so excited to meet everyone that it outweighs any anxious feelings I'm harboring.

"We'll have to get the gifts out after we've all settled in; maybe we can just grab them when all the kids go to bed tonight," Ale tells us just as the door bursts open and three heads pop out. I can hear shouts coming from behind them that sound like little kids yelling something about Uncle Ale. They sound extremely excited about his arrival.

"Hi!" the woman I recognize as Charlie, Ale's sister, shouts from the doorway, waving animatedly at us.

I give her a bright smile and return her greeting. The others in the doorway are Charlie's wife, Rose, and Alessandro's mom, Gloria. They've all got bright smiles plastered on their faces, and it sets me at ease to see how overjoyed they are to meet me.

The guys carry our stuff to the door, dropping it to dole out hugs. "Kassian, you are more and more handsome every time I see you!" Gloria tells him as he bends to give her a hug as she sits in her wheelchair.

"Thank you, Mrs. De Laurentiis; you're even more gorgeous than the last time I saw you."

Ale's mom visibly blushes before swatting his shoulder and telling him, "Now you know what I said, call me Gloria! Mrs. De Laurentiis is my mother-in-law!"

"All right, Gloria," Kas says, winking at her. This poor woman is nearly swooning after my brother's charms. All women love him, young and old. That's a truth that's stood the test of time.

Kas introduces Aiyana to the group, but Aiyana already knows Rose because they work at BioMedics together.

After everyone has been introduced, the women all turn their attention to me. I'm stuck like a deer caught in the headlights, waiting for them to make the first move. Suddenly, I'm engulfed in one giant group hug that seems to be occurring *on* Mrs. De Laurentiis's lap because she's the one who initiated it by pulling me to her.

Charlie and Rose pull away first, leaving Gloria to grasp my cheeks, looking me over intently. She says, "He told me you were gorgeous, but wow." She looks up at her daughter for her to agree.

"Oh, absolutely; pictures don't do you justice, Kat! And that vitiligo? So cool! I always loved the multidimensional look, but I've never seen it affect the hair color too."

Rose is more soft-spoken than Charlie, but she speaks up, advising, "The hypopigmentation of her eyebrow and lashes is actually referred to as poliosis. I've seen it in textbooks but never in person. Gloria's right; it's gorgeous." Rose has a soft and nerdy quality to her that I love already. I could see us being good friends.

"Yeah, other than my mom, I've never met anyone with it. I see people online who cover it up though, so maybe that's why I've never noticed it in real life. I really love it, so I've never bothered," I say with a shrug.

Gloria looks to Alessandro, who's standing in the entryway watching us with a content smile. "My grandbabies with you two are going to be gorgeous! Maybe the best batch yet!"

Bursts of laughter from Charlie and Rose are released as my eyes get big with surprise. "Mom! Don't scare her away, or you won't be getting those grandbabies. Besides, the ones in the house *right now* are perfect as they are, big-headed and all," he says, chuckling.

"No, no. She's right—your babies, if you choose to have them, will be gorgeous, and those babies do have some big ass heads. I have no idea how Arielle pushed out Sammy and Benny; those boys have the biggest heads I've ever seen." Charlie reminds me a lot of Aiyana, always talking and never serious. Qualities I happen to love.

"If we haven't scared you off yet, Kat, come on inside. I'm freezing my nips off out here." Up to this point, I've been able to let all of the quirky comments roll off of me, but that coming from Ale's mom has me keeled over, gasping for breath from the laughter that steals the air from my lungs.

"Oh my god," I huff out between laughs.

Everyone joins in the laughter, and when I straighten, Ale wraps an arm around my shoulder, guiding me into the house. We make it about ten feet inside when a small army of children come running at Ale, catapulting themselves at him and latching onto his legs. "Uncle Ale! You're finally here!" one of them shouts, followed by, "You just saw him last week, Benny, stop whining," from the other little boy, who seems to have more of an attitude.

Ale ruffles the little boy's hair—he looks around nine or ten years old with a mop of curly brown hair. "Sammy, be nice to Benny."

"Sorry, Uncle Ale," Sammy says, casting his eyes downward.

"Who's the pretty lady, Uncle Ale? Ooh, ladies!" The little girl that I know has to be Arlo by her dark, pin-straight hair and striking gray eyes beams up at Aiyana and me.

I crouch down to get eye level with the eight-year-old. "You must be Arlo. Alessandro's told me *all* about you. I'm Katarina, but you can call me Kat." Pointing behind me at Aiyana, I continue, "And that's Aiyana."

"I've heard *all* about you too! Is it true that you're going to marry my uncle?" She's excitedly bouncing, tripping over her own feet as suddenly the entire house goes quiet, seemingly waiting for my answer. Arlo has no idea the bomb she just dropped.

"If he plays his cards right, then maybe one day." I wink at her and hear the chorus of breaths being released around me.

A tall man with black hair comes out of the kitchen wearing a black V-neck T-shirt that shows off his tattooed arms and neck. He's also got on an apron with pink-and-white ruffles that reads, "Kiss The Chef!" with a giant set of red lips over the chest. He looks like the epitome of masculine, and not even the apron could change that.

"All right, kids, let's go watch some TV so the adults can meet everyone too. Stop harassing Kat before she runs screaming out of here." He's rolling his eyes and ushering the kids into the family room, which I now see has a flat-screen TV set up to play *Elf*.

Once the kids are all on the couch, he approaches me, holding his arms out for a hug. I step into his embrace for a fleeting hug and a kiss on each cheek. "You must be the lovely Kat. I'm Dante. You met Sammy and Benny; they're my oldest. My wife Arielle is in one of the guest rooms feeding Lily, our youngest. They'll be down soon. Arielle can't wait to meet you; it's all she's been talking about this whole week." He gives me a warm smile that seems in contrast to his harsh looks. He's all dark hair, dark eyes, and is covered in dark tattoos and dark clothing. He's an enigma, but I remind myself that you shouldn't judge a book by its cover.

"Kat! Get your skinny bum in the kitchen and come help me fill these cannoli," Gloria calls out to me. Never in my life have I been told I had a skinny backside, but there's a first for everything. Following Alessandro, we head to the kitchen. The counters are covered in trays of homemade cookies, cannoli shells, biscotti, and all sorts of other pastries. It looks like some sort of Italian bakery dream come to life right in this kitchen!

"I need help filling these cannoli, and you seem like the type to need to stay busy to avoid feeling anxious, so come on now." She waves me over to her. Somehow, she managed to perfectly pin my personality in the span of five minutes. It makes me wonder just how much Ale's been telling his family about me, and that familiar warmth fills my chest at the thought, especially if he *did* mention marriage to them already.

She shows me how to pipe the ricotta filling into each of the cannoli shells, finishing by dipping the ends in either tiny chocolate chips or crushed pistachios. We get into a rhythm, and a few minutes in, Ale gives me a peck on the cheek before dismissing himself. "I'm gonna go take the kids outside to play soccer. I think I just heard Gianni and Luca arrive, so if I can get Kas and Aiyana to play, we'll have a full team."

"Have fun," I tell him before he exits the kitchen. A moment later, Charlie and Rose enter the kitchen with a gorgeous redhead, who I assume is Arielle, trailing behind them.

I quickly realize that I'm being ambushed. Arielle rushes over to me, grasping my upper arms. "Oh my gosh! I can't believe you're finally here! We never get to meet anyone Ale dates," she gushes as Rose responds.

"That's because Alessandro just doesn't date. He's waiting for a wife and all that." She's waving her hands around dramatically.

"Exactly, which means this is an even bigger deal!" Arielle continues. Clearly, Rose isn't able to dampen the excitement coming from Arielle, and her giddiness is contagious. "I'm Arielle, by the way! Like 'Ar-ie-elle.'" She sounds it out for me, making sure I know her name isn't Ariel.

"Ah, got it—Ariel because of the red hair," I say jokingly because she's made a big show of her name *not* being the same as the Disney princess.

"Funny girl," she says, smirking at me, and I'm glad I didn't have to explain the joke.

"All right, now that we've all been introduced, let's get down to it. Tell us everything about you before my *rattino* comes and steals you away from us."

"Okay, well, I'm twenty-eight. I'm originally from around here but moved to San Diego for school and then stayed for a fellowship in neurology. I'm a physician assistant, and I work at Philly Med in Center City. If you couldn't already tell, Kas and I are twins, and I'm a big fan of sushi, pastries, dogs, and reading romance books." I think that sums up all the major points, but I'm not sure how deeply they expect me to go this soon into our first meeting. Thankfully, I practiced my own elevator pitch, expecting this question.

"Hmm," Gloria hums, looking me over before continuing, "when you say romance books, do you mean smut? Or closed-door romance?" If I were drinking something, I'd have spit it out all over the floor.

"Um," I start before Charlie cuts me off.

"Major brownie points if it's smut. We aren't judging if you read closed-door romances either, but the four of us are smut sluts, so it'd be nice if we could include you in our monthly book club." My shoulders relax despite hearing her refer to herself and her mother as "smut sluts," but I kind of love her already for it.

"I'll accept my brownie points then and the invitation to this book club. I too am a fellow 'smut slut,'" I tell her, realizing quickly that the way to these women's hearts is through brutal honesty and a total lack of a filter.

"Oh, thank god, because I totally lied. We absolutely *would* judge you if they were closed-door!" We all laugh, and I'm finding it easier and easier to relax with these women. They're all so sincere and easygoing.

"I mean, I love a good slow burn, but to read an entire book and there not be *any* spice? That feels like kind of a waste," Rose explains.

"I'd have to agree, but if the sex comes right away, at least between the two main characters, I'll probably lose interest. I have to have something to really look forward to, so that kind of ruins it for me too." They all agree with me, and we continue filling the cannoli.

"Okay, so tell me all about Alessandro's most embarrassing childhood memories before he comes back in and finds us conspiring against him," I say in a fake hushed tone.

For the next hour, they all rattle off stories from Ale's childhood, telling me embarrassing things about each one of the boys as well. Which is how I learned where the nickname *rattino* came from.

When Alessandro was little, he was obsessed with Tom and Jerry, and each night, he'd steal pieces of cheese from the refrigerator, hiding them under his bed, hoping that he could give Jerry the upper hand by leaving him something to eat to gear up for his strenuous day of running from Tom.

Gloria later discovered the cheese a few months in when an actual rat got into the house, and it was found under Ale's bed, along with the assorted, dried, and molded cheese chunks.

I can honestly say that *isn't* what I had expected to hear, but I'm not disappointed by it either.

It sounds like he had a very full childhood filled with so much love, and it really explains why he's so affectionate and giving as an adult.

Everyone heads inside with the kids in tow, and they're all covered in mud and whatever's left of the grass outside. Even Aiyana has dirt on her face and covering her shins and elbows.

"You guys look like you rolled around in a mud pile; go get showered and be ready for dinner in thirty minutes!" Gloria tells them, turning back to stirring the pot of Zuppa Toscana she's been making on the stove.

CHAPTER THIRTY-EIGHT

Alessandro

D ante and I finish getting the kids cleaned up, doing as Mom tells us and avoiding her wrath if they were to come back with even a speck of dirt on them.

Arlo runs down the stairs to join the boys, and I turn to Dante, nodding at him to follow me into the guest room.

He takes a seat on the edge of the bed, and I sit on the ottoman in front of the reclining chair. "How are things with Sammy?"

Dante's brows pull together, but he doesn't seem as defeated as he had weeks prior. "I'm not sure. Ari and I have been taking him to a childhood psychologist in Jersey who came highly recommended to me, and she's the first one he's actually opened up to." Pausing, he chuckles lightly. "That was a strong choice of words. I mean, she's the first person we've taken him to that he's actually *spoken* to."

I nod my understanding. "These things take time, right? That's a good sign, isn't it?"

"It is. She had Arielle and I speak with her extensively too about each person in his life, and she suggested something I'd never honestly considered before, and it's just given us a lot to think about."

"Care to share?" I ask, my words laced with worry. I'm not really sure where he's going with this.

He grunts, "She thinks, after having gotten a little info about each of us, that it might be helpful for Sammy if Gi were to open up and get help. They're a lot alike, but I can't exactly make him do something he isn't ready to do."

"She might have a point, and I think if he's willing to seek help for anyone, it'd be for one of the littles," I tell him hopefully.

"I agree, but I'm just not sure how to bridge that conversation, though I think Sammy's doing better already. I think we just take it day by day and let him take the reins a bit. If it is OCD, then he likely feels he has no control over anything he does, so Arielle and I are starting to let him make a lot more of his own decisions."

"Sounds like a solid plan. Just let me know if you need me to help in any way." He nods his head in response, moving to stand.

I follow suit, and we head out the door. "He's gonna be okay, D."

"I know he is," he agrees in a hushed tone as we enter the living room and make our way to the kitchen.

Chapter Thirty-Nine

Katarina

"How are you holding up so far, *gattina*?" Ale asks me, and I smile up at him.

"Really well. Your family is amazing, Ale. I'm not sure how your dad feels about me because he hasn't spoken much, but everyone else seems to like me, and they've all been really welcoming."

"My dad is a man of few words. He's the opposite of my mom, and we think it's because they balance each other out that their marriage has done nothing but grow stronger through the years. Believe me, he likes you." He lays his hand on my thigh, giving it a squeeze as we follow behind Dante and Luca's SUVs.

We pull up to a dirt road with a sign by the roadside that reads, "Ergle Family Tree Farm." There's a small red brick building in the center of a large field with a porch attached that resembles a horse stable with walls lined with fresh wreaths and shiny ornaments.

The surrounding forest has lights hung all around, with cool-white icicles hanging from the branches and blue flashing lights lining the ground surrounding the trees. There's a light dusting of snow and a huge area behind the main building with rows of Christmas trees just waiting to be cut down. There are families all around, holding axes and handheld saws as they meander through the rows of fir trees, searching for the right one to take home.

"All righty, what size are we looking for?" Kas asks as we all gather together, Mr. De Laurentiis holding the saw.

"We usually go for a six- to seven-foot Frasier fir. Our main criteria are that the kids agree on it, the tree is full, and, of course, it's huggable," he explains to us.

"Huggable?" Aiyana asks him. The group giggles with an inside joke.

"Yep, you've gotta be able to wrap your arms around it, give it a good squeeze, and determine its huggability." Mr. De Laurentiis says it so matter-of-factly that I almost think this must be the standard. Kas and I have always loved the holidays, but we aren't religious, and we never really put up many decorations as kids. But I love the lights, so maybe I'll adopt a new tradition for myself.

"Kid-approved, full, and huggable, got it." Aiyana confirms her understanding of the instructions and starts marching off in the direction of the trees labeled "Frasier fir."

Everyone stares after her before shrugging and following behind her. One thing she definitely knows how to do is command a crowd.

Arlo, Benny, and Sammy run over to us. "Uncle Ale, we're gonna find the best tree yet!" Benny shouts.

"Yeah! The best one we've *ever* had!" Arlo exclaims excitedly.

Ale smiles down at them, wrapping an arm around me and pulling me into his side as he steers me forward. "I agree, guys—not only will it be the best one yet, but I think it'll be good luck for the new year." He winks at them.

They run forward, hot on their parents' heels. Baby Sofia is strapped to Charlie's chest, wearing the cutest little cream-colored beanie with a fuzzy ball on top. Baby Lily is strapped to Dante's chest in a matching beanie but in pink. Again, Dante is such a contrast—doting father and husband but wearing a leather jacket and biker boots, his tattoos peeking out of his neckline. He's quickly becoming someone I admire, and so far, I can say that about all of Alessandro's family. Everyone has been so kind and welcoming.

Ale starts slowing down as everyone else hurries ahead, taking in all the potential options for trees. The kids are shouting, chasing one another, and pointing at the most lopsided trees they can find.

He suddenly grabs my waist, hauling me up his body until I'm forced to wrap my legs around him. Ale quickly ducks us behind a particularly bushy tree, gripping my face firmly with his gloved hand as his lips meet mine. He urgently swipes his tongue into my mouth, deepening the kiss and moving his hand to the back of my head, gripping my hair. He pulls back abruptly when we hear shouts from Benny growing nearer, and he gently places me back on the ground. I press my forehead to his chest, panting and trying to regain control of my breathing.

He grips my chin, tilting my head back to look up at him. "I haven't had my lips on you all day, *gattina*. I just couldn't wait any longer."

He bends to kiss my forehead, and I swear I fall for this man more and more every time he does that. Forehead kisses are my undoing.

Before I can reply, Luca pops his head out from behind the tree and says, "Come on, lovebirds, let's go. You can suck face later. The kids have picked a tree, and they're waiting on Kat to judge its 'huggability.'"

My cheeks redden with the knowledge that we got caught. Ale takes my hand, towing me along toward the kids jumping around a tree that looks around seven feet tall. It's very full and extremely lopsided. I'll be amazed if they can manage to get it to stand upright, but I guess that adds to its charm.

"*Wow,*" I say, dragging out the word, "this tree looks perfect! Great find, guys!" I tell them excitedly as they beam up at me. I catch Ale smiling from beside me, his dimple on full display.

"You've gotta hug it, Aunt Kat!" Benny tells me, my eyes widening. This kid really likes to add a shock factor to conversations.

Sammy shoves him gently, doing his best to whisper, "She isn't our aunt, idiot. She's just Uncle Ale's girlfriend."

"Hey, hey, be nice to your brother, Sammy," Ale scolds.

"You're welcome to call me Aunt Kat if you want, Benny"—I look up at his parents—"if your parents are okay with that." Something about Benny's lack of a filter and seemingly thoughtless comments makes me want to protect him at all costs and ensure he never feels bad about anything. He's such a cute kid with so much light in his eyes. I don't want to see that dulled by anyone or anything.

Benny's face is bright with embarrassment as he gazes down at his feet. Nervously kicking at the dirt beneath him, he mumbles, "Sorry, Aunt Kat, oops." His brows shoot straight up his forehead. "I mean Kat, just Kat. I'm sorry!" he tells me in a rush.

"It's okay, Benny; now, show me how to test the huggability of this super cool tree you guys picked out." I do my best to calm his growing anxiety.

He looks relieved, and his racing mind quickly jumps from nervousness to excitement again as he launches himself at the tree, arms spread wide as he shouts, "Like this! You've gotta give it a big hug!"

He steps away, and that's my cue. I make a show of jumping toward the tree, maybe not as excitedly as Benny, but I think he sees the effort. Everyone is laughing; even Gianni gives me a good-natured chuckle. He, like his dad, is a man of very few words. He seems kind enough, but he looks like he's always in his head with a dark cloud looming over him.

"I think it's perfectly huggable," I say, turning to Alessandro. "Your turn."

He takes a few steps back before giving himself a running start as he leaps toward the tree, nearly knocking it out of the ground with the force. "Very huggable!" he tells everyone.

"It's settled then—time to cut this puppy down," Luca says as he reaches over to his dad, grabbing for the saw.

Mr. De Laurentiis quickly snatches it out of his reach. "You really think I'm letting *you*, of all people, use a sharp object? Absolutely not."

"Yeah, you don't exactly have a good track record with potential weapons. We need not forget the paintball incident of '08," Alessandro tells him.

"What happened in '08?" Aiyana pipes up, asking what I'm thinking.

"Luca's dumbass shot himself in the foot with the paintball gun. *Twice.*" Everyone bursts into laughter as Luca grumbles something under his breath.

"Yeah, yeah, yeah, laugh it up. Let's cut this damn tree down," Luca groans.

Chapter Forty

Katarina

Monday, December 25, 2023

I wake up to warm light peeking through the blinds hanging over the sliding glass doors, my body pressed against a hard chest that I quickly realize is Ale's. He has his heavy arm thrown around my waist, clutching me to him. I peel my eyelids back and look around the room.

We fell asleep on the old floral couch, with Benny, Sammy, and Arlo sleeping in a pillow fort at our feet. The tree is lit with an assortment of ornaments, and the milk and cookies are gone, with nothing but crumbs left behind. Presents are piled around the tree, and it leaves me wondering how they got there without me noticing.

Ale must have brought all of the gifts down after everyone fell asleep, but he was so quiet, I hadn't woken either.

I shift my gaze over him, taking in the flannel pajama bottoms with little dancing Santas and his oversized matching T-shirt. He got everyone in the house a pair, so we're all decked out in the same attire.

His face is relaxed, and his chest is rising and falling softly, a tendril of his dark hair hanging over one eye. Tank is lying on the floor beside the couch, his loud snores reverberating through the small living room.

My heart swells with fondness. This family has shown Kas and me more love in one day than our parents did the entirety of the last year they were both around. We never had traditions or anything to make the holidays feel special, which is fine because we were never religious, but experiencing Christmas as a joyous time to spend with loved ones, following fun traditions, and making memories has been really amazing.

It's given me a new perspective on this time of year. I've always loved the pretty lights, but I thought the decorations were kind of ridiculous and had absolutely nothing to do with the religions that inspired the holiday in the first place. Now I realize that for so many people, this time of year is just about ending the year on a happy note.

Tank's snores stop, his eyes crack open, and when he makes eye contact with me, he stands, tail wagging. I reach down to give him ear scratches, and he huffs contentedly, placing his head on the edge of the couch, his wet nose pressed against Ale's side where his shirt has ridden up.

Ale startles awake from the contact, but his expression quickly transitions to a soft smile that reaches his eyes, crinkling at the corners. "Good morning, *gattina*. Merry Christmas, baby." His hand cups my jaw, and he leans in to press a gentle kiss to the center of my mouth.

He pulls away, chuckling as Tank nudges his side again, lifting his paw on the couch to demand his attention.

A grin spreads across my face. "Merry Christmas, Ale," I whisper, doing my best not to wake anyone, but all hopes of that fly out the window as soon as Tank barks. He stands and barrels toward the sliding glass doors, begging to be let outside to chase the red cardinal perched on the back of one of the white metal patio chairs.

Benny sleeps like a rock, so he doesn't budge, but Sammy and Arlo's heads pop up out of the pillow fort, wide grins splayed across their faces, eyes glittering with excitement. "Merry Christmas!" they shout in unison, Sammy's usual surly demeanor disappearing at the thought of opening gifts.

I smile at them both, climbing out of Ale's lap and padding across the soft carpeted floor to open the door for Tank. He bolts outside, the cardinal flying away.

I close the door, leaving Tank to do his business, and Ale's warm arms wrap around me from behind, his face nuzzling into my neck, lips pressing soft kisses along my jaw, sending tingles down my spine and butterflies rushing to my stomach. I can't help the wide smile that plasters itself across my face, my hands wrapping around the muscular arms holding me to his chest.

A content sigh slips past my lips just as Tank's slobber-covered face smooshes against the glass doors, leaving a huge imprint. The kids erupt in a fit of giggles, so I let Tank inside, who moseys over to Benny. Tank's taken to Benny, so he avoids leaving his side whenever possible. Benny finally stirs awake, bright eyes popping open and a grin lighting his face as Tank scooches closer to him. He tosses his little squishy arm over him and presses a kiss to the top of his furry head.

"Good morning, Benny," I say to him, smiling at the small boy with the mop of curls and deep-brown eyes that look like pools of chocolate. He has such kind eyes and a genuine curiosity that makes me just want to squeeze him into a protective hug.

"Mornin' Kat! Uncle Ale, look." His eyes swing to the pile of presents surrounding the tree, his index finger pointing as he shouts, "Santa really went all out this year! I told you we were good." He's grinning from ear to ear.

"Benny, you are *always* good"—Ale shakes his head, smiling—"and I'm not sure Santa's to thank for all those presents..." He trails off, looking at me accusingly.

Benny catches on quickly, eyes still lit with excitement. "Oh my goodness, Kat! You got us presents." He sounds so jovial, but something about the way he speaks reminds me of a child from a movie I can't seem to recall. He's so thankful for every little thing that comes his way, never expecting good things but always so appreciative.

I smile at him. "Of course I did. I heard you were all so good this year, I figured I'd help Santa out." Sammy watches the encounter, looking at me quizzically before his features smooth, and he gives me the first smile I've seen on his adorable, dimpled face. Sammy's got a chip on his shoulder, and I can't imagine where it comes from. Maybe it's just an older sibling thing, but it seems he's chosen to trust me this once, and I'm not taking that for granted.

It sounds like a herd of wild animals is making their way down the steps, but when I look over, it's just all the adults piling down as Gloria and Angelo head in from their room on the first floor.

Everyone is still dressed in their matching holiday pajamas, and Aiyana's cheeks are noticeably rosy, her hair a messy tangle of raven-black piled high on her head.

"Merry Christmas!" they're all shouting at the kids, the room suddenly pumped full of an energy that wasn't present just moments before.

They all pile into the living room, everyone pulling up chairs and taking seats on the floor or the couch; the room is absolutely packed.

Arielle sits at my feet, her legs crossed, and baby Lily sits in her lap, cooing softly. Arielle looks up at me, her lips softly upturned as she squeezes my thigh for reassurance. Her melodious voice is hushed. "I'm really glad you're here, Kat."

My own smile matches hers as I say, "I am too, and Merry Christmas." She turns her attention back to the tree where Ale is now standing, preparing to hand out presents.

"All right, everyone." His voice is deep, commanding our attention, but his lips crack into a wide grin. "I'm going to hand out the gifts, and for those of you who haven't been here for the holidays, Mom makes everyone watch as you open your gift so she can take pictures and doesn't miss anything."

We all nod our heads in understanding. Kas and Aiyana make their way over to me, standing behind the couch as Ale passes out the gifts, one landing in my lap. Kas squeezes my shoulders, bending his head toward mine, and tells me, "I knew setting you two up was the best idea I've ever had." My head whips back to stare at him, dumbstruck. "Merry Christmas, Kitty-Kat," he tells me, straightening.

My eyes are still wide with the revelation. I *knew* it! He was too damn happy about us meeting, trailing ahead on that hike, inviting him everywhere we went without asking me beforehand. He was playing matchmaker the whole time. I shake my head, eyes cast downward toward the gift in my lap, a small grin tugging at the corners of my mouth.

Once everyone has a gift in hand, we go in order of age, youngest to oldest, unwrapping and sharing what we got. My first gift is from Gloria. It's a box about a foot long and a few inches wide with white wrapping paper covered in gold swirls and topped with a stuck-on gold bow.

Everyone's eyes are on me as I unwrap the gift, being careful not to tear the paper, but Gloria's impatience grows as she says, "Tear it up, Kat! You don't need to save the paper; we have more." She chuckles.

I hurry up, unwrapping it with shaky hands. I don't remember the last time I got a gift from anyone for any occasion, aside from Kas's gifts, though those aren't this formal. Inside the box is a book with a pretty plum cover, a viper in the center, and some other intricate details. The name of the book is *Tremble*. I look up, meeting Gloria's eyes. "It's the book we're reading next month for our book club. I gave you my copy since I hadn't known whether or not you read, so I placed an order for a new one to arrive this week," she tells me cheerily. Then she adds, "The author is also an Italian American woman; she actually lives in the area, so we're excited to support a local!" My eyes crinkle. I'm equally excited to be a part of their book club and to read a book by an author I'm unfamiliar with.

"Thank you." My eyes brim with tears at the sweet gesture, but before they can fall, I notice something else beneath the layer of white tissue paper. I unwrap the thin sheets and find a dozen baby photos of who I assume is Alessandro, his bright-green eyes staring up at me, the single dimple in his cheek on display in every photo. "Oh my gosh, he was so cute!" I gush.

"Hey! *Was?*" he asks, incredulous. Everyone laughs, shaking their heads at his mock outrage.

I stand and give Gloria a hug. She pats my back and plants a kiss on my cheek before I take my seat again.

We do several rounds of the same, Gloria howling with laughter at the heavy stack of smut Arielle, Rose, and Charlie got her, each cover decorated with a different shirtless man. The kids bounce with glee, enjoying all of the Roblox, Lego sets, science kits, and stuffed plushies. Arlo ditches us all as soon as she tears the paper off the Easy-Bake Oven I managed to find online for her. Ale had mentioned that she loves to bake, and that was easily my favorite toy growing up.

We're nearing the end of the stack of gifts when Ale finally hands out the gifts I had gotten for the women.

Gloria looks down at the small gift in her hands before looking back up at me, and she deadpans, "They say the smartest people have the worst handwriting. I'm not sure who 'they' are, but they're right." She giggles, and I can't help the burst of laughter that leaves me.

"Mom!" Charlie shouts at her in reprimand, "You can't insult her *already*."

"Look at that handwriting, Char; really give it a good look before you judge me."

Charlie's gaze casts downward, and her eyes look like they're ready to burst, her cheeks filling with air, and she does her best to hold in the laughter.

"Oh my god," she rushes, "Kat, honey, it's just so *ugly*." She snorts.

My shoulders shake as I see Alessandro standing in the corner of the room, his hand clamped over his mouth as he fights to keep his composure. "She's right," I finally say. "It's really horrendous." I agree. It's just *so* bad. That's why I pretty exclusively type everything, and the time spent without writing anything hasn't done me any favors.

"Now open your gifts!" I urge them.

They're all smiling with childlike glee when they realize what I got them. I had known about their love of books but wasn't sure what genre they read, so I opted for a safe bet and got them each a personalized embosser. They each have a book in the center with flowers corresponding to their birth months pouring out. Everyone but Rose, that is. Her birthday is in August, which isn't a rose, so I opted to go against the theme and have roses sprouting from her book. The top reads, "From the library of..." with their first and middle names.

"This is perfect, Kat!" Charlie's eyes are wild with excitement. "Do you have one of these?"

I shake my head, smiling slightly. "No, I don't, but I saw them in a video on Picturegram and thought they were perfect."

"Okay, that settles it! We have to get you one too—can't leave you out when we're in the same book club," she tells me, rolling her eyes as if I'm absurd for not getting myself one. I appreciate the openness of each one of these women. I always found it difficult to make friends, aside from Aiyana, because I always worried that I had said or done something to upset them, so having women in my life who tell me exactly what they're thinking and show their emotions clearly across their faces settles an unease I hadn't realized I was carrying along with me.

Ale hands me the last gift under the tree and takes a seat next to me, his eyes warm and tender as he watches me. There isn't much room on the couch, so I adjust my position to where I'm practically in his lap with his arms wrapped around my waist, his head resting on my shoulder.

When it's my turn to open my last gift, I untie the small bow made out of curling ribbon and unwrap the bright-red paper. I pull the lid off the small brown box, and sitting inside is a small gold chain bracelet with a single, tiny, light-blue tanzanite stone on one side and another matching one in opal opposite to it. It's so dainty and perfect.

I feel the familiar wave of emotions crash over me and turn my head to look at Ale as everyone watches us. Their eyes all glimmer with unshed tears, and Arielle is sniffling at my feet. The kids have already finished opening their gifts, so they're unaware of the emotional moment the adults are having.

Ale presses a kiss to my temple, reaching for the bracelet and undoing the clasp. He takes my hand, running his lips over my knuckles before fastening the bracelet to my wrist. "Our birthstones, so we never have to be apart." He chuckles lightly. "Sorry, *gattina*, that was almost embarrassingly cheesy," he tells me, grinning.

Luca releases a bark of laughter. "Almost?" he asks jokingly.

Gianni is sitting beside him, and his best friend, Alex, is sitting in front of the unlit fireplace. Gianni never smiles, but right now, his eyes are glimmering with a cheerful, teasing quality that lights me up inside and sends my heart soaring. Gi is quiet and reserved, but I can tell there's more to him than meets the eye.

I shift my gaze to meet his eyes, and his lips crack into his version of a smile. I make it my mission to get a full, genuine one out of him. Gi deserves good things.

We all clean up the gifts, some of us remaining in the living room to play with the kids while others head to the kitchen to work on the rest of the food for the day. Kas takes a seat on the couch, holding baby Sofia as she sleeps on his chest. I've never known Kas to be such a kid person, but I guess we've never really had any family or friends with kids for me to notice. His expression is calm, eyes closed as he relaxes into the worn floral couch cushions, speaking imperceivably softly to her as he rubs her back in small circles.

Aiyana is playing with Arlo in the corner of the room, but her eyes are soft and centered on Kas. I doubt either of them realizes that I've noticed their attraction, but unlike Kas, I don't meddle in people's love lives. Though, if this pining for one another goes on for much longer, I might have to start.

***

The day was jam-packed with activities as soon as the extended family arrived. I'm shocked we were able to fit that many people in here, but they made it work. We set up a large white folding banquet table to extend the dark wooden one in the kitchen and layered them both with dark-green tablecloths with little strands of red glitter twined throughout them.

The food was incredible, as is the theme for all meals where the De Laurentiis family is involved. That's a fact I'm extremely happy about because I can't cook to save my life. Gloria offered to help teach me, and I'm happy to learn from her and enjoy the bonding time, but I have little interest in cooking all of my own meals when Ale's so willing to do it for me.

Angelo and I have developed an unspoken bond, sharing small smiles and quick glances of appreciation toward one another. Like Gianni, he doesn't speak much, but his rumbling laughter sets them apart.

Several aunts, uncles, and cousins from Dante, Gianni, and Charlie's biological family showed up, and they were all really nice. This year, Hanukkah was at the beginning of the month, so the days didn't coincide well, unlike last year, when there was an overlap between the two holidays. Gloria set the table with a Menorah anyway, and they opted not to light it since the holiday had already passed, but it's clear everyone respects each other's beliefs.

Once the house is all cleaned up, Alessandro calls everyone's attention one more time. "We forgot the Elf!"

My eyes widen slightly, looking around the room as everyone's jaws drop slightly. "Oh my gosh, how could we forget?" Gloria asks, and Rose nudges my hip with her own.

"They have a money elf." My brow wrinkles with confusion. "I know it sounds weird, but basically, they have this elf who comes to life on Christmas Eve and hides somewhere in the house holding money. Usually, it's a five-dollar bill, but one year I guess Angelo didn't have change so he hid a twenty." She chuckles with fondness. "They started doing the same with a Mensch on a Bench for the Jewish part of the family."

I nod in understanding but have no idea what a mensch is. "And what's a mensch, and why is he on a bench?"

She laughs softly. "Mensch is a word that means 'good person,' so where people who celebrate Christmas have 'Elf on the Shelf,' Jewish families do 'Mensch on a Bench.' But I've gotta say, my favorite version of that is with Snoop Dogg..." She trails off, glancing at my confused expression with a smirk on her face. "Snoop on a Stoop; he's even holding a blunt and everything. It's incredible—one year, Charlie and I found the elf and replaced it with Snoop." She releases a squawk of laughter, several people pinning her with a confused gaze.

That makes me chuckle, and when Gloria announces that no one's allowed to leave until the Elf, Mensch, *and* Snoop are found, we all run around the house searching.

It takes less than ten minutes before all three are found, and I don't miss that Gianni absolutely found the Elf first but directed Benny toward it as if he had no clue. I knew he was a softy. I could feel it.

We say our goodbyes, and those of us who aren't leaving till the morning get changed into pajamas and then help put the kids to bed. The adults decide to stay up a while longer and start the fireplace, so instead of having the kids sleep in the living room, we set them up in one of the guest rooms.

***

When the kids are all asleep, Gloria and Angelo give us all hugs before heading off to bed.

I'm sitting on the floor in between Ale's legs, a blanket wrapped around us, as Gianni comes out of the hallway pushing a piano on wheels toward the fireplace. Alex is trailing behind him, carrying a small stool that he places behind the cream-colored piano, the worn-down keys showing its age.

Gianni takes a seat, and everyone quiets except for Luca, who groans. Gianni's eyes snap to his, his lips pursed in annoyance.

"What?" Luca asks, feigning innocence, "I just don't want to be here for the impending blood bath when Kat decides to leave Ale for Gianni after hearing his heaven-sent voice." His own voice becomes airy and high-pitched in a mocking tone as he brings his hands together, fingers intertwined, and flutters his lashes.

Gianni grunts, and Ale rumbles with laughter from behind me. "Oh, piss off Luca. Gi's voice *is* heavenly, but I'm pretty confident that Gi's perfect match isn't in this room." He chuckles dismissively. "Go on, Gi, show us what you've got." He smiles at him encouragingly, letting Luca's shit-stirring attitude roll off of him.

Gi straightens in his seat, looking over his shoulder at Aiyana and me. "Any requests?" he asks softly.

"How about 'Hallelujah'?" Aiyana pipes up excitedly.[1]

She loves live music and adores the holidays. I'm glad we got to come here for Christmas because she was really bummed when her parents told her they didn't want to host this year.

He gives a small nod, turning back toward the piano, and his fingers start moving methodically across the keys. His deep baritone reverberates through the room, wrapping us in tendrils of smoke as he sings the most haunted and entirely gorgeous version of that song I've ever heard. My mouth is slightly ajar, Ale's forehead resting between my shoulder blades, and when the song stops, there isn't a dry eye in the room. I hold back a sob, my chest squeezing tightly as the revelation of the moment hits me. That's the first time Gianni has ever let me into his head, and I'm realizing just how dark it is.

Aiyana is actively crying, her beautiful face puffy as she dabs her nose with the edge of her sleeve. "That was incredible," she sobs, "and you play soccer? What the fuck, Gi! You just made me fucking bawl my eyes out, which never happens, mind you." She pauses to catch her breath, Kas's hand slipping over hers, squeezing reassuringly. "You should be performing in music halls, not playing with balls!"

She never fails to break through tension, everyone erupting in laughter, but Gi leans down, tucks a fallen strand of her hair behind her ear, and whispers something that makes both her and Kas smile. Gianni has a tender air about him that you wouldn't notice if you were just passing by him, but his small gestures portray a bigger picture.

Much like Benny, I just want to give Gi a good squeeze. I don't know his story, but there's something there, and I think we could be good friends if he ever decides to let me in.

The next hour or so, Gianni, Kas, and Luca take turns singing, occasionally doing a duet, and Dante finally pipes in, demanding Gi sing one last song with him. He picks a super controversial song that usually makes me cringe, but it seems this is their bit. Dante, with his booming authoritative voice, takes on a high-pitched squeaky quality as he sings the part meant for the female singer, with Gi singing the other part.[2]

The hilarity of the song does wonders to dissolve any tension left over, and everyone either heads to bed or settles in on the couches and the piles of blankets on the floor. Ale kisses the top of my head, pulling me on top of his chest, and Tank takes the opportunity to shuffle closer to us, leaning his weight fully against us. "Goodnight, *gattina*."

"Goodnight, Ale." I fall asleep shortly after, enjoying a peaceful quiet that my mind usually doesn't grant me the pleasure of having.

---

1. **Hallelujah - Pentatonix**

2. **Baby, It's Cold Outside - John Legend (ft. Kelly Clarkson)**

CHAPTER FORTY-ONE

Alessandro

TUESDAY, DECEMBER 26, 2023

The holidays with Kat have been some of the best memories I have. My family absolutely adores her, and I wouldn't have expected anything less, truthfully. She can dish out the banter as well as she can take it, which is a highly coveted trait in my family.

Things have been so nice that I haven't had the heart to tell her that I made an appointment to see Dr. Howell when we get back. I just didn't want to ruin anything or bring the mood down, but I'm starting to have pain again, and it's harder to wake up at a reasonable time.

I also feel like I might be starting to experience some of those overactive reflexes my mom has complained about before. That's been one of my biggest fears because it isn't something I can just power through. People will see it, and there won't be any hiding it. Not from my friends, my family, my team, or Kat.

Chapter Forty-Two

Katarina

Thursday, January 11, 2024

"This has easily been the slowest, most boring hockey game I've ever been to in my life, Kat. Can we just go? I'm sure Ale and your brother will understand if we leave early." It takes a lot for Aiyana to not sit through every second of a hockey game, but she's right. This game has been exhaustingly boring. Neither team is being aggressive, there have been almost no penalties, which is unheard of, and the Scarlets are up four to zero.

There isn't anything that could happen in the next twenty minutes that'll change that. "There are only twenty minutes left, and we're going out to dinner with the team right after anyway. We may as well wait and leave with them."

"God, you're such a good girlfriend. I hate it," she grumbles, arms crossed over her chest.

The next few minutes pass by just as slowly as the first hour or so. I finally decide we can head out now to beat the crowd and meet the guys at dinner, but as I'm standing, I see the other team has tagged in a rookie player who had been on probation for a while. It looks like they wanted to give him a shot tonight since they have no hopes of winning anyway.

This player is already known for his terrible attitude and overly aggressive style, so when I see him gunning for Alessandro, my heart is squeezing so tightly in my chest, I feel like it'll burst.

Alessandro is managing to skillfully sidestep him, expertly avoiding his advances at every turn and pivot. My anxiety is starting to calm down until my greatest fear unfolds.

When your loved ones play contact sports, you know there's a risk of injury. Working in neurology, I know that better than anyone, but it's a whole other thing to see your worst fears play out in front of you.

Alessandro is on his feet, firmly on the ice, maintaining perfect balance one moment, and the next, he's being catapulted into the boards headfirst. His body is thrown several feet before his head smacks into the boards, and his limp body thuds against the ice.

I'm shaking, my heart is pounding out of my chest, and the sound of it is heightened by the silence that has overcome the arena.

The coaches and trainers rush to Alessandro, and I hear screaming coming from the other end of the ice. All of Ale's teammates are yelling at the refs and the rookie.

In this moment, I think I might suffer a heart attack. My heart rate has reached new heights. I'm full of fear like I've never known.

My eyes avert back to Ale a moment later, and just as I thought things couldn't get any worse, he begins convulsing. Seizures are known to occur after a particularly forceful head injury, and my body takes over before my brain can catch up with what I'm doing.

I'm running down the steps and over the sides, the players looking at me in disbelief as I slip and slide across the ice to Ale. The coaches and trainers are just staring at him! They aren't even helping.

"Call nine-one-one and grab the onsite medics!" I shout at them as I kneel at his head, doing my best to gently push his giant bulk away from the wall so he doesn't risk further injury as he seizes.

The seizure stops within seconds, and the medics are rushing over with a stretcher. I speak calmly to him, reassuring him that I'm here and that he's going to be okay, but I'm not getting any response from him. He's entirely too quiet.

"Ma'am, I need you to move out of the way so I can do my job," the lead medic tells me. I won't argue with him. Not now. Not knowing I'm in a horrible frame of mind and I couldn't live with myself if I somehow delayed his care or he ended up with further injury because of me. I get out of their way, staying close enough to continue speaking to him.

It doesn't take long before he's stirring awake, the initial shock wearing off as he becomes more present.

I don't want him to make any jerky movements, so I quickly assure him that I'm here. "Ale, you're okay. You hit your head, but you're going to be okay. I'm gonna stay with you the whole time, okay, baby?" I grab his hand, squeezing it tightly.

"Kat." He says it so quietly, my heart shatters into a million pieces, but I'm filled with a rush of relief that he's speaking at all.

My eyes are welling with tears, my throat tight with emotion. "Yes, baby, I'm right here."

"Don't leave me, okay?" He sounds like he's scared, and that drives the stake that's already residing in my chest even further into my heart.

"Never, baby, I won't leave. You couldn't make me if you tried," I assure him as the paramedics continue to work, getting him onto the stretcher, and soon, we're in the ambulance, heading to my hospital.

Chapter Forty-Three

Katarina

Friday, January 12, 2024

I awake, slightly startled, as I realize I'm not in my bed. Memories of last night start flooding in, and I'm suddenly struck with that same panic I've been consumed with since the moment he went down.

I look around the room, my eyes zeroing in on Ale's sleeping form, looking far smaller in that hospital bed than I've ever seen him. This man is usually so bold and full of life, his personality as big as he is. It kills me to see him like this.

His family arrived last night after they saw everything on TV, and Luca got here after his own game finished. I had one of the nurses help me find a cot so I could stay with him, and I told his family to head home and I'd update them. I figured there was no reason for them all to stay once we knew he was stable and his scans came back clear. He suffered a pretty horrendous concussion, and he's sore all over, but he should be good to go home today as soon as he's cleared.

I sit up, folding the blanket I had sprawled across me, and stand to check on him. He doesn't stir as I approach the bed, but his eyes open, and a smile spreads across his face as soon as I take his hand in mine.

"I love waking up to that beautiful face, *gattina*," he tells me, his eyes bright and hooded.

My eyes well with tears, butterflies taking flight in my abdomen as I battle my warring emotions. I'm so relieved he's okay and so gone for him—it makes me sick to think about losing him. He squeezes my hand tightly, sensing the change in my mood.

"Baby, please don't cry. You know what that does to me." He releases my hand, opening his arms out wide to embrace me. "Come here."

I can't resist this man. I lean over the edge of the bed to hug him, but he lifts me onto his chest so that I'm curled up on top of him. His arms are holding me securely to him, my face pressed into his shirt, and every emotion I've been holding in bursts, my body shaking from the release.

He smooths my hair, whispering to me, calming me down, and eventually, I feel lighter. Every tear releases a bit of the pent-up anxiety, frustration, anger, and fear. I sigh into his embrace, and moments later, I hear a little knock at the door. "Hey Kitty-Kat, we figured we could come check on you guys and bring you your meds."

Peeling myself off of Alessandro, I sit up and get out of the bed to greet Kas and Aiyana. I give my brother a big hug, allowing him to hold me for a while. I step away and gesture toward Ale. "He's doing better," I tell them. "It sounds like he'll be discharged today—just have to wait for his care team to come see him, and then we can break him out of here." I offer Ale a reassuring smile, which he returns.

"I heard *somebody* got into a fight last night, and over little ole me? How you doing, man?" Ale asks Kas, probably wondering if he got in any trouble. He hadn't.

"Me? Nah, I would *never*. I'm a straight arrow, as they say," he replies, giving Ale a wink.

"As much as I love this little bromance that's developed," Aiyana interjects, one hip popped out, "I've gotta get to work. I just wanted to stop by and make sure you guys were all good."

"Yeah, we're good. Thanks for stopping by, Aiyana. I'll see you later today, I'm sure." Ale offers her a small smile that she returns before turning to me and embracing me in a rib-crushing hug.

She takes a step back, gripping my shoulders and staring into my face. "You tell me if you need *anything,* okay?" Then she whispers for only me to hear, "You had me absolutely worried sick last night after you jumped over those boards and I didn't hear from you again for so long."

I'm stricken with a pang of guilt. "I'm sorry," I tell her, my brow furrowing with the memory.

"It's okay, just don't do it again, missy." She tries to lighten the mood, but my head and heart are still trying to catch up.

I give her a weak smile and thank her again for stopping by before she leaves with Kas hot on her heels.

***

"You're sure you can walk?" I ask Ale, knowing he's fine and wouldn't ask for my help even if he needed it.

"*Gattina*, I'm fine. I promise. I just want to get home to Tank and cuddle you both in bed." He looks at me pleadingly, just wanting me to let it go and get us home. I nod in agreement and lead us toward the exit.

"Are you sure there won't be any reporters here today after the accident?"

"No, Ale, I promise. The hospital is really strict about that sort of thing, and security has been keeping an eye out," I assure him.

As soon as we walk through the sliding doors on the bottom level, we're smacked in the face by a gust of frigid wind. It's early, and the sun hasn't fully risen. Thankfully, I was able to get Ale seen first so he could stop taking up a valuable bed for someone who needed it more. Moments later, our ride pulls up, and we hop in. The drive is short, and when we get to our building, the sidewalk is packed with reporters shaking in the cold, waiting to get some kind of response from us.

"You ready?" He looks at me, squeezing my thigh. I nod, grabbing the door handle and greeting the onslaught of nosey reporters.

I'm in fight-or-flight mode, my panic rising again, clawing up my throat and trying to strangle me. This is just too much for me. I don't like being in the limelight, and since being with Alessandro, I've been shoved into it way more than I'd like. I know it isn't his fault, and I'd never blame him. It's just something I need to get used to, but like when we first started dating, the media will get tired of us. At least, I hope.

Ale slides out of the seat behind me and wraps an arm around my waist, ushering me toward our doors where Ralph is waiting for us, fending off the reporters. Does this man ever sleep?

The reporters are scuffling around one another, each shoving their recorders in our faces, begging for information, a comment, an insight, or anything we're willing to give them. Ale pulls me through them, grinding out, "No comment," more times than I can count.

"Good morning, Miss Narvaez"—Ralph tips his chin at me before greeting Alessandro—"Mr. De Laurentiis, I hope you're doing well after that spill last night."

Ale chuckles beside me. "It was quite the 'spill,' Ralph, but I'm okay. Honestly," he adds, giving the older man a small smile.

"I'm glad to hear. Please let me know if either of you needs anything."

"We will, thanks, Ralph." We head upstairs, taking the elevator on autopilot and not saying a word as we make our way to Ale's apartment.

Chapter Forty-Four

Alessandro

M y head is still pounding, and my body aches all over, but my heart is on the verge of shattering. Kat has completely withdrawn from me in the last half hour. She keeps telling me she's fine, but I know she's not. She isn't her chatty self, and she isn't even snuggled into my side. She's just lying a foot away from me, trying to take calming breaths that I see through immediately. I think she might be panicking about the reporters again, and I'm freaking out. I can't lose her because of something I have no control over. If I messed up, that would be on me, but this? I didn't do this. I can't control what the media do, and I know she's scared, but I am too, for entirely different reasons.

I roll over on my side to face her and gently stroke her cheek with the tip of my finger. "*Gattina*, talk to me, please." I'm pleading with her to *let me in*.

"I just need a minute, Ale. I just need to process." She sighs, rolling toward me and popping her eyes open to finally look at me.

"I'm not running, I promise." She says it so softly that I almost sob with relief.

It's at this moment that it becomes glaringly clear that I've fallen in love with her. I'm breathless with the revelation, and the stress still etched into her brow is pulling at my heartstrings. I don't think I'd recover if she were to leave me.

I fully plan to make this woman my wife.

"You'll tell me if you need something, right? Whatever you need, it's yours, Kat. Whatever I have to do to make you happy and comfortable, I'll do it—you just say the word." I'm completely serious. I'd quit my entire damn career for this woman. Even without a Stanley Cup.

She gives me a weak smile that does nothing to appease the rapid beast inside me, gnawing at my chest. She rests her hand over my heart. "I trust you, Ale."

Three little words, *I trust you,* and I'm a goner. A dead man walking. I'll give my life for this woman.

Chapter Forty-Five

Katarina

Saturday, January 13, 2024

The warm steam from my shower helped ease my mind and my aching muscles. I've been wound so tightly, like a string ready to snap from too much tension.

I'm enveloped in my favorite light-green fuzzy robe that Kas got me for Christmas as I pad across my bedroom floor, heading to my nightstand to grab my cell off the charger.

When I reboot it, it takes a moment to load my notifications, but when it does... all the tension seeps back into my muscles, my jaw clenching and my heart racing.

I have texts from colleagues, Dr. Howell included, as well as emails from reporters trying to get a statement from me and missed calls from Alessandro's family. I don't have anything from Ale, Kas, or Aiyana, probably because they're all still asleep.

I start with the text from Dr. Howell that reads, "I'm so sorry, Kat. We don't know how this happened. The hospital is working tirelessly to get it sorted, but a hacker shut down our system last night and released patient files to the public, demanding a large payment if we want them to stop. One of those files was Alessandro's, as I'm sure you know by now. Please call me!"

My heart is in my toes. This could ruin Ale's entire career. No one knows about his illness; I haven't even told my brother.

The message is followed by a screenshot from an article, and the headline reads, "Alessandro De Laurentiis—Good Guy or Selfish Stand-In?"

What the hell are they talking about?

I search the article, and if I didn't think things could get any worse, I was wrong. The article goes into detail about his health history, mentioning his mom and their MS, making statements about his symptoms, and how he had seen me for his treatments. They accused him of using me, and another article says I was black-mailing him into dating me by *threatening* to release information about his condition if he didn't. Others make assumptions about the state of his health and whether his injuries were *really* due to that rookie coming after him or if his legs had suddenly given out. They said he was being selfish by putting his teammates at risk of injury and said I was more concerned with the potential to date a famous hockey player than I was about my own brother's safety.

My thoughts are scattered, panic plaguing my lungs. I can't breathe, and my head is pounding. The edges of my periphery are going dark, and I know I'm having a panic attack.

My hands are shaking as I fumble around my nightstand, grasping at the drawer and finally yanking it open to reveal the medication I take only when absolutely necessary for these panic attacks. It makes me drowsy and unsteady, but I need it now.

I place one on my tongue, chugging the water from my night-stand, and sink to the ground, too weak to climb into bed. Sobs are wracking my body, my eyes swollen from tears, and my stomach in knots.

I lay there for I don't know how long before I hear a knock at my door, but I can't hear who it is over my shaking breaths.

The door opens, hushed voices rushing together frantically, and suddenly, strong arms wrap around me, pulling me off the floor, my face smothered in a warm, firm chest that I immediately recognize as Alessandro from his scent alone. His warmth seeps into me, my shaking limbs slowly calm, and the foghorn blaring in my ears begins to settle.

I lift my head carefully to avoid the spins and pry my swollen lids open. I'm greeted by several pairs of eyes before me—Alessandro holding me, Kas and Aiyana hovering over us, and oddly enough, Dante leaning against the doorframe.

I'm suddenly flushed with embarrassment that so many people just witnessed my panic attack. I know I must look horrendous, but I don't have the energy to apologize.

"Kat, can you talk to us? Tell us you're okay?" Ale is speaking soothingly to me.

"Baby girl, do you want some tea? I can make you a London Fog? Or maybe some chamomile if you want." Aiyana's warm eyes and crinkled brow meet my gaze. Now I know I look like a wreck if she's calling me "baby girl" and treating me like a fragile flower.

"Tea would be nice. London Fog, please." I try to smile at her to calm her own anxiety, but it doesn't reach my eyes, and her brow furrows further.

"Kas, come with me and help me make her some tea. Let's give them some time to talk." Aiyana and Kas head into the kitchen as Ale reluctantly puts me in bed, sitting on the edge once I'm comfortable. Dante gently closes the door and saunters toward me, self-assured. He oozes with a serene aura that immediately works to calm my nerves.

"I'm not sure if Ale has ever told you what I do for a living, but I'm a psychologist. He mentioned that you had been looking for one and asked if I had any recommendations. I wanted to bring those by for you, but given this morning's circumstances, I also wanted to check in on you myself and offer a listening ear if that's something you feel you'd benefit from. Nothing you say to me will be repeated, not even to my brother." That explains why he's always so calm and friendly but never overtly so.

I smile at him, this one more genuine. "I really appreciate that. I actually think that might be a good idea, but do you mind if I talk with Ale first?"

He grins at me. "I'm glad, Kat, and of course. I'll wait in the living room. Come grab me when you're ready." He heads out of my room to wait, closing the door behind him.

"Baby, come here," Ale says, his arms outstretched for me to crawl into. I'm overwhelmed and crave his comfort.

"Is it true?" I can't wait to ask him any longer; I need to know.

"Is what true?" he asks me, confusion etched into his handsome face.

"Have you been experiencing more symptoms and didn't go see Dr. Howell? Could your injury be from your MS and not that rookie?"

He looks like I struck him, his expression hardening momentarily before softening again with a sad quality I don't recognize. "No. I had an appointment with Dr. Howell right after the holidays. Things had gotten worse, and I hadn't told you because I didn't want to worry you or ruin our trip to my parents, but I did see Dr. Howell, and he just had to increase one of my medications and decrease another. The symptoms I was feeling were actually side effects from one of the drugs. It's been working really well now that we made this switch, and I haven't had any pain, numbness, overactive muscles, spasms, or headaches since the first week on the new medications. Dr. Howell and I had a call a few days ago, and we both think we've found the right combination this time." He looks hopeful and confident as he says this, and the worry and resentment that filled me moments before drains out of me.

That's all I needed to know. I lay across him, burying my head in his lap. He strokes my hair instinctually, and I hear him let out a rough breath.

We lay there for a while longer before I sit up, pulling my hair up into a bun and securing it with the elastic I keep on my wrist. "I'm gonna go wash my face. Could you send Dante in, please?"

"Of course." He cups my cheeks with his hands, placing tiny kisses on my forehead, my eyelids, my nose, and finally, my lips. The kiss begins gently, like a butterfly landing on your cheek or the warmth of the sun's rays on your skin. It dissolves into something heady, full of need, and the emotions from the last three days come crashing down around us into this one kiss.

His tongue sweeps the seam of my lips, begging for access, but he's desperate and can't wait any longer, nipping at the corner of my lip, hard enough to draw blood, just like I had that time at the hotel in New York. His tongue swipes out to lick it away, and the metallic taste floods my senses as I'm surrounded by a cascade of Ale. His strength, his emotions, his scent, his lips. It's all so much, my senses in overdrive, overflowing with need.

A moan escapes me, and it's like a switch flips. Ale's rough hands are no longer gently caressing me, and he snaps. Further deepening the kiss, he grips my thighs, tossing me into the center of the bed. I become increasingly aware that I'm wearing nothing but my bathrobe as he prowls over me, his hands on my knees as he spreads my thighs.

His eyes zone in on my core, and he climbs up my body, stopping to let his face hover over me. He ducks his head, and I release a gasp, his nose trailing through my wet folds.

My hands shoot out to my sides, gripping the comforter for dear life. His tongue darts out, lapping at me, and he pays special attention to my clit, knowing exactly what I like.

His eyes never lift from their current focus as he reaches his hand up to pull the tie from my robe loose. The sides fall open, and his hand snakes up my abdomen to my breasts. He alternates kneading them with pinching my nipples, and I can't stop the squeaks and moans that slip past my lips. My hands are in his hair, gripping the roots and urging him on. The rumbles of approval from him act like a vibrator on my most sensitive parts.

I'm moments from coming apart as he lifts himself over me, gripping the sides of his joggers as he pushes them down his massive, toned thighs. His cock springs out, hard and thick and dripping with precum.

This time, he doesn't ask for permission, knowing he has it before he plunges into me. I cry out in pleasure, my cunt milking him as he pounds into me relentlessly. We've had all kinds of sex, but this is needy and rough.[1]

Nothing careful or slow about the brutality of it as he pounds me into the fucking mattress.

He's unusually quiet aside from the rough sounds leaving his throat and the single time he tells me, "That's my good fucking girl, come for me, *gattina*."

I'm screaming his name, unable to remember my own, as he clamps his hand down over my mouth, ineffectively muffling me. We fall apart together, my orgasm drowning me like a rough current, dragging me out to sea.

It takes us a while before we regain control of our breathing, and when we do, he pulls out, a gush of hot come rushing out of me. I have zero embarrassment about it; what I do feel is a new rush of anxiety at the realization that we just had sex while my brother *and* *his* are in the living room right now and likely heard everything.

My cheeks flame with that knowledge. I sit up, hop off the bed, and rush around to get dressed. Ale rights himself, and we head to the living room and realize that no one is here. They all must have stepped out when they heard us going at it like wild animals. My blush claws down my chest, making me look like a tomato, I'm sure.

Ale chuckles. "I'll text Kas and Dante that the coast is clear. They probably just went to my apartment."

1. **Lovin On Me - Jack Harlow**

Chapter Forty-Six

Katarina

I give Dante a tight hug. "Thank you for talking that out with me. And for the recommendations. I think I'll look into them and give them a call on Monday to get scheduled with whoever's available soonest."

He releases me. "You're very welcome, Kat. You're my family now, even if you aren't my children's aunt yet," he tells me with a wink. "I know that's where you and Ale are heading, and I'm in full support of you both. Anything you need, let me know." He heads out, mentioning that he'll see me tomorrow at Sunday dinner.

I've really enjoyed attending these dinners and getting to know his family better, and they've made me feel unbelievably welcome and loved. It's a strange feeling, being that the only real family Kas and I have had is our Lola, and I've only known his family for a short time.

My anxiety has mellowed out a bit as I head back to my apartment. Ale let Dante and I talk at his place to avoid having to let him into my room, which now hosts the come covered duvet that I need to wash.

I plan to just watch movies and relax tonight. Ale and I are going to order in, and Aiyana won't be home.

CHAPTER FORTY-SEVEN

Katarina

MONDAY, JANUARY 15, 2024

This weekend has been such a whirlwind of emotions, both good and bad. The media hasn't let up, and Ale had to hire a guard for his parents' home, as well as the front of our building. Our building has a guard, but press management isn't exactly his forte, though we appreciate the building manager agreeing to having someone else out there.

The stories have become more and more insane with the accusations, and Ale's manager suggested that he make a statement at the team's press conference tonight. They're actually playing an away game against Luca's team in New York, but I won't be attending this one since I work all week. I also just need a bit of a breather. Ale and I have had a bit of cooling down from the series of panic from the last few days, but the overwhelming response from every direction has caused a bit of strain.

And I think Ale has convinced himself that I'm going to bolt if anything else happens. He seems to be waiting for the other shoe to drop, so to speak.

I can't lie. I am too.

I head up to my floor at the hospital, and I'm really excited to see Cindy. She and her fiancé got married over the holidays, so I haven't had her around the last few weeks. The MA that was filling in for her was really efficient, but our personalities didn't mesh as well, and it wasn't as fun as my days with Cindy usually are.

She's sitting at my desk when I walk back to it, and she beams up at me. "Hey! How were the holidays for you?" she asks me, always so excited about any form of human interaction. It's what makes her an ideal medical assistant. The patients love her, and my days with her are never dull.

"They were great for the most part," I tell her, glossing over the way my life imploded the last few days because I'm sure she's aware and will hound me for more information soon anyway. "How was the wedding, and when do I get to see pictures?"

"Oh my gosh, Kat, it was incredible. Everything we ever wanted. Super small, just us and our siblings—we didn't even involve our parents because we just wanted the day to be about us. After having a tiny ceremony in Colorado, we flew to Fiji for our honeymoon, and it was amazing. So warm, and the resort we stayed at was all-inclusive. It was really relaxing." She's glowing with excitement. I've always loved weddings, and I guess I just love love.

I smile at her warmly. "I'm so glad it was everything you wanted. You deserve those sweet moments. But again, where are my pictures?" I ask again. She explains that she doesn't have the edited photos from her photographer yet but that she has some photos she can show me that her siblings took and lots of pictures from her honeymoon. She and Adam, her husband, are madly in love, and it shows in how she speaks about him. We agree to have a double date next month when things calm down a bit because I'd love to meet Adam myself.

The day passes much as it usually does—a blur of patients with a wide variety of illnesses ranging from pain to weakness and loss of function. By the end of the day, I'm wiped and ready to go home, but one of the NPs who usually works from 3:00 p.m. to midnight asked if I could stick around and cover her shift. Her kid is sick, and she's a single mom, so she doesn't have anyone to watch him. I can't imagine how much stress she must be under, so I tell her I'd be glad to.

***

It's almost eleven, and I'm seeing my last few patients of the night, assuming no one new gets admitted to our floor before shift change. I know the press conference is going live shortly, so I step into the staff lounge to watch for a few minutes.

Ale and I hadn't had a chance to discuss what he was going to say, but I'm sure his agent has it covered, and he's good at getting the right message across.

I take a seat after changing the channel on the small TV and making myself a tea. A few moments later, the camera is panned away from the crowd of reporters and is now focused on the guys sitting on a small stage with a Philly Scarlets banner behind them. Matt, the team captain, is there alongside Alessandro, his agent, and Coach Allister. Kas doesn't participate in these press conferences very often, and from what I can tell, Luca isn't allowed to for his team. I can't make out who's sitting at the other team's table though, with the camera being honed in on Ale.

Coach Allister and Matt answer some generic questions about the team, their season, how they're doing, and where they're going. They express their belief that they'll be winning the Stanley Cup this year, and the reporters don't seem to disagree. They're having a remarkably good year, even for their already high standards.

Unfortunately, that was the calm before the storm.

A middle-aged blonde with spiky hair raises her hand to ask a question, and Coach Allister's eyes dart to the side, looking at Ale with concern that fills me with dread.

Some reporters are well-known in the sports community for being problematic and always aiming to cause problems. Even I recognize her as one of them. Her name is Carol Strobof, and she's the one who is constantly in Luca's business.

It feels like she releases an article each week with some catchy headline and images of Luca and whoever his most recent date is. I, for one, don't understand what that has to do with his value to his team. It's his personal business and doesn't hinder him from being named in the top five goalies in the NHL ever since starting with his current team in New York.

So when she opens her mouth to speak, she says, "Alessandro De Laurentiis, is it true that you and your mother have multiple sclerosis?"

He nods. "Yes, it's true." He's keeping his responses to a minimum to avoid leeway for his words to be twisted.

"And is it true that you didn't tell your team about your diagnosis?"

"It's my personal health information. It has no impact on my ability to play, and if it had, I would have resigned." That's not good. He should have stuck with short responses.

"Hmm, well, if it hadn't impacted your ability to play, then why did you end up with your skull through the boards on Friday?"

She's being snarky, and I want to jump through the screen and strangle her for it.

"I ended up injured because of a rookie player with something to prove, and you know that," he tells her with an edge to his voice. He's no longer wearing the fake polite smile he started with.

She smiles at him. "You say he's got something to prove, but so do you. Isn't that right? You need to prove yourself valuable enough to stick around until you win that Cup so you can pay off your 'girlfriend.'" She uses air quotes around the word "girlfriend" before continuing.

His face is tight, eyes flaring with anger, but he keeps his butt planted in his chair. "You have absolutely no idea what you're talking about. She's my girlfriend. There are no contingencies to our relationship, and she is absolutely not *blackmailing* me." He tells her this and realizes as soon as the words come out of his mouth that it was a mistake. I can tell by how his eyes widen, and his brows climb his forehead. The reporter's smile spreads, resembling the Cheshire cat.

"I never said anything about blackmail, Mr. De Laurentiis, but it's clear that's on your mind for some reason," she tells him, looking smug.

He recovers quickly. "Yes, I mentioned blackmail because, contrary to your apparent belief, I actually did read the slanderous article you wrote about my girlfriend on Saturday, where *you* mentioned blackmail. Don't act like that's something I said unprompted."

My heart is hammering out of my chest, and I'm not sure how much more of this back-and-forth I can take. Besides, I need to get back out on the floor to finish up before my shift is over.

To my dismay, it doesn't end there. Not that I had expected it to. Wishful thinking though.

"You're correct. It wasn't unprompted, not from you or me. The records released on your medical condition show that your girlfriend was your healthcare provider. Then suddenly, you swapped providers and started dating her. It all seems very out of the blue since she just moved here. Is it also a coincidence that she and her brother have some very sticky history?"

My stomach plummets to my toes, my mind spinning, and nausea climbing up my throat. I was so focused on the screen that I didn't even hear when one of the doctors came in for a coffee until she was standing next to me, watching the conference unfold.

"That is none of your business. No more questions. You're coming up with crap, and none of it holds any merit." He looks livid, genuinely pissed. I've never seen him so angry before, not even when he was pulling Ante off of me at the bar. "Keep my girlfriend's name out of your mouth and out of your dumbass little made-up stories. Let the record show that I am madly in love with Katarina Narvaez, and I plan to make her my wife. There is no blackmail and no mistrust between us. Our personal lives are not for your enjoyment." He stands to walk off the stage with his agent ushering him away.

I notice Luca hovering nearby, waiting to drag him away, but before he can leave, the reporter drops a bomb on everyone that has the rest of the reporters standing, yelling over one another to ask questions, snapping pictures, and recording everything. The seemingly calm environment of the press conference has erupted into a cacophony of pure chaos.

"Wow, true love must be real if you're willing to deal with all *that* baggage. I mean, what child hides in a closet while their brother witnesses their own father shoot their mother in the head before turning the gun on himself? Stuff like that makes for really fucked-up adults, but I'm sure true love endures, and all that."

She says it, emphasizing every word with more snark as her face contorts into a smug, lopsided smirk.

Every piece of my past and present has been laid out for the world to see, and I feel bare. Naked and raw.

My thoughts are spiraling, my chest is clenching, and this is the last straw. The other shoe that Ale was waiting for. I love him so much it makes me physically ill to think of my future without him, but if being with him means my life is always going to be on display, picked at by vultures, and spread across news stations to be judged by anyone who sees it, I can't do it.

I think of Kas; he must be in shock or pissed. I'm not sure, but this is his reality too, and it's all my fault. I should have just remained Ale's provider and kept my distance from him. But now? I've dragged my brother into this mess, and I can't think of anything worse.

My mother is still alive, and I'm not sure if she even watches the news, but if she does, her information will be spread soon, I'm sure. The last thing she needs is to have reporters knocking down doors at the facility where she lives, disrupting her peace, and making it harder for her just to exist than it already is.

I feel my body shaking, the familiar sensation of panic growing within me, and I let out a scream when Dr. Rebecca Chang places her hand on my shoulder, squeezing and looking down at me with worry.

"Kat, I think you need to head home. You don't have much left to do, right?" she asks with concern.

"No, I just wanted to pop in and check on my patients who are still here, and then I'm done at midnight," I tell her, my breathing erratic.

"I'll check on them for you, okay? But you need to go home, Kat. You can't be here like this. It's not good for you or your patients, and you know that. And based on what I just overheard, soon it may not be easy for you to even get home. Do you need me to order you a ride share?" I appreciate her concern; she's always been really kind to me, but this is an embarrassing situation. Especially since there were recent allegations surrounding the legitimacy of my relationship with Alessandro.

Chapter Forty-Eight

Katarina

Tuesday, January 16, 2024

I head home in a daze—I'm not even sure how I managed to make it to my floor as I stumble into my room. I strip out of my scrubs, leaving my clothing in a heap on the floor before changing into pajamas. I'm too exhausted to shower, even though I know I should. My senses all feel numb and yet heightened at the same time.

I feel like a live wire, buzzing with too much electricity and nowhere to direct it.

I turn off the lights, climbing into bed under my thick duvet. My chest tightens when I realize the bed still smells like Ale from when he cuddled me to sleep last night.

That does me in, sobs wracking my body. I barely hear the light knock at the door before I feel Aiyana slide in behind me, enveloping me in the safety of her embrace. She holds me as I cry. I cry until I think I can't possibly cry anymore, and then I cry some more.

My face is swollen, my voice hoarse, and my skin is coated in a thin sheen of sweat. I finally manage to unwind Aiyana's arms and climb out of the bed.

I head to the bathroom to get cleaned up, wanting to brush my teeth and rinse my face with cold water. The reflection looking back at me is one I don't recognize.

It's been a long time since I've had days like these. Right after everything happened with our parents, Kas went silent for a long time. It had taken months of our Lola's coaxing before he finally spoke again.

He hadn't wanted to interact with anyone, his grades slipped at school, and he was put on probation with the school's hockey team for having a bad attitude and getting into fights with everyone, including his own team. Our grandma set him up with a childhood psychologist, and after seeing how well it worked for him, she got me one too. I had dealt with anxiety long before everything had unfolded with our parents, but it was arguably so much worse after.

Therapy did wonders for us both, but I eventually had to go on medication for the anxiety. I take it every day, and it has been life-changing. I no longer struggle to just get out of bed for fear of something triggering me. I no longer have a sense of constant dread or a looming presence of worry. I also have medication for panic attacks, which I keep on hand for moments like these, but I only take them when I feel one coming on; they aren't an everyday thing.

I had already been comfortable with seeing a psychiatrist because Kas and I were diagnosed with attention-deficit hyperactivity disorder when we were around twelve. While I was the quieter one, we both had trouble concentrating, getting in trouble for going off on tangents in class, and the teachers would call home a lot to complain that we didn't pay attention. Kas would get in fights with kids who made fun of me, saying I was just "slow" and not understanding that my brain is low in a chemical that dictates my ability to concentrate.

Granted, I hadn't understood that either at the time. When we were diagnosed and given stimulant medication, everything started coming together. Our grades improved, our ability to focus in class improved, we were no longer a distraction to the other students, and we could finally sit still without jiggling our legs or bouncing off the walls.

I think the reason the therapist was able to make such an impact on us so quickly is that we already had some familiarity with those sorts of offices and didn't find them as intimidating.

I haven't felt like this in a long time though. It's been years since I've had this level of constant anxiety, and I haven't had a full-blown panic attack in months, not even when shit hit the fan with Ante. Now I'm standing here, puffy-eyed, congested, and aching after my third panic attack in less than a week.

I just wish Alessandro and I could go out on dates, spend time with his family, and build a future together without the prying eyes of the public. But that's seemingly too much to ask for, and this drama is negatively impacting not only me but also him, his family, and my brother. So for everyone's benefit, it's best that I remove myself from the equation.

Chapter Forty-Nine

Alessandro

Friday, January 19, 2024

It's been five days since the press conference that stole everything I've ever wanted and worked so hard for right out from under me.

I'm currently having to undergo rigorous testing to verify that I'm fine to continue playing hockey and that I'm not putting anyone at risk by doing so. So far, that's going okay, but it's a slow process, and I won't be able to play tonight.

Which is probably for the best, considering my head isn't in it. Kat sent me a text with five words that crushed me, and I don't think I've taken a full breath since.

Her text read, "I can't do this anymore." That was it. No explanation as to what "it" is, but I can guess.

She doesn't feel comfortable being in the limelight, and since being with me, she's had to endure so much time being spoken about online and on television. It's not what she signed up for, and even though it became our reality, she can't handle it.

I don't blame her for it, but that doesn't mean I'm not losing my mind over here.[1]

Kas told me he hasn't really spoken to her, which I'm not even sure is true, but at least he doesn't seem to be mad at me. And Aiyana won't let me in the apartment to speak to Kat. I've been texting her and Kat every day, and because I apparently have no self-control when it comes to her, I've been banging on the door, begging to be let in every day as soon as I hear the door to their apartment slam shut.

The most recent time I did it, Aiyana pulled the door open just wide enough to stick her head out and bark at me like a dog with rabies. And yes, I mean, she literally barked at me. Not like a Chihuahua either, she was a full-on Doberman, and it shocked me enough to send me back to my own apartment.

I haven't eaten in days, and I don't remember the last time I showered. My chest is aching, and my jaw is sore from how often I find myself clenching it shut. I can only muster up the strength to do the absolute bare minimum, which means opening the door for the healthcare team performing my physical fitness testing to complete in my apartment and somehow managing to follow their instructions. Anything beyond that is simply not attainable right now. Maybe it will be once the giant gaping hole in my heart has somehow been patched up.

I was finally cleared yesterday, which is a blessing considering I quite literally could not complete those same tasks today after so many days without sustenance.

More than anything, I'm worried about Kat. I just want to know how she's feeling. I want to know if she's coping and taking care of herself, showing up to work, and feeding herself. All things that

I'm not currently doing, but I need her to be because her sanity is the only thing keeping me together.

I just know that if I could *speak to her,* we could work this out. We could figure out a plan and fix this mess.

---

1. **changes - XXXTENTACION**

Chapter Fifty

Katarina

Saturday, January 20, 2024

I peel my eyes open, puffy and crusted together from the tears I've shed this week. I managed to drag myself to work the other day but was sent home by HR when the reporters started piling up, keeping patients from getting in and out of the building when needed.

They asked that I take the week off to allow them time to figure out how to combat the issue and ensure patient safety. If it were possible for me to feel any worse than I already do, the weight of knowing I'm adding another barrier to patient care would do me in. But I'm already at rock bottom. My life is a wreck, splayed out for the world to see, being spoken about as if I'm not a real person with emotions or a right to any kind of privacy.

I'm a shell of the person I used to be, and all in a matter of a week.

***

I hear her rather than see her, not really knowing who it is, but I'm assuming it has to be Aiyana because I haven't seen anyone else in days.

The curtains that were pulled closed are being wrenched back, and next comes my comforter. A chill quivers through my body as the weight of the duvet is tossed to the side.[1]

"Come on, Kat, it's time to get the fuck up." Her voice is strained and full of determination. I'm taken aback at first because she's never spoken to me like this.

I finally look up at her, my arms wrapped around my chest, hugging myself so tightly that it seems I'm physically trying to hold the pieces of myself together.

That's all I am—pieces of a once whole person.

"We can go thrift shopping or drive around for estate sales and look for those ugly ass lamps you and your Lola loved," she pleads with me, and I know she's really trying because Aiyana *hates* estate sales. My throat burns at her mention of my grandmother. If she were here right now, she'd drag me out of bed and help me fix this mess.

But she isn't.

Aiyana's face is laced with worry, her lips are taut, and she has dark bags under her eyes that tell me she's losing sleep over this. Over *me*. I'm being selfish, and I know it. I haven't even reached out to Kas, and it's his life that's imploded too.

And that text I sent Ale? It was a total cop-out. I don't want to end things. I can't imagine my life without him now that I've experienced it for myself. I know I need to clean myself up, speak to him, and fix this mess, but I just *can't.*

That's what I told him, wasn't it? I told him I can't do *this.* I never meant *us.* I meant this situation—I can't live my life in this limelight—constantly under the scrutinizing gazes of those waiting for their next big story surrounding this year's projected Stanley Cup winners.

Aiyana takes a seat at the foot of the bed, resting a hand on my calf. "You can't keep beating yourself up about this, Kat. You and Ale love each other, even if you haven't spoken the words. You know what happened the other day?" She looks at me expectantly.

When I don't answer, she continues with a huff, "I had to bark at him to get him to leave." My eyes widen in surprise, finally meeting hers. "That's right. That poor, broken man came knocking on our door for the hundredth time this week, and I *barked* at him like a damn rabid dog to get him to leave. I don't have many regrets in life, but this is definitely one of them. That man looked like I had just kicked his puppy, and I couldn't let him in, so I barked at him, Kat! Please, please, *please* put us all out of our misery and get the fuck up, wash your nasty ass, get dressed, and march your ass across that hall to come up with a plan."

I want to, I really do. But even if I weren't exhausted in every sense of the word, I don't think I could muster up the emotional strength it would require to see him and deal with the inevitable breakup that would ensue as a result of my selfishness. Of course he wouldn't want to be with me after that. I handled this all wrong.

And it looks like I'm going to keep doing just that...

1. **violet skies - Colette Lush**

CHAPTER FIFTY-ONE

Alessandro

TUESDAY, JANUARY 23, 2024

I still haven't heard from Kat, and I'm playing like shit. I've cost the team two games this week alone. I'm not sure how much more I can take.

The only reason I leave my house at all is to walk Tank. He hasn't left my side, opting to rest his head in my lap as a constant reminder that he's here with me.

Aiyana has stopped being an asshole to me, which actually makes me feel worse. It tells me that Kat is so done with me that even her best friend is pitying me, no longer able to muster up the anger necessary to kick me when I'm down in an effort to distance me from Kat.

I live in a constant state of numbness, and the only thing I seem to feel is the acrid bile rising up my throat from my empty stomach.

I just hope Kat's okay.

Chapter Fifty-Two

Katarina

Friday, January 26, 2024

My chest constantly aches, my head pounds, and my throat is raw with the shed tears and misery that I've been overtaken by.

I miss Alessandro.

I am not okay.[1]

---

1. **Shallow - Lady Gaga & Bradley Cooper**

CHAPTER FIFTY-THREE

Alessandro

I've never been more miserable.

I miss Kat.

CHAPTER FIFTY-FOUR

Katarina

I hear a knock at the front door, but I make no effort to answer.

Aiyana will get it.

Or she won't.

It doesn't matter.

***

I fall back asleep, the medication I've been taking for my panic attacks keeping me drowsy.

***

I wake again, delirious, but hearing whispered words leak in from under my door. If I could get myself up, I could find out who's here and what they're saying.

But I can't.

Chapter Fifty-Five

Aiyana

I've known Kat nearly all my life.

We were inseparable throughout middle school, high school, and beyond. I was there when her heart was shattered into a million pieces when her good-for-nothing, piece-of-shit, sorry excuse of a father took his own life and, for all intents and purposes, ended her mother's as well. I was there when Kas wouldn't speak for *months*.

And yet, this is so much worse.

Kat hasn't left her room in over a week, taking a leave of absence from work, and Gloria tells me that Alessandro hasn't even made it to Sunday dinners. It's time we take matters into our own hands because this can't keep going on. It's clear that time isn't going to fix this mess. The press will forget, and things will slowly shift back to some semblance of normalcy, but by that point, it'll be too late. Ale and Kat won't be able to find their way back to each other as easily, and that just can't happen.

So Gloria and I have devised a plan that we hope works. It has to.

***

Gloria sent me a text this morning letting me know when she'd be stopping by with Dante, and a few hours later, they arrived.

I'm not sure why, maybe because this is for Kat, but I have a firm sense of confidence that this will work. Maybe because it *has* to work.

The usual nerves that come with making a statement to the nosey press are absent, and if I'm being honest, I'm just excited to be doing *something*.

I answer the door, greeting them both and opening the door wide for Gloria to wheel herself in.

"Hi there, handsome, thanks for coming along." I shoot Dante a wry grin, knowing he's already grown comfortable with my teasing. I've quickly become friends with his wife and sister since starting at BioMedics, working with Charlie's wife, Rose.

He smiles at me. "I figured the press might need someone to keep the two of you from tearing them a new one."

"Yeah, yeah, yeah, if the press weren't a bunch of bullies, then they wouldn't be in the path of our wrath anyway. They don't need a mediator, they need a life," she tells us, and I couldn't agree more. "Now, come give your favorite conspirator a hug before we get this show on the road."

***

We finish discussing our plans, call up every news station in the area, and tell them where to be before splitting up to work on getting Kat and Ale cleaned up and out of this damn building.

CHAPTER FIFTY-SIX

Katarina

I'm feeling more human after the shower Aiyana dragged me into, literally.

I finally recognize my face in the mirror, and even though it's a little more gaunt from my lack of appetite the last couple of weeks, my eyes are less puffy.

I work on blow-drying my hair and changing into jeans and a sweater.

Aiyana said we're leaving in thirty minutes, for what I'm not sure. I just know I need to see Ale. I need to apologize and try to mend things between us. This self-loathing pity party I've thrown myself has done nothing but add insult to injury for us all. I've felt like crap, and nothing has improved. I need to get my life back together, go back to work, and hopefully convince Ale to give me another chance.

***

"All right, Kat, it's time to go," Aiyana tells me as I slip my feet into a pair of black ankle-high boots with a wedged heel.

"Are you planning to tell me what exactly it is that we're doing," I ask her, knowing that if she had planned to tell me, she would have already.

She gives me a cheeky smile before cupping my cheeks in her hands, her eyes starting to well with moisture, giving them a glassy appearance. "I'm just so damn glad to have you back," she chokes out.

I give her the broadest smile I can muster and wrap my arms around her in a bone-crushing hug. "I'm glad to be back," I whisper, my voice full of emotion.

She pulls away, opening the door and swatting my butt to urge me forward.

***

Our Uber drops us off in front of Pawsitively Purrfect, my eyes taking in the building surrounded by hundreds of people. Reporters, newscasters, and other bystanders are all gathered around a small platform where Gloria, Dante, and Alessandro are standing with Tank.

I look to Aiyana. "What are we doing here, Aiya?"

"Fixing things. Kas will be here soon."

She leads me over to Ale, and as we approach the platform, I see Louri, the owner of Pawsitively Purrfect, wave at me from a table she's seated at with a sign taped to the front reading, "Adoption

Applications." I give her a small smile and wave back at her before redirecting my attention back to Alessandro, whose face makes me want to cry again. My chest tightens, and the realization that I haven't seen him in so long absolutely crushes me.

His lips are pulled tight, giving nothing away.

Aiyana ushers me forward as she checks the time on her watch. She approaches Gloria, hugging her and giving her a cheeky grin. "It's almost showtime, pretty lady." She winks at her, and Gloria's smile spreads. This is so bad. Aiyana and Gloria working on something together is a dangerous combination.

Gloria's eyes lift to mine, her smile spreading further as she wheels over to me, deliberately knocking gently into my legs. "How's my gorgeous Kat holding up?" she asks me, and a sob chokes me, but no tears flow. We're standing mere feet from Alessandro and Dante, whose scrutinizing gazes wrap around me like a weighted blanket.

I give her my best smile, but I'm unable to speak because there's a frog in my throat. I've put her family through hell, and yet she's still so caring. I envelop her in a hug, holding on for what feels like forever as she pats my back, and when we pull away, my eyes meet Alessandro's again. I go to walk toward him, unable to help myself any longer, but Gloria's fingers wrap around my own, pulling me back to her. "Not yet," she tells me in a hushed tone.

I'm still unsure what she has planned, but the least I can do is comply with her wishes.

CHAPTER FIFTY-SEVEN

Alessandro

Seeing Kat mere feet away with sad eyes and hearing her rough, emotion-laden voice is soul-crushing. I have to fight the urge to rush her, crushing her to my body, and devouring her mouth. I want to be the one to kiss away every tear, swallow every sob.

But I can't. Not yet, anyway. At least not according to Dante, who seems to be one of only four people who know what the hell is going on.[1]

Aiyana and Mom have been scheming together, and it seems that Dante and Kas know about their plans but no one else. Charlie and Rose are at home with the kids, and Gianni is inside playing with the dogs. Louri wrangled him inside when we first arrived, and he still hasn't come out. He likely won't if it means avoiding being in the spotlight or having to answer questions from the press.

***

I can't keep my eyes off of Kat, and it's getting sad. I look nothing short of desperate, but I don't care.

I am desperate.

Suddenly, the crowd grows quiet, and my mom and Aiyana wait until everyone is silent before they begin.

My mom addresses the crowd as a regal would, her shoulders pulled back, head held high, and eyes set forward.

"In the last few weeks, it's become incredibly clear to my family that you all need a story to carry you through. Even going so far as to create ones that don't truly exist." She pauses for dramatic effect, her eyes swinging over the crowd and finally landing on the reporter who antagonized me at the press conference in New York.

She continues, "You've gone through personal health records, breaking the law, and falsifying this information, twisting it to meet your needs so you can get ahead, creating a story your publishers will be happy to continue pushing and resulting in your name being known, but for all the wrong reasons. You've slandered our family's name, making accusations that you know nothing about." She turns to me, her gaze meeting my own. "If you knew anything at all about my son, you'd know that he would never knowingly put his team at risk. He has a heart of gold and would sacrifice his own career to ensure their safety if it came to that. He's been under the care of a fantastic doctor who has successfully been treating his symptoms as they come."

She pauses again, the crowd growing antsy.

"You've taken the childhood trauma of two incredible people and splayed it out as if it has anything to do with you. Newsflash for you, it does not." Her voice is hard and determined.

"You seem to have forgotten that these people are just that. *People.* They have emotions, families who love them dearly, and their own lives that are being negatively impacted by your disgusting lies. So I'm going to tell you what you're not going to do. You're *not* going to carry on talking about my son, his girlfriend, or her brother as if they have no right to privacy. You're *not* going to spread lies and ill will toward them. You're *not* going to continue to add an unnecessary strain to their lives when they should be living happy, content lives. And those of you who continue to do so? Yeah, you're not going to have a job if you do because I mean this wholeheartedly, and yes, I *am* threatening you when I say this—I will personally sue you, ending your career in one fell swoop, just like you tried to end theirs."

The crowd is muttering among themselves, a chill running through them.

Aiyana steps up and begins speaking. "You seem to want to know about Kat and Ale so badly, so I'm going to tell you about them."

Her head is held high like my mother's. "Kat is the kindest person you'll ever meet," she starts, her eyes swinging to my girl.

She continues for several minutes, relaying all of the positives about Kat and myself. My heart clenches seeing Kat's eyes turn glassy again. I want to reach out and crush her to me.

Then Aiyana surprises me by saying, "Kat and Kas used to volunteer at Pawsitively Purrfect for years, and it holds a very special place in their hearts. So much so that Kat brought Alessandro here on their first real date, where he fell in love and adopted Tank." I'm unsure whether she's talking about Tank or Kat when she references me falling in love. I can now see that I started falling for Kat long before I ever admitted it to myself.

"I suggest you all push through the hatred you've found seeping into your hearts and get inside and adopt a pet. Give them a good home and allow their love to transform you since you all seem to be living for the drama you've created. The sweet babies inside need new homes, and I have faith that you all could provide a good life for them if you put your minds to it. The rest of the Philly Scarlets will be here shortly to volunteer for the day. It could be a good opportunity to take some photos of the players and turn over a new leaf, ya know, posting true stories that'll give your readers the warm and fuzzies instead of trying to ruin people's lives." She gives everyone an overexaggerated wink that elicits a few chuckles.

When everyone realizes they're done speaking, cameras begin clicking, and a few brave souls walk over to the adoption table to speak with Louri.

Dante grips my shoulder, leaning in to speak. "I'll hang with Tank; you can go to her now."

And I don't hesitate.

---

1. **Lose Control - Teddy Swims**

Chapter Fifty-Eight

Katarina

My thoughts are rushing through me at breakneck speed, the nervous energy of the crowd blazing through me.

As everyone begins dispersing, Alessandro rushes to me, wrapping his arms around my waist and spinning me in circles, my feet dangling in the air.

My arms instinctively wrap around his neck, my head going to the place between his shoulder and jaw. My lips spread into a smile, laughing at the absurdity of the situation. Joy is bubbling over, the pressure in my chest is releasing, and my thoughts are clearing.

I've missed him so much.

He sets me on my feet, his hands never leaving me but trailing them up my waist and to my arms before he cups my cheeks, staring into my eyes.

His face is thinner, just as mine is, but he's still so damn handsome.

"I've missed you so much, *gattina*; it's like a literal piece of my heart was ripped away," he tells me, and I think I die a little.

"I know the feeling," I tell him honestly, my eyes cast downward in shame. I caused this. I could have prevented all of this by just being open with him and communicating.

"Hey, eyes on me, baby. I haven't seen those beautiful, honeyed eyes in weeks—don't take them away from me now," he tells me, pressing his forehead to mine.

I take a deep inhale, his clean scent filling my lungs, calming me. "I'm sorry, Ale, I'm so, so sorry. I've been selfish and horrible, and I don't deserve you, but I love you so damn much that I'm going to continue being selfish because I want to spend every day, for the rest of my life, with you."

My eyes are clenched shut with emotion, and when I open them to gaze up into his, he's smiling, his eyes crinkled with mirth.

"Sweeter words have never been spoken, *gattina*," he tells me. "I hope like hell nothing like this ever happens again, but there *will* be rough patches in our lives. That's just life. I ask that you actually communicate with me instead of shutting me out. I have absolutely no way of making things better for either of us if I can't reach you. I know you were overwhelmed, but we're a *team*, Kat, and we need all the players we can get if we're going to navigate this crazy life. And I know one thing for sure: I'll *always* want you on *my* starting line." He grins at the cheesiness of what he's just said. My heart flutters in my chest, guilt at my faults still nagging at me, but the joy his words bring me acts as a balm to those wounds.

"I promise to communicate going forward, even when I'm overwhelmed. *Especially* when I'm overwhelmed, actually," I promise him.

Ale's smile widens, and his hand slides into my hair, gripping the roots as he tilts my head so my lips meet his in an agonizingly slow kiss. He's so thorough, exploring every millimeter of my lips before finally slipping his tongue in, teasing and tasting me as if this might be the last time he ever gets to. As if he's memorizing my mouth. His minty taste is sweet on my tongue, making me tingly all over, and as he deepens the kiss, a zing of arousal shoots straight to my core.

We hear the clicks of cameras as we pull back, but I couldn't care less. Let them report on something positive for once; besides, nothing is going to stand in the way of me and this man ever again.

Ale groans, pressing a kiss to my forehead. He whispers, his lips brushing against the shell of my ear, "I need to get you home so we can make up for lost time." Another shot of electricity ripples through me, and I'm nearly panting at the thought. More than just my heart has missed him.

***

The tension has officially dissolved as the rest of the players from the Philly Scarlets arrive, taking dogs on walks and posing for pictures throughout the shelter. By the end of the day, the entire shelter has been cleared out. Nearly everyone adopts a dog or cat, though some of them stay in the shelter for the weekend, allowing their new owners time to get their homes ready for the new addition.

As it turns out, Gianni had fallen in love with a golden retriever mix who he named Pickles. He's taking her home tomorrow.

Ale and Tank haven't left my side—Ale's arm taking up permanent residence around my waist as I speak with Gloria, thanking her for everything she's done.

"You're like a daughter to me, Kat." Her words fill an empty place in the recesses of my heart. "I'd do anything for you," she tells me, her eyes crinkling with affection.

I give Gloria one last hug before Ale hauls Tank and me off to say our goodbyes to everyone before heading home.

***

Ale's hand gripped my thigh tightly the entire drive back to our building, and before heading up, we took Tank on a walk, enjoying being outside, just us, with no one watching for the first time in weeks.

We head up in the elevator, Ale's hand remaining on some part of my body as if he's afraid that if he loses the physical connection, I'll disappear.

We opt to go to his place since he's had a cleaning company come by recently. Meanwhile, my apartment looks like a tornado blew through.

When we step inside, Tank moseys over to his bed in the living room, and Ale releases me for the first time, only stepping a few feet away to prepare Tank's dinner, leaving it out for him to eat when he's ready.

Ale takes my hand, leading me to his room. He stops once he's closed the door, his eyes raking over my body, sending chills down my spine.

The energy in the room has changed; it is suddenly charged with electricity, and I'm filled with need.

"Lift your arms, *gattina*." I do as I'm told, his large, warm hands coming to my waist, pulling the hem of my sweater up and over my head before he tosses it to the floor.

I lower my arms, and he unclasps my bra, letting the weight of my breasts fall. He works at the buttons of my jeans, sliding them down my legs and dragging my panties with them. When he's done, I'm stripped bare, completely at his mercy and dripping with need.

"Get on the bed, and let your head hang off the end for me." Excitement rears through me. I have no idea what he has planned.

He strips naked, his incredible body on full display, and he strokes his heavy cock in his hand; walking toward me, he reaches out with his opposite hand, threading his fingers in my hair.

"I'm going to fuck that pretty throat of yours. Consider it punishment for the weeks of silence I've had to endure from you." His eyes are glimmering with mischief. I know he's not really angry with me, but this game has my skin sizzling and my heart pounding all the same.

I nod at him, and he angles the engorged head of his cock toward my mouth, swiping his precum along my bottom lip. I lick the saltiness off and release a whimper. I hadn't realized how much I missed this until now.

He plunges himself inside my mouth, pressing himself to the back of my throat, controlling the pace entirely himself. I'm just along for the ride.

My jaw is nearly unhinged, and my vision is going blurry as my eyes fill with tears. He pulls out entirely, allowing me to take a deep choking breath before he plunges back in. I'm so wet that I readjust myself on the bed, placing my weight on my left forearm as my right hand snakes down my body, seeking my clit.

Alessandro's hand darts out, fingers wrapping around my wrist as he chuckles, shaking his head. "Not a chance, *gattina;* you won't be touching yourself. Your pussy is all mine tonight."

I release a low moan, my core clenching.[1]

He grips my hair again. "You look so good with my cock in your throat, such a good fucking girl, *gattina*." He continues driving into my mouth with so much force that the bed is shaking. His body stills, going rigid, and I feel him pulse against my tongue. He lets out a long, low groan as hot, salty come drips down my throat, and I suck him completely clean.

He straightens. "Get on your hands and knees at the end of the bed." I push up from my position and crawl along the side of the bed, positioning myself in a tabletop stance with my ass in the air at the edge of the bed.

Ale sinks to the floor behind me, and I feel so vulnerable. All of me is spread out for him to see.

"God, you're fucking gorgeous," he tells me, and I set my nervous energy to the side, allowing myself to fully experience every ounce of pleasure coming my way tonight.

This man is so confusing. He's so unbelievably sweet, and yet he takes control and owns my body with dirty words and actions that have me coming apart around him.

He slaps my ass, the mixture of pain and pleasure shooting straight to my core, and another whimper falls from my lips. Before I have time to recover, his tongue is darting in and out of me. I feel his fingers slide through my slick folds, parting me but not penetrating yet. One hand remains on my ass cheek, steadying me as I rock my body back against his face, unable to hold still.

He brings his hot mouth to me, avoiding putting pressure where I need him most. His tongue delves inside me as his fingers work to keep me splayed open to him before his mouth moves to my clit, sucking and pulling on it as he fills me with three fingers.

I'm stretched to the brim but ready for him to fill me however he wants.

I'm moaning against his mouth, his rumbles of approval vibrating through me. "You want to come?" he asks me, already knowing I do.

My body is on fire, weeks without release built up, driving me to the brink.

His lips leave me again. "I said, do you want to come, *gattina*?" His voice is gruff and filled with desire.

"Yes!" I shout, "please, Ale, let me come." My legs are Jell-O, barely holding me up as need courses through me.

Within seconds, his fingers leave me as he smacks my ass again, eliciting a cry. I feel his thumb slide through my slickness, his mouth returning quickly, coaxing me open as he presses the pad of his thumb against my tight, puckered flesh. I take in a sharp breath, eyes widening with shock and arousal.

He rumbles, "My sweet kitten likes her asshole played with, doesn't she?" My core clenches at his words, and I'm spasming around his hot tongue as it delves into me. My hips continue rocking back, seeking more friction, and Ale's thumb leaves me, sliding to my clit, circling, and finally giving me the pressure I need.

Searing, white-hot heat fires through all of my nerve endings, lighting me up as I come apart around his tongue. He licks away my arousal, his thumb leaving the overly sensitive bundle of nerves.

He stands and gives me one more smack on the ass before gripping my thigh and pushing me over to lay on my back. His eyes are heavy-lidded, the green irises sparkling under the constellations lit on the ceiling. I scooch my body up toward the middle of the bed, and he follows me, prowling up my body, his heavy cock lying against my thighs.

He pushes up, angling his face over mine. I look up at him, my skin still overheated, and a slight smirk spreads across his lips. He bows his head, bringing his lips to mine. The kiss starts gently. He parts my lips, and his tongue dives in after mine, sucking on my tongue before bringing a hand around my throat, pressing lightly as he groans into my mouth.

Arousal floods my core, sticky wetness coating my thighs. I want to wrap my legs around his waist and beg him to let me come again, but I know him. And right now, he needs to be in control, and it makes me even more wet letting him do anything he wants to my body.

His grip on my throat grows tighter as I reach between us, wrapping my fingers around his swollen length.

His head lowers to my ear. "Are you gonna be a good girl and take this cock like I know you can?" My clit aches, and I spasm with desire.

I try to nod, but his thumb presses down more firmly on my windpipe, and I gasp for air. "Use your words," he tells me with a low rumble.

"Yes, I'll be your good girl." His nostrils flare slightly, eyes lighting, and I feel him swell in my palm.

He releases my throat, his forehead resting against mine as he takes a steadying breath, trailing his hand down my chest and squeezing when he reaches my taut nipples.

Looking down at me, his mouth hangs open slightly, taking me in. "Your tits are incredible," he tells me as he lowers his head to suck my nipple into his mouth, biting down hard enough that my nails dig into his back, and he chuckles against me, releasing the sore bud.

"Can I ride you?" I ask him, hoping he'll let me take him as deeply as I want, but a smirk lights his face, and I know the answer before the words leave his mouth.

"So you can take control? I don't think so..." He trails off, lifting his body over mine, and the loss of heat leaves me cold and aching.

Nudging my hand away, he takes himself into his hand, pumping a few times before leaning back to center himself between my folds. "This okay?" he asks me, making sure I'm still on board with him using me however he'd like. I couldn't be more on board if I tried.

A thrill shudders through me. "God, yes," I moan, and that's all the assurance he needs.

He plunges the swollen head of his cock through my dripping heat, his hands coming to my breasts, kneading and toying with my nipples as he punishingly plows in and out of me. My inner muscles are clamping down on him, and he slows his pace. "If you keep taking my cock so well, I'll finish in three seconds," he says, his voice eliciting a chill down my spine.

"Ale," I moan. An unspoken question lingers, and my back arches off the bed as he presses firm circles to my clit, the head of his cock brushing my G-spot with every thrust.

A lock of dark hair falls to his forehead, beads of sweat gather along his brow, and his neck flexes with effort. "Yes, baby?"

His eyes are lit with mischief, knowing exactly what he's doing to me. "I need to come," I whine, need tingling through every nerve fiber already.

He releases a low, condescending chuckle. "I know you do, baby." He lowers his head, nipping at my bottom lip before pulling out of me entirely and rolling over onto his back.

He tips his chin toward his hard length, standing fully erect, bobbing against his flexed abdominal muscles. His lips spread, a huge grin taking up residence on his handsome face, and that playfulness that had vanished is back, his perfectly bright teeth gleaming in the limited lighting. "Take it for a spin, *gattina*," he says with a chuckle.

My brows pinch, but his thumb and forefinger grip my chin, turning my face to his. "Ride my cock and make yourself come all over me."

Biting my lower lip, I lift myself, straddling his lap as he grips the base of his cock and helps me sink onto it.

His hands grip my hips, easing me up and down as he remains partially in control. "It feels so much deeper like this," I tell him, euphoria coating my words.

Ale's eyes are rolling back as he moans each time I sink down onto him, "Fuck, it does."

I shift, rocking back and forth rather than up and down, hitting my G-spot and my clit at the same time; my head feels like it's spinning. My thighs clamp down around his waist, my muscles spasming as I climb toward my release. My legs wobble, molten wetness seeping from my folds, the slap of our bodies gliding together driving me insane, and as if I wasn't already on the brink of shattering, he pinches my clit, and I collapse on his chest, his hips driving up and into me as I ride the wave of my release. Ale's body stills, and he fills me, groaning as I pant against his hard, sweaty chest.

Our breathing slows, and my core aches, stretched beyond what I'm used to. His hand smooths my hair back away from my sticky forehead. He presses kisses to my overheated skin, whispering and mumbling to me, telling me how much he loves me, that I complete him, and that I was made just for him.

Once our muscles are relaxed, he lifts me gently off of him, taking me into his arms and cradling me against his chest as he walks us to the shower.

He turns the shower on and tosses a scented shower bomb in, filling the steam-filled room with eucalyptus and lavender. I step in under the stream, and he follows after me, pulling me into him and pressing chaste kisses along my jaw, his hands resting on my ass cheeks, mine wrapped around his neck.

He whispers into my neck, "Turn around, *gattina*," and when I do, he lets go of me, pumping shampoo into his hands and starting at the roots of my hair. He works the lather through to the ends, massaging my scalp as he does. Removing the shower head, he rinses my hair, being careful not to get shampoo in my eyes. Then he gets to work applying conditioner and repeating the same process, detangling my knotted waves.

When he finishes my hair, I turn around, facing him, and take a few generous pumps of body wash in my hands, lathering and rubbing it along his taut muscles. He groans as I massage his shoulders, and then he does the same to me.

We're both clean and more relaxed than we were when we first arrived home, so he works on drying us off and wraps me in a towel before carrying me to bed.

He places me on my side of the bed and gets a pair of tight black briefs, putting them on before grabbing a T-shirt from his dresser. Ale crawls over to me, smiling, and places a warm hand on my cheek as he gazes adoringly into my eyes. My smile matches his as I let the towel drop from its place around my breasts. I reach out for the shirt, his eyes dancing with arousal already.

My smile spreads, and I shake my head with laughter. "No more tonight; you've broken me," I say as Ale works the shirt over my head, then my arms. I'm swimming in his oversized shirt, his masculine scent surrounding me, and I'm in awe of where these last few months have taken us.

His eyes are bright, and his smirk is so sexy I want to kiss it right off his face. "Damn right I did," he chuckles, nuzzling his head into my neck, breathing me in.

I start to lie back, and his arms wrap around me. He leans across me, turning off the last lamp, and his lips hover over mine, but instead of kissing me, he runs his nose along mine.

Lying back into the plush pillows, he pulls me across his chest, and I rest my cheek on his firm pecs, reveling in the warmth of his hard body under mine.

"I love you, Ale," I tell him, sensing he needs to hear it despite what we've both known for some time now. *I am absolutely gone for Alessandro De Laurentiis.*

"I love you too, *gattina*"—he kisses the crown of my head—"I love you like you're the first and the last breath of fresh air I'll ever take." He presses another kiss to my hair. "Like you're the blood running through my veins," he whispers into my neck. "Please, *never leave me again.*"[2] His voice is choked, and I repress a sob. "I don't think I'd make it."

"*Never,*" I tell him, letting my meaning coat us both in a sticky, sweet softness.

---

1. **Curiosity - Bryce Savage**

2. **Beautiful Things - Benson Boone**

Epilogue: Part One- Alessandro

MONDAY, JUNE 19, 2024

I hear the buzzer before the realization hits me.

We did it.

We actually won the fucking Stanley Cup!

My eyes swing around the ice, catching on Kat as she stands with Aiyana, wearing mine and Kas's jerseys and holding huge signs. They're jumping up and down with excitement in the stands, screaming at the top of their lungs.

I skate toward my teammates, where we all meet in the middle of the rink. We're piling on top of one another, shouting a chorus of obscenities.

It's one thing to think you'll win the Stanley Cup, but it's a whole other to actually do the thing you set out to do so many years ago.

Coach Allister calls us to attention, reminding us that we need to shake hands with the players on the opposing team and show good sportsmanship. His huge grin tells us that he doesn't really care though. His team just won a fucking Stanley!

I'm vibrating with excitement as I exit the ice and head toward the locker rooms. Coach Allister claps me on the back, and, leaning into me, he says, "Come speak to me after the post-game meeting, yeah?" His face still reflects the high of our win, so I'm not too concerned despite everything that went down a few months ago.

***

I get cleaned up and head to Coach's office; his door is closed, so I knock, and he calls out for me to head in.

He's seated at his dark wooden desk, a photo of his wife and daughter sitting on the desk next to his laptop.

"Alessandro," he says, still smiling at me. "I wanted to discuss something with you that I'm hoping you'll be willing to try out."

He's piqued my interest, so I close the door and take a seat. "Yeah, Coach, what are you thinking?" I ask him, wanting him to get to the point so the pounding heartbeat in my ears can calm down.

"You've been an extremely valuable member of our team the last few years, and while I would have appreciated a heads up about your condition"—he pauses, giving me a reprimanding look—"I understand your desire to stay on the team as long as you could."

Of everyone I know, I trust that he understands. He tore his Achilles tendon just three years into going pro, and that wasn't even what kept him off the ice. He developed heart palpitations and lightheadedness that his providers weren't able to explain, so he saw a cardiologist who ended up diagnosing him with hypertrophic cardiomyopathy. It's a super rare heart condition that some people are born with, and it often has no symptoms, but it's most commonly seen in athletes. Young people play sports at their peak fitness and suddenly drop on the field, ice, or track from sudden cardiac arrest. It was too much of a risk for him to keep playing, so he had to give up his dream, and it's made him into a really incredible, no-nonsense coach.

His eyes remain locked on mine. "I see how everyone respects you and follows your lead. I think you'd make a great coach, and since our assistant coach is retiring this year, I'd like to offer you the position."

My eyes are wide with surprise. I hadn't even known Coach Aarons was planning to leave, let alone for me to be offered the spot.

I honestly think I'd be really good at it, and it would allow me to play for fun in league games while also getting to still work with my team.

It's a big decision though, and I want to make sure it's one I make with Kat.

"I'm really honored that you'd think of me for the position, and to be totally transparent, I'd love to take it." I pause, and he cuts in.

"There's a 'but,' isn't there?" He eyes me quizzically.

I give him a sheepish grin. "I've gotta talk to Kat first. I just want to make sure she feels like she's a part of all of the major decisions in my life because, ultimately, it's our life together that matters most, and her opinion's extremely important to me."

He stands up, walks toward me, and then stops and claps me on the back. "You're a good man, De Laurentiis; let me know by the end of the week."

I nod my agreement, getting up and heading out to greet my gorgeous girlfriend as a Stanley Cup winner for the first time, still buzzing with the high of it all.

Epilogue: Part Two - Katarina

SATURDAY, MAY 10, 2025

T he weather is absolutely gorgeous, the trees are full, and the flowers are all in bloom. It's a cool day out, the sun is high in the sky, and there's a light breeze.

I'm getting ready to head out to brunch with Gloria for Mother's Day, so I've chosen a satin dress in my favorite shade of dark-red with a floral pattern. We're meeting everyone at her favorite rooftop café in thirty minutes, and I'm so excited to see her. It's been less than a week since our last Sunday dinner, and I'm already missing the whole family.

They've truly become the family I needed but never had, and they've taken Kas and Aiyana under their wing too, so they've had to buy a new dinner table to accommodate everyone.

I head out of our room and into the kitchen to put my shoes on, but I can't help being distracted as Ale stands in the kitchen with his shirt open, his taut abs on full display as he works on buttoning his shirt up. He hears me enter the room, and his head snaps up, eyes locking on mine with a hooded gaze as his lips pull into a smile I know so well.

"You look gorgeous, *gattina*." His eyes are raking over my body. "I love it when you wear your hair down like that." My whole body tingles. I'll never get over how freely he compliments me.

"You look pretty hot yourself." A smirk spreads across my face. "I just need to put my sandals on, and we can head out."

He finishes buttoning his shirt. "Take a seat, baby," he tells me and walks over to the coat closet, grabbing the tan strappy sandals I had wanted to wear.

I take a seat on the edge of the couch, and he kneels in front of me. Taking my foot, his eyes stay on me as he plants kisses up my calf, stopping just above my knee before he gets to work, putting the sandals on my feet.

"Your legs are so soft," he practically purrs, his voice taking on a seductive quality that sends tendrils of lust swirling through me.

My heart flutters, but he stands abruptly, holding his hand out to me. "We've got to get going, or we'll be late."

I know he's right, but I deflate a little anyway.

He smirks at me, helping me right myself. "Don't look so disappointed, *gattina*, we'll have our fun later."

His ability to shift from ooey-gooey sweet to complete sex god with me will never stop making my heart pound. I love it.

I love *him*.

Epilogue: Part Two– Alessandro

K at looks so damn gorgeous, I can't stand it. I wish I could superglue my hands to her body so I never have to go another second without touching her.

Her long, wavy hair is swaying behind her as she walks ahead of me, hurrying to catch the elevator that will lead us to our surprise engagement and subsequent party.

She has no idea because she thinks this brunch is a celebration for Mother's Day, though that's not technically wrong. My mom practically begged me to do this—it was her idea to do it today anyway. She said all she wants for Mother's Day is for her eldest son to *finally* propose to his perfect girlfriend. She's not wrong. Kat really is *flawless*.

The only reason I've waited this long is that Kat didn't see a reason to rush anything. We moved in together shortly after things died down from the crazy press bullshit, then I took on the job as assistant coach for the Philly Scarlets, and she was still adjusting to her new position at the hospital. There was a lot of change in a short period of time, and married or not, there wasn't anything pressing that would have changed for us. We wanted to take our time so everything else could smooth out first; that way, the wedding planning could be enjoyable and not just one more thing on our plate.

However, we've discussed it more and more because we're both ready to start the paperwork for adoption, and it's easier to get approved if you're married or at least engaged.

We take the elevator to the rooftop, and I open the door for Kat to walk in ahead of me.

My whole family is seated around a long, dark-stained wood table, along with Kas and Aiyana. Everyone is in dress pants and a button-down or a sundress of some kind. There's soft music playing all around, and the table is set with the perfect combination of red and pink peonies, Kat's favorite.

Everyone turns to us, acting casually as they pretend to read their menus and greet Kat with smiles that to anyone else would seem fake or like they're hiding something. However, since they all adore Kat and act pretty strangely just in general, it doesn't seem to set any alarm bells off for her.

She smiles at them, stopping by each of them for a hug or kiss on the cheek.

I pull her chair out, and she takes a seat, still blushing every time I do.

I take my own seat, my hands starting to get clammy despite knowing she's going to say yes. There's not a doubt in my mind. I can already picture her satiny tan skin covered in white lace lingerie as she waits for me, lying in a lush bed, with floor-to-ceiling windows overlooking the clear blue Fiji water on our honeymoon.

She's going to say *yes*.

***

We've all eaten, and when the waitress comes out with dessert menus, everyone agrees to take a look. Kat leans over to whisper in my ear before taking her menu; she quirks a brow and gives me a small smile. "We should come here more often, dessert with brunch?" She makes it sound like the most incredible combination, and if I didn't know any better, I'd think she might have figured out my surprise, but Kat's a sucker for dessert at any time of the day.

In my periphery, I can see Dante struggling to signal for the kids to get out their handmade signs, so to bide some more time, I lean further into Kat, capturing her lips in mine for a chaste kiss that still manages to leave me dizzy.

She's smiling, her cheeks flushed and eyes cast downward. I see the kids getting into position, so I wrap my hand around her thigh that's closest to me, give her a squeeze, and whisper, my lips feather light against the shell of her ear, "The only dessert I want right now is you, *gattina*, but given the company, I'm gonna need you to pick between a cannoli and the tiramisu."

Her eyes shoot up to mine, blazing as she purses her lips and shifts back in her seat to grab hold of the menu.

She starts reading, and I know the moment she gets to the print beneath the cannoli that's only on her menu, which reads, "I cannoli think about marrying you, *gattina*..."

Her head snaps to me, and then she shifts her gaze around the table, finally noticing that Sammy, Benny, Arlo, Sofia, and Lily seated across from her are holding signs that each read a different word in the sentence, "Will you marry our uncle?"

I push my chair back, stand, and reach into my pocket for the black velvet box that's been burning a hole in my pocket for hours. I kneel in front of her, her soft bottom lip caught between her teeth, eyes glassy with unshed tears.

I open the box and steel my resolve, hoping I don't cry in the middle of this.

"Katarina Narvaez, you came into my life when I least expected it, and in a way I could never have guessed." I pause as everyone chuckles, remembering how we met in that hallway a year and a half ago. I smile brightly up at her. "You've managed to make me the happiest man alive, filling me with pride each and every single day, overcoming every battle we've faced, and giving me a love that outdoes every expectation I've ever set for what a relationship could mean."[1]

The tears are spilling over, and she knows how that breaks me. I reach up, unable to stop myself, as I use the pad of my thumb to swipe away the stray tears, smiling at her and sliding my hand down her smooth arm. I take hold of her left hand and continue, "Will you do me the honor of continuing to make me the happiest man alive and marry me?"

A sob racks her body as she falls forward into my arms, her own swinging around my neck as I catch her, steadying her body as she whispers a chorus of yeses over and over. The stress of planning this and hoping it all went perfectly finally clears, and my own tears spill over out of pure fucking joy.

I'm elated.

She pushes off my chest, dark waves strewn around her shoulders, pieces of hair splayed across her forehead, and the brightest smile that could light up all of Philadelphia is displayed across her now puffy face. I smooth her hair back, and everyone asks, "She said yes, right?"

They're all looking at one another with confusion. Our tears and her whispered response were not what they had expected.

Kat throws her hand in the air, almost in a "raise the roof" fashion, and shouts, "Yes! A million times, yes!"

Everyone cheers excitedly as I work the yellow gold band with a four-carat, emerald-cut garnet stone and three leaf-shaped clear diamonds on either side out of the box, placing it on Kat's slim finger.

Her mouth pops open slightly. "It's perfect," she tells me, admiring it.

I smile at her. "Just like you, *gattina*."

---

1. **Conversations in the Dark - John Legend**

Epilogue: Part Three— Katarina

SATURDAY, MARCH 20, 2027

I feel like I haven't slept in months since we started working on this project a couple of years ago, but it was so worth it. My body is practically vibrating with nerves and excitement.

This is the day we've all been working tirelessly toward:

The opening of Philadelphia's first completely free clinic with a covered and enclosed bus stop out front for accessibility. There's an attached greenhouse where we've found volunteers to teach classes daily on how to grow food from items found around people's homes, providing them with seeds that were donated to us. We were even able to link up with a few local co-ops that are going to give us all of the produce they can't sell. There's nothing wrong with it—it just looks a little ugly.

I'm ecstatic to be able to provide the community with quality healthcare regardless of their socioeconomic status, but being able to help them learn how to prevent certain illnesses at their root through proper diet, and being able to make that more accessible for them is truly the icing on the cake.

I was even able to get set up with someone on social media who helps teach black, indigenous, and people of color how to overcome the hurdles placed in front of them and become MDs, DOs, PAs, and NPs regardless of those things. She has a link on her page where people in the area can sign up to volunteer or work at the clinic for their healthcare and patient experience hours, as well as volunteer hours. It helps bridge the gap for those with a desire to work in healthcare, as well as provide an invaluable service to this clinic by doing so.

***

I've just finished getting all the lights turned on to showcase the facility and start taking patients immediately, so it's officially time!

Heading outside, the nerves start to overwhelm me, but I close my eyes, centering myself and remembering everything my therapist and I have spoken about over the last few years. The nerves subside, and I no longer feel the need to bolt, so I wipe my damp hands on my dress pants and head outside.

Alessandro's entire family is here, beaming with pride. They should be proud of themselves too; none of this would have been possible without them, and I am eternally grateful for their dedication to this project.

Ale is speaking to Kas and Aiyana, keeping a watchful eye on Nataly and Oliver as they sit at a picnic table set up with crayons and coloring books.

We adopted Nataly last year after her mother passed away from breast cancer. She turned fifteen today and practically begged to have the opening on her birthday. We told her that we could wait as we didn't want her to feel like we were blowing over something as wonderful as the day her incredible mom brought her into this world, but she said it would only make the day more special for her. I think she also wanted the distraction. It's her first birthday without her.

We adopted Oliver when one of Dante's patients had begged him to help her find someone to adopt her son. She was so young, and her parents didn't believe in abortive care. She didn't have the means or the desire to care for him, but she wanted to ensure he lived a good life and was able to contact her and have access to all of his biological family's information if he ever wanted it.

Dante had known we were waiting for the adoption agencies to call us, but the process is so long, usually taking over two years. We had already been waiting just over a year before he called to talk to us about Oliver. He was almost three years old because Carmen had to wait until she was eighteen to give him up for adoption. He was a shy little guy, but his bright-green eyes looked just like Alessandro's, and our hearts instantly melted.

When we adopted Nat, we weren't sure how she'd get along with a four-year-old, but they've been best buds. She looks out for him, and with every milestone he reaches, she comes out of her shell a little bit more to meet him there.

My heart is so full, some days I think it might burst.

Ale's eyes catch mine, his lips spreading into a wide grin, his dimple peeking out at me.

He motions for me to get over there. Checking the time on my watch, I realize it's just one minute until we cut the ribbon, and I'm supposed to give a small speech to the hundreds of people staring at me. The last time I was a part of something like this, my heart was broken into a million pieces. But not this time. Now, my heart is sewn so perfectly together that I feel it glowing in my chest.

As soon as I'm within a foot of Ale, his arm wraps around my waist, bringing me in for a kiss on the top of my head. He mumbles into my hair, "I'm so fucking proud of you, *gattina*."

I'm absolutely beaming.

Aiyana walks over to me, baby Jer on her hip, as she brings me the giant scissors she insisted I needed for the ribbon-cutting ceremony. "You're gonna do great, babe; I'm so proud of you." She smiles at me, knowing how nervous I've been about this.

The reporters from the various news stations we invited to cover the opening in hopes of attracting donors to keep us up and running all raise their cameras, focusing on me. I smile brightly, my hands shaking, but Ale's steady arm supports me. "Thank you all so much for coming out today. I can't even begin to express how much it means to me." I continue telling them about the building, everything we offer, and why it's so important to have a place like this, especially in big cities.

When it's time, Ale's warm hand shifts to mine, gently squeezing before bringing my knuckles to his lips for a reassuring kiss. He releases my hand, allowing me to walk forward. I cut the ribbon, turning back to smile at the cheering crowd, knowing many of these people I get to call my family.

My family.

Something I had never truly had before, and now I have in spades.

What an incredible life.

The end.

Afterword

Quiver was almost entirely finished when I decided to look into whether there had been any hockey players with MS. I know, I probably should've looked into that sooner, but the ideas for *Quiver* just came so freely that there wasn't much I researched until long after my first manuscript was already written. When I found Bryan Bickell's story, I knew I wanted to share a little piece of it with you all and encourage you to donate to his foundation if you have the means.

Another coincidence (or fate, however you'd like to see it) was that Tank, the worse-for-wear pitbull in need of a good home, was inspired by my parents' pitbull (also named Tank). As it turns out, prior to Bryan's diagnosis, he had started a foundation for pitbulls in need of some TLC! Alessandro and Tank really *are* soulmates! I've provided links to both of these foundations below.

https://www.bickellfoundation.org/main
https://www.us.bickellfoundation.org/

***

While Kat's free clinic isn't a reality yet, it is very much a real dream of mine, down to every last detail depicted in the epilogue. I hope that one day you'll all be able to join me in celebrating the opening, though that is several years in the future. I hope that *Quiver* will inspire others to start something similar in their area, and if you live around Philadelphia, I'd love to discuss any ideas or suggestions you may have.

<3

***

If you'd like to see more of Kat and Ale, hold tight for Kas and Aiyana's book! You'll also get to see their wedding... eventually <3

Acknowledgements

Thank you to the friends who pushed me to write **Quiver** in the first place. Without you, it wouldn't exist at all.

To my favorite person on the planet, thanks for marrying me and letting me spend all the money you made at work to cover my tuition and write this book! You're the bestest, and I love you more than words could ever explain. This means it must be complicated since... well... I AM a published author now.

To my mom, who keeps asking to read this book. *The answer is still no*, but I appreciate the support and love the enthusiasm!

To Sarah @HockeySmutBookClub, who had the absolute misfortune of me sliding into her DMs on a whim, begging for help with content creation despite the fact that she doesn't even offer those services. What can I say? I liked the vibes. Our absolutely unhinged voice memos at night are literally what kept me going most days, and I look forward to them forever!

To Suz, who learned pretty quickly that I need to be told in the most forward way possible if something is a complete dumpster fire; thanks for not letting me suck!

To Evelyn Leigh. (You should definitely read her novel, **Elevator Pitch**, when it releases on August 30, 2024!) Thank you for the support you've shown me from the very beginning, your willingness to share with me and never gatekeep, and, of course, for our chaotic, anxiety-ridden conversations. Thank you for dealing with my breakdowns and helping me dig myself out of the very deepest depths of self-doubt. Imposter syndrome is a bitch, but so are we, and we showed it who's boss.

To Kat's Literary Services. Thank you for ensuring my book baby is a work of art. Unfortunately, I have a serious love for commas in place of periods. What can I say? Commas just hit different.

And last but certainly not least, a massive THANK YOU to my incredible readers and Booksta fam; literally no one would be reading this right now if it weren't for you!

About the author

Giuliana Victoria is an author based in Pennsylvania who shares her readers' deep love of all things romance. She's a full-time physician assistant student currently in the clinical phase of her program. By the time *Quiver* is published, she'll be almost graduated and ready to join the healthcare workforce once again!

The idea for *Quiver* came about when she was reading another book where the FMC worked in healthcare and thought to herself, "I don't think I've ever even SEEN a romance book with a physician assistant in it..."

She searched high and low and found absolutely nothing! So she decided to write her own, and she hopes she did all of the incredible PAs out there justice.

When Giuliana isn't writing swoon-worthy book boyfriends, she can be found seeing patients, hiking with her three large breed rescue dogs, and, of course, curled up with a good book beside her husband.

She hopes you'll love *Quiver* as much as she enjoyed writing it, and she looks forward to sharing all of her future works with her incredible readers.

Also by

GIULIANA VICTORIA

Book #2 in the Philia Players Series: Coming Soon!
Sign up for my newsletter for a sneak peek at Kas and Aiyana's
story.

.

Printed by Amazon Italia Logistica S.r.l.
Torrazza Piemonte (TO), Italy